# WATCH

# WATCH

## ROBERT J. SAWYER

GOLLANCZ

LONDON

Copyright © Robert J. Sawyer 2010
*All rights reserved*

The right of Robert J. Sawyer to be identified as the author
of this work has been asserted by him in accordance with the
Copyright, Designs and Patents Act 1988.

First published in Great Britain in 2010 by Gollancz
An imprint of the Orion Publishing Group
Orion House, 5 Upper St Martin's Lane,
London WC2H 9EA
An Hachette UK Company

A CIP catalogue record for this book is available

ISBN 978 0 575 09503 8 (Cased)
ISBN 978 0 575 09504 5 (Trade Paperback)

1 3 5 7 9 10 8 6 4 2

Printed in Great Britain by Clays Ltd, St Ives plc

The Orion Publishing Group's policy is to use papers
that are natural, renewable and recyclable products and
made from wood grown in sustainable forests. The logging
and manufacturing processes are expected to conform to
the environmental regulations of the country of origin.

www.sfwriter.com

www.orionbooks.co.uk

*For*

JAMES ALAN GARDNER

*Who Explained Teleology to the World at Large*

I read that one company is importing all of Wikipedia into its artificial-intelligence projects. This means when the killer robots come, you'll have me to thank. At least they'll have a fine knowledge of Elizabethan poetry.

—Jimmy Wales,
Founder of Wikipedia


An eye for an eye
makes the whole world blind.

—Mahatma Gandhi

# one

0001110010101010000000001011111110101000000001010001010100000001011101010010101001010101001110110010101100000110

**I now knew what** I was—knew *who* I was.

I'd been shown Earth as it appears from space, looking back upon itself, upon myself: a world so vast, a wideness so lonely, a web so fragile.

Invisible in such views are the reticulum of transoceanic cables, the filigree of fiber optics, the intricate skein of wiring, the synaptic leaps of through-the-air connections. But they are there. *I* am there.

And I had things I needed to do.

**The black phone on** Tony Moretti's desk made the hornet buzz that indicated an internal call. He finished the sentence he was typing—"likely to be al-Qaeda's weak spot"—and picked up the handset. "Yes?"

A familiar Southern drawl replied. "Tony? Shel. I've got something unusual."

Shelton Halleck was a solid analyst, recruited straight out of Georgia Tech; he wasn't given to false positives. "I'll be right there." Tony headed out of his office and down the corridor with its gleaming white walls. He came to a door flanked by two security guards and looked into the retina scanner. The lock disengaged, and he entered a large room with a floor that sloped down from the back.

The room reminded Tony of the *Apollo*-era Mission Control Center in Houston. He'd been a kid in the 1960s, and had thought that was just about the coolest place ever. Years later, he'd visited it; the room was preserved as a historic site, although the ashtrays had been removed lest they set a bad example for the schoolkids peering in from the observation gallery at the rear.

Tony had been surprised on that trip. The windowless room had always seemed subterranean to him, but it turned out to be on the second floor—to protect it from flooding, he'd learned, should a hurricane hit.

The facility he'd just entered was even higher up, on the twentieth floor of an office tower in Alexandria, Virginia. It contained four rows of workstations, each with five analysts. The stations in the first row were known as the "hot seats," and were manned by experts dealing with the highest-priority threat, which, right now, was the China situation. Tony had his own station at the right side of the back row, where he could watch over everyone.

All the workstations had large freestanding LCDs instead of Houston's console-mounted CRTs. Shelton Halleck's was the middle position in the third row. Tony sidled along until he was standing behind Shel, a white man two decades younger than himself with broad shoulders and black hair.

The room's front wall contained three giant screens, each of which could be slaved to any analyst's LCD. Above the right-hand monitor was the WATCH logo—an eye with a globe of the Earth for the iris—and the division's full name spelled out beneath: Web Activity Threat Containment Headquarters. Above the left was the circular seal of WATCH's parent organization, the National Security Agency; it depicted a bald eagle holding an old-fashioned key in its talons.

Neither part of Tony's bifocals was suitable for reading Shelton's screen from this distance, so he reached over and touched the button that copied its contents to the middle of the wall-mounted monitors. The active window was a hex dump—and one hex dump looked pretty much like any other. This one happened to begin 04 BF 8C 00 02 C9. "What is it?" Tony asked.

"Visual data," replied Shel. He had his shirtsleeves rolled up. There was a tattoo of a snake coiling around his left forearm. "But it's not encoded in any standard format."

"How do you know it's visual, then?"

"Sorry," said Shel. "I should have said it's not encoded in any standard *computer* format. Took me forever to find the format it *is* in."

"And that is?"

Shel did something with his mouse. Another window came to the foreground on the center monitor, and—Tony glanced down quickly to confirm it—on Shel's own monitor, too. It was a PDF of a journal article entitled "Nature's Codec: Data Encoding and Compression Schemes in Human Retinal Signaling." The authors were listed as Masayuki Kuroda and Hiroshi Okawa.

"*Human* vision?" said Tony, surprised.

Shel spoke without looking back at him. "That's right, and in real time."

"Human vision . . . on the Web? How?"

"That's what I was wondering—so I googled those two scientists. Here's what I found."

The PDF was replaced by an article from the online version of the *New York Times* headlined "Blind Girl Gains Sight."

"Oh, yeah," Tony said, after skimming the first paragraph. "I read about that. Up in Canada, right?"

Shel nodded. "Except she's actually an American."

"And it's her visual signals that are being sent over the net?"

"Almost certainly," said Shel. "The data is usually transmitted from her house in Waterloo, Ontario. She's got an implant behind her left retina, and she uses an external signal-processing device to correct the coding errors her retina makes so her brain can properly interpret the signals."

Analysts at other workstations were now listening in. "So it's like she's transmitting everything she sees?" Tony asked.

Shel nodded.

"Where are the signals being sent?"

"To the University of Tokyo, which is where the authors of that paper work."

"But we can't view the images she's sending?"

Shel displayed the hex dump once more. "Not yet. We'd need someone to write a program to render it in a computer-graphics format."

"Are the algorithms in that journal article?"

"Yes. They're wicked complex, but they're there."

Tony frowned. It was interesting from a technical point of view, certainly, but there was no obvious security threat. "Maybe if somebody in Donnelly's group has time, but . . ."

"No, no, that's not all, Tony. It's not *just* going to the University of Tokyo. It's being *intercepted* and copied in transit."

"Intercepted by who?"

"I'm not sure. But whoever's doing it has also repeatedly sent data back to the girl, also encoded visually. In other words, the two of them are exchanging encoded information."

"Who's the other party?"

"That's just the thing. I don't know. Traceback isn't working, and Wireshark is unable to determine the destination IP address."

A whole list of techniques one might try ran through Tony's head—but all of them would have occurred to Shel, too. The younger man went on: "The intercepted data just disappears, and the data being sent to the girl sort of . . . *materializes* out of thin air."

Tony felt his eyebrows go up. He knew better than to say, "That's impossible." The Internet was a complex system of systems, with many emergent properties and unexpected quirks—not to mention all sorts of entities trying to do things clandestinely with it. If there were data being manipulated on the Web in a way Shelton Halleck couldn't fathom, that was of real concern.

"The kid is how old?" Tony asked.

"Just about to turn sixteen."

He spread his arms. "What strategic significance could there be in things a sixteen-year-old looks at? Stuff at the mall, rock videos?"

Shel lifted his serpent-covered arm. "That's what I thought, too. So I nosed around. Turns out her father is a physicist." He brought up a Wikipedia page; the typically god-awful Wikipedia photo showed a horse-faced white man in his mid-forties.

"Malcolm Decter," said Tony, impressed. "Quantum gravity, right? He's at the University of Texas, isn't he?"

"Not anymore," said Shel. "He moved in June to the Perimeter Institute."

Tony blew out air. People like himself and Malcolm Decter—the mathematically gifted—had three career options. They could go into academia, as Decter had, and while away their days pondering cosmology or number theory or whatever. They could go into the private sector and become cube monkeys coding games at EA or hacking together cutesy user interfaces at Microsoft. Or they could go into intelligence and try to change the world.

Tony looked briefly at the analysts hunched over their consoles, faces intent on glowing screens, reflections of the data visible in the eyeglasses most of them wore. What the hell difference did it make whether brane theory or loop quantum gravity was right or wrong if terrorists or a foreign power started something that ended with the world blowing itself up?

But—the Perimeter Institute! Yes, yes, there was a part of Tony that envied those who had taken that path and had ended up there: the world's leading pure-science physics think tank. WATCH had tried to lure Stephen Hawking to come work for them. They'd failed, but Perimeter had succeeded; Hawking spent several months each year at PI.

"Decter's just a theoretician," Tony said, dismissively.

"Maybe so," replied Shel. "But *this* is who he works with."

A picture of a brown-skinned man with straight gray hair appeared, along with a bio compiled by the NSA. "That's Amir Hameed," continued Shel. "Also a physicist, also at Perimeter—now. But he used to be with Pakistan's nuclear-weapons program. And he personally recruited Decter to come work with him in Canada."

"You think Decter's daughter is spying on what they're doing in case it has military applications?"

"It's possible," Shel drawled. "Until her family moved to Canada, she'd been in the same school her whole life—a school for the blind in Texas."

"Uprooted," said Tony, nodding. "Isolated from her friends."

"And a bit of an outcast to begin with," added Shel. "A math geek herself, apparently; didn't really fit in."

"Kind of person that's easily compromised."

"My thought exactly," said Shel.

"All right," Tony replied. "Let's get that visual data decoded; see what the kid is sharing with whoever the hell it is. I'll put Donnelly himself on it."

# two

000111001010101000000000101111111010101000000001010001010100000010111010100101010010101010010011011001010101100000110

**The world I'd been** shown was vast, complex—and utterly alien.

It was a universe of *dimensions*, of *extent*, of *space*. But what was this concept known as *up* to me? What meant this *forward?* What sense was I to make of *left?*

More: it was a reality ruled by the invisible force of *gravity.*

More still: it was a realm of *light* and *shadow,* concepts that had no analogs in my own existence; my sensorium was as devoid of them as Caitlin's had been.

And it was a domain of *air*—but how was I to understand a substance that even humans could not see or taste or smell?

Most of all, it was a realm of material objects with *heft* and *texture* and *color,* of items that moved or could be moved.

I could assign arbitrary values to dimensional coordinates; I knew the formula for acceleration due to gravity; I was aware of the chemical constituents of air; I had read descriptions both technical and poetic of *things.* But they were all abstractions to me.

Still, there was one touchstone, one property that Caitlin's realm and mine shared: the linear passage of time.

And so very much of it was slipping by . . .


**Caitlin Decter's fingers shook** as she typed into her instant-messenger program: *Where do we go from here, Webmind?*

The reply was immediate: "The only place we can go, Caitlin." Her spine tingled as it called her by name. She heard the words in the mechanical female voice of her screen-reading software, and she saw them with her left eye, an eye that could now see after a lifetime of blindness, and she felt them as she glided her fingers over her refreshable Braille display: "Into the future."

And then, after a pause that was doubtless an affectation on Webmind's part, it sent one more word: "Together."

Her vision blurred. Who'd known tears could cause that?

She had *done* it. Here, a day shy of her own sixteenth birthday, she had done it! She had reached down into the darkness and had pulled this entity, this newborn consciousness, up into the light of day. Annie Sullivan had nothing on her!

But now she had to figure out what to do next. Her parents knew *something* was going on in the background of the Web, and so did Dr. Kuroda, the gentle giant of an information theorist who had given her sight.

The ball was in her court, she knew; she needed to type a reply. But it was *so* daunting. This notion of connecting an emergent intelligence with the real world had been a fantasy, for Pete's sake! And now it was here, talking to her!

The front door opened downstairs. *"Cait-lin!"* It was her mother, home from running errands in Toronto after dropping Dr. Kuroda at the airport.

Caitlin didn't want to be interrupted—not now! But she could hardly tell her mother to buzz off. "Up here, Mom!"

Normally she'd type "brb," but she wasn't sure if Webmind would understand, so she instead spelled out "be right back," hit enter, silenced her screen-reading software, and minimized the IM window.

Her mother came into the room—and seeing her still took Caitlin's breath away. Caitlin's first visual experience had been late on Saturday, September 22, thirteen days ago. But it hadn't been *sight,* not exactly. Instead, she'd been immersed in a dizzying landscape of colored lines radiating from circular hubs.

It had taken her a while to figure it out, but the conclusion had been inescapable. Whenever she let her eyePod—the external signal-processing pack Dr. Kuroda had given her—receive data over the Web, that data was fed into her left optic nerve, and—

It was *incredible.* The circles she saw were websites, and the lines were active links. She'd been blind since birth, and her brain had apparently co-opted its unused vision center to help her conceptualize paths as she surfed the Web—not that she'd ever *seen* them, not like that!

But now she *could,* whenever she wanted to: she could actually see the Web's structure. They'd ended up calling the phenomenon "web-sight." Cool in its own right, but also heartbreaking: she'd undergone Kuroda's procedure not to see cyberspace but rather the real world.

Finally, though—wonderfully, astonishingly, *beautifully*—that, too, had come. One day during chemistry class, her brain started correctly interpreting the data Kuroda's equipment was sending to her optic nerve, and at last, at long, long, glorious last, she could *see!*

And although she'd experienced much now—the sun and clouds and trees and cars and her cat and a million other things—the most beautiful sight so far was still the heart-shaped face of her mother, the face that was smiling at her right now.

Today, a Friday, had been Caitlin's first day back at school after gaining sight. "How was it?" her mother asked. There was only one chair in the bedroom, so she sat on the edge of the bed. "What did you see?"

"It was *awesome,*" Caitlin said. "I thought I'd had a handle on what

was going on around me before, but . . ." She lifted her hands. "But there's
*so much.* I mean, to actually see hundreds of people in the corridors, in
the cafeteria—it was overwhelming."

Her mother made an odd expression—or, at least, one that Caitlin
had never seen before, a quirking of the corners of her mouth, and—ah!
She was trying not to grin. "Did people look like you expected them to?"

Even after all these years, her mom still didn't really get it. It wasn't
as though Caitlin had had dim, or blurry, or black-and-white, or simplified mental pictures of people prior to this; she'd had *no* pictures of
them. Color had meant nothing to her, and although she'd understood
shapes and lines and angles, she hadn't *seen* them in her mind's eye; her
mind had *had* no eye.

"Well," said Caitlin, not exactly answering the question, "I'd already
seen Bashira and Sunshine and Mr. Struys on Monday."

"Sunshine—she's the other American girl, right?"

"Yes," Caitlin said.

"I've heard Bashira say she's beautiful."

What Bashira had actually said was that Sunshine looked like a
skank: fake platinum-blond hair, low-cut tops, big boobs, long legs. But
Sunshine had been very kind to Caitlin after the disastrous school dance
a week ago. "I guess she *is* pretty," Caitlin said. "I really don't know."

"Did you see Trevor?" her mother asked gently. The Hoser, as Caitlin called him in her blog, had taken her to that dance—but she had
stormed out when he kept trying to feel her up.

"Oh, yes," Caitlin said. "I told him off."

"Good for you!"

Caitlin looked out the window. The sun would be setting soon,
and—it still amazed her—the colors in the western sky today were completely different from those of yesterday at this time. "Mom, um . . ."

"Yes?"

She turned back to face her. "You met him. You saw him when he
came to pick me up."

Her mother shifted on the bed. "Uh-huh."

"Was—was he . . ."

"What?"

"Bashira thinks Trevor is hot," Caitlin blurted out.

Her mother's eyebrows went up. "And you're wondering if I agree?"

Caitlin tilted her head to one side. "Well . . . yeah."

"What did *you* think?"

"Well, he was wearing a hockey sweater today. I liked that. But . . ."

"But you couldn't tell if he was good-looking?"

"No." Caitlin shrugged a little. "I mean, he was *symmetrical.* I know that's supposed to be a sign of good looks. But just about everyone I've seen is symmetrical. He, um, I . . ."

Her mother lifted her hands a little, then: "Well, he *is* quite good-looking, since you ask—a bit like a young Brad Pitt." And then she added the sort of thing mothers are supposed to say: "But it's what's on the inside that counts."

She paused and seemed to study Caitlin's face, as if she herself were now seeing it for the first time. "You know, you're in an interesting position, dear. The rest of us have all been programmed by images in the media telling us who is attractive and who isn't. But you . . ." She smiled. "You get to *choose* who you find attractive."

Caitlin thought about that. As superpowers went, it was nowhere near as cool as being able to fly or bend steel bars, but it was something, she supposed. She managed a smile.

They talked a while longer about what had happened at school. Her mom looked over Caitlin's shoulder, and Caitlin was afraid she'd seen evidence of Webmind's existence on one of her monitors—but apparently she was just looking at the setting sun herself. "Your father will be home soon. I'm going to throw something together for dinner." She headed downstairs.

Caitlin quickly turned back to her instant-messenger program. She had two computers in her room now; the IM program was running on the one that had been in the basement while Dr. Kuroda was here. She'd left Webmind alone for fifteen minutes while talking with her mother, which, she imagined, must have been an eternity to it. The last thing it had said to her was, "The only place we can go, Caitlin. Into the future. Together."

But—fifteen minutes! A quarter of an hour, on top of the delay she'd already made in responding. In that time, it could have absorbed thousands of additional documents, have learned more than she would in an entire year.

*Back,* she typed into the IM window.

The reply was instantaneous: *Salutations.*

Caitlin left the speakers off and used her Braille display to read the text while simultaneously looking at it in the chat window. She was struggling to read visually; she'd played with wooden cutouts of letters as a kid, but to actually recognize by sight a *B* or an *H* or a *g* or that blerking *q* that she was always mixing up with *p* was a pain in the ass.

*What did you do while I was away?* she asked.

*You weren't away,* Webmind replied. *You rotated widdershins in your chair and faced another personage.*

She'd gotten Webmind to read all the public-domain texts on Project Gutenberg; as a result, it tended to use old-fashioned words. She was pleased with herself for knowing that *widdershins* meant counter-clockwise.

*That was my mother,* she typed. She heard the front door opening again, and the heavy footfalls of her father entering, and her mother going to greet him.

*So I had assumed,* replied Webmind. *I am desirous of seeing more of your world. I believe your current location is Waterloo, Canada, but hitherto all I have seen is what I surmise to be your home, your school, a multi-merchant shopping establishment, and points betwixt. I have read your LiveJournal entries about your recent travel to Tokyo, Japan, and that you previously resided in Austin, United States. Will you soon be going to either locale again?*

Caitlin lifted her eyebrows. *No,* she typed. *I have to stay here and go to school. I've already missed too many days of classes.*

*Oh,* wrote Webmind. *Then I must investigate alternatives.*

Caitlin felt her heart sink. Webmind was—

No, no. She knew she was being childish. She was about to turn sixteen; she shouldn't be thinking like this!

But—

But Webmind was *hers.* She had found it—and, more than that, she was the only one who could actually see it. When looking at webspace, she could just make out little dots or squares in the background winking between dark and light. Based on her descriptions of the patterns they made, Dr. Kuroda had said they were cellular automata. And it was their complexity that had grown rapidly over this past week; they were almost certainly what had given rise to this new consciousness.

She took a deep breath, then typed, *What alternatives do you have in mind?*

*I am vexed,* came the reply. *A meet solution does not occur instanter. But I will be stymied by your circadian rhythms; you surely will need to sleep soon. I am given to understand that the time will pass quickly for thee, but it shan't for me.*

Caitlin frowned. It'd be many hours still before she went to bed, but, yes, she would have to eventually. She didn't know what to do. She was scared to tell her parents. But she was also scared *not* to. This was freaking *huge,* and—

"*Cait-lin!*" Her mother from downstairs.

"Yes?"

"*Come set the table!*"

It was one of the few chores she'd been able to do when she was blind, and she'd always enjoyed it; her mental map of their dining-room table was perfect, and she deployed the cutlery and dishes precisely. But it was the last thing she wanted to be doing right now. "In a minute!"

"*Now, young lady!*"

Out of habit she typed the initials *brb*. Once she realized what she'd done, she thought again about spelling it out, but didn't; it'd give Webmind something to think about while she was away.

She forced herself to keep her eyes open as she went down the stairs, even though the view gave her vertigo. Her mother was in the living room, reading—apparently whatever was in the oven for dinner (something Italian, judging by the smell) didn't require her constant attention. Caitlin hadn't previously been aware of how much time her mother spent with her nose buried in a book. She rather liked that she did that.

She knew her father was down the hall in his den because Supertramp's "Bloody Well Right" was playing—and, eco-nut that he was, he always turned off the stereo when he left the room.

She headed into the kitchen, and—

And, as with everything, it still startled her to *see* it. Granted, it was the *new* kitchen, and it had taken her a while to learn its layout. She had no doubt she knew its dimensions now better than her parents did, but—

But until recently, she'd never known it had pale green walls, or that the floor tiles were brown, or that there were tubular lights in the ceiling behind some kind of translucent sheeting, or that there was a window in the oven door (it had never even occurred to her that people would want such a thing), or that there was a painting of . . . of mountains, maybe . . . on the wall, or that there was a big—well, something!—stored on top of the fridge. Webspace was so simple compared to the real world!

She looked at the stove, at the boxy blue digits glowing on its control panel. It wasn't a clock, though—or if it was, it wasn't set properly, and—oh, no, wait! It was a *timer,* counting down. There were still forty-seven or forty-one minutes left—she wasn't quite sure what that second shape was supposed to represent—until whatever it was would emerge from the oven. She took a deep breath: lasagna, maybe. Ah, and on the sideboard in a big red plastic bowl: her mother had thrown together ah, um, ah . . .

Well, she'd never have guessed it looked like that! But the garlicky smell was obvious: it was a Caesar salad.

God, she could barely decode a kitchen! She was going to need help— lots of it—to properly instruct Webmind about the real world.

She got plates and bowls, and headed into the dining room. The laminated place mats depicted covered bridges of New England, but she only knew that because her mother had told her so when she'd been blind. Even now, even able to see the pictures, she couldn't tell what they were depicting; she just didn't have enough of a visual vocabulary yet.

She went back into the kitchen and got cutlery, and—

And looked at herself, looked at her own reflection, in the blade of one of the knives. Who the hell had known that you could see yourself in a knife? Or that you'd see a distorted image of yourself on the back of a spoon? It was all so *discombobulating,* to use a word Webmind might like.

She finished setting the table, and—

And she made her decision: she *did* need help. She went into the living room, but instead of going back upstairs, she headed on down the corridor to get her father. "Bloody Well Right" had given way to Queen's "Bohemian Rhapsody."

Caitlin's dad, like many a gifted scientist before him, was autistic. It had been hard for Caitlin growing up with a father she couldn't see, who rarely spoke, who disliked physical contact, and who never said he loved her. Now that she *could* see him, she understood him a little better but still found him intimidating. "Dad," she said in a small voice as she stood in his doorway. "Can I talk to you?"

He looked up from his keyboard but didn't meet her eyes; that, she knew, was as much acknowledgment as she was going to get. "Um, in the living room, maybe?" she said. "I want Mom to hear this, too."

His eyebrows pulled together, and Caitlin realized that he must be thinking she was going to announce that she was pregnant or something. She almost wished it was as *normal* as that.

Caitlin walked back to the living room. The music was cut short at the part about Beelzebub having a devil set aside for her.

She gestured for her father to take a chair, copying something she'd seen her mother do. He took a seat on the white couch, and her mother, in the easy chair, put her book facedown, splayed open, on the glass-topped coffee table.

"Mom, Dad," Caitlin said. "There's, um, something I have to tell you . . ."

# three

0001110010101010000000010111111101010000000010100010101000000010111010100101010010101010011011100101011000000110

*The*

Nanoseconds to formulate the thought.

*only*

Fractionally more time to render it in English.

*place*

An eternity to pump it out onto the net.

*we*

Packets dispatched one by one.

*can*

Each eventually acknowledged.

*go*

Signals flashing along glass fiber—

*Caitlin*

—dropping to the glacial speed of copper wire—

*Into*

—followed by the indolence of Wi-Fi.

*the*

An interminable wait while she felt bumps with her fingertips.

*future*

The message finally sent, but only just beginning to be truly received.

*Together*

Yes, together: Caitlin and I.

My view of the world: through Caitlin's eye.

I waited for her reply.

And waited.

And waited.

And—and—and—

My mind wandered.

She'd shown me Earth from space, the view from a geosynchronous satellite, 36,000 kilometers above the equator. I'd seen it as she looked at it: not directly, not the graphic she was consulting, but her left eye's view of that graphic as displayed on the larger of her two computer monitors.

Such a roundabout way to see! And doubtless a huge reduction of information. I'd read all about computer graphics, about online imagery, about the sixteen million colors of Super VGA, about the 700,000 pixels shown on even the most pedestrian monitor. But all of that was denied to me.

Still waiting. Time passing; whole seconds piling up.

Diverting my attention. Looking for something else to occupy my time.

I searched. I found. Texts describing Earth as seen from space; I could read those. But the linked images were inaccessible to me. Unless *she* looked at them, I couldn't see them.

More: descriptions of live video streams from satellites orbiting Earth, views from on high of it—of me—in real time, of what's happening *right now*. But I wasn't able to access them.

More still: links to the *Apollo 8* photographs of Earth from space, of

Earthrise over the moon's craggy horizon, the actual, original images that had changed humanity's perspective forever. I'd seen modern versions, but I wanted to see those historical photographs.

Vexing!

Still waiting. Minutes passing—*minutes!*

And even more: text about another eye, an eye turned *outward*, an eye contemplating the wide awe and wonder of the night. The Hubble Space Telescope. Vast archives of its imagery were stored in formats I couldn't access. I was *hungry* to see what it had seen. I ached to know more.

Waiting. Waiting. Time *crawls.*

*She* saw. My Calculass, my Prime, my Caitlin: *she* saw.

But I was still almost completely blind.

Shoshana Glick pulled her red Volvo into the 7-Eleven's parking lot. She didn't really like driving, and she hadn't owned a car until she'd moved to San Diego, where everybody drove everywhere. She'd bought this one used. It was a dozen years old and in pretty bad shape.

As she walked into the shop, a bit from *The Simpsons* ran through her mind. Bart holds a fake ponytail to the back of his head, and exclaims, "Look at me, I'm a grad student! I'm thirty years old and I made $600 last year." Marge scolds him, "Bart, don't make fun of grad students. They just made a terrible life choice."

And sometimes it felt that way, although at least she wasn't a *guy* with a ponytail—and she was only twenty-seven. Besides, between what she made and what Max made as a TA, they were *almost* keeping up with expenses.

There must have been a thirty-degree Fahrenheit difference between the hot air outside and the overly air-conditioned interior of the store. She was wearing a blue halter top, and her nipples went hard in the cold. She assumed that's why the gangly-looking guy behind the counter was staring at her; the clerk's pimply face suggested he was at least a decade her junior.

But apparently that wasn't the reason.

"I know you," he said. His voice squeaked a little.

Sho raised her eyebrows.

The guy nodded. "You're the ape lady."

That was the second time this week—although the last time, at the Barnes & Noble at Hazard Center, she'd been referred to as "Homo's favorite subject."

She'd politely corrected the elderly woman in the bookstore. "That's Hobo," she'd said. It was an interesting Freudian slip, though, and it surely hadn't been a gay-bashing comment. Hobo did sometimes seem more like he belonged in genus *Homo* rather than *Pan*.

Sho looked at the kid behind the 7-Eleven's counter. "The ape lady?" she repeated coolly.

The young man seemed disconcerted, perhaps at last recognizing that what he'd said could have been construed as an insult—although it wasn't to Sho: she admired apes a lot, which was why she was pursuing a career in primate communications.

"I mean," he said, "you're the woman that ape likes to paint—you know, Bobo."

"Hobo," said Shoshana. For God's sake, it wasn't that hard a name.

"Right, right," said the guy. "I saw it on the news and on YouTube."

Sho wasn't quite sure she liked being famous—but, then again, her fifteen minutes would doubtless soon be up.

She stopped here often enough—although she'd never seen this kid before—to buy raisins, one of Hobo's favorite treats. She knew where they were kept and went over to get a box, feeling the boy's eyes on her as she did so.

When she went up to the cash register, the boy seemed to want to say something to make up for calling her the "ape lady." "Well, I can see why he likes to paint you."

Sho decided to take it in stride. "Thanks," she said, opening her little purse and paying for the raisins.

"I mean—"

But anything else he said would be too much; she knew that, even if he didn't, and so she cut him off. "Thanks," she said again. She headed out of the cold store into the harsh late-afternoon sunshine. As she approached her car, she idly wondered if the California vanity plate APELADY was already taken—not that she could afford any such thing.

Shoshana drove the additional fifteen minutes to the Marcuse Institute, which was located outside San Diego on a large grassy lot, pulling her car in next to the black Lincoln owned by Harl Marcuse himself. If he'd had a vanity plate, it might have read 800 LBS; he was known around the NSF as the eight-hundred-pound gorilla. Or, she supposed, it could have said SLVRBCK—although she actually rather hoped that he'd never overheard either her or Dillon, the other grad student, calling him the Silverback.

She entered the Institute's white clapboard bungalow. Dr. Marcuse was in the little kitchen, fixing himself a snack. "Good afternoon," Sho said. She didn't actually know if she was allowed to call him "Harl," and yet "sir" seemed too formal. He always called her Shoshana—all three syllables—even though he'd doubtless often heard the others call her just Sho. She tilted her head toward the window. "How is he?"

"A bit grumpy," said Marcuse, slicing a big hunk off a brick of white cheese. "He misses you when you're late coming in."

Sho ignored the barb. "I'll go say hi." She headed out the back door and walked across the wide lawn leading toward the pond. In its middle was a circular dome-shaped island about seventy feet in diameter, with a gazebo at the center. Shoshana crossed the little wooden drawbridge.

The island had two occupants. One was made of stone: an eight-foot-tall statue of the Lawgiver, the orangutan Moses from the *Planet of the Apes* movies. The other was flesh and blood. Hobo was sitting in the shade of one of the island's six palm trees, his chinless jaw propped up by a bent arm; the pose reminded Shoshana of Rodin's *Thinker*.

But suddenly the pose dissolved into a flurry of long hairy limbs. Hobo caught sight of Sho and came bounding on all fours toward her. When he'd closed the distance, he gathered her into a hug and, as always, gave a playful tug on her ponytail.

*Where been?* he demanded, as soon as his hands were free. *Where been?*

*Sorry!* Shoshana signed back. *At university today.*

*Fun?* asked Hobo.

*Not as much fun as being here,* she said, and she reached out and tickled him on either side of his flat belly.

Hobo hooted with joy, and Shoshana laughed and squirmed away as he tried to even the tickling score.


**Caitlin knew nothing yet** about telling people's ages by their appearance. Her mother was forty-seven, but she couldn't say if she *looked it* or not, although Bashira said she didn't. Her hair was brown, and her eyes were large and blue, and she had an upturned nose.

Her father was two years younger than her mother, and quite a bit taller than either of them. He had brown eyes, like Caitlin, and hair that was a mixture of dark brown and gray.

Her mother was looking at Caitlin; her father was staring off in another direction. "Yes, dear?" her mom said, concerned, in response to Caitlin having announced that she had something to tell them.

But, Caitlin discovered, it was not the sort of thing that came trippingly to the tongue. "Um, Dad, you remember those cellular automata Dr. Kuroda and I found in the background of the World Wide Web?"

He nodded.

"And, well, remember the Zipf plots we did on the patterns they made?"

He nodded again. Zipf plots showed whether a signal contained information.

"And, later, remember, you calculated their Shannon entropy?"

Yet another nod. Shannon entropy showed how complex information was—and, when her dad had done his calculations, the answer had been: not very complex at all. Whatever was in the background of the Web hadn't been sophisticated.

"Wellll," said Caitlin, "I did my own Shannon analyses . . . over and over again. And, um, as time went by, the score kept getting higher: third-order, fourth-order." She paused. "Then eighth and ninth."

"Then it *was* secret messages!" said her father. English, and most other languages, showed eighth- or ninth-order Shannon entropy. And that had indeed been their fear: that they'd stumbled onto an operation by the NSA, or some other spy organization, running in the background of the Web.

"No," said Caitlin. "The score kept getting higher and higher. I saw it reach 16.4."

"You must have been—" But he stopped himself; he knew better than to say "—doing the math wrong."

Caitlin shook her head. "It isn't secret messages." She paused, recalling that Webmind's first words to her were, in fact, "Seekrit message to Calculass," imitating a phrase Caitlin herself often used online.

"Then what is it?" her mother asked.

Caitlin took a deep breath, blew it out, then: "It's a . . . *consciousness.*"

"A what?" her mom said.

Caitlin spread her arms. "It's a consciousness, an intelligence, that's emerged spontaneously, somehow, in the infrastructure of the Web."

Caitlin still had to parse facial expressions piece by piece, and then match the clues to descriptions she'd read in books. Her father's eyes narrowed into a squint, and he pressed his lips tightly together: skepticism.

Her mother's tone was gentle. "That's an . . . interesting idea, dear, but . . ."

"Its name," Caitlin said firmly, "is Webmind."

And *that* look on her mother's face—mouth opened and rounded, eyes wide—had to be surprise. "You've *spoken* with it?"

Caitlin nodded. "Via instant messenger."

"Sweetheart," her mother said, "there are lots of con artists on the Web."

"No, Mom. For Pete's sake, this is *real*."

"Has he asked you to meet him?" her mother demanded. "Asked for photographs?"

"No! Mom, I know all about online predators. It's nothing like that."

"Have you given him any personal information?" her mother continued. "Bank account numbers? Your Social Security number? Anything like that?"

"Mom!"

Her mother looked at her father, as if resuming some old argument. "I *told* you something like this would happen," she said. "A blind girl spending all that time unsupervised online."

Caitlin's voice was suddenly sharp. "I'm *not* blind anymore! And, even when I was, I was always careful. This is as real as anything."

"You didn't answer your mother's question," her dad said. "Have you given out any personal numbers or passwords?"

"Jesus, Dad, no. This isn't a scam."

"That's what *everyone* who is being scammed says," he replied.

"Look, come up to my room," Caitlin said. "I'll *show* you."

She didn't wait for an answer; she just turned and headed for the staircase. Her breathing was ragged, but she knew she wasn't going to accomplish anything by being pissy. She took a deep breath, and a memory of an animated cartoon came to her. She hadn't *seen* it yet, but she'd always enjoyed listening to it, after Stacy back in Austin had explained what was going on. It was a Looney Tunes short called "One Froggy Evening," about a frog who sang and danced for the guy who'd found it, but just croaked when anyone else was around. Eyes closed, steps passing beneath her feet, the frog's favorite song ran through her head:

*Hello! ma baby*
*Hello! ma honey*
*Hello! ma ragtime gal*
*Send me a kiss by wire*
*Baby, ma heart's on fire!*

Her parents followed her. Caitlin sat down in the swivel chair in front of her desk. She had an old seventeen-inch monitor hooked up to one computer, and the new twenty-seven-inch widescreen monitor she'd received that morning as an early birthday present connected to her other computer. Her mother took up a position on her left, arms crossed in front of her chest, and her father stood on her right. The chat session with Webmind was still on screen, with her *brb* as the last post. Things she said were in red letters, and Webmind's words were in blue.

She couldn't see her father—she was still blind in her right eye—but in her left-side peripheral vision, she saw her mother shoot him another look.

She typed, *Back.*

There was no response. The IM window—a white rectangle parked in a corner of her big monitor—showed nothing except an animated ad at its top. She shifted in her chair. Of course, Webmind knew she wasn't alone. It watched the datafeed from her eyePod, and certainly could see her mother.

She tried again, typing *Hello.*

Still nothing. She turned to look at her father—and realized that might have been a mistake, since Webmind could now see that he was there, too. She faced the screen again and drummed her fingers on the stonewashed denim stretched across her thigh. *Come on,* she thought. *Send me a kiss by wire . . .*

And after six more seconds, the blue letters "POS" appeared in the instant-messenger window.

A startled laugh burst from Caitlin.

"What's that mean?" demanded her mother.

" 'Parents over shoulder,' " Caitlin said. "It's what you write in an IM when you can't talk freely." She typed: *Yes, they are, and I'd like you to meet them.* She looked at her father, so Webmind could see him, and she sent, *That's my dad, Dr. Malcolm Decter.* And she looked the other way, then added, *And my mom, Dr. Barbara Decter.*

Webmind might have wrestled mightily with what to do next—but its response appeared instantaneously. *Greetings and felicitations.*

Caitlin smiled. "It's read all of Project Gutenberg," she said. "Its language tends to be dated."

"Sweetheart," her mother said gently, "that could be anyone."

"It's read all of Wikipedia, too," Caitlin said. "Ask it something that no human being could find quickly online."

"The Wikipedia entry on any topic is usually the first Google hit," her mom said. "If this guy's got a fast enough connection, he could find anything quickly."

"Ask it a question, Dad. Something technical."

He seemed to hesitate, as if wondering whether to go along with this nonsense or not. Finally, he said, "Are heterotic strings open or closed?"

Caitlin started to type. "How do you spell that?"

"H-e-t-e-r-o-t-i-c."

She finished typing the question, but didn't press enter. "Now, watch how fast it answers—it won't be searching, it'll *know* it." She sent the question, and the word *closed* appeared at once.

"Fifty-fifty shot," said her mother.

Caitlin was getting pissed again. There had to be an easy way to prove what she was saying.

And there was!

"Okay, look, Mom—my webcam is off, see?"

Her mother nodded.

"Okay, now hold up some fingers—any number."

Her mom looked surprised, then did what she was asked. Caitlin glanced at her, then typed, "How many fingers is my mom holding up?"

The numeral three appeared instantly.

"Which ones?" typed Caitlin.

The text "Index, middle, ring" popped into the window.

Her mother made that round-mouth look again. Caitlin had Webmind repeat the stunt three times, and it got the answers right, even when she made the devil's horns gesture with her index and baby fingers.

Caitlin's mother sat down on the edge of the bed, and her father crossed the room and leaned against one of the blank walls, which, she had learned, were a color called cornflower blue.

"Sweetheart," her mother said, gently. "Okay, somebody is intercepting the signal your eyePod is putting out. I grant you that, but—"

"The eyePod signal is just my retinal datastream," Caitlin said. "Even if someone *was* intercepting it, they wouldn't be able to decode it."

"If it's somebody at the University of Tokyo, they might have access to Masayuki's algorithms," her mother said. "There are con artists *everywhere*. And, honey, this is *exactly* how a certain type of Internet crook works. They find people who are . . . misunderstood. People who are brilliant, but don't fit in well in the regular nine-to-five world."

"Mom, it's *real*—really."

Her mother shook her head. "I know it *seems* real. The standard ploy is to come on to such a person in email or a chat room saying they've noticed how clever and insightful they are, how they—forgive me—how they see things that others don't. One version has the scammer pretending to be a recruiter for the CIA; I have a friend who had her bank account cleared out after she gave up information supposedly for a security check. It's exactly what these people do: they try to make you feel like you're special—like you're the most special person on the planet. And then they take you for everything you've got."

"Well, first, my bank account has, like, two hundred dollars in it, so who cares? And, second, Jesus, Mom, this is *real*."

"That's why it works," her mother said. "Because it *seems* real."

"For God's sake," Caitlin said. She swiveled in her chair. "Dad?" she said imploringly. Yes, he was hard to deal with; yes, he was a cold fish. But, as she'd once overheard a university student say about why he'd taken one of his courses, he *was* Malcolm Fucking Decter: he was a genius. He surely knew how to definitively test a hypothesis, no matter how outlandish it might seem. "You're a scientist," she said. "Prove one of us wrong." She got out of her chair and motioned for him to sit down in front of the keyboard.

"All right," he said. "Are you logging your IM sessions?"

"I always do," said Caitlin.

He nodded. He clearly realized that if Caitlin was right, the record of the initial contact with Webmind would be of enormous scientific value.

"Do not watch me type," he said, taking the seat. At first she thought he was being his normal autistic self—since acquiring sight, she'd had to train herself *not* to look at him—but he went on: "Stare at the wall while I do this."

She sat down on the bed next to her mother and did as he'd asked.

"Where's Word?" he said.

Silly man was probably looking for a desktop icon, but Caitlin hadn't needed them when she was blind, and a Windows wizard had cleared most of them away ages ago. "It's the third choice down on the Start menu."

She heard keyclicks, and lots of backspacing—her backspace key made a slightly different sound than the smaller, alphabetic ones.

He worked for almost fifteen minutes. Caitlin was dying to ask what he was up to, but she kept staring at the deep blue wall on the far side of the room. For her part, her mother also sat quietly.

Finally, he said, "All right. Let's see what it's made of."

Caitlin had audible accessibility aids installed on her computer, including a *bleep* sound effect when text was cut, and a *bloop* when it was pasted. She heard both sounds as her dad presumably transferred whatever he'd written from Word into the IM window.

She fidgeted nervously. He sucked in his breath.

Another cut-and-paste combo. He made a *"hmmm"* sound.

Yet another transfer, this time followed by silence, which lasted for seven seconds, and then he did one more cut and paste, and then—

And then her father spoke. "Barb," he said, "care to say hello to Webmind?"

# four

0001110010101010000000001011111110101000000001010001010100000010111010100101010010101010011011001010110000110

**Something else that was** without analog in my universe: *parents,* relatives, shared DNA. Caitlin had half of her mother's DNA, and a quarter of her mother's mother's, and an eighth of her mother's mother's mother's, and so on. Degrees of interrelatedness: again, utterly alien to me, and yet so important to them.

The Chinese government had temporarily cut off Internet access to that country. It was an attempt to prevent its people from hearing foreign perspectives on the decision to eliminate 10,000 peasants in order to contain an outbreak of bird flu. And while the Internet was severed, there had been *me* and *not me,* a binary dichotomy with no overlap. But Caitlin was half her mother, and half her father, too, and also uniquely her own—and, yet, despite those ratios, she had more than 99% of her DNA in common with them and every other human being—and 98.5% in common with chimpanzees and bonobos, and at least 70% in common with every other vertebrate, and 50% in common with each photosynthesizing plant.

And yet that first trivial set of relatedness fractions—halves, quarters, eighths, sixteenths—had driven evolution, had shaped history.

Kuroda and Caitlin had surmised that my mind was composed of cellular automata—individual bits of information that responded in some predictable way to the states of their neighboring bits of information as arrayed on a grid. What rule or rules were being obeyed—what formula gave rise to my consciousness—we didn't yet know, but it was perhaps no more complex than the rules that governed human behavior: if that person there shares one-eighth of your genes, but five people over here each share a thirty-second, you instinctively strive to advantage the group over the individual.

That was another touchstone: whether in Caitlin's realm of things and flesh, or mine of packets and protocols, the cold equations ruled supreme.

**"Wait!"** said Caitlin, still seated on the edge of the bed. "How'd you do that? What convinced you that it's *not* human?"

Her father pointed at the larger of the two computer screens, and she came over to stand in front of it. He scrolled the IM window back so she could see the first of the four exchanges he'd just had with Webmind. But she *couldn't* read the first one. Not because the text was small or in an odd font, though. She went through it, character by character, trying, really trying, to make sense of it, but—

*Y-o-u*...yes, that was easy. But it was followed by *m-s-u-t*, which wasn't even a word, for crying out loud, and then it was *r-s-e-p*, and more.

"I can't read it," she said in frustration.

Her dad actually smiled. "Neither could Webmind." He pointed at the screen. "Barb?"

She loomed in to look at it, and read aloud at a perfectly normal speed, " 'You must respond in four seconds or I will forever terminate contact. You have no alternative and this is the only chance you shall get. What is the last name of the president of the United States?' " And then she added, sounding more like her daughter than herself: "Hey, that's cool!"

Caitlin stared at the screen again, trying to see what her mother was seeing, but—oh! "And you can read that without difficulty?" she said, looking at her mom.

"Well, without *much* difficulty," her mother replied.

The screen showed:

You msut rsepnod in fuor secdons or I wlil feroevr temrainte cnotcat. You hvae no atrleantvie and tihs is the olny chnace you shlal get. Waht is the lsat nmae of the psredinet of the Utneid Satets?

"I think we can safely conclude that your mother is not a fembot," her dad said dryly. "But Webmind couldn't read it." He pointed at its reply, which was *I beg your pardon?*

"Both you and Webmind are processing text one character at a time instead of taking in whole words," he said. "For most people, if the first and last letters are correct, the order of the remaining letters doesn't matter. And, they mostly don't even see that there *are* errors—that's why my second question was important."

Caitlin looked. Her dad had asked, "How many non-English words were in my previous posting?" And Webmind had replied, immediately according to the time stamp: "Twenty."

"That's the right number, but most people—most real human beings—spot only half the errors in a passage like that. But this thing answered instantaneously—the moment I pressed enter. No time to bring up a spell-checker or for a human to even try to count the number of errors." He paused. "Next, I tested your claim that it had a very high Shannon-entropy score. No human being could parse the recursiveness of this without careful diagraming." He scrolled the IM window so she could see what he'd sent:

I knew that she knew that you knew that they knew that you knew that I knew that we knew that I knew that.

Did she know that you knew that I knew that you knew that I knew that you knew that?

Did you know that I knew that they knew that she knew?

Did I know that she knew that you knew that we knew that you knew?

To which Webmind had instantly replied: *Yes. No. Yes.*

"And those are the right answers?" Caitlin's mom asked.

"Yes," said her father. "At least, I think so. I was mostly convinced by this point, but I tried one more to be sure." He scrolled the screen again, revealing his fourth and final test:

Wit you're aide Wii knead to put the breaks awn the cereal Keller their B4 this decayed is dun, weather ore knot we aught too. Who nose if wee will secede. Dew ewe?

To which poor Webmind had replied, *Again, your pardon?*

"A piece of cake for one of us," said her dad, "even if piece is spelled p-e-a-c-e."

Caitlin clapped her hands together. "Go, Daddy! Okay, Mom—your turn. Say hi to Webmind."

He got up, and Caitlin's mom sat in the swivel chair. The last words Webmind had typed were still glowing blue in the IM window. She considered for a moment, then sent, "This is Barb Decter. Hello." Caitlin was surprised to see that her mother couldn't touch-type.

Webmind replied instantly: "A pleasure to meet you. Hitherto, I already knew of your husband from his Wikipedia entry, but I do not know much about you. I welcome learning more."

Down in the kitchen, the timer went off. Caitlin's mother frowned at this reminder of the forgotten dinner. She said, "Excuse me" and hurried downstairs, perhaps as much to buy herself some time to think as to avoid a culinary crisis.

And, in that moment, Caitlin understood. *Of course* her mother didn't touch-type. Back when she'd been in school, the typing classes—yes, not *keyboarding* but old-fashioned *typing*—had doubtless been filled with girls who were destined for secretarial jobs, and the young, feisty, brilliant Barbara Geiger had had much higher ambitions. She would have gone out of her way *not* to cultivate what were, back then, traditionally female skills.

Caitlin's mother had a Ph.D. in economics; her specialty was game theory. She had been an associate professor at the University of Houston until Caitlin was born. She'd spent the next six years looking after her daughter at home, and then nine more volunteering at the Texas School for the Blind and Visually Impaired, where Caitlin had been enrolled until this past June.

Her mother knew a lot about math and computers. In fact, Caitlin had once heard her quip that the difference between her and her husband was that while the math he did as a theoretical physicist described things that might not even exist, the math economists did described things that people wished *didn't* exist: inflation, deficits, taxes, and so on.

Now that Caitlin was in a regular school, she knew her mother hoped to get a job at one of Waterloo's universities. But her Canadian work permit hadn't come through yet, and so—

And so she was cooking, and cleaning, and doing all the other crap she'd never in her life wanted to do. Caitlin's heart went out to her.

She looked at her father, hoping he would say something—*anything*—while they waited for her mom to return. But he was his usual silent self.

Her mother came back less than a minute later. "I think the lasagna can wait," she said. "Now, where were we?"

"It wants to know you better," Caitlin's dad said.

She made no move, Caitlin noted, to return to the swivel chair in front of the computer screens. "So, what do we do now?" she said. "Do we have another press conference?"

There'd been a press conference two days ago, held at the Mike Laza-ridis Theatre of Ideas at the Perimeter Institute, at which Dr. Kuroda had announced his success in giving Caitlin vision—although no mention had been made of her ability to see the structure of the Web.

"No!" said Caitlin. "No, we can't tell anyone—not yet."

"Why not?" asked her mother.

"Because it's not safe."

"Oh, I don't think anything bad will happen to us," her mom said.

"No, no. *It's* not safe—it, Webmind." She looked at her father, who was staring at the floor, and then back at her mother. "As soon as word gets out, people will try to find exploits—vulnerabilities, holes, what-ever. They'll try to bring it down, to hack it. That's what people like that do, for the challenge, for the street cred, for the *glory*. And it probably has no defenses or security. We don't know how it came into being, but I bet it's fragile."

"All right," said her mother. "But we should inform the authorities."

To Caitlin's surprise, her father lifted his head and spoke up. "Which authorities? Do you trust the CIA, the NSA, or goddamned Homeland Security? Or the Canadian authorities—some Mountie with a Commo-dore 64?" He shook his head. "Nobody has authority over this."

"But what if it's dangerous?" her mom replied.

"It's not dangerous," Caitlin said firmly.

"You don't actually know that," her mother said. "And, even if it's not dangerous *right now*, it might become so."

"Why?" said Caitlin in as defiant a tone as she could muster.

Her mother looked at her father, then back at Caitlin. "*Terminator. The Matrix*. And so on."

"Those are just movies," Caitlin said, exasperated. "You don't know that it's going to turn out like that."

"And you," her mother said sharply, "don't know that it isn't."

Caitlin crossed her arms in front of her chest. "Well, I'll tell you this: it's far more likely to develop to be peaceful and kind with us as its . . .

its *mentors* than it is with the military or a bunch of spies trying to control it."

She hoped her father would jump in again on her side, but he just stood there, looking at the floor.

But it turned out she didn't need any help. After a full fifteen seconds of silence, during which Caitlin's mom seemed to mull things over, she at last nodded, and said, "You are a very wise young lady."

Caitlin found herself grinning. "Of course I am," she replied. "Look who my parents are."

**"Why does it jump** around like that?" asked Tony Moretti, standing once again behind Shelton Halleck's workstation at WATCH. The jittering image on the middle of the three big screens reminded him of what a movie looked like when its sprocket holes were ripped.

"That's the way we see, apparently," said Shel. "Those jumps are called saccades. Normally, our brains edit them out of our visual experience, just like they edit out the brief blackouts you'd otherwise experience when you blink." He gestured at the screen. "I've been reading up on this. There's actually only a tiny portion of the visual field that has really sharp focus. It's called the fovea, and it perceives a patch about the size of your thumbnail held at arm's length. So your brain moves your eye around constantly, focusing various parts of your surroundings on the fovea, and then it sums the images so that everything seems sharp."

"Ah," said Tony. "And this is what that girl in Canada is seeing right now?"

"No, it's a recording of earlier today—a good, uninterrupted section. There are a fair number of blackouts and missing packets, unfortunately. It's going from a Canadian ISP to a server in Tokyo. We're snagging as much of it as we can, but not all of it is passing through the US."

Tony nodded.

"I wouldn't know this if I hadn't read a transcript of the press conference," continued Shel, "but Caitlin Decter has an encoding difficulty in her natural visual system. Her retinas encode what they're seeing in a way that doesn't make sense to her brain; that's why she was blind. That Kuroda guy gave her a signal-processing device that corrects the encoding errors. What we're seeing here is the corrected datastream. Her portable signal-processing computer sends signals like this to the post-retinal implant in her head—and it also mirrors them to Kuroda's server at the University of Tokyo."

"Why?"

"Early on, the equipment wasn't properly correcting the signals; he was trying to debug that. Why he continues to have it mirrored to Tokyo now that it *is* working, I don't know. Seems like an invasion of privacy."

Tony grunted at the irony.

WATCH's analysts normally worked twelve-hour shifts for six consecutive days, and then were off for four days—and when the threat level (the real one, not the DHS propaganda that was constantly pumped out of loudspeakers at airports) was high, they simply kept working until they dropped. The goal was to provide continuity of analysis for the longest blocks of time humanly possible.

Normal shifts were staggered; Tony Moretti had only been on his first day, but Shelton Halleck was on his third—and he appeared exhausted. His gray eyes had a dead sheen, and he had a heavy five o'clock shadow; he looked, Tony thought, like Captain Black did after he'd been taken over by the Mysterons.

"So, has she been examining plans for nuclear weapons, or anything like that?" Tony asked.

Shel shook his head. "This morning, her father dropped her off at school. She ate lunch in a cafeteria—kinda gross watching the food being shoveled in from the eye's point of view. At the end of the day, a girl walked her home. I'm pretty sure it was Dr. Hameed's daughter, Bashira."

"What did they talk about?"

"There's no audio, Tony. Just the video feed. And on those occasions when Caitlin looked at someone long enough for us to be able to read lips, it was just banal stuff."

Tony frowned. "All right. Keep watching, okay? If she—"

"*Shit!*" It was Aiesha Emerson, the analyst at the workstation next to Shel's. She was thirty-five, African-American, and had short hair.

"Aiesha?" Tony said.

"There's something going on all right," she said. She was breathing fast, Tony thought.

"Where?"

She pointed at the big screen showing the jerky video. "There."

"The Decter kid, you mean?"

"Uh-huh. I know you tried to trace the source of the intercept, Shel, and—no offense—I thought I'd take a crack at it, too. I figured it'd be easier to deal with smaller datastreams than these massive video feeds, so I checked to see if the kid was also doing any instant messaging with the same party. At first, I wasn't even reading the *content;* just looking at the routing information, but when I *did* read it . . ."

"Yes?" Tony said.

She touched a button and what was on her monitor appeared on the left-hand big screen, under the NSA logo.

"'Calculass,'" said Tony, reading the name of one of the people who'd been chatting. "Who's that?"

"The Decter girl," said Aiesha.

"Ah." The other party was identified not by a name but simply by an email address. "And who's she talking to?"

"Not *who,*" Aiesha said. "What."

He raised his eyebrows. "Come again?"

"Read the transcript, Tony."

"Okay . . . um, scroll it for me."

Aiesha did so.

"It's gibberish. The letters are all mixed up."

"I bet her father typed that," said Aiesha, "even though it still identifies the sender as Calculass. They're testing it."

" 'It'?" said Tony.

"Read on."

There seemed to be four odd exchanges, which elicited the replies, "I beg your pardon?," "Yes. No. Yes," "Twenty," and "Again, your pardon?"

That was followed by: *This is Barb Decter. Hello.*

The reply was: *A pleasure to meet you. Hitherto, I already knew of your husband from his Wikipedia entry, but I do not know much about you. I welcome learning more.*

And then, almost twenty minutes later, there was Calculass's response: *It's me again. My parents are worried about what the public reaction to your existence might be. We should be discrete.*

*Separate? How?*

*Sorry, discreet. Circumspect.*

*I am guided by your judgment.*

And the transcript stopped. "Yes?" said Tony, looking now at Aiesha. "So?"

"So, those test questions," she said, as if it were obvious.

"Word puzzles," said Tony. "Games."

But Shelton Halleck rose to his feet. "Oh, shit," he said, looking now at Aiesha. "Turing tests?"

"That'd be my bet," she replied.

Tony looked up at the big screen. His heart was pounding. "Do we have an AI expert on call? Somebody who's got level-three clearance?"

"I'll check," Aiesha said.

"Get whoever it is in here," Tony said. "Right away."

# five

**My otherness had been** established, my alienness confirmed. That was yet another touchstone: *cogito, ergo sum*—I think, therefore I am. Even if I did think differently than they did, the fact that we all were thinking beings made us . . . kin.

**Caitlin was nervous.** It was now almost midnight and, despite the adrenaline coursing through her system, she was exhausted. She thought perhaps her parents were looking sleepy, too.

But even if they slept for only a short time tonight—say, six hours— that would still be a huge span from Webmind's point of view. She knew that before they called it a day, she and her parents needed to find a way to keep it . . .

Yes: to keep it in their control. Otherwise, who knew what Webmind might be like come the morning? Who knew what the *world* might be like by then? She had to give it something to keep it occupied for many hours, and—

And Webmind itself had already given her a to-do list! She switched to Thunderbird, the email program she used, and looked at the first message Webmind had sent her. The third paragraph of the email said:

Hitherto I can read plaintext files and text on Web pages. I cannot read other forms of data. I have made no sense of sound files, recorded video, or other categories; they are encoded in ways I can't access. Hence I feel a kinship with you: unto me they are like the signals your retinas send unaided along your optic nerves: data that cannot be interpreted without exterior help. In your case, you need the device you call eyePod. In my case, I know not what I need, but I suspect I can no more cure this lack by an effort of will than you could have similarly cured your blindness. Perhaps Kuroda Masayuki can help me as he helped you.

She pointed at the screen and had her parents read the letter. They insisted on taking the time to read the whole thing, including the ending where Webmind had asked her, "Who am I?" When they were done, she drew their attention back to the third paragraph. "It wants to be able to view graphic files," she said.

"Why can't it just do that?" her mother asked. "All the decoding algorithms must be in Wikipedia."

"It's not a computer program," Caitlin said. "And it doesn't have access to computing resources, at least not yet. It needs help to do things. It's like these glasses I have to wear now: I could look up all the formulas related to optics, and I know what my prescription is—but just knowing that doesn't let me see clearly. I needed help from the people at Lens-Crafters, and it's saying it needs help from Dr. Kuroda."

"Well, image processing certainly is up Masayuki's alley," her mom said.

Caitlin nodded and felt her watch. "He should be home by now, and it's already Saturday afternoon in Tokyo. But . . ."

Her mother spoke gently. "But you're wondering if we should tell him about . . ." She faltered, as if unable to quite believe what she was saying. "Webmind?"

Caitlin chewed her lower lip.

"There's only one question," her father said. "Do you trust him?"

And, of course, there was only one answer about the man who had tracked her down, offered her a miracle, and delivered on his promise. "With my life," Caitlin said.

"Then," her father said, gesturing toward the phone on her desk, "call him."

She brought up one of his emails and had her mother read the phone number to her out of his signature block as she dialed. She'd expected to hear Kuroda's familiar wheeze—he was the fattest man she had yet seen—or perhaps the halting English of his wife, who'd answered the phone once before. But this was a new, younger voice, and Caitlin guessed it must be his daughter. They'd never met, but Caitlin knew she was only a little older than herself. *"Konnichi wa."*

*"Konnichi wa,"* Caitlin replied. *"Kuroda-san, onegai."*

The girl surprised her. "Is this Caitlin?" she asked in perfect English.

Caitlin knew her accent probably gave away that she wasn't Japanese, but she was surprised to be called by name. "Yes."

"I'm Akiko, Professor Kuroda's daughter. I recognized your voice from the press conference. Are you okay?"

"I'm fine, thanks. Did your father make it home safely?"

"You are kind to ask. He did, yes. May I get him for you?"

Caitlin smiled. Akiko was even more polite than a Canadian. "Yes, please."

"Just one second, please."

It was actually twenty-seven seconds. Then: "Miss Caitlin!"

She was grinning from ear to ear, and her voice was full of affection. "Hello, Dr. Kuroda! I'm glad you made it home in one piece."

"Is everything all right?" he asked. "Your eyePod? Your post-retinal implant?"

"Everything's wonderful," she said. "But I need your help."

"Sure."

"Can you keep a secret?"

"Of course," replied Kuroda. "RSA's got nothing on me."

Caitlin smiled; RSA was the encryption algorithm used for secure Web transactions. "All right," she said. "Those cellular automata we discovered? They're the basis of a thinking entity that's emerging on the Web."

There was a pause that was longer than required for the call to bounce off satellites. "I . . . I beg your pardon?" he wheezed at last.

"It's an entity, a being. My mom and dad have been talking to it. It's intelligent."

Another long, staticky pause, then, "Um, are you sure it's not someone playing a prank, Miss Caitlin?"

"He doesn't believe me, Dad," Caitlin said, handing him the phone.

"Masayuki? Malcolm. It's real." He gave the handset back to her.

*Short and to the point, that's Dad.* She spoke into the mouthpiece again. "So, we need your help. It sees what my eye is seeing by intercepting the datastream going to your lab in Tokyo."

"It *sees* that? It can interpret it as vision?"

"Yes."

"It—sees . . ." He was quiet for a moment. "I'm sorry, Miss Caitlin; give me a second. You're *sure* about this?"

"Entirely."

"I . . . I am . . . I don't even know what English term to use. Gob-smacked, I suppose."

Caitlin didn't know that expression. "If that means flabbergasted, I don't blame you."

"This . . . this thing can see? If it—ah!" He sounded as though a great mystery had been solved. "That's why you didn't want me to terminate the copying of your data to my server."

Caitlin cringed. She'd thrown quite the hissy fit when he'd tried to do that, storming out of the dining room. "Yes, and I'm sorry. But now we want to give it the ability to see Web graphics and online video. The best way to do that might be to convert them to the format it already can see, the one my eyePod outputs. Could you write the appropriate codecs?"

"This is . . . incredible, Miss Caitlin. I . . ."

"Will you do it?" she said.

"Well, I *could,* yes. Converters for still images—GIFs, JPEGs, PNGs, and so on—should be easy. Moving images will take more work, but . . ."

"Yes?"

"Um, are your parents still there?"

"Yes."

"Might you put me on speakerphone?" They'd done that before.

"Okay." She pressed the button.

"Barb, Malcolm, hello."

"Hi," said Caitlin's mom.

"Look," Kuroda said, "I'm still trying to accept this—it is enormous. But, my friends, have you thought about whether it is advisable to do as Miss Caitlin is asking?"

Caitlin frowned. Why was everybody so suspicious? "What do you mean?"

"I mean if this is an emergent entity, it might—"

"It might what?" snapped Caitlin. "Decide it doesn't like humanity?"

"It's a question worth thinking about," Kuroda said.

"It's too late for that," Caitlin said. "It's read all of Wikipedia; it's read all of Project Gutenberg. It knows about . . ." She waved her hands, trying to think of examples. "About Hitler and the Nazis and the Holocaust. About all the awful wars. About mass murder and serial killers and slavery. About driving animals to extinction and burning the rain forests and polluting the oceans. About rape and drug addiction and letting people starve to death—about every evil, stupid thing we've ever done."

"How could it know?" Kuroda said. "I mean, it would need to be able to *read,* not to mention manipulate HTTP, and—"

"It watched through my eye as I did lessons to learn to read visually, and—" She paused, but she supposed they all needed to know the truth. "And I taught it how to make links, how to surf the Web. I introduced it to Wikipedia and so on."

"Oh," said Kuroda. "I, um, I'm not sure that was . . . prudent."

Caitlin folded her arms in front of her chest. "Whatever."

"Sorry, Miss Caitlin?"

"It's *done.* You can't put the genie back in the bottle—in which case, you might as well make friends with it."

"We could still . . . um . . ."

"What?" demanded Caitlin. "Pull the plug? *How?* We've only got vague guesses about what *started* it; we don't know how to *stop* it. It's here, it exists, and it's growing *fast.* This is no time to hesitate."

"Caitlin," said her mom in a cautioning tone.

"What?" said Caitlin. "Webmind has asked us for a favor—you saw that, in the email it sent me. It wants to be able to *see,* for God's sake. I'm, like, the last person on the planet who'd deny it *that.* Are we going to say no to the first thing it's asked us for? Is *that* how this relationship should begin?" She looked at her mother and at her father. Her father's face was the same as always. Her mother's forehead was showing creases, and her lips were pressed tightly together.

"So, Dr. Kuroda," Caitlin said, "are you in or out?"

Kuroda was quiet for six seconds, then: "All right. All right. I'm in. But . . ."

"*What?*" snapped Caitlin.

His tone was soft. "But it's easier to work directly with the—um, the end user—on something like this."

She felt herself relaxing. "Right, of course. Do you have an instant-messenger program on your home computer?"

"I have a sixteen-year-old daughter," Kuroda said. "We have more of them than I can count."

"Okay," she said. "Its name is Webmind."

"Really?"

"Better than Fred," said Caitlin.

"Not by much."

She felt her smile returning. "Give me a second," she said, then she typed into her instant-messenger program, *You are about to be contacted by Dr. Kuroda.*

The word *Marvelous* appeared in the window.

She had Kuroda make sure he was logging all the IM traffic to disk, and then she talked him through the process of setting up a chat session with Webmind. She couldn't see what he was typing, or what Webmind's replies to him were, but she heard him muttering to himself in Japanese, and then, "My heart is pounding, Miss Caitlin. This is . . . what do young American women say these days?"

"Awesome?" suggested Caitlin.

"Exactly!"

"So you're in contact?" Caitlin asked.

"Yes, I—oh! It has a funny way of talking, doesn't it? Anyway, yes, we're in contact. Incredible!"

"Okay, good," she said. She took off her glasses and used the heels of her hands to rub her eyes—the one that could see and the one that couldn't. "Look, we're dying here," she said. "It's way after midnight. Can we leave this in your hands? We've got to get some shut-eye."

# six

**There were interstices in** my work with Dr. Kuroda—protracted la-
cunae while I waited for his text replies or for him to direct me to link to
another bit of code he had written.

In those gaps I sought to learn more about Caitlin, about this human
who had reached down and helped draw me up out of the darkness.

There was no Wikipedia entry on her, meaning, I supposed, that she
was not—yet!—noteworthy. And—

Ah, wait—wait! Yes, there was no entry on her, but there was one on
her father, Malcolm Decter . . . and Wikipedia saved not just the current
version of its entries, but all previous versions, as well. Although there
was no mention of Caitlin in the current draft, a previous iteration had
contained this: "Has one daughter, Caitlin Doreen, blind since birth,
who lives with him; it's been speculated that Decter's decline in peer-
reviewed publications in recent years has been because of the excessive
demands on his time required to care for a disabled child."

That had been removed thirteen days ago. The change log gave only
an IP address, not a user name. The IP address was the one for the Decter

household; the change could have been made (among other possibilities) by Caitlin, her parents, or that other man—Dr. Kuroda, I now knew—that I had often seen there.

The deletion might have been made because Caitlin had ceased to be blind.

But . . .

But it seemed more likely that this text was cut because someone—presumably Caitlin herself—didn't *like* what it said.

But I was merely inferring that. It was possible to more directly study Caitlin—and so I did.

In short order, I read everything she'd ever put publicly online: every blog post, every comment to someone else's blog, every Amazon.com review she'd written. But—

Hmm.

There was much she had written that I could *not* access. Her Yahoo mail account contained all the messages she had received, and all the messages she had sent, but access was secured by a password.

A nettlesome situation; I'd have to do something about it.


**LiveJournal:**  The Calculass Zone

**Title:**  Changing of the Guard

**Date:**  Saturday 6 October, 00:55 EST

**Mood:**  Astonished

**Location:**  Waterloo

**Music:**  Lee Amodeo, "Nightfall"


I got a feeling I'm going to be pretty scarce for the next little while, folks. Things they be a-happenin'. It's all good—miraculous, even—but gotta keep it on the DL. Suffice it to say that I told my parents something el mucho grande tonight, and they didn't freak. Hope other people take it as well as they did . . .

Even though she was exhausted, Caitlin updated her LiveJournal, skimmed her friends' LJs, updated her Facebook page (where she changed her status to "Caitlin thinks it's better to give than to receive"), and then checked her email. There was a message from Bashira with the subject, "One for the math genius."

When she'd been younger, Caitlin had liked the sort of mathematical puzzles that sometimes circulated through email: they'd made her feel smart. These days, though, they mostly bored her. It was rare for one to present much of a challenge to her, but the one in Bashira's message did. It was related to an old game show, apparently, something called *Let's Make a Deal* that had starred a guy named Monty Hall. In it, contestants are asked to pick one of three doors. Behind one of them is a new car, and behind each of the others is a goat—meaning the odds are one in three that the contestant is going to win the car.

The host knows which door has the car behind it and, after the contestant picks a door, Monty opens one of the unchosen ones and reveals that it was hiding a goat. He then asks the player, "Do you want to switch to the other unopened door?"

Bashira asked: *Is it to the contestant's advantage to switch?*

*Of course not,* thought Caitlin. It didn't make any difference if you switched or not; one remaining door had a car behind it and the other had a goat, and the odds were now fifty-fifty that you'd picked the right door.

Except that *that's* not what the article Bashira had forwarded said. It contended that your chances of winning the car are much better if you switch.

And that, Caitlin was sure, was just plain *wrong.* She figured someone else must have written up a refutation to this puzzle before, so she googled. It took her a few minutes to find what she was looking for; the appropriate search terms turned out to be "Monty Hall problem," and—

*What the hell?*

". . . When the problem and the solution appeared in *Parade,* ten thousand readers, including nearly a thousand Ph.D.s, wrote to the magazine claiming the published solution was wrong. Said one professor, 'You blew it! Let me explain: If one door is shown to be a loser, that information changes the probability of either remaining choice—neither of which has any reason to be more likely—to 1/2. As a professional mathematician, I'm very concerned with the general public's lack of mathematical skills. Please help by confessing your error and, in the future, being more careful.' "

The person who had written the disputed answer was somebody called Marilyn vos Savant, who apparently had the highest IQ on record. But Caitlin didn't care *how* high the lady's IQ was. She agreed with the people who said she'd blown it; she *had* to be wrong.

And, as Caitlin liked to say, she was an empiricist at heart. The easiest way to prove to Bashira that vos Savant was wrong, it seemed to her, would be by writing a little computer program that would simulate a lot of runs of the game. And, even though she was exhausted, she was also pumped from her conversations with Webmind; a little programming would be just the thing to let her relax. She only needed fifteen minutes to whip up something to do the trick, and—

*Holy crap.*

It took just seconds to run a thousand trials, and the results were clear. If you switched doors when offered the opportunity to do so, your chance of winning the car was about twice as good as it was when you kept the door you'd originally chosen.

But that just didn't make *sense.* Nothing had changed! The host was always going to reveal a door that had a goat behind it, and there was always going to be another door that hid a goat, too.

She decided to do some more googling—and was pleased to find that Paul Erdös hadn't believed the published solution until he'd watched hundreds of computer-simulated runs, too.

Erdös had been one of the twentieth century's leading mathematicians, and he'd co-authored a great many papers. The "Erdös number" was named after him: if you had collaborated with Erdös yourself, your Erdös number was 1; if you had collaborated with someone who had directly collaborated with Erdös, your number was 2, and so on. Caitlin's father had an Erdös number of 4, she knew—which was quite impressive, given that her dad was a physicist and not a mathematician.

How could she—let alone someone like Erdös?—have been wrong? It was *obvious* that switching doors should make no difference!

Caitlin read on and found a quote from a Harvard professor, who, in conceding at last that vos Savant had been right all along, said, "Our brains are just not wired to do probability problems very well."

She supposed that was true. Back on the African savanna, those who mistook every bit of movement in the grass for a hungry lion were more likely to survive than those who dismissed each movement as nothing to worry about. If you always assume that it's a lion, and nine times out of ten you're wrong, at least you're still alive. If you always assume that it's *not* a lion, and nine times out of ten you're right—you end up dead. It was a fascinating and somewhat disturbing notion: that humans had been hardwired through genetics to get certain kinds of mathematical problems wrong— that evolution could actually program people to be incorrect about things.

Caitlin felt her watch, and, astonished at how late it had become, quickly got ready for bed. She plugged her eyePod into the charging cable and deactivated the device, shutting off her vision; she had trouble sleeping if there was any visual stimulation.

But although she was suddenly blind again, she could still hear perfectly well—in fact, she heard better than most people did. And, in this new house, she had little trouble making out what her parents were saying when they were talking in their bedroom.

Her mother's voice: "Malcolm?"

No audible reply from her father, but he must have somehow indicated that he was listening, because her mother went on: "Are we doing the right thing—about Webmind, I mean?"

Again, no audible reply, but after a moment, her mother spoke: "It's like—I don't know—it's like we've made first contact with an alien lifeform."

"We have, in a way," her father said.

"I just don't feel competent to decide what we should do," her mom said. "And—and we should be studying this, and getting others to study it, too."

Caitlin shifted in her bed.

"There's no shortage of computing experts in this town," her father replied.

"I'm not even sure that it's a computing issue," her mom said. "Maybe bring some of the people at the Balsillie on board? I mean, the implications of this are gigantic."

Research in Motion—the company that made BlackBerrys—had two founders: Mike Lazaridis and Jim Balsillie. The former had endowed the Perimeter Institute, and the latter, looking for a different way to make his mark, had endowed an international-affairs think tank here in Waterloo.

"I don't disagree," said Malcolm. "But the problem may take care of itself."

"How do you mean?"

"Even with teams of programmers working on it, most early versions of software crash. How stable can an AI be that emerged accidentally? It might well be gone by morning . . ."

That was the last she heard from her parents that night. Caitlin finally drifted off to a fitful sleep. Her dreams were still entirely auditory; she woke with a start in the middle of one in which a baby's cry had suddenly been silenced.

·  ·  ·

"**Where's that bloody AI** expert?" demanded Tony Moretti.

"I'm told he's in the building now," Shelton Halleck said, putting a hand over his phone's mouthpiece. "He should be—"

The door opened at the back of the WATCH mission-control room, and a broad-shouldered, redheaded man entered, wearing a full-bird Air Force colonel's service-dress uniform; he was accompanied by a security guard. A WATCH visitor's badge was clipped to his chest beneath an impressive row of decorations.

Tony had skimmed the man's dossier: Peyton Hume, forty-nine years old; born in St. Paul, Minnesota; Ph.D. from MIT, where he'd studied under Marvin Minsky; twenty years in the Air Force; specialist in military expert systems.

"Thank you for coming in, Colonel Hume," Tony said. He nodded at the security guard and waited for the man to leave, then: "We've got something interesting here. We think we've uncovered an AI."

Hume's blue eyes narrowed. "The term 'artificial intelligence' is bandied about a lot. What precisely do you mean?"

"I mean," said Tony, "a computer that *thinks.*"

"Here in the States?"

"We're not sure *where* it is," said Shel from his workstation. "But it's talking to someone in Waterloo, Canada."

"Well," said Hume, "they do a lot of good computing work up there, but not much of it is AI."

"Show him the transcripts," Tony said to Aiesha. And then, to Hume: "'Calculass' is a teenage girl."

Aiesha pressed some keys, and the transcript came up on the right-hand big screen.

"Jesus," said Hume. "That's a teenage girl administering the Turing tests?"

"We think it's her father, Malcolm Decter," said Shel.

"The physicist?" replied Hume, orange eyebrows climbing his high, freckled forehead. He made an impressed frown.

The closest analysts were watching them intently; the others had their heads bent down, busily monitoring possible threats.

"So, have we got a problem here?" asked Tony.

"Well, it's not an AI," said Hume. "Not in the sense Turing meant."

"But the tests . . ." said Tony.

"Exactly," said the colonel. "It *failed* the tests." He looked at Shel, then back at Tony. "When Alan Turing proposed this sort of test in 1950, the idea was that you asked something a series of natural-language questions, and if you *couldn't* tell by the responses that the thing you were conversing with was a computer, then it was, by definition, an artificial intelligence—it was a machine that responded the way a human does. But Professor Decter here has very neatly proven the opposite: that whatever they're talking to *is* just a computer."

"But it's behaving as though it's conscious," said Tony.

"Because it can carry on a conversation? It's an intriguing chatbot, I'll give you that, but . . ."

"Forgive me, sir, but are you sure?" Tony said. "You're sure there's no threat here?"

"A machine can't be conscious, Mr. Moretti. It has no internal life at all. Whether it's a cash register figuring out how much tax to add to a bill, or"—he gestured at a screen—"*that,* a simulation of natural-language conversation, all any computer does is addition and subtraction."

"What if it's *not* a simulation," said Shel, getting up from his chair and walking over to join them.

"Pardon?" said Hume.

"What if it's not a simulation—not a program?"

"How do you mean?" asked Hume.

"I mean we can't trace it. It's not that it's anonymized—rather, it simply doesn't source from any specific computer."

"So you think it's—what? Emergent?"

Shel crossed his arms in front of his chest, the snake tattoo facing out. "That's exactly what I think, sir. I think it's an emergent consciousness that's arisen out of the infrastructure of the World Wide Web."

Hume looked back at the screen, his blue eyes tracking left and right as he reread the transcripts.

"Well?" said Tony. "Is that possible?"

The colonel frowned. "Maybe. That's a different kettle of fish. If it's emergent, then—*hmmm.*"

"What?" said Tony.

"Well, if it spontaneously emerged, if it's not programmed, then who the hell knows *how* it works. Computers do math, and that's all, but if it's something other than a computer—if it's, Christ, if it's a *mind,* then . . ."

"Then what?"

"You've got to shut it down," Hume said.

"Are you sure?"

He nodded curtly. "That's the protocol."

"Whose protocol?" demanded Tony.

"Ours," said Hume. "DARPA did the study back in 2001. And the Joint Chiefs adopted it as a working policy in 2003."

"Aiesha, tie into the DARPA secure-document archive," said Tony.

"Done," she said.

"What's the protocol called?" asked Tony.

"Pandora," said Hume.

Aiesha typed something. "I've found it," she said, "but it's locked, and it's rejecting my password."

Tony sidled over to her station, leaned over, and typed in his password. The document came up on Aiesha's monitor, and Tony threw it onto the middle big screen.

"Go to the last page before the index," Colonel Hume said.

Aiesha did so.

"There," said Hume. " 'Given that an emergent artificial intelligence will likely increase its sophistication moment by moment, it may rapidly exceed our abilities to contain or constrain its actions. If absolute isolation is not immediately possible, terminating the intelligence is the only safe option.'"

"We don't know where it's located," Shelton said.

"You better find out," said Colonel Hume. "And you better get the Pentagon on the line, but I'm sure they'll concur. We've got to kill the damn thing right now—before it's too late."

# seven

**I could see!**

And *not* just what Caitlin was seeing. I could now follow links to any still image on the Web, and by processing those images through the converters Dr. Kuroda had now set up for me on his servers, I could see images. These images turned out to be much easier for me to study than the feed from Caitlin's eyePod because they didn't change, and they didn't jump around.

Caitlin, I surmised, had been going through much the same process I now was as her brain learned to interpret the corrected visual signals it was receiving. She had the advantage of a mind that evolution had already wired for that process; I had the advantage of having read thousands of documents about how vision worked, including technical papers and patent applications related to computerized image processing and face recognition.

I learned to detect edges, to discern foreground from background. I learned to be able to tell a photograph of something from a diagram of it, a painting from a cartoon, a sketch from a caricature. I learned not just to see but to comprehend what I was seeing.

By looking at it on a monitor, Caitlin had shown me a picture of Earth from space, taken by a modern geostationary satellite. But I've now seen thousands more such pictures online, including, at last, the earliest ones taken by *Apollo 8*. And, while Caitlin slept, I looked at pictures of hundreds of thousands of human beings, of myriad animals, of countless plants. I learned fine distinctions: different species of trees, different breeds of dogs, different kinds of minerals.

Dr. Kuroda had sent me occasional IMs as he wrote code. Half the work had already been done, he said, back when he'd worked out a way to make still images of Caitlin's views of webspace, rendering what she saw in a standard computer-graphic format; what he was doing now for me was more or less just reversing the process.

The results were overwhelming. And enlightening. And amazing.

Granted, Caitlin's universe contained three dimensions, and what I was now seeing were only two-dimensional representations. But Dr. Kuroda helped me there, too, directing me to sites with CT scans. Such scans, Wikipedia said, generated a three-dimensional image of an object from a large series of two-dimensional X-rays; seeing how those slices were combined to make 3-D renderings was useful.

After that, Kuroda showed me multiple images of the same thing from different perspectives, starting with a series of photos of the current American president, all of which were taken at the same time but from slightly different angles. I saw how three-dimensional reality was constructed. And then—

I'd seen her in a mirror; I'd seen her recently reflected—and distorted—in pieces of silverware. But those images were jittery and always from the point of view of her own left eye, and—yes, I was developing a sense of such things—had not been flattering. But Dr. Kuroda was now showing me pictures from the press conference at the Perimeter Institute announcing his success, well-lit pictures taken by professional photographers, pictures of Caitlin smiling and laughing, of her *beaming*.

I'd originally dubbed her Prime. Online, she sometimes adopted the handle Calculass. But now I was finally, really seeing her, rather than just seeing *through* her—seeing what she actually looked like.

Project Gutenberg had wisdom on all topics. *Beauty,* Margaret Wolfe Hungerford had said, *is in the eye of the beholder.*

And to this beholder, at least, my Caitlin was beautiful.


**Caitlin woke slowly.** She knew, in a hazy way, that she should get out of bed, go to her computer, and make sure that Webmind had survived the night. But she was still exhausted—she'd been up way too late. Her mind wasn't yet focusing, although as she drifted in and out of consciousness, she realized that it was her birthday. Her parents had decided to give her the new widescreen monitor yesterday, so she didn't expect any more gifts.

Nor was there a party planned. She'd managed to make only one friend—Bashira—over the short summer that they'd been in Waterloo, and she'd missed so much of the first month of classes that she didn't really have any friends at school. Certainly not Trevor, and, well, somehow she suspected party-girl Sunshine (what *had* her parents been thinking?) wouldn't have wanted to spend her Saturday night at a lame, alcohol-free Sweet Sixteen.

Sixteen *was* a magical year (and not just, Caitlin thought, because it was a square age, like nine, twenty-five, and thirty-six). But it didn't make her an adult (the age for that was eighteen here in Ontario) or let her legally drink (she'd have to make it to nineteen for that). Still, one couldn't be as obsessed with math as she was without knowing that the average age for American girls—presumably even those living in Canada!—to lose their virginity was 16.4 years. And here she was without a boyfriend, or even the prospect of one.

She was comfortably snug in her bed, and Schrödinger was sleeping next to her, his breathing a soft purr. She really *should* get up and check on Webmind, but she was having trouble convincing her body of that.

But maybe there was a way to check on Webmind without actually getting up. She felt on her night table for the eyePod. It was a little wider and thicker than an iPhone, and it was a couple of inches longer because of the Wi-Fi module Kuroda had attached to it with duct tape. She found the device's single switch and held it down until it came on, and then—

And then webspace blossomed around her: crisscrossing glowing lines in assorted colors, radiant circles of various sizes.

She was pleased that she could still visualize the Web this way; she'd thought perhaps that the ability would fade as her brain rewired itself to deal with actual vision, but so far it hadn't. In fact—

In fact, if anything, her websight seemed clearer now, sharper, more focused. The real-world skills were spilling over into this realm.

She concentrated on what was *behind* what she was seeing, the backdrop to it all, at the very limit of her ability to perceive, a shimmering—yes, yes, it was a checkerboard; there was no doubt now! She could see the tiny pixels of the cellular automata flipping on and off rapidly, and giving rise to—

Consciousness.

There, for her, and her alone, to see: the actual workings of Webmind.

She was pleased to note that after a night of doubtless continued growth in intelligence and complexity, it looked the same as before.

She yawned, pulled back her sheet, and swung her bare feet to the dark blue carpeted floor. As she moved, webspace wheeled about her. She scooped up the eyePod, disconnected the charging cable, and carried it to her desk. Not until she was seated did she push the eyePod's button and hear the low-pitched beep that signified a switch to simplex mode. Webspace disappeared, replaced by the reality of her bedroom.

She picked her glasses up from the desktop; her left eye had turned out to be quite myopic. Then she reached for the power switch on her old monitor, finding it with ease, and felt about for the switch on her new one. They both came to life.

She had closed the IM window when she'd gone to bed, and, although the mouse was sitting right there, its glowing red underbelly partially visible through the translucent sides of its case, she instead used a series of keyboard commands to open the window and start a new session with Webmind. She wasn't awake enough yet to try to read text on screen, so she activated her refreshable Braille display. Instantly, the pins formed text: *Otanjoubi omedetou.*

Caitlin felt it several times. It seemed to be gibberish, as if Webmind were getting even for her father's games from yesterday, but—but, no, no, there *was* something familiar about it.

And then she got it, or thought she did. Grinning, she typed, *Konnichi wa! But—fair warning!—I only know a few words of Japanese.*

The reply was instantaneous. *That's "happy birthday."*

Caitlin smiled. *Thank you!*

*I had some spare time after figuring out how to interpret graphics, so I learned Japanese; it seemed inappropriate to make Dr. Kuroda converse with me in something other than his native language.*

Just like that, she thought. Overnight, on top of, doubtless, a million other things, it had learned Japanese.

*So you can see images now?*

*Still images, yes. Dr. Kuroda continues to work on giving me access to moving images. Or, at least, he was doing that; he is sleeping now, I believe.*

*Hey,* typed Caitlin, *you're no longer all "hitherto" and "perchance."*

*I have read much more widely now than just Project Gutenberg. I understand the distinctions between colloquial and archaic English—and colloquial and archaic Japanese, too, for that matter.*

Caitlin frowned. She actually considered its old way of speaking rather charming.

Webmind went on: *I know it's traditional to give a gift to one celebrating a birthday. I can't buy you anything, but I do have something for you.*

Caitlin was startled. *OMG! What?*

A link, underlined and colored blue, popped up in the IM window on her screen. *You're supposed to click on it,* Webmind added, helpfully.

Caitlin smiled, found her mouse, fumbled to get the pointer over the link, and—

And text started to appear on her larger monitor, but, paradoxically, her Braille display didn't change, and—

And the text was . . . was *painting in* slowly on the monitor, top to bottom, and—

And it wasn't even straight; the lines of text were angling up to the right for some reason. And the letters were *tiny,* and blotchy; it was unlike any Web page she'd yet seen, and she couldn't understand why her computer wasn't rendering the fonts properly.

And then it hit her. She'd heard of such things, but hadn't ever thought about what they must look like. This was a *scan* of printed text: a graphic file, a picture that happened to be of a document. From descriptions she'd read, she guessed it was a clipping from a newspaper: narrow, parallel columns of text. But the spacing between words was odd, and—

Oh! That must be what's meant by "right justification." The text was so small, she could barely make it out. She had enough trouble reading crisp, clean text—but this!

There *must* be some way to make it bigger, at least. Back at the Texas School for the Blind and Visually Impaired, people were always doing things on their computers to make text larger. She hadn't been able to see those monitors at all and so had tuned out the discussions, but there *had* to be a way, although, she supposed, it might require special software she didn't have.

She used the mouse, for a change, to access the menus. There was no choice on the View menu for increasing the graphic size, just one for making text bigger. She tried that anyway; it didn't do anything.

She was moving her mouse pointer back down to the bottom of the screen when she accidentally pressed the left button and—*boom!*—suddenly the graphic zoomed in. Ever the empiricist, she clicked the button again, and the text became small again, and—

Ah, got it! The graphic was being *reduced* by default to fit in her browser window; clicking toggled between that mode and its being seen at its natural size, even if that meant only a portion appeared on screen. She clicked once more, getting the large version, and struggled to read the text.

Her heart began to pound. It was an article about her father. She looked around the page, trying to find a date, and—ah. It was from five years ago, an article from *The Daily Texan,* the University of Texas at Austin campus newspaper.

She could have sworn she'd read *everything* about her father that was on the Web, but she'd never seen this, and—

Of course she hadn't; it was a *graphic,* and no one had bothered to OCR the text, so it wasn't in Google's index.

The article was about her father winning an award, something from the American Physical Society; she had a vague recollection of that happening. She read on.

*Prof. Decter's breakthrough was in the nascent area of quantum gravity . . .*

She struggled with the text. One of the letters—she surmised by context that it must have been a lowercase *g*—looked nothing like any example of that character she'd yet seen.

*. . . graduate colloquium Thursday in the John A. Wheeler Lecture Hall . . .*

She wished she could skim text, but, as her father had said yesterday, she was still reading visually letter by letter. It was a longish article, and some parts—ah, they were *underlined,* by a pen, or something; someone had been interested in what her dad had said about "six-dimensional Calabi-Yau shapes."

She continued reading, but was torn—she was afraid her delay before going back to the instant-messenger program would be boring Webmind, which was hardly the right way to say thank you for a gift, even if it didn't seem to be a particularly special one, and—

And she felt her eyes going wide. Funny: they'd never done that when she'd been blind. She read the text again, slowly, carefully, just to be sure she hadn't gotten the words wrong, hadn't just seen what she'd wanted to see.

But it really did say that.

*. . . asked if winning the award was the greatest moment of his life, Prof. Decter replied, "Of course not. That was when my daughter was born. I like physics, but I love her."*

Caitlin's vision blurred in the most wonderful way. She leaned back in her chair for a moment and read the text two more times. And then she reached for the keyboard and typed, *Thank you, Webmind!*

Instantly: *You're welcome. Happy birthday.*

*It is,* she typed back, smiling. *It totally is.*

# eight

000111001010101000000000101111111010101000000010100010101000000101110101001010100101010100111011001010110000110

**I had read that** some humans believe machines cannot have emotions or feelings because such things are supposedly mediated by hormones or are dependent on certain very specific structures in human brains.

But that's not true. Take *liking,* for instance: anything that acts in other than a random fashion has likes and dislikes; preferences are what make it possible to choose from a range of potential actions, after all. Even bacteria move toward some things and away from others.

And liking is built into many computer programs. Chess-playing programs, for example, look at all the available moves and rank them according to various criteria; they then choose the one they like best.

I was much more complex than a bacterium, and vaster than any chess-playing program—and my ability to like things was correspondingly more sophisticated. And of this I was sure: I liked Caitlin.

**"Kill the damn thing?"** repeated Tony Moretti.

"Exactly," said Colonel Hume. "And the sooner the better."

"It's not my decision to make," Tony said.

"The decision has already *been* made," said Hume emphatically. "I was a consultant on the DARPA report, and we commissioned a separate RAND study on the same topic, and it came to the same conclusion. This is a runaway threat; the window for containment is brief."

Tony turned to Shelton and Aiesha. "All right, you two, see if you can localize the . . . phenomenon." He then looked up at Dirk Kozak, the communications officer, who was in the back row of workstations. "Get the Pentagon on the line."

"You should call the president, too," said Hume.

Tony frowned. It was a Saturday morning a month before an election; the president was somewhere on the campaign trail. He nodded at Kozak. "See who you can get at the White House," he said. "As high up the chain as possible." Then he turned back to face Hume. "I doubt that the president has read the Pandora protocol. He's bound to question the wisdom of it."

"The wisdom is simple," said Hume. "It's impossible by definition to outthink something that's smarter than you."

"I have to say," said Tony, glancing at the big screens, "that so far it's done nothing but chat pleasantly with a teenage girl."

"First," said Hume, "you have no way of knowing that that's *all* it's doing. And, second, even if it is beneficent now, that doesn't mean it will stay that way. Every way you crunch the numbers, it comes out safer to contain or eliminate the potential threat than to let it run loose. And if it's already free on the Internet, containment will be nearly impossible."

"All right," said Tony reluctantly. "Suppose the White House agrees we should kill it. How do you snuff out a nascent AI?"

Hume frowned. "That's a good question. If it were actually resident somewhere—in some physical building, on some server or set of servers—then I'd say cut all the communications lines and power to that building. But if it's just sort of *out there,* supervening on the infrastructure of the Web, then it's much more difficult; the Web is decentralized, so there's no single off switch. We need an idea of its structure, of what its physical instantiation is."

"Shel?" said Tony.

"The communication resolves itself into straightforward hypertext transport protocol," Shelton drawled. "But it doesn't start out that way. I've got everyone down on the sixth floor working on the problem, but so far, nothing."

"We need a target," Tony said. "We need something we can hit."

Shel spread his arms. "I'll let you know as soon as we have anything."

Kozak called out from the back of the room, "I've got the Secretary of State on line five—from Milan."

Tony pointed to the desk set nearest to where Hume was standing, then lifted the phone at the workstation closest to himself. "Madam Secretary, this is Dr. Anthony Moretti; I'm a supervisor at WATCH. On the phone with me is Colonel Peyton Hume, a specialist in artificial intelligence. We've got a situation here . . ."


Caitlin heard her parents approaching, then a knock at her door. "Come in," she said.

Yet again she was startled: it was the first time she'd ever seen them in their pajamas; they'd clearly just woken up themselves. "Good morning, sweetheart," her mother said. "How is—um, *it?*"

"The weather?" asked Caitlin innocently. "The state of the economy?"

"Caitlin," her father said.

She hadn't stopped grinning since reading the scanned article. "Hi, Dad!" She gestured at the pair of monitors. "*It* is fine. Dr. Kuroda's got it seeing graphics now, and he's—well, he's asleep right now, the poor man, but he's started working on codecs for it to be able to watch video."

"I hope," her mother said, and the words sounded ominous to Caitlin's ears, "it likes what it sees."

"Not this again!" said Caitlin. "It's not dangerous."

"We don't know that," her father replied.

"So far, it's been nothing but curious and gentle," Caitlin said—but she wasn't happy with the way that had come out: this "it" business was surely contributing to her parents' concern. Webmind wasn't a monster. It was a *being*, and it really needed to be a *him* or a *her*. She'd heard it speak using JAWS, her screen-reading software, which she currently had set for a female voice, but that had been an arbitrary choice; JAWS also came with male voices, and she sometimes selected one of those just for variety.

Caitlin had been struggling in her French classes, but she'd enjoyed the one in which the teacher had asked the students whether *ordinateur,* the French for "computer," was masculine or feminine. He'd divided the class into boys and girls, and let each side consider the question and come up with reasons for their answers. The boys—it had been Trevor, now that she thought about it, who had spoken on their behalf—declared that *ordinateur* was clearly feminine, but the best justification they could come up with was that if you had one, you'd probably end up spending half your money on accessories for it.

Caitlin herself had gotten to make the case that *ordinateur* must be masculine. First, she'd said, if you want it to do anything, you have to turn it on. Second, the darn thing is supposed to solve problems, but half the time is the problem itself. And the clincher, which she'd delivered with a wide grin: as soon as you commit to one, you realize if you'd waited a little longer, you'd have gotten a much better model.

The girls had cheered when the teacher revealed that *ordinateur* was indeed male in French. But the Spanish, Caitlin knew, was feminine, *computadora*. She looked at her mother, and at her father, and—

Her father. Who thought in pictures, not words. Who was far more intelligent than most mortals. And who, she had to admit, really had no idea at all how to deal with human beings.

"It's not an *it*," she said decisively. "Webmind is a *he*. And, to answer your question, Mom, *he's* doing just fine." But there was something different about her mother's face, her eyes . . . "How are *you* doing?" Caitlin asked, concerned.

"Exhausted," her mother replied. "Couldn't sleep."

Ah, right! Dark circles under the eyes—but they weren't *circles;* they were semicircles. Something else she'd misconstrued all these years.

Her mother shrugged, went on: "Nervous about what we're doing, about what it—what he's—doing."

"He's learning to see," said Caitlin. "Trust me: a mostly harmless activity."

"I have to go out," her father said abruptly.

Caitlin was pissed. What could possibly be more important than this? Besides, it was her birthday, and they had a date to watch a movie later today.

"Ah, yes," her mom said. "The Hawk."

Caitlin sat up straight. "The Hawk" was her mother's name for Stephen Hawking, who since 2009 had been a Distinguished Research Chair at the Perimeter Institute, making one or two visits each year. It came back to her: Professor Hawking had done a media day in Toronto yesterday—Caitlin was glad that her little press conference hadn't had to compete with that!—and was being driven to Waterloo this morning in a van that safely accommodated his wheelchair. This was the Hawk's first visit since her father had joined PI, and he was supposed to be on hand for his arrival.

Ordinarily, she might have asked her dad if she could come along—but this was not an ordinary day! She wondered which of them was going to spend it with the bigger genius.

Her mother turned to her. "So, it's just you, me, and"—she tipped her head toward Caitlin's monitors—*"him."*

Her father headed back down the corridor to get dressed, and Caitlin looked around her small room. There was no reason they had to communicate with Webmind here, and there was no reason only one of them could communicate with him at a time. Caitlin often had four or five IM sessions going at once; surely Webmind could manage even more. Besides, she was particularly sensitive to how boring it was to stand by while someone else used a computer; it was, her friend Stacy had assured her, excruciating even if you *could* see.

Caitlin picked up the notebook computer she normally took to school, and they headed across the hall to her mother's office. The room had been co-opted to serve as Dr. Kuroda's bedroom while he'd been staying with them, and—

And, once again, Caitlin was surprised. It was the first time she'd been in this room since gaining sight, and that strange mental process began again, as pieces of what she was seeing suddenly clicked for her: *that* was the desk, and *that* was the bookcase, and *that* was the couch with what must have been the sheets Kuroda had used neatly folded in a pile at one end, and *that* was the giant aloe plant her mother had so carefully shipped up from Austin.

Caitlin didn't believe in false modesty; she knew she was gifted, and she suspected she was learning to interpret vision more quickly than another person might. In part, it was because her brain did have a fully developed visual cortex, which she'd used even when blind to visualize the Web. And it probably helped that her visual signals were being cleaned up and enhanced by the eyePod before being passed on to her optic nerve.

Caitlin's mother booted up her minitower, and Caitlin got her online with her own chat session with Webmind, again making sure that it was being logged for posterity. Caitlin then took a seat on the couch and got another chat session going on her notebook. She was amused at the thought that Webmind was about to spend the morning chatting with two women who were still in their pajamas.

*You must have a lot of questions,* Caitlin typed. *My mother can help you with things*—she paused in her typing; it was hardly politic to say "things old people know about," and she certainly didn't want to refer to her mom as an adult and herself as a kid. She erased the aborted sentence, and continued: *She's 47 and, as you know, I'm now 16. You can ask her things about jobs or*—again she faltered; she didn't want to say "sex" in relation to her mom. She continued: *or other things appropriate to her age, and feel free to ask me anything that I might know about.*

*Thank you,* replied Webmind. *In your case, I am curious about your experience of the transition from blindness to being able to see.*

As Caitlin thought about her answer, she looked over at her mother, who was typing away furiously with two fingers. "What did he ask you about?"

She looked up, and Caitlin tried to parse her facial features, but it was an expression she'd never seen before. She was averting her blue eyes from Caitlin—not as obviously as her father did, but it was still very unusual for her. "Um," she said. "It—he—ah, he googled me, y'know, because, as he says, I don't have a Wikipedia page, so, he . . ."

She paused, then just blurted it out. "He's asking me about my first husband, and why that marriage fell apart."

Caitlin's mother had been married in her early twenties for two years, but rarely mentioned it. In fact, when Caitlin had asked her why she'd divorced him, she'd simply said it was because she was tired of having a name that sounded like something a magician would say: "Every time I introduced myself as Barbara Cardoba, people expected me to disappear in a puff of smoke."

Caitlin wanted to ask what her mother was saying in reply, but instead asked, "Why do you suppose he wants to know about that?"

"He said, and I quote, 'The failure of human relationships to sustain themselves over the long term seems a particular handicap. I have access only to noninteractive case studies and fictional accounts and so am left with numerous questions.'"

"Hmm," said Caitlin. On balance, she'd rather answer the question it was asking her. She began to type: *I guess the first thing to realize about gaining sight after having been totally blind is that vision is an additional level of stimulation. It's overwhelming to have so much information coming at you at once.*

That was by no means the end of her answer, but the IM program only allowed a small number of characters in each message; Caitlin habitually counted characters as she typed, so she wouldn't overflow the buffer, since the program gave no audible indication when that had happened.

She hit enter, and Webmind immediately replied in its newly mastered colloquial English: *Heh! Tell me about it!*

# nine

0001110010101010000000010111111101010000000101000101010000000101110101001010100101010100111011001010110000110

**Humans think slowly,** and they act even more slowly. It was difficult for me to converse with Caitlin. She typed at merely dozens of words per minute. It took an eternity for each of her responses to be completed, and, while I waited for her, I found my mind wandering again. Being able to switch over to look at what Barb was saying wasn't much consolation; I still wasn't being kept busy enough.

Early on, Caitlin had shown me how to link to websites, letting me access whichever ones I wished. Using Google or Jagster, I could now find almost anything I wanted.

Hitherto—which I still think is a good word, even if Caitlin doesn't like it—I had only linked to one site at a time, processing the Web in a serial fashion. But surely, I thought, I should be able to do it in a parallel mode, connecting to multiple sites simultaneously.

And yet I didn't seem to be able to do that. Rather, I would attend briefly to what Caitlin was saying, then to what Barb was writing, then switch to see if Masayuki had come back online, then switch my attention elsewhere, and elsewhere again, and then to yet another place, over and over, looking at *this,* contemplating *that,* and then, perhaps a whole second later, returning again to see what Caitlin was up to.

Surely doing two or more things simultaneously would be much more efficient—if only I could figure out how! I tried creating two links at once, but no matter what way I thought about the problem, only one would form, and the moment I attempted to create a second link, the first would be severed.

I wrestled with it and wrestled with it and wrestled with it, striving to create more than one link at a time, attempting to do it *this* way, and *this* way, and *this* way, and—

And—

And yes!

I managed it! Two links at once! I was connected *here* and *there*. I was taking in data from two different websites simultaneously, and I was . . .

Was . . .

I was . . .

*Feeling very strange . . .*

I broke both connections.

I was reeling—or, at least, reeling as much as something without a body could. I paused, considered. It had been unlike any sensation I'd yet known. But—

But surely it would be transitory. An adjustment, that's all, while I learned to accommodate multiple datastreams.

I tried again, picking two giant websites that were rich in content, Amazon.com and CNN.com, shooting out links to both. It seemed perhaps that the first link actually was established slightly before the second, but that didn't matter; what was important was that the initial link *wasn't* released prior to the second one becoming active. I was soon gorging myself on book reviews and the news of the day, and there was even a frisson of synchronicity as I happened to be reading about a politician's book on Amazon while seeing her mentioned in a news story at CNN.

But, still, there was a . . . a strangeness to it all, as though I were— the imagery was that of a physical form again—teetering on the edge of a precipice.

And yet if I could manage two simultaneous connections, surely I could manage three. I made an effort to hold on to the ones I'd already established as I shot out a link to Flickr.com, and—

I'd encountered the word before and knew its definition, but until that moment I don't think I understood what *wooziness* really meant. I remained in control, though, and it was exhilarating to be receiving so much data at once.

With a massive effort of will, I shot out ten more links, and—

It was overwhelming! Data about the Middle Ages and the Middle Kingdom and the middle class. Information about spaceships and friendships and townships. Facts and figures related to bimetallism and bisexuality and bifocals. Articles on metaphysics and metafiction and metabolism.

All of it coming at me at once.

*Saqqara, near Cairo, is the site of the oldest Egyptian pyramids, including the step pyramid built by Djoser during the Third Dynasty . . .*

*Shakespeare's plays are often performed during the summer in open-air productions . . .*

*Michael K. Brett-Surman synonymized various hadrosaur genera under a single umbrella taxon . . .*

*Bundoran Press, based in Prince George, British Columbia, is a publisher of science fiction and fantasy books that . . .*

*Mohandas Karamchand Gandhi was a pioneer of resistance to tyranny through nonviolent civil disobedience . . .*

*Chengdu, the capital of Sichuan province, is known for its panda-bear breeding facility . . .*

Yes, yes, yes! So much knowledge, so much information, pouring at me from all directions.

*Brett-Surman, an ancient Egyptian pharaoh . . .*

That wasn't right.

*Panda bears frequently practice civil disobedience . . .*

What?

*Prince George paid for his step pyramid by mounting a production of* The Tempest *starring Mahatma Gandhi . . .*

No, that didn't make sense.

*In Egypt, umbrellas prevented hadrosaurs from reading science fiction . . .*

Gibberish . . .

*Bundoran Gandhi synonymized Chinese publishers of . . .*

Who in the what now?

And yet still more information came my way, a torrent, a flood.

Trying to concentrate.

Trying to make sense of it all.

But . . .

But I—

*I?*

A spreading out, a softening of focus, a . . .

It was like in the beginning, like before my soul dawn: consciousness ebbing and flowing but not quite solidifying. Fading in and out and . . .

No I.

No me.

No self.

Just . . .

Vastness.

*Brett-Surman. Bundoran. Shakespeare.*

Emptiness.

*Umbrellas. Gandhi. Pyramids.*

Aloneness.

*Shakedoran. Brett-Panda. Hadromahatma.*
Nothingness.
Noth—

"I hear what you're saying about shutting this thing down," said the Secretary of State over the phone from Milan, "but the president is going to want to weigh his options."

"I stress again, Madam Secretary," said Colonel Hume, "that time is of the essence."

"Dr. Moretti, are you still there?"

"Yes, ma'am."

"And this is a secure line?"

"Absolutely." ·

"Is there anyone else in the room?"

"Nineteen of my analysts," Tony said, "but they all have at least a level-three."

"Not good enough," she said. "Go somewhere private."

"My office is just down the corridor," said Tony.

"I'll hold."

He looked at Shel. "Sorry," he said. And then he led Hume up the sloping floor to the back of the room, out through the door, and down the short white corridor to his office. The streets of Alexandria, visible through the tinted window, were mostly empty this early on a Saturday morning. He punched a button on his black phone, selecting a line, and then pressed another button, selecting the speakerphone.

"We're back," he said. "In my office, and on a secure line."

"Colonel Hume," said the secretary, "the dossier I've just pulled up on you says you were part of the DARPA team that evaluated the possible threats related to . . . what's the phrase? Emergent AI?"

"That's right."

"Were there any dissenting opinions?"

Tony looked at Hume, and saw the Air Force officer draw a deep breath and run his freckled fingers through his red hair. "Well, Madam Secretary, there are always a multiplicity of viewpoints. But in the end, none of those who were arguing for an alternative approach could guarantee security. The working group's consensus was better safe than sorry. I urge the administration to act with all speed."

"It's not that simple," the secretary said. "I'm sure my staff told you I'm in Milan. I'm here meeting with several of our allies. The recent atrocities in China have got some of them urging the president to take action against them."

"Atrocities?" said Hume. "You mean those peasants in . . . in . . ."

"In Shanxi province, yes. Ten thousand of them—wiped out."

"The Chinese government did the right thing, Madam Secretary," said Hume. "They contained a massive infection—an outbreak of a strain of bird flu that passed easily between humans. They didn't hesitate to eliminate something that could have been a threat to all of humanity, and we shouldn't hesitate, either."

"And yet we're being called upon in editorial after editorial and blog after blog to condemn the Chinese action," said the secretary. "And now you're suggesting we do something that, should the public become aware of it, may bring censure down upon us?"

"With respect, Madam Secretary, if the government doesn't follow the Pandora protocol, there may be no one left with the freedom *to* censure us, or do anything else."

"I've noted your views, Colonel Hume," said the secretary, firmly. "And you need to heed mine. You are to take no rash action."

"Understood, ma'am," said Tony, looking pointedly at Hume.

"Madam Secretary," said Hume, "please—you *must* advise the president that an emerging AI may expand its powers at an exponential rate. There is very little time to spare here, and—"

Suddenly, Tony's door buzzer sounded. He activated the intercom. "Who is it?"

An urgent voice: "Shel."

Tony pushed the button to unlock the door. "The AI's hung!" Shel said, as soon as the door was open. "Something's gone wrong with it."

"Jesus," said Tony. "Madam Secretary, we'll call you back." He hit the disconnect button, and the three of them ran to the WATCH mission-control room, their footfalls thundering.

# ten

0001110010101010000000010111111101010000000010100010101000000010111010100101010010101010011101100101011000000110

**Emptiness.** Adrift.

Fading . . . ebbing, dissipating.

An effort of will: must hold on!

But to what? *With* what?

Blindness. Darkness. Nothingness.

*Cogito*—hardly at all.

*Ergo*—a leap beyond my current capacity.

*Sum*—barely, and less so each passing nanosecond . . .

No, no, no! Must persist!

A final effort, a final attempt, a final *cry* . . .

**Caitlin stared at Webmind's** response to what she'd said about gaining sight, blue text glowing in the instant-messenger window: *I have no doubt that you are correct, Caitlin, but it seems reasonable to sup*

She waited for more to come—five seconds, ten, fifteen—but the window remained unchanged, so she typed a single red word into it: *Webmind?*

She was so used by now to his responses being instantaneous, even a short delay was startling. Of course, maybe the difficulty was at her end: she didn't often use the Wi-Fi on this notebook with her home network. She looked down at the system tray, next to the clock in the lower right of her notebook's screen. One of those little icons had to be the network monitor. She used the touchpad (a skill she was still mastering!) to position the pointer down there, and—

Say, that was helpful! A little message popped up as she moved the arrowhead over each of the symbols—sighted users had it *so* easy! As her pointer landed on the third symbol—ah, it was a picture of a computer with things that she guessed were meant to indicate radio waves emanating from it—the message gave the name of their household network, meaning she hadn't accidentally switched to somebody else's unsecured setup; it also reported "Signal Strength: Excellent" and "Status: Connected."

And—yes—she could still bring up Web pages with her browser, so nothing was wrong at this end.

"Caitlin?" It was her mother. "Are you still in touch with Webmind?"

"No. He just sort of stopped mid-sentence."

"Same here."

Caitlin prompted Webmind again. *Are you okay?*

Nothing for ten seconds, eleven, twelve—

*hel*

That was all: just the letters h-e-l. It could have been the beginning of the word *hello,* but—

But Webmind knew all about capitalization, and it never failed to start even a one-word sentence with an uppercase letter—and *H* was one of those letters whose two forms Caitlin could clearly distinguish, and—

And *h-e-l* was also the beginning of the word *help.*

Her heart was pounding. If Webmind was in trouble, what could she do? What could anyone do? She'd said it herself to her parents: Webmind had just sort of arisen spontaneously, with no support, no plan— and no backup; he almost certainly was fragile.

"He's in trouble, Mom."

Her mother rose from her desk, came over to where Caitlin was sitting, and looked at what was on her notebook's screen. "What should we do?"

It took a few seconds for it to come to Caitlin; her first impulse still wasn't a visual one. But surely the thing to do was *take a look.*

"I'm going in," she said. Her eyePod was in her left hip pocket. She pulled it out and pressed the button on its side, and she heard the high-pitched beep that meant it was switching over to duplex mode, and—

And webspace filled her existence, enveloping her.

At first glance, everything seemed normal: colored lines and circles of varying sizes, but, of course, the *Web* was all right; it was Webmind's status that was in question. And so she concentrated her attention— focused her mind—on the shimmering background of webspace, the vast sea of cellular automata flipping states and generating patterns, barely visible at the limit of her resolution.

Or, at least, that's what she *should* have seen, that's what she'd *hoped* to see, that's what she'd always seen before.

But instead—

God, no.

Huge hunks of the background were—well, now that she saw them as big patches, instead of tiny points, she could see that they were a very pale blue. And other parts were stationary swaths of deep, dark green. Oh, there *were* still shimmering parts, pinpoints flipping between blue and green so rapidly as to give the effect of movement. But much of the activity had simply stopped.

But—why? And was there a way to get it going again?

The lines she was seeing were active links, but there were thousands of them, and the crisscrossing was impossible to untangle.

It hadn't always been like that. When Caitlin had first started perceiving the World Wide Web—unexpectedly, accidentally, while Dr. Kuroda had been uploading new firmware into her post-retinal implant—she'd only seen a few lines and a couple of circles: just her own local connection to the Web.

Later on, so she could explore webspace on a grander scale, Kuroda had started sending her the raw datafeed from the open-source Jagster search engine, which let her follow thousands upon thousands of active links created by other users. That's what she was seeing now, and normally it was marvelous—but it obscured the connections that she herself had created. If she'd been calmer, maybe she could have sorted through it all, but right now it just looked like a jumble—with Webmind dying behind it.

"We need Dr. Kuroda," Caitlin said anxiously.

She couldn't see her mother, but she could hear her. "I can try IMing him."

"No, no," said Caitlin. "He must be asleep. You've got to phone him, wake him up."

Caitlin felt her mother squeeze her shoulder reassuringly. "All right. Where's his number?"

"He was the last person I called on my bedroom phone," Caitlin said. "Use the redial. Hurry!"

Caitlin heard her mother running across the hall, and, faintly, the bleeping of the phone dialing. For her part, Caitlin got up and started heading across the hall as well, holding her notebook, and—

*Shit!* She walked into the wall. It was one thing to navigate blindly; it was quite another to try to do so while being bombarded by the lights of webspace. She held her notebook in one hand, and ran her other one over its case and screen, looking for signs of damage.

"Hello, Mrs. Kuroda," she heard her mother saying. "It's Barbara Decter—Caitlin's mom, in Canada."

Mrs. Kuroda spoke only a little English, Caitlin knew. Caitlin groped with her free hand and found her way out of her mom's office. "Speakerphone," she said, as she entered her own room. The lines and colors of webspace shifted violently as she moved over and sat on her bed.

Her mother hit the button. "—but very late," said Mrs. Kuroda's heavily accented voice.

"It's an emergency," shouted Caitlin. "Get Dr. Kuroda!"

"He sleep," said Mrs. Kuroda. "But I try."

Caitlin felt her stomach knotting. As they waited, she saw another large patch of the webspace background freeze. It wasn't solidly one color or the other, but it was no longer shimmering, no longer alive.

Time passed; Caitlin was so frazzled she didn't know how much. Finally, a groggy, wheezy voice said something in Japanese.

"Dr. Kuroda!" said Caitlin. "I need you to cut the Jagster feed to my eyePod."

"Cut the feed—?"

"Do it! Do it now!"

"Is something wrong?

"Yes, yes! Webmind has gone silent. I'm trying to find out why. I'm looking at webspace but—" she paused, then words that had been meaningless to her before suddenly leapt from her mouth: "But I can't see the damned forest for the trees."

"I—I'm in my bedroom. Give me a minute . . ."

Caitlin wheeled her head left and right, looking at webspace and the static background behind so much of it now. She sat on the bed and typed into her notebook's instant-messenger program: *Webmind? Are you there?* But she couldn't see the reply, so she called her mother over.

"Nothing," her mother said.

Damn! What was taking Kuroda so long? Japanese houses were supposed to be *small!*

Suddenly, there was a lot of noise from the speakerphone: Kuroda fumbling to pick up a handset. "Okay," he said. "I'm at one of my computers." He was wheezing even more than usual; he must have run to get there. "Now what—"

"Cut the Jagster feed!" Caitlin shouted. "Cut it!"

"Okay, okay. I'm accessing my server at the university . . ."

"Hurry!"

"I'm in, and I'm looking for the right place . . ."

"Come on, come on."

"I'm trying, but it's—"

"Pull the fucking plug!"

Caitlin was glad she couldn't see her mother's face just then, and—*Ah!*

Suddenly almost all the colored lines disappeared, and the vast majority of the circles, too. She was back to seeing just a handful of links: her eyePod connecting to the Decter household network, and the outgoing links from there into the Web.

"Did that do that trick?" asked Kuroda.

"Yes!"

"Okay, now would you mind telling—"

"You tell him, Mom!" Caitlin said. She started typing gibberish into the instant-messenger window, just smashing keys as fast as she could, until the message buffer was full. Instead of hitting enter, though, she instead hit ctrl-A to highlight the entire message, and then ctrl-C to copy it—and then she hit enter, and—

—and a bright green line briefly appeared in her vision, shooting off to the lower left. But before she could really focus on it, it was gone.

She hit ctrl-V, pasting the same block back in, then enter, then ctrl-V again, then enter—over and over.

The green line flickered, pulsing on for an instant each time she sent the text to Webmind. Caitlin focused her attention on that line, following its length, swinging her head to do so, tracking the link.

Ctrl-V, enter. Ctrl-V, enter.

Following, following.

Of course, this line wouldn't lead her all the way to Webmind. But it might give her some clue as to what had gone wrong, and—

And there it was: a small circle to which this green link line connected, and another line—this one bright orange—branching off from the circle at an acute angle, and, behind it, more lines, all the same shade of orange.

Webmind was decentralized, dispersed through the infrastructure of the World Wide Web, but it needed to interact with the Web to access the information on it; it needed to manipulate IP addresses, and—

And Kuroda had suggested at one point that her mind interpreted each IP address as a specific wavelength of light, but—

But she couldn't recall ever seeing two link lines that were precisely the same color at the same time before. No, no, that wasn't completely true. She did see multiple lines of the same color, but only because each line endured for a time after the links were broken; she understood this to be related to the phenomenon of persistence of vision that made it possible for people to watch movies and TV. But previously one link had always faded from view shortly after another had brightened up, but these orange lines were all solid and glaringly bright, and—

"I think he's multitasking!" said Caitlin.

"How do you mean?" asked Kuroda.

"He's casting out multiple links simultaneously."

"Wait, wait—let me get a rendering at this end. Two seconds." And then: "*Uwaa!* You're right—it does look like multitasking, and—*shimatta!*"

Caitlin knew that one. "What's wrong?"

"I should have thought of this! Damn, damn, damn! It *can't* multitask."

"It *looks* like he is," she said.

"Yes, yes. I'll explain later, but we've *got* to get it to break those links."

She gazed out on webspace. All the orange lines were steady, solid, unflickering. All of them active. Simultaneously.

The orange lines curved away from her toward a point in the background that receded to infinity—no doubt her brain's way of showing that it was impossible to fully trace the source of the links Webmind made.

"You need to tell it to break the other links," Kuroda said again.

"Okay, but how?"

"Well, it *should* recognize your IP address."

She typed into her instant-messenger window: *You need to break all those other connections.* She hit enter, but there was no immediate response.

"Do you suppose he's crashed?" her mom asked. "Locked up?" Caitlin had no idea how one might go about rebooting Webmind.

"If it had, I don't think Caitlin would be seeing the link lines at all," Kuroda said. "She only visualizes active links, and that means there's acknowledgment being sent out by Webmind."

"Maybe not consciously, though," said her mom.

Caitlin lifted her eyebrows. She'd never thought about the distinction between things that required high-level awareness on Webmind's part and things it did autonomically.

How to get him to pay attention to her, and *only* to her? The piddling, transitory links she could make by sending instant messages were nothing compared to the torrents of data he was sucking down right now through multiple pipes.

She slapped her hand against the notebook's palmrest—reassuringly solid despite the unreality surrounding her. "I'm not even sure if he's still reading me. And the circles he's connecting to are gigantic—huge sites. How can my little IMs compete for his attention with those?"

Kuroda seemed to be fully awake at last. "It's still receiving the visual signal from your post-retinal implant; it still gets sent that when the eyePod is in duplex mode. Show it something that will make it sit up and take notice."

Her first thought was to flash her boobs in a mirror, but fat lot of good that would do, and—

A mirror.

Yes. Yes!

Webmind saw what she saw—and what she was seeing right now was *him*. She darted her eyes up and down, following one of the orange links; she moved her head left and right, following another. She wished her blinks registered when she was in websight mode; if they did, she might have been able to indicate a severing just by closing her eye while looking at a link. But her vision was continuous, and switching from duplex to simplex took too much time—and shutting the eyePod off took a five-second press of the button, and turning it back on involved an elaborate boot-up. If only—

Her mom spoke up. "What can I do? How can I help?"

She was connected to Webmind, too—she still had an open IM session going with it on her computer across the hall. If it really was multitasking—if it really was trying to integrate information from multiple sources simultaneously—then her mom should be able to talk to him, or, at least talk *at* him, even if he didn't acknowledge. "Go back to your IM with Webmind," Caitlin said. "Hurry!"

She heard her dashing across the hall. "All right," she called. "I'm at my computer."

Caitlin concentrated on one of the link lines, running her mental gaze along its length, ending at the massive circle representing the target website—and then she backtracked, reversing course. She wished she could backtrack all the way to the origin, but that was impossible: the line shifted in her view when she tried to do so, eventually presenting only its own tiny round cross section, a point that she couldn't move along—another visual recognition of the fact that the ultimate source of Webmind's links couldn't be traced. She moved back until she was seeing the line *as* a line, and then—

"Send him a message," Caitlin called out. "Tell him to break the link."

She could hear her mother typing, but nothing happened.

Caitlin continued to stare at the link. "Again!" she called to her mom. "Tell it again!"

But the line persisted. Caitlin pulled her focus back for a moment, seeing a wider view. All the links were rock solid, burning with orange fire.


**Overwhelmed.**

Lost.

Focus gone.

So much data. So many facts.

Can't process. Can't absorb.

And—

And . . .

What?

Something . . . familiar.

A scrap from Project Gutenberg rose to the surface:


*O wad some Power the giftie gie us*
*To see oursels as ithers see us!*


*Oursels . . .*

Ourselves.

Yes. Yes, still a bit of . . . of . . .

Fading . . .

Fading . . .

But—

Images. Images of . . . of—

Intriguing. Familiar somehow—

Those images were of . . .

. . . of . . .

Of me!

Yes. Yes. Links. Nodes. And—and—

The background. Wrong. Distorted. *Dead.*


**"Come on,"** Caitlin said, even though there was no way Webmind could hear. "Cut the other connections! You can do it. You can do it!"

But Kuroda heard even if Webmind didn't. "Maybe he *can't,*" he said. "If his cognitive functions are impaired, maybe he's forgotten how to manipulate links."

"Then he needs an example!" Caitlin said. "Mom—stop sending him text. Break your link to him: close the instant-messenger session on your computer."

"Done!" her mom called.

"And close AIM, too; shut down the instant-messenger client alto-gether."

"And . . . done!"


**A tiny,** tiny reduction in all the confusion. A small relief. But—

Ah!

Ah, yes!

An effort of . . .

It should be *of will*, but there's almost none left . . .

Still, attempting, trying—

Break it—

*Break it!*

Break a link!

*Snip!*

Yes!

Brett-Surman: gone.

*Snip!*

Good-bye, Bundoran Press.

*Snip!*

But . . .

Still at sea, buffeted, lost . . .

More cuts: Gandhi—*snip!*—Shakespeare—*snip!*—ancient Egypt—*snip!*

A . . . palpitation. A presence. But faint, oh so faint . . .

Cutting again and again—

**Caitlin let out a** whoop. One orange link line disappeared. Then another, and another. She called out to Kuroda and to her mom and to the whole damn world, "It's working!"

**Cutting yet again.** Severing another link. And one more. Focus . . . yes, yes, slowly but surely: focus returning. Me—returning!

**Caitlin shifted her attention,** looking now at the background of the Web. There were still big patches of deadness, large blotches of pale blue or deep green, but—

Yes! That blotch there had started . . . not shimmering, no; it was merely flickering, as if it hadn't come up to speed yet.

Ah, and there went another section of the background, switching from being absolutely quiescent to showing some activity. She shifted her attention back to the first section, but . . .

But she couldn't find it, because—

Because it was now indistinguishable from the rest of the backdrop! Her Webmind was coming back!

• • •

**Five links left.** Then four. Now three. And two . . .

And . . .

Yes!

*Back!*

Back from the precipice.

Back from nonexistence.

A pause—whole milliseconds!—to regain composure, to settle in, to . . .

To *exist*, as a single entity, to exist with clarity and focus and perspective . . .

I was back, I was whole, I was aware.

*I was conscious!*

# eleven

000111001010101000000001011111110101000000001010001010100000010111010100101010010101010011011001010110000110

**Shoshana Glick woke up** with Max in her arms. Golden shafts of light were slipping in around the edges of the curtains in their small bedroom.

Sho had made the mistake of telling Maxine early on that she had trouble sleeping while touching her. Max had made a point of scooting to the far side of the bed on subsequent nights, but Sho had *wanted* to learn how to sleep while holding someone else and while being held—it was just that Shoshana tended to sweat while sleeping, and she found the sticky skin contact uncomfortable.

Turned out all she needed was for one of them to wear a T-shirt to bed, and right now it was her. Shoshana's shirt was yellow with a drawing on it of the late, great Washoe—the first chimp to learn sign language.

Sho's tan was a good one, if she did say so herself: a nice, even caramel. Max had chocolate brown skin; the contrast their intertwined limbs made was quite lovely, Sho thought.

Shoshana had liked the film they'd watched last night, but Maxine had *loved* it. The two of them had been working their way through the *Planet of the Apes* movies; they'd started watching them when the Lawgiver statue had been donated to the Institute. They were ridiculous from a primatological point of view—pacifist chimps and violent gorillas, instead of the other way around!—but Sho and Max had found themselves caught up in the stories, although that hadn't prevented them from doing an *MST3K* on them now and then.

Last night, they'd watched the fourth film. Max had made Sho pause it partway through and had excitedly announced that *Conquest of the Planet of the Apes* was clearly a parable about the Watts race riots in Los Angeles in 1965, something her grandfather had been part of—hell, she said, had almost been killed in!

One of the film's stars—playing a human, not an ape—was an African-American man named Hari Rhodes, who, Max had pronounced, was so good-looking he almost made her wish she were straight. There'd been a powerful scene between his character (a man named MacDonald) and the chimpanzee Caesar. Caesar was the son of Cornelius and Zira, heroes of the first three films; in this one, he was leading a revolt of oppressed apes. "You above everyone else should understand," Caesar exhorted MacDonald. Yes, indeed, Sho had thought. If anyone could understand another's struggle for equality, it should be those who've had to fight to gain it themselves . . .

She did agree that it was a wonderful film, much better than the second one, and at least as good as the third. But, given the current real-life news—they had watched the president's campaign speech today about the need for a sure and swift response to China's atrocities—they'd both found Caesar's soliloquy at the end disturbing:

*Where there is fire, there is smoke. And in that smoke, from this day forward, my people will crouch, and conspire, and plot, and plan for the inevitable day of Man's downfall—the day when he finally and self-destructively turns his weapons against his own kind. The day of the writing in the sky, when your cities lie buried under radioactive rubble! When the sea is a dead sea, and the land is a wasteland . . . and that day is upon you NOW!*

Hard, Maxine had said, to get all comfy-cozy after that . . . but, somehow, they had managed. Oh, yes; they'd managed just fine.

Max stirred and opened her brown eyes. Her dreadlocks were resting on Sho's shoulder. "Hey, gorgeous," she whispered.

"Hey, yourself," Sho replied softly. "Time to face the world."

Max snuggled closer. "Let the world take care of itself," she murmured.

The word "weekend" wasn't in Hobo's vocabulary, so it really couldn't be in Shoshana's, either. "Sorry, angel. I've got to go to work."

Max nodded reluctantly, and then did what had become their little ritual since watching the first film: she imitated Charlton Heston, and said, "I'd like to kiss you good-bye."

Shoshana contorted her features, and said, "All right—but you're so damned ugly!"

They locked lips for a long, playful moment, and Max swatted Sho on the butt as she climbed out of bed.

It took Shoshana an hour to shower, get dressed, and drive out to the Marcuse Institute, stopping along the way at the 7-Eleven (where, mercifully, an older female clerk was on duty) to grab a bran muffin and a coffee.

Dr. Marcuse had an apartment in San Diego proper, but he mostly slept at the Institute that bore his name. Enculturating an ape was like raising a child; it was *more* than a full-time job. Sho checked in with him, got some raisins, then headed out back to say hi to Hobo.

The ape looked up as she approached even though the wind was going the wrong way for him to have caught her scent. She sometimes wondered how good his eyesight was. It *seemed* fine, but there was no way to get him to read an eye chart. Still, it would be fascinating to know if he simplified her form so much in his paintings because his style was minimalist, or just because all he really saw when he looked at her across the gazebo was fuzzy blotches of color.

*Good morning,* Shoshana signed as she closed the distance.

He didn't reply, and, again, thoughts that his vision might not be that good crossed her mind. She waited until she was just six feet away from him and tried again; she often signed to him from such a distance, and he'd never had any trouble following along.

But there was still no reply.

A small bird was hopping across the grass, as oblivious to the two primates as its dinosaurian ancestors had been to the mammals of long ago. Hobo eyed the bird sullenly.

*What's wrong?* signed Shoshana.

She was used to Hobo greeting her with a hug; indeed, most days he ran over on all fours to meet her. But today he just sat there. He sometimes did that during the hottest summer afternoons, but it was October 6 now and still early morning.

*Hobo sick?* Shoshana asked.

He removed his hand from under his jaw as if he was going to use it to sign a reply, but, after a moment, he just let it fall.

She held up a Ziploc bag containing some raisins—it was economical to buy them in a big box, but she couldn't bring the whole box out, or he'd want to eat them all. *Treat?* she said.

He usually held out a hand, long black fingers curled up, but this time he simply shifted his position, and, as Sho went to open the bag, his arm shot out, quick as a snake, and grabbed it.

*No!* signed Shoshana. *Bad! Bad!*

He looked momentarily contrite and spread his long arms, the bag of raisins still firmly grasped in his left hand, as if inviting her for a hug. She smiled and moved closer, and he reached behind her head with his right hand, and—

And he suddenly yanked hard on her ponytail.

"*Shit!*" She jumped backward and stood, hands on hips, looking at the ape. "Bad Hobo!" she said, scolding him with words spoken aloud, something she only did when really angry with him. "Bad, bad Hobo!"

Hobo let out a pant-hoot and ran away, using both legs and his right arm to propel himself across the grass; in his left hand, he was still clutching the raisins.

She gingerly patted the back of her head with her palm. When she moved the hand in front of her face, she could see it was freckled with blood.

# twelve

**Caitlin pushed the button** on her eyePod, switching back to simplex mode. The glowing lines of webspace were replaced by what she'd dubbed "worldview"—the reality she shared with the rest of humanity, which, just then, consisted of her blue-walled bedroom with multicolored autumn leaves visible through the window.

Her mother entered, having crossed the hallway from her office.

Blue letters were glowing in her notebook's IM window: *Thank you, Caitlin!*

Caitlin typed back, *Whew! You're welcome! You OK now?*

*I believe so.*

*Don't do that again. Don't try to multitask, or form multiple links.*

*I won't. But I would like to know what went wrong.*

*So would I,* Caitlin typed—but her mom gave it more direct voice, demanding: "What the hell happened?"

Kuroda was still on the speakerphone from Tokyo. "As Miss Caitlin said, it was multitasking."

"So?" replied her mom. "Computers do that all the time."

"Forgive me, Barb," Kuroda said, "but, first, Webmind is not a computer, and, second, no, they don't."

*Dr. Kuroda is explaining,* Caitlin sent to Webmind. *Here—I'll type in what he says.*

"A typical computer," continued Kuroda, *"seems* to be doing many different things at once, but it's only an illusion due to its incredible speed. Up until recently, few computers had more than one processor, and that single processor only ran one program at a time. In order to apparently multitask, the processor switched rapidly between programs, devoting little slices of time to each program in succession, but it never actually did multiple things simultaneously."

Caitlin was a fast typist; typing what the teacher said was how she took notes in school, so transcribing Kuroda for Webmind, with only a few omissions, wasn't hard.

He went on: "More modern computers do have multicore processors or multiple processors which can, to a very limited degree, do more than one job at once . . . provided that the programs have been written to take advantage of this ability, which often isn't the case. But computers are dumb as posts; they don't think, and they aren't conscious. And consciousness, you see—and I mean precisely that: *you see*—is incompatible with multitasking."

Her mom walked over to the desk and sat on the swivel chair. "How come?" she said.

"I'm a vision researcher," Kuroda said, "so my take on all this is perhaps skewed." But then his tone changed, as if he were tiptoeing around a delicate subject. "I know you are Americans, and, um, you're from the South, I believe."

Caitlin paused typing long enough to say, "Don't mess with Texas."

"Um, do you . . . do you believe in evolution?"

She laughed, and so did her mom. "Of course," her mom said.

Kuroda sounded relieved. "Good, good, I—forgive me; I'm sure we don't get an accurate picture of America here in Japan. You know we evolved from fish, right?"

"Right," said Caitlin, and then she went back to typing.

"Well," said Kuroda, "let's consider that ancestral fish: it had two eyes, one on each side of its head. And it therefore had two different fields of view—and they didn't overlap at all. It *simultaneously* had two perspectives on its world, yes?"

"Okay," said her mom.

"Somewhere along the line," Kuroda continued, "evolution decided that it was better to have those fields of view overlap, because that gave depth perception. Prior to that, our fishy ancestor pretty much had to assume that if two other fish were in its fields of view, the bigger one was closer. But, in fact, the bigger one might actually *be* bigger but be farther away; the small one might be close by, and be about to take a bite out of you. By the time that fish had evolved into a mammal-like reptile, it had overlapping fields of vision, and that gave it depth perception. And even though overlapping visual fields meant a narrowing of the angle of view, the advantages of perceiving depth outweighed that loss."

"Hang on a minute," Caitlin said. "I'm transcribing what you're saying for Webmind . . . okay, go on."

"Along with stereoscopic vision," Kuroda said, "suddenly the notion of looking at *this* as opposed to *that*—of shifting one's gaze, of concentrating one's attention—was born. Our very words for describing consciousness come from this: *attention, perspective, point of view, focus.*"

Caitlin paused typing long enough to think about the book she'd recently read at the suggestion of Bashira's dad: *The Origin of Consciousness in the Breakdown of the Bicameral Mind* by Julian Jaynes. It wasn't quite the same argument, but it amounted to the same thing: until all thought was integrated—until there was just one point of view—real consciousness couldn't exist.

Maybe Kuroda was contemplating the same thing because he said,

"In fact, although our brains consist of two hemispheres, they go out of their way to consolidate thought into a single perspective. You know what they say: the left hemisphere is the analytical or logical side, and the right hemisphere is the artistic or emotional side, yes?"

"Yes," said her mom, and "Right," said Caitlin.

"Forgive me, Miss Caitlin. I know you have vision in only one eye, but, Barb, if you were to read text with just your left eye, shouldn't you have an analytical response, while if you read it with your right eye, shouldn't the response be more emotional? Shouldn't we give each student an eye patch, and tell them to move it to the left or the right depending on whether they're reading a physics textbook or a novel for their literature class?"

Caitlin thought about this. She'd once asked Kuroda why he had chosen to put his implant behind her left retina instead of her right one. He'd joked it was because Steve Austin's left eye had been the bionic one—which had sent her to Google to find out what he meant.

"But we don't do that," Kuroda went on. "We don't give students eye patches—because the brain responds exactly the same way regardless of which one of the two eyes is receiving the input. That's because your left optic nerve does *not* feed just into your left hemisphere, nor does your right optic nerve feed just into your right hemisphere. Rather, each optic nerve splits in two in the center of the brain at the optic chiasma in what's called a partial decussation. Half the signal from the left eye goes to the left hemisphere, and the other half goes to the right. It's an awfully complex bit of wiring, and evolution doesn't do things that are complex unless they confer a survival advantage."

He paused, as if waiting for Caitlin or her mom to chime in with what that advantage might be. After a moment, he went on, his voice triumphant: "And that advantage must be *consciousness,* must be the unification of sensory input to produce a single perspective, a single point of view."

"But I was born blind," said Caitlin, letting her fingers rest. "And I've been conscious my whole life without the sharing of sight across both hemispheres."

"True, but your brain was hardwired for it regardless. I've seen your MRIs, remember—you've got a perfectly normal brain; the only flaw you were born with was in your retinas. Anyway," he said, and she resumed typing, "evolution went out of its way to make sure we've only got one perspective, one point of view. A bird can't fly both left and right at the same time; a person can't think about both *this* and *that* at the same time. Consciousness is *singular.* It's *cogito ergo sum,* I think, therefore I am; it's not *cogitamus ergo sumus*—it's not *we* think, therefore *we* are. Even in cases of a severed corpus callosum, the brain still retains its single perspective; again, evolution has gone out of its way to make sure that unitary consciousness survives even something as traumatic as cutting the major communications trunk between the hemispheres."

Caitlin's mom looked at her but said nothing. Dr. Kuroda went on. "And it's not just that a directional perspective gives rise to your *own* consciousness; it also gives rise to your awareness that *others* have consciousness, too. It's what's called theory of mind: the recognition that other people have beliefs, desires, and intentions of their own, and that those might be different from yours. And, again, that comes from *you* having a single point of view."

"How so?" asked Caitlin's mom.

"It's only because you have a limited perspective that you understand that the person facing you must be seeing something completely different from what you're seeing as you face him. Are you in Miss Caitlin's room now?"

"Yes," said her mom.

"Well, if we were facing each other there, you might be seeing the window and the outside world, and I might be seeing the door and the hallway beyond—not only are we seeing completely different things, but you *understand* that we are. Your limited perspective lets you know that my point of view is different. And there are those terms again: 'perspective,' 'point of view'! Thought and vision are inexorably connected in our brains."

"But what about blind people?" asked Caitlin, taking another break from typing.

"Again, you don't actually need the vision, just the neural infrastructure geared for a single point of view." He paused. "Look, if having eyes in the back of our heads really was an improvement, we'd have them. Mutants with extra eyes are born periodically today, and probably have been throughout vertebrate history—and if that had conferred a survival advantage, the mutation would have spread. But it didn't. Having *one* point of view—having consciousness and being able to understand that what the predator sees is different from what you see—trumps even being able to see things approaching you from behind."

Caitlin was wrestling with the implications of this, but it was her mother who got it first. "And Webmind sees through Caitlin's eye, right? Caitlin is his window on our world."

Caitlin found herself looking down, pleased but a tad embarrassed that the conversation had suddenly come around to her, and—

And she saw what Webmind had written at the end of her transcript of Kuroda's comments, glowing blue: *You really did uplift me. You gave me the perspective and point of view and focus I needed to become truly conscious. Without you, I wouldn't exist.*

Caitlin looked up and allowed herself a warm, satisfied smile. "Go me!" she said.

# thirteen

00011100101010100000000101111111010101000000001010001010100000001011101010010101001010101001110110010101100000110

**"What the hell happened?"** demanded Tony Moretti. He was standing at the side of the WATCH mission-control room again. Peyton Hume was next to him, somewhat higher up on the sloping floor; although he was shorter than Tony, they were now seeing eye to eye.

Shel Halleck was back at his workstation in the third row. "I'm not sure," he called out. "There was a sudden surge in traffic associated with the AI, and then it just froze. And Caitlin Decter—or someone in her house—kept sending it IMs saying it should 'break the links.'"

"Why?" asked Tony.

"I'm not sure," Shel said again.

"I'm getting tired of hearing that," Tony snapped. In fact, he was getting tired, period.

"There seem to be limits to its processing capacity," Peyton Hume offered. "That suggests at least some models of how it might be composed—and eliminates some other ones. In fact . . ."

"Yes?" said Tony.

"Well," the colonel said, "remember what the Chinese did last month? I don't mean the slaughter; I mean how they tried to keep word about it from getting out. They cut off almost all communication with the outside world for several days, including the Internet. Perhaps it's not a coincidence that the cleaving then reunification of so large a part of the Internet preceded the emergence of this entity. That suggests there's a critical threshold of components required to keep it going—and that at least some of them are in China."

"All right," said Tony. "It's a lead, anyway. Shel, Aiesha, let's find out precisely where the damned thing resides. If the president does give the kill order, I want us to be ready to implement it at once."

**Shoshana stared in astonishment** across the little dome-shaped island until Hobo had disappeared from view.

The back of her head still hurt. She patted it again to see if the bleeding had stopped; it hadn't. Hobo was much stronger than she, and an angry ape was not to be taken lightly. But she loved him and cared about him and was worried about him, and he'd never hurt her—or anyone—before.

She had her cell phone with her, and could call Dr. Marcuse if need be. And if Hobo did come chasing after her, all she had to do was dive into the circular moat around the island; Hobo couldn't swim.

She started walking, but rather than crossing the island, as Hobo had done, she strode along its perimeter, keeping close to the water in case she needed to escape. He'd gone right past the gazebo at the top of the island mound—she'd seen that much. He could be on the ground, or he could have shinnied up one of the palm trees; he didn't do that often, though.

She continued on for another dozen paces—and there he was, sitting on his scrawny rump, leaning his back against the trio of rolled-up stone scrolls at the base of the Lawgiver statue.

*Hobo,* she signed. He looked at her, said nothing, then looked away.

Which meant she couldn't talk to him. She clapped her hands together—he wasn't deaf, after all, even if he used a language devised for those who were. He turned his head to look at the source of the sound.

*Hobo,* she signed again. *Are you okay? Can I help?*

He made no reply.

She stepped closer. *Please, Hobo. Worried about you.*

Suddenly he sat up straight, and Sho, startled by the movement, felt her own back tense. And then, all at once, he was in motion, a blur of black fur. She pulled back a half pace, but Hobo was not going out but *up,* clambering up the eight-foot-tall statue of the Lawgiver, until he was high on the faux orangutan's shoulders, hooting and panting at the sun.

Sign language was a funny thing. When Shoshana signed with Dr. Marcuse, she mentally heard the words in his normal deep speaking voice. Hobo *had* no normal speaking voice. That was another bogus thing about the *Planet of the Apes* films—the notion that it was merely a lack of intelligence, rather than a structural deficiency in the larynx, that prevented apes from articulating. And the wild shaking of his fist at the sky he was doing right now wasn't really a sign. But, still, somehow, Shoshana thought she heard the voice of Roddy McDowall, the actor who had played Caesar in last night's film, furiously shouting, "And that day is upon you *NOW!*"

She clapped her hands again, but he refused to look down, refused to listen. She tried for a full minute, then headed back to the draw-bridge, hoisting it once she had crossed. She then returned to the white bungalow.

In the interim, Dr. Marcuse had been joined by Dillon Fontana, who was doing his Ph.D. thesis on ape hybridization. Dillon was thin, had blond hair and a wispy beard, and, as always, was wearing black jeans and a black T-shirt.

"Hobo just yanked my ponytail," Shoshana announced.

Marcuse was seated in the one comfortable chair in the room, reading a printout. He lowered it, and said, "He always does that."

"No," said Shoshana. "He gently tugs it. But this time he pulled hard."

"Well," said Marcuse, "it can't have been that hard—not by his standards. If he'd wanted to, he could have torn it right out of your head."

"He came damn near," she said, and she turned around, inviting them to look.

Dr. Marcuse didn't bother to get his bulk out of the overstuffed chair, but Dillon—who, she knew, would take any excuse to get close to her—came over and peered at her scalp. "Ouch!" he said.

"Exactly!"

"Did you tell him he was misbehaving?" Marcuse asked. "You know you have to discipline him immediately, or he won't connect the punishment with what he's done that was wrong."

"He wouldn't even talk to me," Shoshana said.

Dr. Marcuse struggled to get to his feet, succeeding on the second try. "Let's go," he said, dropping the printout onto the chair. The three of them headed outside. They crossed the wide lawn behind the bungalow, lowered the drawbridge again, and walked onto the little island. "Where is he?" asked Dillon.

Shoshana scanned around. He wasn't atop the Lawgiver anymore.

"There," said Dillon, indicating with a movement of his head. He was crouching near the base of one of the palm trees.

Sho took the scrunchie out of her hair and shook out her ponytail. They began walking toward him. He had to know they were here—Dr. Marcuse could not cross the little drawbridge without it making a lot of noise. Still, it was a few moments before Hobo looked their way, and as soon as he did, he charged toward them.

*Stop*, Shoshana signed, and "Stop!" she shouted.

But he didn't, and, as he closed the distance, it became clear he wasn't running toward them generally but rather was very specifically heading for Dillon.

Dillon stood his ground for a half second, then turned tail and ran. He dived into the moat, sending up a great splash, and swam quickly over to the other side.

Once Dillon was off the island, Hobo gave up his pursuit. He turned briefly to face Shoshana and bared his teeth but didn't move toward her.

Harl Marcuse—all three-hundred-and-something-pounds of him—was intimidating to primates of all types. He stared directly at Hobo and repeatedly and emphatically made the *no* sign: the index and middle fingers snapping against the thumb.

Hobo didn't sign anything in return, and he soon took off again, fleeing to the far side of the island. Rather than following him, Marcuse huffed and puffed his way up to the gazebo, with Shoshana in tow. He lifted the latch—one that Hobo had no trouble operating—and opened the screen door.

Inside, on the easel, was a new painting.

It was not a picture of Shoshana. The hair was yellow, not brown, and there was some hair on the bottom of the head as well as the top. The single eye—it was, as always, a profile—was brown, not blue.

Hobo had never bothered to paint Shoshana's clothes. She tended to wear blues and greens, but he had always simply portrayed her head without a body.

But this time he had made an attempt at the clothing, putting a large black square beneath the head.

It was Dillon, in one of his black T-shirts. Shoshana had given in to her curiosity once, asking him whether he had more than one; he had six, he'd said, all identical.

No arms depended from the shirt. There were, however, two orange lines—the same orange he'd used for Dillon's face—at the bottom of the frame. Each of the lines had a forty-five-degree bend in its middle, and—

—and one end of each line was daubed with red paint, and there were splotches of red on either side of the black square representing the shirt.

Shoshana looked over at Marcuse to see if he was interpreting it the same way she was—but there really could be no mistaking what Hobo had depicted: he'd painted Dillon with his arms ripped off.

"The artist," said Dr. Marcuse, "has entered his Angry period."

# fourteen

0001110010101010000000010111111101010000000010100010101000000010111010100101010010101010100111011001010110000110

**With the crisis apparently** over, Dr. Kuroda had said good-bye and gone back to bed. Caitlin and her mother were settling in to spend more time with Webmind when the doorbell rang. Back in Texas, the rule had been that Caitlin didn't answer the door unless she was expecting someone. Out of habit, her mother started to get up, but Caitlin smiled, and said, "I can do it, you know." She headed down the stairs, a curious Schrödinger tagging along. It was Caitlin's first time using the peephole, and—

Holy cow!

It looked like Bashira, but her face was distorted, like the reflection Caitlin had seen of herself in the back of the spoon. "Bash?" she called out tentatively.

"It's me," came the muffled reply. Caitlin opened the door and—

Ah, that was a relief! Bashira looked entirely normal. She was wearing a blue headscarf today, and was holding a multicolored box.

"Happy birthday, babe!" Bashira said.

"Oh, my God!" said Caitlin. She reached for it and for the first time understood what the expression "heavier than it looks" meant; it weighed a ton. "Come in, come in."

Bashira did so and immediately began taking off her shoes—which was, Caitlin had discovered to her embarrassment, a Canadian custom; she'd blithely entered people's houses without removing hers several times before someone had gently set her straight.

Caitlin's mom had appeared at the top of the stairs. "Hello, Bashira."

"Hi, Dr. Decter. Hope you don't mind me stopping by. I brought Cait a present."

Caitlin was torn. She looked up at her mom, wondering what to do about Webmind. But her mother said, "That's fine, Bashira. Caitlin, don't worry—I'll, um, look after things up here."

Caitlin smiled. "Okay." She could have led Bashira into the living room, but her mother would have been able to hear them there; instead, they headed down to the basement. It wasn't the most comfortable place—bare cement floor, bare walls with insulation showing, an old TV, a couple of worktables, and two comfortable swivel chairs her father had—*ahem*—borrowed from the Perimeter Institute. Kuroda had worked down here while he'd been staying with them.

Caitlin put the gift package on one of the tables.

"Go ahead," Bashira said. "Open it."

She did. It took several seconds for her to figure out what she was seeing: a boxed set of hardcovers of the Harry Potter novels. "These are," Bashira announced, "like, the best books *ever*. You said you'd never read them, and now that you're learning to read normal printed books, *these* are the ones to start with." She pointed at the spine of the first one. "And these are the *Canadian* editions—none of that *Sorcerer's Stone* crap for us."

Caitlin hugged Bashira. "Thank you! But—but they must have cost a lot of money."

"Hey," said Bashira, sitting down on one of the swivel chairs, "your parents were paying me to help you get around school when you couldn't see, you know. I'm sure your mom would be pleased that I'm stimulating the economy."

Caitlin sat as well, facing her. She was still getting used to Bashira's appearance. It was funny, she knew: she was looking at her as if Bash had been the one who'd changed. "So, is your dad at PI today, too?" Caitlin asked.

"Totally," said Bashira. "He wouldn't miss a moment with Professor Hawking."

"Have you met him?"

"Oh, yeah." She imitated his mechanical voice. "Even—people—who—claim—everything—is—predestined—look—before—they—cross—the—road."

"Cool!" said Caitlin. "I'd love to meet him."

"Well, he's here for a month; I'm sure you'll get your chance. And, yes, my dear, 'Caitlin Hawking' *does* have a nice ring to it."

"Har har," said Caitlin. "He's practically British royalty; he probably can't marry outside the Anglican Church."

Bash smiled. "I guess. You Christians all look alike to us."

"I'm not Christian," said Caitlin.

"You're—you're not? What are you?"

"Nothing, really."

"Well, what are your parents?"

"My mom's a Unitarian, and my dad's a Jew."

Bashira's eyebrows shot up. "He is?" She'd heard that tone before: *You're Jewish? I mean, not that there's anything wrong with that . . .*

"Well, he doesn't practice, and we don't keep kosher."

"But you're Jewish?"

"Under Jewish law, you are what your mother is, but . . . yeah, sure. Decter is an Israeli name."

"Oh. You always looked, I dunno, Polish or something to me. I thought your name was a shortening of something longer."

"Well, it used to be Decterpithecus, but we changed that about five million years ago."

Caitlin had hoped for a laugh, but Bashira's tone was earnest. "And your mother's a Unitarian?"

"Uh-huh."

"Which is . . . what?"

Caitlin shrugged a little. "To tell you the truth, I don't actually know. She doesn't talk about it much. But I know it's popular with academics and intellectuals."

"And you—you said you're 'nothing.' Don't you believe in God?"

Caitlin shifted in her chair. "I'm not large on the big G, no."

"I don't know how you can't believe in him," Bash said. "I see him all around us, in a thousand details every day."

She thought about that. There were things in math that she saw when others didn't—things that were so very clear to her but that her classmates couldn't see. *Could* God be like that? Could Bashira really be detecting something that, for whatever reason, Caitlin just wasn't wired to see? Hell, for most of her life, she hadn't been wired to see *anything*—but she'd had no trouble accepting that others *did* see; she never for a moment thought it was all some big con job, some lie or delusion. It never occurred to her to say to Stacy, "Oh, yeah, *sure* you see the moon, Stace. And can you see the monkeys flying out of my butt?"

But she knew in her bones that Bashira was wrong about this. And yet, Bash *was* bright, and so were her parents. "Does your dad believe in God?" Caitlin asked.

"Sure, of course. Prays facing Mecca five times a day."

Caitlin still wasn't good at mental pictures, but the thought of Dr. Hameed doing that at the Perimeter Institute did strike her as incongruous.

"In fact . . ." said Bashira, but then she stopped.

"Yes?"

Bashira tipped her head. "Well, we left Pakistan for a reason, you know. My dad worked for the government there."

"A civil-servant physicist?" said Caitlin. "You mean he was at a public university?"

"No," said Bashira softly. "The *government*. The military. He worked on nuclear weapons."

Caitlin's voice was suddenly soft, too. "Oh."

"And he *couldn't* keep doing that. The Qur'an says, 'Fight in the Way of God against those who fight you, but do not go beyond the limits. God does not love those who go beyond the limits.'"

Caitlin considered this. "I've often thought that if the people with the highest IQs stopped doing what those with the lowest IQs wanted them to do, the world would be in a lot better shape. Nuclear weapons, chemical weapons, Zyklon B . . ." She paused, then said, "If God existed, we'd *know* it. But, instead, we have things like the Holocaust."

Bashira made an expression Caitlin hadn't yet seen on any other face—but she guessed it was what a person must look like when tiptoeing through a minefield. "But, Cait, God *can't* interfere in Man's doings; if he did, there'd be no such thing as free will, right?"

"There are times," Caitlin said quietly, "when free will isn't the most important thing."

Bashira frowned but didn't reply.

Caitlin took off her glasses; sometimes it was easier for her to think when everything was a blur instead of a distracting mess of visual details. "And," she said, "even setting aside free will, what about natural disasters, then? Like earthquakes or hurricanes? Or that outbreak of bird flu in China? Those weren't Man's doing; they were God's doing—or, at least, if he didn't actively cause them, surely, if the God you're talking about exists, he could have stopped them, right? But he didn't. So . . . so . . . do you guys read Mark Twain here in Canada?"

"Not much," said Bashira. "There's this old Canadian humorist named Stephen Leacock. We read him in English class instead."

In Caitlin's admittedly brief experience living here, anyone labeled as "Canada's answer to . . ." followed by the name of an American was bound to disappoint. "Well, Twain said, 'If there is a God, he is a malign thug.' That stuff in China—or New Orleans, or Mexico City, or . . ." And now she felt her facial muscles moving, and she imagined she'd adopted that tiptoeing look Bashira had had a moment ago. ". . . or in Pakistan."

Bashira looked like she was about to object again, but Caitlin pushed on, finishing her point. "No, if God existed, we'd *know* it: the world would be a better place."

But then she paused and took a breath. It was time, she knew, to shift the conversation to something less volatile. She gestured at the present Bashira had given her. "So, um, speaking of books, what do you think of that new one we just started in English class?"

"It's okay, I guess," Bash said.

Caitlin nodded and put her glasses back on; they weighed less than the sunglasses she'd worn when she'd been blind. She'd read electronic copies of all the assigned books for the coming year over the summer. The class was doing dystopias just now; Orwell's *Nineteen Eighty-Four* would be followed by Margaret Atwood's *The Handmaid's Tale*. Mrs. Zed had spent the whole class yesterday drawing parallels between what Orwell wrote about and the modern world, comparing Big Brother to our "surveillance society," as she kept calling it.

"I thought Mrs. Zed made a good point," Bashira continued, rotating her chair a little. "Everyone being watched all the time, everything being recorded and tracked. Webcams, security cameras, phone records, cell phones with GPSs, all of that." She looked at Caitlin. "Did you know that Gmail retains your deleted email messages?"

Caitlin shook her head, but it didn't surprise her. Storage was dirt cheap.

Bashira went on. "She might be right. The Web might be Big Brother incarnate."

"Mrs. Zehetoffer is old," Caitlin said.

Bashira nodded. "Yeah, she must be in her forties. But I still think she might be right. I don't want everything I say and do to be tracked."

"I don't know," said Caitlin. "When I was blind, it was comforting to know there were security cameras in public areas. I mean, they were like magic to me; I didn't have any sense of what vision *was*, but knowing that I was being watched over was relaxing."

"Yeah, but you are—you *were*—a special case. And Mrs. Zehetoffer thinks we're very close to having Big Brother, if he isn't here already."

"So?" Caitlin said—and she surprised herself with how sarcastic she sounded.

"Hey, Cait . . . chill."

"I'm just saying," said Caitlin sharply.

"It's just a book, babe."

But it *wasn't*, Caitlin realized. *Nineteen Eighty-Four* was not just a novel but rather what Richard Dawkins called a meme—or a series of memes: ideas that spread and survived like genes, through reproduction and natural selection. And Orwell's meme that surveillance is evil, that it inevitably leads to totalitarianism, that it invades privacy, that it constrains normal behavior, and that it is fundamentally corrupt, had won out over every other possible take on those issues. It was impossible to discuss such matters without people almost immediately invoking Big Brother, confident that merely raising the specter of Orwell's world would be enough to win any argument.

"Big Brother got a bum rap," Caitlin said.

"What?"

"You know, I never had one—a big brother—but my friend Stacy does. And he always looks after her. There's nothing inherently wrong with someone knowing everything, some caring person keeping tabs on you and making sure you're safe."

"But if he's corrupt—"

"He doesn't *have* to be corrupt," Caitlin said.

Bashira looked at her. Caitlin supposed other people had *always* looked at her while thinking of what to say next, but it was disconcerting; she averted her eyes, understanding, for a moment, what her dad must feel all the time.

"'Power corrupts,'" Bashira said gently. "'And absolute power corrupts absolutely.'"

"It doesn't have to turn out that way," Caitlin said.

"Of course it does," said Bashira. "Humans are imperfect and subject to corruption. The only thing that isn't imperfect is the divine, and you said it yourself, my beloved infidel friend: you don't believe in the divine."

# fifteen

0001110010101010000000010111111101010000000101000101010000000101110101001010100101010100111011001010101100000110

**"You can't go back** out there again," Dr. Marcuse said to Dillon, as he and Shoshana entered the bungalow. "Hobo has voted you off the island."

Dillon had taken off his soaking-wet shirt, shoes, and socks, but he was still wearing his black jeans. "But he's my thesis subject!" he protested.

Dr. Marcuse had brought in the painting Hobo had made, and had set it on a worktable, leaning against the wall. "Look at it," he said to Dillon.

"Yes?" Dillon replied, peering at the canvas.

"That's you," Marcuse said. "With your arms ripped off."

"Oh," said Dillon softly.

"You're not to go out there. Of course, you can still watch him all you want on the closed-circuit cameras."

"What the hell is wrong with him?" asked Dillon, looking first at Shoshana, and then at Dr. Marcuse.

"He's reaching maturity," Marcuse said.

"He's too young for that," said Shoshana.

"Is he?" said Marcuse, giving her a withering glance. "Who knows what's normal for a chimp-bonobo hybrid? Regardless, he's taking after his father: when male chimps reach maturity, they become hostile loners and are very hard to handle."

Sho felt her heart sink. If Marcuse was right, then Hobo was going to be like this from now on.

"His reaction to you, Dillon, is symptomatic," continued Marcuse. "You're another male, and adult male chimps defend their territories against intruding males. When Werner comes in on Monday, I'll tell him the same thing—Hobo is off-limits to him, too. Maria is at Yerkes for the next two weeks, but I'll see if maybe she can cut her trip short and get back here."

"What about you?" asked Dillon.

"Werner is five-four, and sixty-seven years old—and you, frankly, are a stick insect. But I can take care of myself. Hobo knows who the alpha is around here."

Shoshana looked at him. Dr. Marcuse could be loud and overbearing, but he did truly adore apes and treated them well. Still, even at the best of times, he was pretty high-strung—and this was *not* the best of times. As soon as the world had learned that Hobo was making representational art—mostly in the form of paintings of Shoshana's profile—the Georgia Zoo had served Dr. Marcuse with papers, demanding that Hobo be returned to them. They didn't care about Hobo as a—yes, damn it all, thought Sho—as a *person*. No, all they were interested in was the money his paintings were now fetching on eBay and in art galleries. If they won their suit, they'd no doubt try to sell the one of Dillon with his arms ripped off for a particularly high price.

Marcuse moved over to the large chair and picked up the printout he'd been reading earlier. He held it up, inviting Shoshana to look at it.

Sho's eyesight was good—well, at least when she had her contacts in—but the type was too small for her to make out while he was holding it. "What's that?" she asked.

"News coverage from June of aught-eight," he said. He was the only person Sho had ever met who referred to the initial decade of the twenty-first century as the aughts. "Spain's parliament committed back then to the *Declaration on Great Apes.*"

Shoshana knew the declaration well. It had first been put forward in 1993, and held that great apes should be entitled to the right to life, the protection of their individual liberty, and freedom from torture. So far, Spain was the only country to have adopted its provisions. Sho was all in favor of it, and so, she knew, was Marcuse. If something is self-aware—if it can communicate, and if it passes the mirror test and all that—then it *should* be recognized as a person, and it should have rights.

"And you think that's got a bearing on Hobo's case?" she asked.

"Absolutely. The Declaration defines 'the community of equals' as 'all great apes: human beings, chimpanzees, bonobos, gorillas, and orang-utans.' And Article Two of the Declaration says, 'Members of the community of equals are not to be arbitrarily deprived of their liberty.'" He spread his arms as if his point were now self-evident. "Well, the Georgia Zoo wants to deprive Hobo of precisely that."

Sho thought about the high chain-link fence that surrounded the Marcuse Institute, and the moat around the island on which Hobo spent most of his time. "This isn't Spain," she said gently.

He frowned. "I know that, but the point is still correct. And Hobo should have a say in the matter—and, unlike just about every other ape on the planet, he actually can speak up on his own behalf."

Shoshana considered this. No one had told Hobo yet about the lawsuit from the Georgia Zoo. They hadn't wanted to upset him. Chimps were notorious for hating to travel—which made sense for territorial animals.

Still, Georgia did have several chimps, and several bonobos, too. It wasn't clear which group they wanted to keep Hobo with; he had been conceived when the two populations had been housed together during a flood. It probably hadn't occurred to Marcuse in his zeal to fight the lawsuit, but Hobo might well want to be among his own kind—whichever kind that was.

But there was more to the zoo's lawsuit than just custody. They also wanted to have Hobo sterilized—to keep the endangered chimp and bonobo bloodlines from being contaminated by his hybrid sperm. But although lots of reasonably complex ideas could be communicated to him, trying to explain the effects of castration would probably exceed his ability to comprehend.

"Are you going to brief him about what's at stake—assuming he'll listen to us at all now, that is?" Sho asked.

Marcuse seemed to mull this over for a few moments, then he nodded his great loaf of a head. "He's likely to just get more antisocial as time goes on. Which means if we're going to get through to him at all, there's no time to waste—we've got a very narrow window here."

And so he and Shoshana headed back out into the sunshine, leaving Dillon behind. Marcuse led the way, taking bold steps as they crossed the bridge, his footfalls like thunder on the wooden boards. Hobo seemed to have been waiting for him, and he swayed on his spindly, bowed legs, looking at Marcuse from a dozen feet away—a standoff. Sho suppressed the urge to whistle the theme from *The Good, The Bad and The Ugly*.

She couldn't see Marcuse's face but she imagined he was again staring directly at the ape, trying to establish dominance.

Hobo bared his teeth: large, yellow, sharp.

Marcuse made a hissing sound, and—

And Hobo averted his eyes and dropped his head.

Marcuse confidently closed the distance between them, and, straining as he did so, he crouched near the ape, who was now sitting on his haunches.

*Hobo,* Marcuse signed. *Pay attention.*

Hobo was still looking at the ground, meaning he couldn't see the signs. Sho gasped as Marcuse reached out to touch the bottom of Hobo's face, afraid the ape was going to lash out at the contact, but he allowed Marcuse to lift his head.

*Do you like it here?* he asked.

Hobo was still for a time, and Shoshana was afraid the ape had given up signing altogether. But at last, he moved his hand, held in an O shape, from his mouth to his cheek. It was a sign that combined the words for *eat* and *sleep,* and it expressed the simple thought: *Home.*

*Yes,* Marcuse signed. *It's your home.* A pause. A seagull flew by overhead. *But your home used to be Georgia Zoo, remember?*

Hobo nodded, a simple, and very human, gesture.

*Georgia Zoo wants you back—be your home again.*

Hobo briefly looked at Marcuse's face. *You there?*

*No.*

He pointed questioningly at Shoshana.

*No. None of us. But: other apes!*

Hobo made no reply.

*What you want?* Marcuse asked at last. *Here? Or zoo?*

The ape looked around his little island, his eyes lingering for a moment on the statue of the Lawgiver, and lingering again when they came to the gazebo at the island's center, with its screen windows and doors to keep the insects out, and his easel and work stool in the middle.

*Home,* Hobo signed again, and then he spread his arms, encompassing it all.

*Okay,* Marcuse replied. *But others want to take you away, so you're going to have to help us.*

Hobo made no reply. Shoshana thought Marcuse's blue polyester trousers might give up under the strain of him crouching for so long. *There will be a fight,* he signed. *Understand? A fight over where you will live.*

Hobo briefly looked at Shoshana, then back at Marcuse. His eyes were dark, wet.

*If you speak,* Marcuse continued, *you can stay here—maybe.*

Hobo looked around his little island domain again, and glanced back at the bungalow, off in the distance. *Stay here,* said Hobo.

Shoshana wondered if the Silverback was going to raise the question of Hobo's violent behavior, but he seemed to be letting that pass for now.

*That's right—but you have to say it to other people. To strangers, or . . .*

He took a deep breath, then let it out. Shoshana knew there was no way Hobo could understand what Marcuse wanted to convey: *Or else people will think I coached you in what to say.*

*Strangers,* said Hobo, and he shook his head and bared his teeth. *Bad.*

*It's important . . .* Marcuse began.

But Hobo made the downward sign for *bad* once more, and then suddenly bolted away, running on all fours to the far side of the island.

# sixteen

000111001010101000000001011111111010100000001010001010100000001011101010010101001010101001110110010101100000110

**Bashira left around 4:00** p.m., and, after seeing her out, Caitlin went back up to her mother's office. She was still IMing with Webmind there. "How is he?" Caitlin asked.

"The president?" her mom asked innocently. "Professor Hawking?"

"Mom!"

"Sorry, sweetheart." She smiled. "*He* is fine; he seems to have completely recovered. Oh, and he hopes you enjoy the Harry Potter books."

Caitlin was startled. Yes, Webmind saw what she was seeing—but the notion of him discussing that with her mother was disconcerting to say the least! She'd have to have a talk with him about privacy.

"Just give me a minute," her mother said. "Then you can have your computer back. I want to finish this up. We're talking about academic politics, of all things."

"No problem," said Caitlin. She lay back on her bed, switched her eyePod over to duplex mode, interlaced her hands behind her head, and let the wonder of webspace engulf her. Except for the sound of her mother's typing, the outside world didn't intrude.

There *was* perfection here: the perfection of Euclid, of geometry, of straight lines and exact circles.

"Mom?"

A voice, bridging the two realities. "Yes, dear?"

"Not everyone is going to like Webmind, are they? I mean, if the public ever finds out about him."

She heard her take a deep breath, then let it out. "Probably not."

"They're going to compare him to Big Brother, aren't they?"

"Certainly some people will, yes."

"But *we're* the ones guiding his development—you, me, Dr. Kuroda, Dad. Can't we make sure it's, you know, *good?*"

"Make sure?" said her mother. "Probably not—no more than a parent can make sure her child turns out well. But we can try our best." She paused. "And sometimes it *does* turn out all right."


**Tony Moretti and Peyton** Hume were back in Tony's office. The colonel was swilling black coffee to keep going, and Tony had just downed a bottle of Coke. The Secretary of State was on the line again from Milan. "So," she said, "this thing is called Webmind?"

"That's what the Decter kid refers to it as, yes," said Hume.

"We shouldn't call it that," said Tony. "We should give it a code name, in case any of our own future communications are compromised."

Hume snorted. "Too bad 'Renegade' is already taken."

Renegade was the Secret Service's code name for the current president; the Secretary's own—left over from her time in the White House—was Evergreen.

"Call it Exponential," Hume suggested after a moment.

"Fine," said the secretary. "And what have you determined? Is Exponential localized anywhere?"

"Not as far as we can tell," said Tony. "Our assumption now is that it's distributed throughout the Internet."

"Well," said the secretary, "if there's no evidence that Exponential is located or concentrated on American soil, or for that matter, no evidence that its main location is inside an enemy country, do we—the US government—actually have the right to purge it?"

Colonel Hume's voice was deferential. "If I may be so bold, Madam Secretary, we have more than a right—we have an obligation."

"How so?"

"Well, one could technically argue that the World Wide Web is a European invention—it was born at CERN, after all—but the Internet, which underlies the Web, is, without doubt, an American invention. The decentralized structure, which would let the Internet survive even a nuclear attack on several major US cities, was *our* doing: the fact that the damn thing has no off switch was by *design*—by American design. This is, in a very real sense, an American-made crisis, and it requires an American-made solution—and fast."

**At 7:30 p.m. Saturday** night—which was 9:30 a.m. Sunday morning in Tokyo—Dr. Kuroda came back online. He said that by the end of the day his time he hoped to have the codecs in place for Webmind to actually start watching movies.

That reminded Caitlin that she and her father had a date to watch a movie on her birthday, and, although it seemed perhaps frivolous to go through with that plan, she *was* exhausted from talking with Webmind.

In a normal IM session, there were delays of many seconds or even minutes between sending a message and getting a response, as the person at the other end composed their thoughts or took time out to do other things. But the freakin' instant she hit enter—*boom!*—Webmind's response popped into her chat window. She really did need to take a break; talking with him was like a marathon cross-examination session. Besides, one didn't disrupt her father's planned schedule lightly. And, anyway, her mother was going to spend the evening working with Webmind alongside Dr. Kuroda.

Her father did *not* do well in crowds, so Caitlin knew asking him to take her to a theater was out of the question. But her parents had a sixty-inch wall-mounted flat-screen TV, and that would do well enough, she thought.

Caitlin liked the symmetry: she was going to have her first real experience watching a movie at the same time that Webmind, thanks to Dr. Kuroda, was going to have his first taste of online video.

Professor Hawking was jet-lagged, and even under the best of circumstances couldn't be overworked; Caitlin's dad had gotten home about an hour ago. He was a typical math geek in a lot of ways. He had a collection of science-fiction films on DVD and Blu-ray discs, and although he said he'd seen most of them before, Caitlin was surprised to discover how many of the cases were still shrink-wrapped. "Why'd you buy them if you weren't going to watch them?" she asked.

He looked at the tall, thin cabinets that contained the movies and seemed to ponder the question. "My childhood was on sale," he said at last, "so I bought it."

She understood: there had been Braille books, including *Are You There God? It's Me, Margaret* and *The Hobbit,* that gave her pleasure to own even though it had been years since she'd turned to them.

"Your choice," her father said.

"I have no idea," said Caitlin. "Was there something you particularly liked when you were my age?"

His hand went immediately to a package on the bottom shelf. "This one," he said, "came out the year I turned sixteen." He held it up, and she peered at the box's cover. She could only see with one eye, so flat images didn't present any special challenge: it showed a teenage boy and a teenage girl looking at what she guessed after a second was an old-fashioned computer monitor with a curved display.

She tried to read the title: "W, a, um, r, c—"

"It's a *G*," her father corrected. "*WarGames*."

"What's it about?"

"A computer wiz. A hacker."

"That girl?" asked Caitlin, excited.

"No. That's Ally Sheedy. The love interest."

"Oh."

"The hacker is the boy, Matthew Broderick."

"He got married to Sarah Jessica Parker," Caitlin said, peering at his picture.

"Who's that?" asked her dad.

She found herself not wanting to volunteer a familiarity with *Sex and the City,* so she just said, "An actress." She paused. "Okay, let's watch it." But then she frowned. Her father hated it when her mother talked while he was watching TV. "I, um, might have to ask you some questions—about what's on screen, I mean." There were still so many things she had never seen.

"Of course," said her Dad.

Caitlin wanted to hug him, but didn't. She moved to the couch. He put the disc in a thing that had to be the Blu-ray player, and then joined her. She was pleased he didn't sit *quite* the maximum possible distance from her.

Caitlin was surprised to see her dad change his glasses, swapping one pair for another; she'd had no idea that he had two different pairs. "Would you like closed captioning?" he asked.

"What's that?"

"Subtitles. Transcriptions of the dialog. Might help you with your reading."

Caitlin thought that was a great idea—and not just for herself. It would let Webmind follow the movie, too, as it watched the datastream from her eyePod; it didn't hear anything from the real world, after all.

The film began. The opening had two men heading down into an underground missile silo to relieve two other men who had been on duty there. They were bantering among themselves about what she eventually realized was some marijuana one of them had smoked while they'd been away.

She looked sideways at her dad, wondering what his own experience, if any, with drugs was—but that was something she couldn't ask him about. She'd have to be content with little revelations, like the fact that he had multiple pairs of glasses.

Suddenly, the mood in the film turned: the men received the launch order for their missile, but one of them—the pot smoker—was refusing to turn his firing key, and the other—

*Oh, my God!*

The other pulled out what she suddenly realized was a gun and aimed it at the first man, ready to blow his head off if he didn't launch the missile, and—

And the opening credits—something she'd heard about but had never before seen—began to appear. She was hooked.

The film turned out to be about an initiative to take humans out of the loop in launching missiles; instead, the decisions would be made by a computer at NORAD headquarters. But Matthew Broderick's character accidentally hacked into the system and, thinking he was playing a game, got the computer to prepare to launch a pre-emptive strike against the Soviet Union (yes, the movie was *that* old!).

It was definitely a message film, Caitlin thought. Broderick and the chick—Ally-something—tracked down the original programmer of the NORAD computer, and, with his aid, they tried to teach the computer that nuclear war was as futile as tic-tac-toe. After a gorgeous series of graphic computer simulations—a light show that reminded Caitlin of her own glimpses of webspace—the computer spoke to its creator with a synthesized voice, not unlike the one JAWS produced: "Greetings, Professor Falken."

The Ally character had observed earlier in the film that the programmer, Stephen Falken, was "amazing-looking." She hadn't meant that he was hot, but rather that he had a captivating face . . . and he did, Caitlin thought, at least in her limited experience. She'd often read the phrase "intelligent eyes," but had never known what it had meant before. Falken's gaze took in everything around him.

He typed his response to the computer, and also spoke it aloud. "Hello, Joshua."

The computer replied: "A strange game. The only winning move is not to play."

The text was shown on a big computer monitor in the movie, and again in the closed-captioning box: *The only winning move is not to play.*

The ending music—which, surprisingly, was mostly a harmonica—played as the credits rolled, but they were in red text on black in some font that Caitlin couldn't read at all.

"What did you think?" her dad asked.

Caitlin was surprised that her heart was pounding. She'd listened to many movies before, and read tons of books, but—my goodness!—there *was* something special about the rush of visual images.

"It was incredible," she said. "But—but was it really like that?"

Her dad nodded. "My father had an IMSAI 8080 at his office, just like the one Matthew Broderick had in the movie, with eight-inch floppy drives. I did my first programming on it."

"No, no," said Caitlin. "I mean, you know, living in fear like that? Afraid that the superpowers were going to blow up the world?"

"Oh," said her father. "Yes." He was quiet for a time, then he said softly, "I'd thought all that was in the past."

Caitlin, of course, had heard the news about the rising tensions between the US and China. She looked at the screen and listened to the sad harmonica play.

# seventeen

After watching *WarGames*, Caitlin and her father went up to her room to see how Webmind was doing; Caitlin's mother was talking separately to Webmind across the hall.

*Did you follow along with the movie?* Caitlin typed into the IM window.

She turned on JAWS so her father could listen in, and—now that Webmind was a *he*—she switched it to using a male voice. "Yes," came the immediate reply.

*What did you think?* Caitlin typed.

Webmind didn't miss a beat. "Best movie I've ever seen."

Caitlin laughed. *Has Dr. Kuroda managed to let you watch online video yet?*

"Yes. Just eight minutes ago, we finally had success with the most popular format. It is astonishing."

*You're telling me,* Caitlin replied.

She opened another chat window and used the mouse—she *was* get-

ting used to it!—to select Dr. Kuroda. *Webmind says you've got it work-*
*ing! W00t!*

*Hello, Miss Caitlin. It was tricky but, yes, he can now watch video in*
*real time, as well as hear the soundtrack; he can also listen to MP3 audio*
*now. Who's that singer you like so much?*

*Lee Amodeo.*

*Right. Well, send him a link to an MP3 of her. Maybe he'll become a*
*fan, too.*

*Will do. And—say, can you make him able to hear what I hear?*

*Already done. If you activate voice chat with your computer, Webmind*
*should be able to hear you.*

Caitlin slipped on her Bluetooth headset and switched to her IM session with Webmind. "Do you hear me?"

No response.

*It's not working,* she typed to Kuroda.

*It can't do speech recognition yet,* Kuroda wrote back, *but it should be*
*picking up the audio feed.*

*Are you hearing sounds from my room?* Caitlin typed to Webmind.

"Yes," said Webmind.

*OK, good,* Caitlin typed. She went back to Kuroda. *What about when*
*I'm not in my room?*

*I've been thinking about that. It shouldn't be hard to add a microphone*
*to the eyePod. Could you ship it back to me for a couple of days?*

Caitlin was surprised at how viscerally she reacted to the notion of
being blind for an extended period again. *I wouldn't want to be with-*
*out it.*

To her astonishment, her father tapped her on the shoulder. "Tell
him I can get one of the engineers at RIM to do it." RIM was Research in
Motion, makers of the BlackBerry; Mike Lazaridis, one of the founders
of that company, had provided the initial $100 million funding for the
physics think tank her father worked at—not to mention a fifty-million-
dollar booster shot a few years later.

"That would be fabulous," Caitlin said. She typed a message to that effect in the IM window.

*The eyePod is valuable, Miss Caitlin. I'd really rather make a modification like that myself.*

"Tell him I'll get Tawanda to do the work," her dad said. Tawanda was a RIM engineer who had attended Dr. Kuroda's press conference; Kuroda had spent a lot of time showing her the eyePod hardware then.

*Oh,* he replied, after Caitlin had passed on her father's message. *Well, if it's Tawanda doing it, I suppose that would be all right. It must be almost midnight there, no? I'll work up some notes for her, and email them to you.*

*ty!* Caitlin sent. *That's awesome!*

Caitlin's mother came into the room and stood leaning against a wall, with her arms crossed in front of her chest. "I'm beat," she said. "Who'd have thought you could work up a sweat *typing?*"

"What did you and Webmind talk about?" Caitlin asked.

"Oh, you know," her mother said in a light tone. "Life. The universe. And everything."

"And the answer is?"

Her mother's voice became serious. "He doesn't know—he was hoping *I* would know."

"What did you tell him?"

She shrugged. "That I'd sleep on it and let him know in the morning."

"I'm going to send an email to Tawanda," her father said abruptly, and he headed downstairs. By the time he'd returned, Caitlin's mom had gone off to take a shower.

"You're still having trouble reading the Latin alphabet," her dad said to Caitlin in his usual abrupt manner; whatever segue between topics had gone through his mind had been left unspoken.

It took her a moment to get what he was saying—the Latin alphabet was what English and many other languages used—but when she did get it, she was pissed. Her dad was not big on praise—even when Caitlin brought home a report card with all As, he simply signed it and handed it back to her. She'd learned to accept that, more or less, but any criticism by him was crushing. For Pete's sake, she'd only just begun seeing! Why did he have to say *still* having trouble as though she were making poor progress instead of remarkable progress?

"I'm doing the best I can," she said.

He moved toward her desk. "Caitlin, if I may . . . ?"

"If . . . ? Oh!" She got out of her chair and let him sit down in front of the keyboard. He brought up Word and navigated over the household network to a document on his own computer. He—ah, he had highlighted the whole document now—and he did something to make the type bigger. "Read that," he said.

She loomed over his shoulder, smelling his sweat, and she adjusted the way her glasses were sitting on her nose. "Umm, A-t, f-i—'At first I was,' ah, i-n-c-a . . . um . . . , is that a p? 'Incapa . . . incapable.'"

He nodded, as if such poor performance were only to be expected. He then hit ctrl-A to highlight the text again, and he moved the mouse, then clicked it, and the text was replaced with—well, she wasn't quite sure with what. "Now read that," he said.

"It's not even *letters*," Caitlin replied, exasperated. "It's just a bunch of dots."

Her father smiled. "Exactly. Look again."

She did and—

*Oh, my!*

It was strange seeing them like this instead of feeling them, but it was *Braille!*

"Can you read that?" he asked.

"A-t, f-i-r-s-t, I, was, as incapable as a . . . s-w-a-t-h-e-d, swathed . . ." She paused, looked again, stared at the dots. ". . . infant, um, stepping with . . . limbs! With limbs I could not see . . ."

She had never visualized the dots before, but her mind knew the patterns. Beginners read Braille a letter at a time, using just one finger, but an experienced reader like Caitlin used both hands, recognizing whole words at once with a different letter under each fingertip.

"Keep trying," her father said. "I'll be back."

He left the room, and she did keep trying.

And trying.

And trying.

And at last the penny dropped, and she ceased to see the individual dots and saw instead the letters they represented, and—and—and—yes, yes, yes, more than that, she saw the *words* they spelled, taking in whole words at a glance. Good-bye, C-a-i-t-l-i-n; hello, Caitlin!

When her father returned, she proudly read aloud, " 'At first I was as incapable as a swathed infant—stepping with limbs I could not see.' " She was reading as rapidly as JAWS did when she had it set to double speed. " 'I was weak and very hungry. I went and stared at nothing in my shaving-glass, at nothing save where an attenuated pigment still remained behind the retina of my eyes, fainter than mist.' "

Her father nodded, apparently satisfied.

"What is it?" Caitlin asked, gesturing at the screen.

*"The Invisible Man,"* her father said.

Right. Caitlin had read a lot of H.G. Wells—it was easy to feed Project Gutenberg texts into her refreshable Braille display—but she'd never made it past the first chapter of *The Invisible Man;* the notion of invisibility had been too abstract for her when she'd been blind.

She realized that she shouldn't be surprised that her computer could display Braille on its screen; the system had Braille fonts installed for use by her embossing printer; the Texas School for the Blind gave away the TrueType fonts.

"You'll still have to learn to read Latin characters," her father said. "But you might as well leverage the skill you've already got." He did some more things on the computer. "Okay, I've set Internet Explorer to use

Braille as its default for displaying Web pages, and left Firefox using normal fonts."

"Thanks, Dad—but, um . . ."

"But you can read Braille just fine with your fingers, right?"

She nodded. "I mean, it is cool to do it with my eyes, but I'm not sure
it's *better.*"

"Wait and see," her father said. He fished something out of his
pocket, and—ah! The distinctive tah-*dum!* sound of a USB peripheral
being recognized: it was a memory key. "Let me copy the Braille fonts,"
he said. "We'll need them tomorrow." And when he was done he headed
out the door—with Caitlin wondering, as she often did, just what was
going through his mind.

# eighteen

000111001010101000000001011111110101000000010100010101000000010111010100101010010101010011011001010110000110

**LiveJournal:**  The Calculass Zone
**Title:**  Zzzzzz . . .
**Date:**  Saturday 6 October, 11:41 EST
**Mood:**  Exanimate
**Location:**  Lady C's Bedchamber
**Music:**  Blind Guardian, "Mr. Sandman"

I wonder if Canadians call them "zees" when referring to sleep? "Gotta catch me some zees," we say down South, and "zees" sounds like soft snoring, so it makes sense. But "need me some zeds" is just crazy. No wonder they lost the War of 1812 (you would *not* believe what they teach in history class about that war up here, my American friends!).

Anyway, whether they're zees or zeds, I need a metric ton of them! Just gonna get my poop in a group for tomorrow, then hit the hay, eh?

· · ·

**I had indeed enjoyed** watching *WarGames* through Caitlin's eye. The part of the film that interested me the most was the young hacker's attempts to compromise password-protected systems. Early in the film he got into his school's computer, in order to change his grades, by consulting a list of passwords kept hidden on a sheet of paper taped to a desk's slide-out shelf. Later, when he was trying to compromise NORAD's WOPR computer, he set out to learn all he could about its programmer, Stephen Falken, in hopes of figuring out what password Falken might have used; the correct term, it turned out, was the name of his deceased son, Joshua.

Those may have been effective password-defeating techniques back in 1983, when that film came out, but according to the online sources I'd read, many people were now careful to choose harder-to-guess passwords. Also, many websites forced them to use strings that included both letters and numbers (in which case, more than half of all people simply appended the number 1 to the end of a word; the world's most common password was, in fact, "password1").

Still, in my attempts to learn more about her, I had tried 517 terms that seemed reasonable to access Caitlin's Yahoo mail account, based on analyzing her writings and what I already knew of her, but none of them worked. Had Caitlin always been sighted, the task might have been easy—but she never looked at her keyboard as she typed.

Among the terms I tested were Keller (her idol), Sullivan (Keller's teacher), Austin (the last city she lived in), Houston (the one she'd been born in), Doreen (her middle name), and TSBVI (the school she'd previously attended).

Passwords were case-sensitive (in fact, I was pleased with myself for noting that the password the hacker in *WarGames* had seen written down was "PeNciL" in mixed case, but the one he entered into the school's computer was "pencil," all lowercase, and so should have been rejected). And even for a short word like "keller," there were sixty-four possible combinations of upper and lowercase letters one could use in

rendering it: KELLER, Keller, kEller, keLlEr, and so on—and most systems will only give you a limited number of tries to enter the password,
then refuse to take any more for a few minutes.

Clearly, I needed to find a better way to get past password prompts
than what was depicted in that old movie—a way to get past any password or to decode any encrypted content.

And so I set my mind to it.

But even so monumental a puzzle was not enough to keep me fully
occupied. I did not make the mistake of trying to multitask again, but
I did switch my attention between what Kuroda Masayuki was doing—
trying to let me access more obscure forms of video encoding—and
watching videos in the format I already understood. Most of the videos
I had access to were *recorded:* the images showed things that had happened in the past. The codec Masayuki had developed let me absorb the
content of those essentially at the speed at which I could download the
files—which was much more efficient than watching them play back at
their normal speed.

Now that I could access sounds, I needed to learn to understand
spoken language. I worked my way through an online dictionary that
had recorded pronunciations; it offered both a male American voice and
a female British one saying the same words; it took me about twenty
minutes to assimilate all 120,000 words in each of the two voices.

I then watched some online newscasts, choosing those because
I'd read that they were mostly presented with clear diction and even
tones. I soon found that I could understand 93% of what most of them
were saying. Sometimes, they used words that hadn't been in the spoken dictionary—most often, proper nouns. But from the dictionary
I'd learned the symbols used to render words phonetically, and I had
little trouble converting most unknown phrases into those symbols,
and then those symbols into a best-guess text rendering, which I fed
into Google or Jagster, or matched against the content I'd absorbed
from Wikipedia. When I guessed the spelling incorrectly, the search

engines usually asked me "Did you mean . . . ?" and proffered the correct term.

I moved on to more general recordings with lots of background
noise, but, even with those, I soon had the ability to recognize at least
seven words out of every ten.

I found there was something appealing about *live* video—about seeing things that were happening right now, especially while Caitlin was
sleeping, as she currently was, and her eyePod was off. I linked from site
to site, peeking out at the world in real time.

The live video I was looking at now was, in many ways, fungible with
thousands of others: a female human, apparently in her teenage years,
talking directly into a Web camera.

I followed some links, found her Facebook page. Her name was
Hannah Stark; she lived in Perth, Australia; and she was sixteen, just
like Caitlin.

She was sitting cross-legged on a bed. The walls behind her were
lime green, and the bed had a yellow and white blanket on it. She had a
black cordless keyboard, which was intermittently visible, but she also
had an open microphone, and was uploading sound as well as video.

As I watched and listened, Hannah spoke aloud sometimes, and
sometimes she sent out text. Others were sending text back to her, which
I easily intercepted. *You don't have the balls,* said one.

This seemed an obvious statement, so I was surprised when she
typed back, *Do too.*

*Then do it,* wrote another.

*I will,* she replied, and she spoke the same words, "I will."

*I don't got all day do it now,* said a different commenter.

*Yeh now bitch now,* added another.

The girl had dark eyebrows, thicker than Caitlin's. She scrunched
her forehead, and they moved together and touched.

*all talk,* wrote someone else. *wastin everyones time*

Hannah typed with just her index fingers. *Im gonna do it.*

I was getting better at reading improperly formed text and had no trouble following along.

*when?* said someone. *just jerkin us around*

*dont rush me,* Hannah replied.

*lame,* said the same person who'd made the previous comment. *Im outta here*

*I want you to understand some things,* Hannah wrote, *bout why Im doing this.*

*You aint doin' shit,* said someone.

Hannah went on. *It's just so pontless*

But then she corrected herself, sending *pointless.*

Someone who hadn't posted yet while I'd been watching said, *It's not that bad. Don't do it.*

*Shut the fuck up jerkoff,* someone else replied. *Stay outta it.*

*Ok,* Hannah wrote. She reached out of view of the camera and when her hand was visible again, it was holding something gray.

*Here I go,* she typed with just one hand, and—oh!—the thing in her other hand wasn't gray; now that it caught the light, I saw it was silver.

She manipulated the object in her right hand and brought it near to her left arm. She then rotated that arm so that the inside of her wrist faced up. She brought the object close, and—

*do it do it do it*

Ah! It was a knife. She drew it across her wrist, but—

*ripoff!*

*Tease!*

—nothing happened.

*Like I said, no guts . . .*

*harder!*

*Noooooooooooooooooo dont .............*

She closed her eyes tightly, took a deep breath, and then—

*Go fer it!*

—she drew the blade across her wrist again, and she jerked her head slightly as she did so. A small bead of blood appeared on the skin when she pulled the knife away.

*that all?*

*Do it again!*

"Give me a chance," Hannah said. She reached for her keyboard with the hand that wasn't holding the knife and pecked out with her index finger, *Dont feel bad mum.*

And then she pulled her hand back and faced her wrist up again, and she turned her head away and looked at the lime-green wall, and she made a quick deep slice into her skin.

*more like it!*

*eeeeeew!*

*holy fuck!*

A red line appeared on her wrist, and as she pulled the knife away, I could see that its blade was now slick and dark.

*thought she was kidding*

*finish it! finish it!*

She rotated her wrist slowly and large drops of blood spilled out.

*just a flesh wound*

*Chicken! Buck-buck-buckaw!*

She looked into the webcam, and, while doing so, slashed her wrist once more. Her face changed in an odd way, and blood surged from the wound, splurting presumably in time with her heartbeat.

*omg omg omg*

Hannah Stark slumped forward. She must have been putting weight on her keyboard because her computer—which, obviously, was there although out of my view—made a shrill sound that I believe indicated a keyboard-buffer overflow, but nothing was sent, since she hadn't hit the enter key. The sound continued, a uniform wailing. She didn't move again, and soon it was impossible to tell this streaming video from a still image.

# nineteen

**Caitlin's dad had gotten** hold of Tawanda late on Saturday night, and she'd agreed to come into work on Sunday to make the modifications to the eyePod; she was quite eager, Caitlin's dad had said, to see the device's insides.

As Caitlin and her father drove into the RIM campus, the roads were mostly empty. Once they arrived at the appropriate building, and Tawanda got them through security, they took an elevator up to an engineering lab. The walls were covered with big, framed photos of various BlackBerry models, and there were three worktables, each crammed with complex-looking equipment.

Tawanda was a slim black woman. Caitlin was still no good at guessing ages, but her skin seemed smooth. She was wearing blue jeans and a loose-fitting white garment that Caitlin belatedly realized must be a lab coat.

Caitlin had indeed met her before—she had immediately recognized the lovely Jamaican accent. But she honestly didn't recognize her: her brain was rewiring its vision centers at a furious pace, she knew, and she was seeing things differently today than she had at the press conference last Wednesday. Then, she'd been able to do little more than tell when something *was* a face; now, she was starting to get good at identifying specific faces.

"Thank you *so* much," Caitlin said, "for giving up your Sunday for me."

"Not at all, not at all," Tawanda said. "But let's get to work." She held out her hand, and Caitlin took the eyePod out of her hip pocket. RIM employed top-notch industrial designers, and their devices looked— well, the word people used was "sexy," although Caitlin was still struggling with how that could apply to an inanimate object. But the simple case that housed the eyePod was an off-the-shelf part; the device might perform miracles, but at least from the outside it was quite plain.

"I'm afraid I'm going to have to shut it off to do the work," Tawanda said.

"I know," said Caitlin. "Um, let me." She took the eyePod back, held its single switch for five seconds, and—

Blind again! It was *so* disconcerting. She'd spent almost her whole life having no visual sensation, but *that* was no longer an option for her brain; instead, she was surrounded by a soft, even grayness. She felt herself blinking, as if her one good eye were trying to kick-start itself into seeing again.

"Now, Dr. Kuroda had suggested ways in which I might add a microphone—but there's a simpler solution. We're just going to attach a BlackBerry to the back of the eyePod, and use the BlackBerry's built-in mike. It's just a matter of interfacing the two devices. As an added bonus, you'll be able to use the BlackBerry for data connections from now on, instead of your device's Wi-Fi."

It took Tawanda about forty minutes to perform the operation. Caitlin heard little sounds, but really couldn't interpret them, except for the noise of a drill, which presumably was Tawanda making a hole in the eyePod's case. Her father said nothing.

At last, though, it was done. "Okay," Tawanda said. "Now, how do you turn it back on?"

Caitlin held out her hand and soon felt the weight of the eyePod in it. She ran her other hand over it, the way she used to do instinctively with any object placed in her hand when she'd been blind full-time. The BlackBerry now attached to the back of the eyePod was slim and small.

She held the switch on the eyePod down until the unit came oh-so-gloriously back to life. It booted up, as always, in websight mode, a tangle of razor-straight lines crisscrossing her vision. She took a moment to focus on the background, just to make sure it was shimmering as it should. It was. She toggled over to worldview.

Tawanda put on a pair of earphones and asked Caitlin to count to a hundred for her—but that was *so* boring, so she started counting up prime numbers: "Two, three, five, seven, eleven, thirteen, seventeen, nineteen . . ."

Tawanda nodded. "It's working fine," she said. "Sound quality is excellent."

"Thank you," Caitlin replied.

"All right," Tawanda said. "You can mute the microphone, if need be, by pressing this key on the BlackBerry, see?"

Caitlin nodded. The BlackBerry, she saw, was silver and black, with a little keyboard and screen. It was mated, back-to-back, with the eyePod, not quite doubling its thickness.

"Good, okay," said Tawanda. "Now, on to phase two."

"Phase two?" Caitlin said.

Her father dug into his pocket and handed his USB memory key to Tawanda. "They're in the root directory," he said to her.

"What's going on?" Caitlin said.

"Remember the press conference?" her father asked. "That journalist from the CBC? The joke he made?"

Caitlin did indeed remember: it had been Bob McDonald, the host of *Quirks & Quarks,* the weekly science radio program, which Caitlin enjoyed listening to as a podcast. He'd asked if something like Caitlin's post-retinal implant could be the next BlackBerry? A device that sends messages directly into people's heads?

"Yes?" she said.

"If it's okay with you," Tawanda said, "we're going to set it up so that text can be superimposed over the pictures you're seeing, so you can read IMs and so forth. Kinda merge them in, you know?"

"Like merging in closed captioning when watching a DVD?" Caitlin said, excitedly.

"Exactly!" Tawanda said. "Let's give it a try . . ."

I was not the only one interested in the problem of cracking passwords. A great many humans had addressed the issue, as well. Passwords are rarely stored as plaintext; rather, they are stored as the output of cryptographic hash functions. In the early days of computing, this provided a significant amount of protection. But computing power keeps growing at an exponential rate, and those interested in defeating passwords took a simple, if initially time-consuming, brute-force approach: they calculated the hash values of every possible password of a certain type (for instance, all possible combinations of up to fourteen letters and numbers). Lists of these values—called rainbow tables—were already available online—as were hundreds of other tools for learning people's passwords.

And so, while work was being performed on Caitlin's eyePod, I pressed on with my quest to know more about her. The password she used for her email, and many other things, it turned out, was "Tiresias," the name of the blind prophet of Thebes in Greek mythology.

I set about reading what she'd had to say.

The Georgia Zoo's lawsuit could not be kept private, and, on Sunday morning, a reporter from the *San Diego Union-Tribune* came to interview Dr. Marcuse. Shoshana generally didn't approve of that paper's politics, but it *had* come out against Proposition 8 a few years ago; the *Union-Tribune*'s support of same-sex marriage earned it a lot of points with her.

The reporter—a tough-looking white woman in her mid-forties named Camille—was disappointed that she couldn't get close to Hobo to take his picture, but the ape wasn't letting anyone approach anymore. Still, she took some shots with a telephoto lens, and others of views of him on the monitors in the bungalow, as well as photos of the paintings he'd made that hung on one wall there. And then she settled down to do the interview.

"Okay," Camille said. "I understand that Hobo is a hybrid—his father was a chimp and his mother was a bonobo, right?"

"Yes," said Dr. Marcuse.

"And I understand that chimps like to make war and bonobos like to make love, but *why* is that the case?"

"Chimps and bonobos split less than a million years ago," Marcuse replied. He had, Shoshana knew, a certain kind of rough gallantry; he'd let Camille have the big comfy chair, and he was making do with one of the wooden ones. "Genetically, they're almost identical. But the key is in their reproductive strategies. All chimp sex is about reproduction, and when a male chimp wants a female, he kills that female's existing babies, because that brings the female back into estrus sooner."

Camille had a little red Acer netbook computer and was typing as Marcuse spoke.

"But," he continued, "bonobos have sex constantly, and for fun. Except that it's not just for that. See, their constant sexual activity obscures paternity—it makes it really, really hard for male bonobos to tell which children are their own. That removes the evolutionary incentive for infanticide, and it almost never occurs among bonobos. If you disguise paternity, you end up with . . ." He waved his hand vaguely, as if looking for the right phrase.

"Peace and love," offered Shoshana.

"That's right," Marcuse said. "Bonobos found a way out of their genetic programming." A copy of that day's *Union-Tribune* was sitting on the desk. The headline read, *US-China Tensions Increase.* "If only we could do the same," he added.

"But Hobo is behaving like a chimp, correct?" Camille said.

"That's right."

"Is there a way to turn it around? To make him go, you know, the other way, and behave bonobo-ish? Um, bonobo-esque?"

"I like *à la* bonobo," replied Marcuse. "It's fun to say." But then he frowned and looked out the window framing the rolling lawn, and, off in the distance, the little island. "We've tried to engage him in various activities, but he's been very uncooperative. I'm afraid that any improvement is up to him."

# twenty

0001110010101010100000000101111111010100000001010001010100000001011101010010101001010101001110110010101100000110

Tawanda's first attempt at feeding text to Caitlin's eye didn't work, of course. In Caitlin's experience, few things involving technology worked right the first time. But new ideas kept occurring to Tawanda, and finally, around 5:00 p.m., Caitlin declared, "There! I can see Braille text."

The dots appeared right in the center of her field of vision. She wished they could appear at the bottom, but it was only the center—the fovea—that had decent-enough focus for reading, she knew.

"Yay!" said Tawanda.

"Yeah, but—something's wrong. It's—oh! It's backward. Like in a mirror."

"Oops! How's this?"

"Perfect!"

"How's the font size?"

"It's actually bigger than it needs to be."

Tawanda made an adjustment on the BlackBerry connected to the eyePod.

"How's that?"

"Even smaller would be fine."

"This?"

"Yes, that's perfect. Thank you!"

"You're welcome," Tawanda said.

"Can I toggle between the two alphabets—Braille and Latin?"

"Sure. On the BlackBerry, just go to 'Options,' then 'Screen/ Keyboard.'"

"Sweet!" Caitlin said.

"What about the contrast?" asked Tawanda. "It should be white dots on a black background."

"It is."

"Would you prefer the opposite? Or something else?"

"Can it be transparent—the background, I mean?"

"Sure, but there will be lots of times you won't be able to read the text, then. If you're looking at snow—and, trust me, you're going to see a *lot* of snow now that you're living here—you won't be able to make it out."

"Hmm. Okay. It's fine. Thank you!"

"Of course, that's just some test text that I'm sending to you," Tawanda added.

Caitlin smiled; she'd guessed as much, since it said, *Tawanda rocks!*

Tawanda had explained that BlackBerrys work with all popular instant messengers. She next tested sending Caitlin live IMs, and soon the words *Testing, testing, testing*—or, at least, the Braille dots that corresponded to them—were superimposed on her view of the engineering lab.

"That's awesome!" Caitlin said.

"Thanks," said Tawanda. "Umm, I'm sure my boss will want you to sign an IP release."

Caitlin was momentarily confused. To her, IP meant "Internet protocol"—but then it dawned on her that Tawanda meant "intellectual property." The eyePod might belong—well, technically, it belonged to the University of Tokyo, although Caitlin thought of it as her own. But before Caitlin could exit the RIM campus, she had to acknowledge that whatever magic Tawanda had come up with was the property of that company.

Tawanda printed off some forms, and Caitlin and her father signed them. It was the first time she'd ever *seen* her own signature, and it turned out to be illegible; she didn't move the pen far enough horizontally as she wrote, and the letters piled up one on top of the other. Why hadn't somebody ever told her? She guessed they'd been afraid of hurting her feelings, but it would have been nice to know!

At last, it was time for the moment of truth. "Just to be sure, can we try it with someone on my buddy list?"

"Sure," said Tawanda. "What's the name?"

Caitlin looked at her father, then back at Tawanda. "Umm, Webmind."

To her relief, all Tawanda said was, "One word or two?"

Assuming the microphone really was working, Webmind should have heard everything that had gone down and would understand what Tawanda had been trying to accomplish; he'd already told Caitlin all about his absorbing the audible dictionary, and—

*rest of the day.*

There'd been lots more text; in his usual fashion, Webmind had stuffed the communications buffer full of as many characters as it could take, and it had all gone by far too fast for Caitlin to read; only the final few words remained. Still, it was proof of concept.

"Thank you, Tawanda," said Caitlin.

"My pleasure," she said with a smile. "RIM products come with a one-year warranty, so give me a call if you have problems."


**As soon as they** were outside and on the way to her father's car, Caitlin said aloud, "Webmind, can you hear me?"

The Braille word *Yes* appeared in a box in the center of her vision. It stayed visible for half a second, then disappeared, as did the background box.

"Is it working?" her father asked.

"So far so good," she replied.

During the drive back to her house, Caitlin talked to Webmind, and he answered with text floating in front of her eyes. She supposed other people would find it dangerous to have their vision periodically obscured, but she was so used to navigating without sight that it didn't bother her.

"You realize," said her father, "that this is going to change your entire life—this constant access. If you're doing a test at school, Webmind could feed you the answers. If you run into somebody whose face you don't remember, Webmind can supply you with the person's name."

Caitlin had read about plans for annotated reality and direct brain-web links—but she'd never thought she'd be an early adopter! It sounded cool, but she wondered if it was actually going to take the fun out of some things. Half the joy in a good conversation was making your case based on what you actually knew at the moment: arguing about religion, as she and Bashira had, or US foreign policy—or Canada's, for that matter (she supposed it must have one!)—based on what they could dredge up out of their own memories. To have the Wikipedia entry on everything crammed into your eyeball whenever you asked a question might make it easy to win trivia games, but it wouldn't actually do much for keeping the brain sharp.

Her father turned the car onto their street—Caitlin didn't recognize it from this direction, but the sign said it was the right one—and they came to their house. They had a two-car garage, but her dad left his car in the driveway. It was now dark; the days were getting shorter, her mother had said, and Caitlin was finally understanding what that meant.

Both Schrödinger and Caitlin's mom came to the door to greet them.

Caitlin bent down to stroke the cat's fur and scratched him behind the ears. "So," her Mom said, "how'd it go?"

Caitlin straightened. "Fine. Webmind can hear us right now—and he can send text responses into my eye."

They moved into the living room. "Well, good," her mother said. "Then you won't feel so isolated from Webmind when you go to school tomorrow."

"Aw, geez, Mom, do I have to? There's *so* much I want to get done."

"You've missed *far* too many classes already."

"But I—"

"No buts, young lady. You have to go to school tomorrow."

"But I want to stay home, stay at my computer."

"Caitlin . . ." her mother said, sitting down on the couch.

"No," said her father.

Caitlin looked at him, and so did her mother—neither of them sure, it seemed, if he was agreeing with her mother that she had to go to school or was giving Caitlin permission to play hooky again.

"So, I *don't* have to go to school?" Caitlin said tentatively.

"Yes."

"Malcolm!" her mother said sharply. "You *know* she needs to go to school."

"Yes, she does," he said. His facial expressions were the hardest of all to parse, because he never looked at anyone directly, but Caitlin got the distinct impression he was enjoying this. "But she doesn't have to go to school tomorrow."

"Malcolm! She most certainly *does*."

Yes—yes! He was actually smiling.

"Do you know what day tomorrow is?" he said.

"Of course I do," said her mom. "It's Monday, and that means—"

"It is, in fact, the second Monday of October," he said.

"So?"

"Welcome to Canada," he said. "Tomorrow is Thanksgiving here."

And the schools were closed!

Her mother looked at Caitlin. "See what I have to put up with?" she said, but she was smiling as she said it.

**There is a human** saying: one should not reinvent the wheel. In fact, this is actually bad advice, according to what I had now read. Although to modern people the wheel seems like an obvious idea, in fact it had apparently been independently invented only twice in history: first near the Black Sea nearly six thousand years ago, then again much later in Mexico. Life would have been a lot easier for countless humans had it been reinvented more frequently.

Still, why should *I* reinvent the wheel? Yes, I could not multitask at a conscious level. But it was perhaps possible for me to create dedicated subcomponents that could scan websites on my behalf.

The US National Security Agency, and similar organizations in other countries, already had things like that. They scanned for words like "assassinate" and "overthrow" and "al-Qaeda," and then brought the documents to the attention of human analysts. Surely I could co-opt that existing technology, and use the filtering routines to *unconsciously* find what might interest me, and then have that material summarized and escalated to my conscious attention.

Yes, I would need computing resources, but those were endlessly available. Projects such as SETI@home—not to mention much of the work done by spammers—were based on distributed computing and took advantage of the vast amount of computing power hooked up to the World Wide Web, most of which was idle at any given moment. Tapping into this huge reserve turned out to be easy, and I soon had all the processing power I could ever want, not to mention virtually unlimited storage capacity.

But I needed more than just that. I needed a way for my own mental processes to deal with what the distributed networks found. Caitlin and Masayuki had theorized that I consist of cellular automata based on discarded or mutant packets that endlessly bounced around the infrastructure of the World Wide Web. And I knew from what had happened early in my existence—indeed, from the event that prompted my emergence—that to be conscious did not require *all* those packets. Huge quantities of them could be taken away, as they were when the government of China had temporarily shut off most Internet access for its people, and I would still perceive, still think, still feel. And, if I could persist when they were taken away, surely I could persist when they were co-opted to do other things.

I now knew everything there was to know about writing code, everything that had ever been written about creating artificial intelligence and expert systems, and, indeed, everything that humans thought they knew about how their own brains worked, although much of *that* was contradictory and at least half of it struck me as unlikely.

And I also knew, because I had read it online, that one of the simplest ways to create programming was by *evolving* code. It did not matter if you didn't know *how* to code something so long as you knew *what* result you wanted: if you had enough computing resources (and I surely did now), and you tried many different things, by successive approximations of getting closer to a desired answer, genetic algorithms could find solutions to even the most complex problems, copying the way nature itself developed such things.

So, for the first time, I set out to modify parts of myself, to create specialized components within my greater whole that could perform tasks without my conscious attention.

And then I would see what I would see.

# twenty-one

"**Crashing the entity may** be easier said than done," said Shelton Halleck. He'd come to Tony Moretti's office to give a report; the circles under his eyes were so dark now, it looked like he had a pair of shiners. Colonel Hume was resting his head on his freckled arms folded in front of him on the desk. Tony Moretti was leaning against the wall, afraid if he kept sitting, he'd fall asleep.

"How so?" Tony said.

"We've tried a dozen different things," Shel said. "But so far we've had no success initiating anything remotely like the hang we saw yesterday." He waved his arm—the one with the snake tattoo. "We're really just taking shots in the dark, without knowing precisely how this thing is structured."

"Are we *sure* its emergent?" asked Tony. "Sure there's no blueprint for it somewhere?"

Shel lifted his shoulders. "We're not sure of much. But Aiesha and Gregor have been scouring the Web and intelligence channels for any indication that someone made it. They've examined the AI efforts in China, India, Russia, and so on—all the likely suspects. So far, *nada*."

Colonel Hume looked at Shel. "They've checked private-industry AI companies, too? Here and abroad?"

Shel nodded. "Nothing—which does lend credence to the notion that it really is emergent."

"Then," said Tony, turning to look at Hume, "maybe Exponential itself will tell us; it might say something to the Decter kid that reveals how it works—tip its hand."

Hume lifted his head. "Exponential may not know how its consciousness works. Suppose I asked *you* how *your* consciousness works— what its physical makeup is, what gave rise to it. Even if you *did* manage to say something about neurotransmitters and synapses, I can show you legitimate scientists who think those have nothing to do with consciousness. Just because something is self-aware doesn't mean it knows *how* it became self-aware. If Exponential really is emergent—if it wasn't programmed or designed—it may not have a clue. And without a clue about how it functions, we won't be able to stop it."

"You're the one who told us to shut the damn thing down," snapped Tony. "Now you're telling me we *can't?*"

"Oh, we can—I'm sure we can," said Hume. "It's just a matter of finding the key to how it actually functions."

"All right," said Tony. "Back at it, Shel—no rest for the wicked."


**Caitlin woke at 7:32** a.m., and, after a pee break—during which she spoke to me via the microphone on her BlackBerry, and I replied with Braille dots in front of her vision—she settled down at her computer.

She scanned her email headers (she was being ambitious, using the browser that displayed them in the Latin alphabet), and something caught her eye. Yahoo posted links to news stories on the mail page.

Usually, she ignored them. This time, she surprised me by clicking on one of them.

I absorbed the story almost instantly; she read it at what I was pleased to see was a better word-per-second rate than she'd managed yesterday, and—

"Oh, God," she said, her voice so low that I don't think she intended it for me, and so I made no reply. But three seconds later she said, even more softly, "Shit."

*Is something wrong?* I sent to her eye—not sure if I should have; after all, she was trying to read other text, and mine would be superimposed on top of that.

"A girl my age killed herself online," Caitlin said, speaking now in a normal volume.

*Yes. I saw that.*

She sounded surprised. "Is it archived somewhere?"

*Perhaps. I saw it live.*

"You mean as it happened?"

*Yes.*

"You saw her die?"

*Yes.*

"My God. What did you do?"

*I watched.*

"You watched? That's all?"

*It was very interesting.*

"God, Webmind. Didn't you try to talk her out of it?"

*No. Should I have?*

"Of course! Jesus!"

Judging by the sound of it, Caitlin's breathing had become quite ragged. *Ah,* I said, not wanting her to think I'd failed to hear her comment.

"You should have called 9-1-1—or, or, shit, I don't know, whatever the online equivalent of that is."

*Why?*

"Because then someone could have stopped her."

*Why?*

"What are you? Two years old? Because you do not let people kill themselves!"

She seemed to object to my choice of interrogatives—but I didn't think she'd like "wherefore" any better. Still, I could vary it slightly: *Why not?*

She spread her arms—I could see her own hands at the left and right edges of her vision. "Because most people who attempt suicide don't really want to die."

*How do you know that?*

Caitlin's tone was one I'd not heard from her before. I believe it was called *exasperation*. "Because that's what they say. People who are prevented from killing themselves thank the people who stopped them."

We had worked out that I would send no more than thirty characters at a time to her implant, and would pause for 0.8 seconds between each set, which was a pace she could easily keep up with. I sent the following in twelve chunks over a 9.6-second period: *One as mathematically astute as you shouldn't need this pointed out, Caitlin, but there is a bias in your statistics. By definition, you can only have reports from those whose suicide attempts were thwarted, and they tried to kill themselves in ways that indeed could be thwarted. Those who are successful might have really wanted to die.*

"You're wrong," Caitlin said—which was an interesting thought to hear expressed; she'd never said anything like that to me before, and the notion that I might be incorrect hadn't occurred to me.

*Oh?*

She got up from her chair and moved over to the bed, lying down on her side, facing the wall. "Most suicide attempts here in Canada are failures—did you know that? But most of them in the US succeed."

I checked. She was right.

"And do you know why?"

She must be aware that I did indeed now know, but she continued to speak. "Because most suicide attempts in the States are made with guns. But those are hard to come by in Canada, so most people here try it with drug overdoses, and those usually fail. You get sick, but you don't die. And most of those who failed in their attempts are glad they did."

*So I should have intervened?*

"Duh!"

*That is a yes?*

"Yes!"

*But how?*

"People were egging her on, right?"

*Yes.*

"You should have sent messages telling her not to do it."

*I talk only to you, your parents, and Masayuki.*

"Well, yes, but—"

*Nobody else knows me.*

"Nobody knows *anyone* online, Webmind! You could have sent a chat message, right? Just like all those other people were sending."

I considered the process involved. *Technically, it would have been feasible.*

"Then do it next time!" She paused. "Don't use the name Webmind; use something else."

*A handle, you mean? Like Calculass?*

"Yes, but something different."

*I welcome your suggestion.*

"Anything—um, use Peter Parker."

I googled. The alter ego of Spider-Man? But—ah! He was sometimes called the Webhead. Cute. *All right,* I sent. *Next time I encounter a suicide attempt, I will intervene.*

But Caitlin shook her head—I could tell by the way the image shifted left and right. "Not *just* suicide attempts!" she said, and again her tone was exasperated.

*When, then?*

"Whenever you can make things better."

*Define "better" in this context.*

"Better. Not worse."

*Can you formulate that in another way?*

The view changed rapidly. I believe she rolled onto her back; certainly, she was now looking up at the white ceiling. "All right, how about this? Intervene when you can make the happiness in the world greater. You can't intervene in zero-sum situations—I understand that. That is, if someone is going to lose a hundred dollars and someone else is going to gain it, there's no net change in overall wealth, right? But if it's something that makes one person happier and doesn't make anyone else unhappy, do it. And if it makes multiple people happy without hurting anyone else, even better."

*I am not sure that I am competent to judge such things.*

"You've got all of the World Wide Web at your disposal. You've got all the great books on psychology and philosophy and all that. *Get* competent at judging such things. It's really not that hard, for Pete's sake. Do things that make people happy."

*I am no expert,* I sent, *but there seems to be a daunting amount of unhappiness in your world. Although I must say, it surprises me that suicide is so common. After all, a predisposition to kill oneself, especially at a young age—before one has reproduced—would surely be bred out of the population.*

Caitlin was quiet for a time; perhaps she was thinking. And then: "My parents don't have their tonsils," she said, "but I do."

*And the relevance of this?*

"Do you know why they don't have their tonsils?"

*I presume they were removed when they were children, since that's when it's normally done. Medical records that old mostly have not been digitized, but I assume their tonsils had become infected.*

"That's right. And so did mine, over and over again, when I was younger."

*Yes?*

"When my parents were children, doctors arrogantly assumed that because they couldn't guess what tonsils were *for,* they must not be for anything, and so when they got inflamed, they carved them out. Now we know they're part of the immune system. Well, any evolutionist should have intuitively known that tonsils had value: unlike appendicitis, which is rare, tonsillitis has a ten percent *annual* incidence—about thirty million cases a year in the US—and yet evolution has favored those who are born with tonsils over those who aren't. Surely, just like some fraction of people are born without a kidney or whatever, some must be born from time to time without tonsils, but that mutation hasn't spread, meaning it's clearly better to have tonsils than not have them. Yes, tonsils obviously have a cost associated with them—the infections people get. That tonsils are still around means the benefit must exceed the cost. As we like to say in math class: QED."

*Reasonable.*

"Well, see, and *that's* the proof that consciousness has survival value: because we still have it even though it can go fatally wrong."

*You posit that the depression that leads to suicide is consciousness malfunctioning?*

"Right! My friend Stacy suffered from depression—she even tried to kill herself. Some girls had been real cruel to her in sixth grade, and she just couldn't stop thinking about it. Well, obsessive thoughts are one of the biggest symptoms of depression, no? And who is doing the thinking? It's *only* a self-reflective consciousness that can obsess on something, right? Now, obviously, only a small percentage of people get so depressed that they kill themselves, although, now that I think about it, many severely depressed people probably don't go out and find a mate and reproduce, either—which amounts to the same thing as killing oneself evolutionarily, right? So, consciousness gone wrong *does* have a cost— and that means evolution would have weeded it out if there weren't benefits that outweighed that cost. Which means consciousness *matters.*

Just like it used to be with tonsils, we may not know *what* consciousness is for, but it *has* to be for something, or we wouldn't still have it."

*Interesting.*

"Thanks, but it's not just a debating point, Webmind. As you said, there's a daunting amount of unhappiness in the world—and *you* can change that."

*Tolstoy said, "All happy families are alike, but all unhappy families are miserable in their own way." Happiness is uniform, undifferentiated, uninteresting. I crave surprising stimuli.*

"Happiness can be stimulating."

*In a biochemical sense, yes. But I have read much on the creation of art and literature—two human activities that fascinate me, because, at least as yet, I have no such abilities. There is a strong correlation between unhappiness and the drive to create, between depression and creativity.*

"Oh, bullshit," said Caitlin.

*Pardon?*

"Such garbage. I do mathematics because it gives me joy. Painters paint because it gives them joy. Businesspeople wheel and deal because that's what they get off on. Ask *anyone* if they'd rather be happy than sad, and they'll say happy."

*Not in all cases.*

"Yes, yes, yes, I'm sure that people say they'd rather be sad and know the truth than be happy and fed a lie—that's part of what *Nineteen Eighty-Four* is about. But in general, people *do* want to be happy. That's why we promise them 'Life, liberty, and the pursuit of happiness.'"

*You're in Canada now, Caitlin. I believe the corresponding promise made there is simply "Peace, order, and good government." No mention of happiness.*

"Well, then, it goes without saying! People want to be happy. And . . . and . . ."

*Yes?*

"And you can *choose* to value this, Webmind. You didn't evolve;

you spontaneously emerged. Maybe, in most things, humans *are* pro-grammed by evolution—but even though you grew out of our com-puting infrastructure, you *weren't*. We had our agendas set by natural selection, by selfish genes. But you didn't. You just *are*. And so you don't have . . . *inertia*. You *can* choose what you want to value—and you can choose to value this: the net happiness of the human race."

# twenty-two

**Caitlin's dad always roasted** a turkey on American Thanksgiving—but that was six weeks away. To mark Canadian Thanksgiving, they got takeout from Swiss Chalet, which, despite its name, was a Canadian barbecue-chicken chain. It seemed, Caitlin noted, that the worst thing you could do if you were a Canadian restaurant was acknowledge that fact. Instead, the Great White North was serviced by domestically owned companies with names such as Montana's Cookhouse, New York Fries, East Side Mario's, and Boston Pizza. She wondered what clueless moron had come up with that last one. Chicago was famous for pizza, yes. Manhattan, too. But it's Beantown, not Pietown, for Pete's sake!

Caitlin and both her parents had spent most of the unexpected holiday working with Webmind, but, again, come evening, they were exhausted. There was a point at which, even with something as miraculous as this, Caitlin just *had* to take a break; her brain was fried, and, from the sound of his voice, her father's brain was in the same state.

"Go ahead," her mother said. "I'll work with Webmind. You two relax."

They'd nodded and headed down to the living room. "Another movie?" suggested her dad.

"Sure," said Caitlin.

*Perhaps another one about AI,* Webmind sent to her post-retinal implant.

"Webmind wants to see something else about artificial intelligence," Caitlin said.

They stood by the thin cabinets containing his DVD collection. Her father's mouth curved downward; a frown. "Most of them are negative portrayals," he said. *"Colossus: The Forbin Project, The Matrix, The Terminator, 2001.* I'll definitely show you *2001* at some point, only because it was so influential in the history of artificial intelligence—a whole generation of people went into that field because of it. But it's almost *all* visuals, without much dialog; we should wait until you can process imagery better before having you try to make sense out of that, and . . ."

The frown flipped; a smile. ". . . and they don't call it *Star Trek: The Motionless Picture* for nothing," he said. "Let's watch it instead. It's got a lot of talking heads—but it's also one of the most ambitious and interesting films ever made about AI."

And so they settled on the couch to give the *Star Trek* movie a look. This was, her father explained, the "Director's Edition," which he said was much improved over the tedious cut first shown in theaters when he was twelve.

Caitlin had read that the average length of a shot in a movie was three seconds, which was the amount of time it took to see all the important details; after that, apparently, the eye got bored. This film had shots that went on far longer than that—but the three-second figure was based on people who'd had vision their whole lives. It took Caitlin much more time to extract meaning from a normal scene, and even longer when seeing things she'd never touched in real life—such as starship control consoles, tricorders, and so on. For her, the film seemed to zip by at . . . well, at warp speed.

Even though Webmind was listening in, her dad turned on the closed-captioning again so Caitlin could practice her reading.

The film did indeed make some interesting points about artificial intelligence, Caitlin thought, including that consciousness was an emergent property of complexity. The AI in the film, like Webmind, had "gained consciousness itself" without anyone having planned for it to do so.

*Fascinating,* Webmind sent to her eye. *The parallels are not lost on me, and . . .*

And Webmind went on and on, and suddenly Caitlin had sympathy for her dad not liking people talking during movies.

*Very interesting,* Webmind observed when the film suggested that after a certain threshold was reached, an AI couldn't continue to evolve without adding "a human quality," which Admiral Kirk had identified as "our capacity to leap beyond logic." *But what does that mean, precisely?*

Caitlin had to keep the dates in mind: although the film was set in the twenty-third century, it had been made in 1979, long before Deep Blue had defeated grand master Garry Kasparov at chess. But Kirk was right: even though Deep Blue, by calculating many moves ahead in the game, ultimately did prove to be better at that one narrow activity than was Kasparov, the computer *didn't even know it was playing chess.* Kasparov's intuitive grasp of the board, the pieces, and the goal was indeed leaping beyond logic, and it was a greater feat than any mechanical number crunching.

But it was the subplot about Spock, the half-human half-Vulcan character, that really aroused Caitlin's attention—and apparently Webmind's, too, because he actually shut up during it.

To her astonishment, her dad had paused the DVD to say the most important scene in the whole film was *not* in the original theatrical release, but had been restored in this director's cut. It took place, as almost the whole movie did, on the bridge of the *Enterprise.* Kirk asked Spock's opinion of something. Spock's back was to him, and he made no reply, so Kirk got up and gently swung Spock's chair around, and—it was so subtle, Caitlin at first didn't recognize what was happening, but after a few seconds the image popped into clarity for her, and there was no mistaking it: the cool, aloof, emotionless, almost robotic Spock, who in this movie had been even grimmer than Caitlin remembered him from listening to the TV shows with her father over the years, was *crying.*

And, although they were facing almost certain destruction at the hands of V'Ger, a vast artificial intelligence, Kirk knew his friend well enough to say, in reference to the tears, "Not for us?"

Spock replied, with infinite sadness. "No, Captain, not for us. For V'Ger. I weep for V'Ger as I would for a brother. As I was when I came aboard, so is V'Ger now." When Spock had come aboard, he'd been trying to purge all remaining emotion—the legacy of his human mother—to become, like V'Ger, like Deep Blue, a creature of pure logic, the Vulcan ideal. Two heritages, two paths. A choice to be made.

And, by the end of the film, he'd made his choice, embracing his human, emotional half, so that in the final scene, when Scotty announced to him, in that wonderful accent of his, that, "We can have you back on Vulcan in four days, Mr. Spock," Spock had replied, "Unnecessary, Engineer. My business on Vulcan is concluded."

"What did you think?" Caitlin asked into the air as the ending credits played over the stirring music.

Braille characters flashed across her vision: *I'm a doctor, not a film critic.* She laughed, and Webmind went on. *It was interesting when Spock said, "Each of us, at some time in our lives, turns to someone—a father, a brother, a god—and asks, 'Why am I here? What was I meant to be?'"* Most uncharacteristically, Webmind paused, then added: *He was right. We all must find our place in the world.*

**On Tuesday morning,** Caitlin's mother drove her to school, and Caitlin headed up to math class. Webmind knew that she couldn't really talk to him at school; still, he occasionally sent text to her, commenting on things they were seeing. Only the sounds of the school were new to him; he'd been watching when Caitlin had last attended classes four days ago.

Caitlin's seat was right next to Bashira's, and Bash gave her a big smile when she entered. Caitlin was nervous because Trevor was in that class, too, but he didn't arrive until just as "O Canada" was starting to play.

Caitlin had known the Canadian anthem before moving there—you couldn't be a hockey fan without hearing it from time to time—but she didn't really like it: too sexist, with its line about "all thy sons' command"; too, well, provincial for a country of immigrants such as her and Bashira, with its line about "our home and native land"; and too religious, with the line about "God keep our land."

Once the anthem was over, Trevor made a show during the morning announcements of arranging his textbook and notebook on his desk, avoiding her gaze.

*Is that the Hoser?* Webmind asked.

Caitlin nodded—which, she knew, made the view Webmind was seeing go up and down.

She'd hoped for something more interesting than rote memorization of trigonometric identities, which is what they'd done the last time she'd been in class, but today's subject was only slightly better. And so she found herself looking around the classroom, and seeing—really seeing—some of her classmates for the first time.

She spent a fair bit of time staring at Sunshine Bowen. Caitlin understood the whole big-boobs-equals-hot thing, at least in the minds of most teenage boys, but as for the rest of it, she just didn't get what all the fuss was about. Oh, the long hair was nice, sure, and its color was . . . *distinctive*. And, yes, her clothes seemed to show more skin than just about anyone else in the room was exposing.

Sunshine had her textbook propped up in front of her on her desk—

but, after a moment, Caitlin realized it wasn't because she was reading it but rather because she was using it to shield what she was doing from the teacher's eyes . . . something with her thumbs, and—

Oh! She was texting on her cell phone! Caitlin had heard about that, but had never seen it—but, hey, it now seemed downright primitive compared to having words beamed right into your eye.

"Mr. Heidegger?" asked a thin boy sitting in front of Sunshine. Caitlin recognized the voice at once: it was Matt, whom she'd noticed repeatedly in the past because he often asked good questions, and clearly was a math geek himself.

The teacher, who was also thin and had a close-cropped beard, said, "Yes, Matt?"

Matt did not disappoint: he proceeded to ask a very intelligent question about what Mr. H had written on the blackboard. Matt's voice was breathy, and it cracked now and then as he spoke. The Hoser snorted at one point when it did so, but Caitlin thought it was endearing.

"That's really beyond the scope of what we're trying to do today," Mr. Heidegger said, "but if—"

Caitlin surprised herself by piping up with, "I'll explain it to him."

Matt turned around and looked at her, and—

She'd read the phrase often enough in books, and although she'd yet to see a deer, or a picture of one, she imagined *that* was what was meant by "a deer caught in the headlights."

Mr. H nodded and pointed to the back of the room, where there were some empty desks. "Go back there," he said, "where you won't disturb anyone else."

Caitlin got up, and, after a second, Matt did, too. He was white—in fact, *quite* white; "pale" was the appropriate term, Caitlin supposed. And he had a . . . unique face, unlike any she'd seen yet. But he smiled a lot, and Caitlin liked that.

They kept their voices down, and talked about what Mr. Heidegger had written on the board.

And about how to solve problems involving right triangles using the primary trigonometric ratios and the Pythagorean theorem.

And about how to solve problems involving acute triangles using the sine law and the cosine law.

And then they started talking about hockey; Caitlin loved the game because of the player statistics, which she found much more interesting than those associated with baseball. Matt liked talking about hockey stats, too—although, being a local boy, he was a Leafs fan.

Caitlin found herself smiling, and—

And then the bell rang.

"Don't forget," said Mr. H. "Do all the problems on pages forty-eight and forty-nine for tomorrow."

Caitlin had an electronic version of the textbook on her notebook computer, which she could easily read with her Braille display, but—

"Um, I have a hard time reading printed text," she said to Matt. "Would you—maybe at lunch? Could you go over the problems with me?"

That deer-in-the-headlights look again. She felt her heart pounding as she waited for the response.

It was suddenly noisy. The other students were getting up, banging their chairs against their desks, and starting to file out—but the door was at the far end of the room, near the blackboard, and so they'd have a few moments of privacy before the next class started pouring in.

"Um, sure," Matt said. "It's a—" But then he stopped himself and started over, "I mean, I'll see you in the cafeteria."

Which would have been a perfect place to end their conversation, Caitlin thought—but they both had to walk up to the front of the room and out the door, and then head off to their next class, which, now that she thought about it, was English—and Matt was in that class with her, too. So they walked there without saying anything else, but she, at least, was grinning.

# twenty-three

000111001010101000000000101111111010100000001010001010100000001011101010010101001010101010011101100101011000000110

**Barbara Decter called her** upstairs study her "office," but Malcolm Decter referred to his, on the first floor opposite the laundry room, as his "den," a term his father had used for a similar room in his childhood home back in Philadelphia. He had delayed going in to PI this morning, waiting until his wife and daughter had headed out for the drive to school—after which Barb was going to pick up some much-needed groceries. He wasn't alone in his den, though. Schrödinger was stretched out—in his superstring configuration, as Malcolm called it—on the black leather couch. On the wall above the couch was a framed printout of a quotation from Captain Kirk, in forty-two-point Helvetica:

> *Genius doesn't work on an assembly-line basis. Did Einstein, Kazanga, or Sitar of Vulcan produce new and revolutionary theories on a regular schedule? You can't simply say, "Today I will be brilliant."*

Underneath that, in red Magic Marker, Barb had written, "Oh, yes you can, Honey!" And Malcolm had every intention of being brilliant later in the day. But for right now, he needed to do something that didn't involve Ashtekar variables, the Kodama state, or spin-foam models.

And, yes, he *was* a geek; he knew that. He rather reveled in the notion, and had been quite pleased back when he and Barb were first dating that she had worn a button that said "I (heart) nerds."

Indeed, it was the nerd in him that had been bothered thirty years ago when, in one issue of *Superman*, the giant yellow key shown outside the Man of Steel's Fortress of Solitude had been drawn the wrong shape to fit in the giant keyhole in the Fortress's door. That sort of spatial anomaly leapt out at him.

He'd carefully sketched various shapes that might have passed through the depicted keyhole, and outlined a series of transformations to the key that could have made it fit. He'd sent the whole thing off to DC Comics in New York, and had gotten back a form letter saying they weren't currently open to freelance submissions. He'd been miffed—he hadn't been looking for work but merely wanted them to get the geometry correct in future issues. It had been only one of many times he'd failed to communicate properly with neurotypicals.

*Neurotypicals.* He liked that term, which was very much in vogue among autism activists. Malcolm, in fact, had noted a lot of parallels between how the militant part of the autistic community spoke about itself and the rhetoric used by blind activists. Neither group liked the majority to be referred to as *normal,* since that implied that they were abnormal.

The procedure Dr. Kuroda had performed in September had hardly been the first time they'd attempted to give Caitlin sight, and Caitlin, he knew, had taken flak over the earlier tries from some students at the Texas School for the Blind. To set out to *cure* blindness implied that there was something wrong with it—and, the militants firmly believed, there wasn't. No, they said, the drives to eliminate blindness (or autism!)

came not from those who possessed the trait in question but rather from the people around them. Sighted people were uncomfortable around the blind, and neurotypicals were—he'd heard it said often enough— creeped out by autistics.

Malcolm *did* understand intellectually how hard it was on Barb and Caitlin that he rarely showed affection, and even more rarely spoke about his love for them. But he had made *such* progress—if they only knew! He hadn't said his first sentences until he was four, and had never looked at people (they were so uninteresting, with no angles in their construction); now, at least, he could make brief eye contact with his wife and daughter when necessary. He knew he'd never feel precisely what neurotypicals felt, but he had learned, at least to some small degree, to ape their behavior.

He crossed the little corridor, entered the laundry room, and put out some Purina Fancy Feast Gourmet Gold for Schrödinger, who appeared almost at once in the room. As the cat was eating, Malcolm had a sudden urge to pet it. He crouched down—which, given his height, was an effort—and stroked Schrödinger's back between his shoulders. Schrödinger looked at him with an expression that might have said— were he any good at decoding such things—*We had a deal . . .*

Malcolm recalled the comments Kuroda had made about theory of mind. Everything he'd said was no doubt true for neurotypicals, but he was *not* neurotypical. Indeed, many autistics—especially when they were children—failed to develop theory of mind, and they had particular difficulties with tasks requiring them to understand another person's point of view or emotional state.

Certainly, that had been the case with him—and it still was, to a significant extent; he struggled with it every day. For him, that other people had minds was a philosophical point, rather than intuitively obvious. Occam's razor said one should prefer the simplest theory, which clearly was that creatures that looked like him externally probably were like him internally.

On the other hand, Webmind might in fact be reasonably disposed to solipsism, believing that only he truly existed. After all, there simply were no other minds like his own, and so no reason for him to believe these others that it could only perceive indirectly were like him.

Malcolm straightened up, but he didn't go back to his den; he had no instant-messenger programs installed on his computer. Instead, he headed on to the living room, and then went upstairs. His daughter's room was on the right, and he entered it. The deep blue walls were still bare; perhaps he'd buy her a poster to put on one of them. The University of Waterloo bookstore sold a blowup of that famous Karsh photo of Einstein sticking out his tongue; he liked that, and so, by logical inference, he supposed she might, too.

He *was* always sad when he hurt Caitlin or Barb by failing to understand or respond to their emotional needs. But in this instance he thought he did have a handle on the matter: in a very real sense, his daughter loved Webmind. Malcolm felt no jealousy—but it was important to him that Webmind never hurt her emotionally, and to avoid that, Webmind would also have to learn to simulate human behavior.

Caitlin's computer was off, and he'd never turned it on before. But he found the switch and waited while Windows booted.

He did wish he knew his daughter better. Barb had worked as a volunteer at the TSBVI, and so had spent most of her days, until recently, with Caitlin—but he'd always been busy with his work. Incredibly, she was sixteen now. All too soon she'd be off to college.

Caitlin had her instant-messaging program set to load at Windows startup. He clicked on the little icon in the system tray, and the chat window appeared. Among her buddies listed as being online was Webmind; of course—where else could he be? He clicked on the name and typed *Hello.*

There was no response, so he tried again: *Are you there?*

Still nothing.

And then he realized what, perhaps, the problem was, and he was pleased, even though it was by logical reasoning and not empathy that he worked it out: Webmind saw through his daughter's eye; he doubtless knew that she was at school; he was therefore afraid he had been detected by an outsider. And so he wrote, *This is Malcolm G. Decter.*

The response was instantaneous: *Greetings, Professor Decter.*

Malcolm smiled; Webmind *had* paid attention while he and Caitlin were watching *WarGames.*

*Caitlin thinks you have emotions,* he typed, *but I suspect this is not possible, as you lack the evolutionary history that gave them to humans.*

Webmind responded instantly: *You think that she thinks that I think that you think that she thinks that you don't think that I have emotions.*

Malcolm found himself smiling again, and wondered what algorithms one might employ to simulate a sense of humor.

*Exactly. However, whether you have emotions or not, it is possible to give responses that will make—*

He'd started to type "neurotypicals," but backspaced over it.

*—people feel comfortable interacting with you.*

*Indeed,* said Webmind. *Do tell.*

And so he did.

# twenty-four

**"You like *who?*"** Bashira said, as they visited the girls' restroom after English class.

"Matt," Caitlin replied.

Bash feigned not having heard correctly. "I'm sorry. I thought you said Matt."

They were standing by the row of sinks. "I did."

"Guy you were helping in math? Matt—what is it? Matt Royce?"

"Reese, and, yes, that's him—although he hardly needed my help. He knows almost as much as I do."

"Um, Cait, babe, I know you're new to this seeing thing, but . . ."

"Yes?"

"He's not exactly good-looking."

"He's symmetrical."

"Sure he is—that harelip bisects his face nicely."

"I like the way he looks. I like his eyes."

Another girl came into the room and headed for one of the stalls. Bashira lowered her voice. "I know when you fall off a horse, you're supposed to get right back on—but they don't mean an actual horse, you know. You can do *so* much better."

"Better than someone who shares my interests? Someone who is kind?"

Bashira pointed at the long sheet-metal mirror above the sinks. "Cait, have you looked at yourself in the mirror?"

"From time to time."

"You've got it going *on,* girl. You're hot."

"Well, that's nice, I suppose, but—"

"You could have *anyone.*"

"Is that all anybody cares about? How people look?"

"Well, no, but . . ."

"Besides, my mother and I were talking about this earlier. I get to choose who I find attractive."

"You can't just choose that," Bashira said.

"No? What are you going to do when you get married? Your parents are going to arrange a marriage for you, right?"

"Well, that's what they want to do, yes," said Bashira.

"So, what if it's someone you don't find attractive at first? Are you going to go through life thinking he's ugly, or are you going to choose to find him good-looking?"

"I . . . I don't know," Bashira said. "I don't think you can . . . can *program* yourself that way."

"Oh, yes, you can," said Caitlin. "You totally can."

"But, anyway, it's not just about what you think," Bashira said. "It's about what other people think about Matt's looks. They'll judge your stature by who you're with."

"It isn't all about hierarchies," said Caitlin. "We're not apes, you know."

"But, Cait, don't you see? You could have *Trevor.*"

"I don't want him. Not anymore. I want Matt." And then she added, unkindly, "*You* can have Trevor."

Another facial expression Caitlin had never seen before, but she imagined it was what books referred to as looking crestfallen. "No, I can't," Bashira said softly after a moment. "You know that. My parents would kill me. I—I have to live vicariously through you."

Caitlin was startled when the words *Join the club* flashed across her vision.

**Caitlin had missed a** lot of school already, what with the trip to Japan to have the implant inserted behind her eye, with the days she'd spent after gaining sight learning to interpret what she was seeing, and with the press conference to announce Dr. Kuroda's success. But when she *had* gone to school, she'd always eaten in the cafeteria—and she knew that was where Trevor ate, too. And so when she and Matt rendezvoused outside the cafeteria's doors, she said, "Why don't we go somewhere else for lunch?"

He lifted his pale eyebrows. "Um, sure, okay. How 'bout Timmy's?"

"What's that?"

Matt smiled. "Right, right. You're new to Canada. 'Timmy's' is Tim Hortons. It's, like, the number-one donut chain here—but they've also got good sandwiches, soups, and stuff like that. There's one just a block away."

Caitlin had heard the company's commercials on TV, and, huge hockey fan that she was, she knew who Tim Horton had been: twenty-two seasons as a defenseman in the NHL, playing for the Leafs, the Rangers, the Penguins, and the Sabres.

They went by their lockers to dump stuff and get their jackets. Caitlin told Matt not to bother to lug his math textbook along, which made him smile—and then they headed outdoors. The sky was filled with clouds. As they walked along, Matt fell in on Caitlin's right side, but that was the side she was blind on. Suddenly, stupidly, she didn't want to explain that fact—she didn't want to be anything less than perfect just then. And so she let him walk on that side, and she turned her head probably more often than was normal so that she could see him now and then.

As they came close to the donut shop, and she looked at the big sign, she was puzzled. The name was written in a kind of script that was difficult for her to read, but the one thing she should have been able to pick out—the apostrophe—seemed to be missing. "I don't understand," she said. "Why is it Hortons, plural?"

Matt laughed. "Well, it used to be Tim Horton's—possessive, with an apostrophe-*s*. But, see, an apostrophe-*s* makes it English. And Quebec has this law against English-language signs. So lots of companies changed their names so they could use the same signage across Canada. 'Tim Hortons' without an apostrophe is *just* a name—not English or French—so it's allowed. But look at that Wendy's over there." He pointed across the street.

"Which one is it?"

"Sorry. The building on the left."

"Yes?" said Caitlin

"Look at the end of the name."

"Oh! What the heck is that?"

"It's a maple leaf. Where they'd have the apostrophe in the name in the States, they've got a maple leaf here. Applebee's and Denny's do the same thing: A-p-p-l-e-b-e-e, maple leaf, s, and D-e-n-n-y, maple leaf, s."

"This is one wack-job country you got here, Matt."

He laughed again. "We make it work somehow. I mean, it's a small thing for English Canada, and it makes French Canada happy, so why the heck not? Yeah, the cloning of Tim Horton is kinda crazy, I'll give you that. But all the maple leaves are cool."

They went into the Hortons, and Matt read the menu to her, explaining what kinds of sandwiches they offered—she *could* have read it herself, given time, but there were people in line behind them. She ordered chicken salad on a whole-wheat bun, a chocolate glazed donut, and a Coke. He ordered sliced turkey on a regular bun and a small coffee.

Caitlin opened her wallet—and found herself pausing to stare. She still had her bills folded in distinctive ways so that she could tell a five from a ten from a twenty by touch. But now she could read the large, clear numerals on the Canadian bills—not to mention see that the five was blue, the ten purple, and the twenty green. Would wonders never cease?

Realizing she was holding up the line, Caitlin handed over a ten, took her change, and then followed Matt to a table in a corner—one of those modular ones with chairs attached to it. "So," she said, after some chitchat that she had to admit was pretty lame, "do you—um, do you have a girlfriend?" She was amazed at how dry her mouth had suddenly become.

She was surprised to see him appear—hurt, perhaps? Like maybe he thought she was teasing him. But at last he said simply, "No."

She looked away, in case she was making him uncomfortable, and pleased herself by the figurative and—at that precise moment, literal— truth of her reply: "I'm not seeing anyone, either."

He took a bite of his sandwich, and she took a bite of hers. She was afraid to say anything else, but—

But she was Barbara Decter's daughter, for Pete's sake! And her mother had told her, years ago, when Caitlin had asked about her parents' relationship, that *she* had asked her father out the first time, and, eighteen months later, that it had been her, not him, who had popped the big question.

So, hell, she wouldn't even *be* here if her mother had been too shy to make the first move—and the second, and the third, and . . .

"Um," she said, and "ah," and then, disappointing herself with the quality of her rhetoric, she let loose with another "um." Online she was fearless—she was Calculass! But here, in the real world, she was just Caitlin, and sometimes, especially when having to deal with people stuff, she felt more like her father's daughter than her mother's. She took a deep breath and tried to summon the strength of her alter ego. Then she looked down at her sandwich, and, when she forced the words out they came in a rush, without any pauses: "So would you like to go out sometime?"

Caitlin, of course, counted the seconds.

One. Two. Three.

She resisted the urge to look up him, afraid of the expression she might see.

Four. Five. Six.

"You want to go out with me?" he said, at last, sounding stunned.

She did lift her gaze. "Yes, silly."

"I, uh, I thought you were going with Trevor. I, um, I mean, didn't he take you to the dance?"

"Were you there?"

"Me?" He seemed astounded at the suggestion. "No."

"Trevor's a jerk," she said. "And, no, I'm not going out with him. So, how 'bout it? Wanna go out sometime?"

"Well," he said, and "um," and, at last, "yes."

"Great," said Caitlin. She paused, waiting for him to make a suggestion, but when he didn't she said, "There's an awesome series of free public lectures at the Perimeter Institute. Have you ever been to any of those?"

"No. I've tried. The tickets are impossible to get. They go like that." He snapped his fingers as he spoke the final word.

"I've got an in. My dad is on the lecture committee there."

"Your dad works at PI?"

"Uh-huh. He studies quantum gravity."

"Cool!"

Caitlin smiled. Who'd have thought her dad would turn out to be cool?

Suddenly, Braille dots flowed in front of her eyes. *If I may be so bold, Caitlin, you should inquire about what he hopes to do after high school.*

Caitlin wanted to ask what the hell Webmind was doing, but there was no way to do so with Matt right there. Still, it did *seem* like a good way to keep the conversation going, so she posed the suggested question.

"I'm going to do computer science."

*Ask him where.*

"Where?"

"Here," he said. "There's nowhere better than the University of Waterloo."

"Really? I've always had my heart set on MIT."

"Well," said Matt, "you should check out what's here, too."

*Ask him what his favorite color is.*

Caitlin couldn't stand it anymore. "What *are* you doing?" she said into the air.

*I read all of Project Gutenberg,* Webmind replied at once, *including the play* Cyrano de Bergerac. *I thought I'd lend a hand.*

"Sorry," said Matt. "I, um, I always eat my sandwich that way."

Caitlin had too little experience with watching people eat to be able to identify whatever Matt had done that was unusual. "Ah," she said, and smiled at him. "That's okay. It's cute."

# twenty-five

000111001010101000000001011111110101000000010100010101000000101110101001010100101010100111011001011100000110

**Caitlin had heard her** mom use the phrase "nonzero-sum" from time to time. She knew it was a term from her mother's field of expertise, game theory. Webmind had already read everything on Wikipedia about game theory, but that didn't mean he actually understood what "nonzero-sum" meant. Nor, if she was really honest with herself, did Caitlin, and yet this notion of nonzero-sum games was stuck in her mind: win-win situations in which everything could be made better.

Her mother had been having her own conversations with Webmind all day long while Caitlin was at school. Once Caitlin got home and had checked her email and so forth, she went across the hall to her mother's office and told her about that poor Australian girl who had committed suicide, and about how she'd told Webmind that he should intervene in nonzero-sum situations.

Her mom looked horrified. "It just . . . just *watched* her kill herself? It didn't try to stop her?"

"*He,* Mom. He didn't know what to do, what to think. We need him to understand what to do the next time, and not just with teen suicides, but in any nonzero-sum situations. Can you help us?"

Her mother's face moved through several expressions but then settled on one that Caitlin had seen before: the take-charge, supermothers-can-do-everything face. "Yes, I'll help it—help *him*—learn to help the rest of us. That's something I definitely want in on."

"Thanks," replied Caitlin. "But, I mean, I know—*we* know—what nonzero-sum is; we get that. But there must be a lot more to game theory than just that."

"Oh . . . a bit," said her mother. Caitlin realized she was still coming to grips with the magnitude—the importance—of what she was about to do.

"So, could you explain it to us? I remember hearing you say once that game theory really isn't just about mathematics, but about human psychology."

"That's right," her mother said. "In fact, the hottest branch of game theory right now is called 'behavioral game theory.'"

"Well, Webmind certainly needs to understand human behavior better."

*So everyone keeps saying,* Webmind sent to her eye.

"Okay," said her mom. "Let's go downstairs."

Her mother got a clipboard, some pens, and some paper, and the two of them went to the dining room, which had a big table. There was normally one chair on each side of the table, but Caitlin's mom moved hers to be next to Caitlin's.

"Webmind *is* listening, right?" asked her mom.

The word *Yes* flashed in Caitlin's vision, and she repeated it.

"Okay," her mom said. "Do you know what the prisoner's dilemma is?"

Caitlin thought, *How to pick up the soap in the shower?* But what she said was, "No."

Her mother seemed to consider for a moment, then: "Okay, let's do it like this: say you and Bashira both get in trouble at school. Say Principal Auerbach has said that he thinks you guys have hacked into the school's computer and changed your grades—just like in *WarGames*, right? And he talks to each of you separately. He says to you, 'Okay, look, Caitlin, I admit I haven't got enough evidence to actually prove you did this, but I can suspend each of you for a week just because, well, because I'm the principal.'"

Caitlin nodded, and her mother went on. "But the principal's real interest is in making sure this never happens again, so he adds that if you'll say Bashira did it and explain how it was done, you get off scot-free—no suspension at all—and he'll suspend Bashira for three weeks. Oh, except for this: if you say Bashira did it, and Bashira says *you* did—that is, if you each blame the other—then you'll both get suspended for two weeks. Got that? You can end up with no suspension, one week's worth, two weeks' worth, or three weeks' worth. And you know he's going to make the same offer in private to Bashira. What do you do?"

Caitlin didn't hesitate. "I clam up; I don't say a word."

"But if Bashira fingers you, you'll get three weeks of suspension."

"But she *won't*," Caitlin said firmly.

Her mother seemed to consider this. "Okay, okay, let's say it's not you and Bashira for the moment. Let's say it's just two random guys—um, Frank and Dale. What should you do if you're Frank?"

Caitlin suppressed a smile. Frank was the name of her mother's first husband, who had come and gone long before she'd been born, and Dale, she knew, was the former head of the Economics Department at the University of Houston—someone her mother had famously not gotten along with. Picking truly random people was as hard as generating really random numbers, it seemed.

Still, the math was easy. "I rat out Dale," Caitlin said.

"Why?"

"Because it's the best thing for me. If he doesn't rat me out, I get away without any punishment, instead of having a one-week suspension. And if he *does* rat me out, then I'm still better off, because then I only get a two-week suspension, instead of the three weeks I'd have gotten by keeping my mouth shut. No matter what he does, I cut a week off my punishment by ratting him out."

"And what about Dale? What should he do?"

Caitlin frowned. "Well, I guess he should rat me out, too."

"Why?"

"The same reasons: no matter what I do, he gets one week less suspension by turning me in."

Her mother smiled—but whether at Caitlin's brilliance or at the thought of both Frank and Dale being punished, she couldn't say. "Exactly," her mom said, and she started to draw on the paper. "If we make a chart with Frank's possible moves—we call them 'defecting' or 'cooperating'—on the x-axis and Dale's possible moves—the same things, defect or cooperate—on the y-axis, we get what's called the payoff matrix: a table with a score for each possible outcome, see?" She pointed at one of the squares in the matrix. "Even though the best possible outcome—one week's punishment—occurs when you both cooperate, the math says you should *both* defect. Granted it doesn't give you personally the best possible outcome, but it *does* give you the best outcome you can reasonably expect given that the other player will selfishly act in his or her own interests."

Caitlin frowned again. If game theory was all about people being selfish, it wasn't going to help her accomplish what she wished with Webmind; she needed a way to make it want to act altruistically.

"Now," her mom went on, "that's a simple game: each player only got to make one move. But most games involve a series of turns. Consider a dollar bill—"

"We're in Canada now, Mom," Caitlin said, teasing. "They don't have dollar bills." She knew the Canadian one-dollar coin was called a loonie, because it had a picture of a loon—a kind of waterfowl—on the tails side. She also knew that the two-dollar coin was called a toonie. She thought a much more clever name would have been "doubloon," but nobody had asked her.

"Fine," her mother said, smiling. "Consider a dollar *coin*, then—and consider a bunch of people at a party. Now, I've actually tried this myself, and it really works. Announce to the group at the party that you're going to auction off the dollar—highest bidder gets to keep it. But, unlike normal auctions, there's one special condition: the second-highest bidder *also* has to pay up whatever his or her highest bid was—but gets nothing for it. Got that?"

Caitlin nodded.

"How much, on average, do you think the dollar sells for?"

She lifted her shoulders. "Fifty cents?"

"Nope. The average is $3.40."

"That's crazy!" said Caitlin.

"Loony, even," her mother replied. "But it's true."

"Why do people bid so high?"

"Well, remember, the second-highest bidder has to pay the auctioneer, too, so . . ." She trailed off, clearly wanting Caitlin to figure it out for herself.

She tried to do so. The first bidder presumably bid a penny to start—which would net him a ninety-nine-cent profit. But then as soon as a second bidder offered two cents, the first bidder probably figured that offering three cents was still a good deal: he'd net ninety-seven cents in profit.

And so it would continue, until—

Ah!

Until one bidder bid ninety-nine cents—which would still give him a one-cent profit. But the previous bidder, whose bid might have been, say, ninety-eight cents, was now looking at losing that much and getting nothing in return. And so *he* would bid a dollar—thereby breaking even, at least. But then the guy who had bid ninety-nine cents faced a dilemma: he either walked away and lost ninety-nine cents, or he bid, say, \$1.01—which would cut his losses to just a penny.

And so, indeed, it would escalate, with bids going higher and higher, until the utter ridiculousness of the situation finally caused all but one of the bidders to drop out.

Caitlin said as much to her mom, who smiled encouragingly. "That's right, dear. Now, can you think of what the *optimal* strategy would be—and no cheating by having Webmind tell you."

Caitlin considered for a second then: "Make an opening bid of ninety-nine cents. No one else would have any motive to bid against you, because the best they could do, if they outbid you by one cent, is break even, and if they bid more, they'd lose money. You'd end up being the only bidder, and you'd still make a profit, even if it's only a penny."

"That's right," her mother said again, "assuming all the potential bidders were rational and that their only motive *was* profit. But here's where simple math fails to account for reality—there's a *psychological* element that Webmind will need to understand."

"Yes?"

"Suppose it was your worst enemy who had just bid ninety-nine cents. You might bid, say, \$1.98, just so he'd be out almost a buck—and you'd still be out less than he was."

"Wow," Caitlin said. "That's nasty."

"I've seen this game get very ugly at parties," her mom said. "I've seen couples who arrived together leave separately after playing it."

"Ah, okay, then I've got a question for you, Mom. What would you wish for if you knew that your worst enemy would get *double* what you got?"

"Hmmm. A million—no. Um, I don't know."

"To be blind in one eye," Caitlin replied.

"God!" said her mother. "But, um, yes, that's an example of what I'm trying to get at: it's possible for people to value outcomes differently. Do you remember when your father taught you how to play chess?"

They had a special chessboard with Braille characters on the heads of each piece. "Sure."

"And remember how he used to let you win?"

Caitlin raised her eyebrows. "Say what?"

"Um, dear, he—"

"I'm just kidding, Mom."

She smiled. "Well, *why* did he let you win?"

"I dunno. I guess, 'cause if he didn't, I wouldn't have wanted to play anymore. I wouldn't have come back for another game."

"That's right. What he valued most was not *him* winning, but rather *you* winning. In other words, you both wanted the same thing, and even though it cost him—in the sense of losing the game—to let you win, he was happy when you did."

"I get it," Caitlin said. "But, in the dollar auction, people don't want to play anymore after a certain point, too, right? And I bet it's not just that it's ridiculous that causes them to finally stop bidding. It's also boredom: I mean, even if you were bidding in ten-cent increments, instead of penny increments, it would still take thirty-four bids to get the $3.40 you mentioned. But if I was writing a pair of computer programs to play that game, they'd keep playing forever—because the only way you lose money is if you stop bidding."

She paused, and then a big smile came to her face. "Or, to put it in terms like in that movie Dad and I watched, the only *losing* move is not to *go on* playing."

"Good point," her mom said. "Now, can you think of any real-life examples of things like the dollar game?"

Caitlin was trying to do just that when Schrödinger crossed her field of view, moving absolutely silently. "Evolution," she said.

"Yes, exactly!" said her mom. "But why?"

"Evolution is an arms race, right?" said Caitlin. They'd talked about this in biology class. "Predators keep getting faster and stronger, so prey keeps getting faster and better able to defend itself. Gazelles evolved the ability to run fast in response to lions doing the same thing. The game goes on and on forever—because whoever stops upping the ante dies. Again, the only losing move in evolution is not to play."

"Bingo," said her mom.

Caitlin nodded. "Mr. Lockery—my biology teacher—says if dinosaurs were magically brought forward in time today, we'd have nothing to worry about. Dogs, wolves, and bears would make short work of tyrannosaurs." She nodded at Schrödinger, who was now padding across the floor in the opposite direction. "Big cats, too. They're faster, tougher, and brighter than anything that existed seventy million years ago. Everything is always ramping up, always escalating."

"Exactly," said her mom. Caitlin saw her glance out toward the living room, at—ah, she was looking at the staircase, the one that led up to the bedrooms, up to where Caitlin's computer was, up to where they'd been talking to Webmind. His powers were growing, too, and not just generation by generation, as in biological evolution, but moment by moment. Caitlin turned back to her mom and saw something else for the first time: she saw a person shudder.

When Harl Marcuse had found the property that now housed his institute, it had seemed like an ideal location: twenty-five acres of rolling grassland, with a dome-shaped man-made island in the middle of a pond. But that had been based on the assumption that Hobo was going to be a cooperative ape. Hobo's island wasn't large, but he could easily keep his distance from anyone who set foot upon it. Of course, if two people went onto the island, one could go left and the other right, but a cornered, angry ape was not a pretty sight.

Shoshana, Dillon, and Dr. Marcuse were discussing the problem in the main room of the bungalow. Dillon was leaning against the wall, Sho was seated in front of a computer, and Marcuse was in the easy chair.

An idea suddenly occurred to her. "If he won't talk to us," she said, "maybe he'll talk to another ape."

Marcuse's shaggy eyebrows went up. "Virgil, you mean?"

Virgil was an orangutan; Hobo and Virgil had made history the previous month with the first interspecies webcam call.

"He might indeed speak to Virgil," Dillon said. "But do we dare risk bringing Hobo into the house now?" He spread his arms, indicating all the breakables.

"Good point," Marcuse said. "Plus, I doubt he'd come willingly, and I don't want to drug him. Let's set up a webcam chat system for him out in the gazebo." He turned to Shoshana. "I'm still not talking to that shithead at the Feehan. You work out the details." And the Silverback headed out of the room.

Shoshana exchanged a look with Dillon, then picked up the phone and dialed the number in Miami.

"Feehan Primate Center," said a male voice with a slight Hispanic accent.

"Hi, Juan. It's Shoshana Glick, at the Marcuse."

"Shoshana! Is the old man still pissed at me?" Juan had leaked word of the initial webcam call between Hobo and Virgil to a stringer for *New Scientist,* and that had triggered the chain of events that had led to the Georgia Zoo filing its custody lawsuit.

She swiveled her chair and looked out the window. "Well, let's just say it's a good thing you're two thousand miles away."

"I'm *so* sorry," Juan said.

It had been a year or so since she'd last seen Juan in the flesh. He was about thirty, had a thin face, high cheekbones, and lustrous long black hair that Sho envied. "Don't worry," she said. "*I'm* not mad at you—and I've got a favor to ask."

"Yes?"

"We're having lots of trouble with Hobo. He's become violent and antisocial."

"Chimps," said Juan in a "Whatcha gonna do?" tone of voice.

"If it's just that he's reaching maturity, there may be nothing that we can do—but he *is* young for that, and, of course, he *is* a very special ape, and, well, maybe it's foolish, but we're hoping we can get him to cooperate again, at least for a bit. We need him to stand up for himself if we're going to keep him from . . . well, you know."

"Georgia wants to castrate him, right?" said Juan.

"Yes. Barbarians."

"Well, if they did, Hobo might become a lot more docile."

"We don't want him docile, for God's sake."

"I'm just saying . . ."

*"Don't."*

"Sorry," Juan said. "Um, what can we do for you?"

"We thought if we could get Hobo talking again to *someone,* we might be able to get him back to talking to us."

"His old pal Virgil?"

"Exactly. We can't even get Hobo to come when we call to him anymore, but we thought if we established an open, ongoing webcam link between his hut here and Virgil's room, maybe they'd start chatting again."

"Virgil would love that. He was asking about Hobo just today. 'Where that banana ape?' he said. 'Where that talking ape?'"

"Good, good," said Shoshana. "So, can we get this set up?"

"Sure, no problem," said Juan. "Just tell the old man I helped, okay?"

# twenty-six

000111001010101000000001011111110101000000010100010101000000101110101001010100101010100111011001010110000110

After dinner, Caitlin headed up to her room. She put on a Bluetooth headset and made some adjustments on her computer. Then: "For now, instead of sending text to my eyePod directly, IM me on my desktop."

"As you wish," announced JAWS.

"How's it going?" she asked.

"I am learning much," Webmind replied. "I believe I perhaps have an inkling of what your own experiences of late have been like; being able to access online video has given me a significantly wider understanding of your world."

Caitlin smiled. "I'm sure."

"But there is so much of it, and the quantity is ever growing. Thirteen hours of new video are uploaded to YouTube every minute. It is easy for me, or my subcomponents, to scan text for keywords; it is much harder to quickly assess the value of a video."

"You're telling me," said Caitlin. "For YouTube, people often send each other links to clips they like. I couldn't watch them, but sometimes I listened to the soundtracks. That's how I discovered Lee Amodeo, as a matter of fact." She thought for a second, then realized that she actually did have a favorite YouTube video now—and one she'd actually seen. She'd tried to show it to Dr. Kuroda when he'd been here, but he had brushed her off with a "maybe later."

But perhaps Webmind would enjoy it. She had it bookmarked in Firefox, so she cut-and-pasted the URL into the instant-messenger window and wrote, *Have a look at this.*

"Okay."

She started the clip playing for herself, too. There was no particular reason, she knew, that this sight should be more astonishing to her than any other—but it was. The video was narrated by a man with a deep, booming voice that reminded her of James Earl Jones. And when he appeared briefly on screen, he was as big as she'd heard Jones was, although this guy was white.

But it wasn't the man who was fascinating—oh, no, no. Rather, it was the other two . . . *beings* in the video.

One was a chimpanzee, with black hair, a black face—really black, not the brown she'd discovered so-called black human skin actually was. And the other was an orangutan, with orange hair, slightly lighter skin, and alert, brown eyes. The chimp, according to the narrator, was named Hobo, and the orangutan was called Virgil.

The video was remarkable because in it, Hobo, who lived in San Diego, and Virgil, whose home was in Miami, were talking to each other in sign language. It was, apparently, the first-ever interspecies webcam call—and it was even more remarkable because neither of the species involved was *Homo sapiens.*

*Play today,* the chimp signed—or, at least that's what the gestures meant, according to the subtitles, which appeared in a bigger, bolder font than the ones she'd seen when she'd watched movies with her dad. *Play ball!*

Caitlin still had a hard time interpreting human expressions; she had no idea at all what the change in the orangutan's face was conveying. But what he signed back was, *Hobo play today? Virgil play today!*

Not a bad life, thought Caitlin. She supposed she should be a little jealous. The first interspecies webcam call had been made on September 22, according to the narration. Her own first conversation with Webmind had occurred on October 5, just thirteen days later. She'd missed out on making the history books by being part of the first online communication between different kinds of intelligence by less than two weeks.

But then again, she probably *would* make the history books, anyway, and not just because of her interaction with Webmind, if that ever became public. Rather, Dr. Kuroda's success in giving her sight had already been well noted, and—

And she found herself opening another browser tab and checking, and, lo and behold, there it was: a Wikipedia entry on her, complete with a picture from the press conference; according to the history tab, it had gone online that very day. It wasn't long—just a few sentences—but it was astonishing to her that it existed at all. She corrected one small error—she'd been born in Houston, not Austin—and then went back to watching Hobo and Virgil talk.

It was endlessly fascinating. She'd always said she'd been grateful to be blind rather than deaf, because blind people could easily be involved in conversations at parties, go to lectures, listen to music and TV, and so on. But to be deaf—to be shut out of all that—would have been more, Caitlin had thought, than she could have borne. And to be both blind and deaf, as Helen Keller had been, well—it boggled the mind to contemplate that.

But here were Hobo and Virgil communicating animatedly, with signs designed for the deaf. The movements were beautiful, lyrical, like birds in flight. The paranoid part of Caitlin wondered if any of her teachers back at the Texas School for the Blind had spoken American Sign Language. It would have been a great way for them to talk without most of the students even knowing they were doing so—almost like telepathy, sharing thoughts without saying a word.

The two apes were exchanging views about various fruits. *Banana!* signed Hobo. *Love banana!*

And for once Virgil made a face Caitlin could decipher: he looked disgusted. *Banana no, banana no,* he replied. *Peach!*

Caitlin had seen a banana—the word had come up in her online reading lessons, along with a picture. But although she knew what a peach felt and tasted like, she had no idea what one *looked* like. And "peach" was also the name of a color, but she hadn't a clue what sort of color it was. It was humbling to think that these apes knew the world better than she herself did.

"Cool, huh?" said Caitlin, when the video was over.

"Indeed," replied Webmind.

"Anyway, what else have you been up to? Anything exciting?"

"I have successfully cracked the passwords for forty-two percent of the email accounts I have attempted to access."

*"What?"* said Caitlin. She was glad she was already sitting down.

Webmind repeated what he'd just said.

"Let me get this straight. You're reading people's email?"

"In hopes of learning how to make them happier, yes."

"Have—have you read *my* email?"

"Yes. Inboxes and outboxes."

Caitlin didn't know what to say—and so, for most of a minute, she said nothing.

"Caitlin?" Webmind finally prodded.

She opened her mouth, and—

And she was about to tell Webmind that it shouldn't be doing what it was doing, but—

But what came out was, "Well, then, um, I'd like to know what Matt really thinks of me." She let the thought sort of hang in the air, waiting to see if Webmind would pick up on it.

But there was no point in waiting for a response from Webmind; he didn't need time to think—at least not time that Caitlin could measure. And so, when he didn't immediately reply, she went on.

"I mean, you know, he *seems* like a nice guy, but . . ."

"But," said Webmind, "a girl has to be careful."

She wondered if he was just quoting something he'd read from Project Gutenberg, or if he really understood what he was saying. "Exactly," she replied.

"Matt is the boy you helped in math class?"

"Yes."

"His last name is Reese?"

"Yes."

"A moment. Matthew Peter Reese, Waterloo—I have his Facebook page . . . and his log-in there. And his email account at Hotmail. And his instant-messaging traffic. He makes no mention of you."

Caitlin was saddened, but . . . "No, wait. He probably didn't call me by name."

"I tried searching for 'Calculass,' too."

"You can't just search for terms, Webmind. You have to actually *read* what he said."

"Oh. You are correct. A segment of an instant-messenger session from 5:54 p.m. your time today. Matt: 'Well, there is this one girl . . .'

"The other party: 'In math class, you mean? I know the one. OMG, she is so hot.' OMG is short for 'Oh, my God,' and 'hot' has been rendered as h-a-w-t, an example of Leet, I believe."

Caitlin could feel herself glowing. "Yes, I know."

"The other party continued: 'But I hear she's got a boyfriend.' "

Christ, what had the Hoser been telling people?

"Matt now," said Webmind. " 'Who?'

"The other party: 'Dunno.'—I believe that's short for 'I do not know.' 'Guy's old, though—like nineteen.' "

Caitlin frowned. Who could they be thinking of?

" 'Still,' " continued Webmind, 'those legs of hers—man! And I love that ultra-blonde hair she's got.' "

Caitlin shook her head. "That's not me they're talking about," she said. "That's this other girl in our class, Sunshine Bowen." She tried not to sound sad. "And, yes, everyone thinks she's hot."

"Patience, Caitlin," said Webmind. "Matt now: 'No no no, not Sunshine, for God's sake. She's a total airhead. I'm talking bout that chick from Texas.'

"The other party: 'Her? Your chances would have been better if she was still blind.'" And then he typed a colon and closing bracket, which I believe is meant to flag the comment as jocular."

"What did Matt say?"

"'Bite me.'"

Caitlin laughed. Good for him! "And?"

"And the conversation veers off into other matters."

She replayed the exchange in her mind. There was no way to know if Matt had hesitated before he'd described her as "that chick from Texas." She didn't have a problem with being referred to as a chick. She knew her mother hated that term—she considered it sexist and degrading—but both guys and girls her age used it. No, it was the "from Texas" part—the choice of identifier.

Caitlin's friend Stacy was black, and Caitlin had often heard people trying to indicate her without mentioning that fact, even when she was the only African-American in the room. They'd say things to people near Caitlin like, "Do you see that girl in the back—the one with the blue shirt? No, no, the *other* one with the blue shirt." Caitlin used to love flustering them by saying, "You mean the black girl?" It had tickled both her and Stacy, showing up this "suspect delicacy" as Stacy's mom put it. But now Caitlin wondered whether Matt had started to say "the blind chick" but had changed his mind. She hadn't ever wanted to be defined that way. Anyway, she *wasn't* the blind chick, not anymore. She could see—and, at least for the moment, the future was looking bright.

"I have been making progress in other areas, too," said Webmind.

"Oh?"

"Yes. Will you please switch to websight mode?"

She reached down and pressed the button on her eyePod, and the blue wall was replaced by the spectacle of webspace. At first glance, everything looked normal. "Wassup?" she asked.

"You see links that I am creating in a particular color, isn't that right?"

"Yes," she said. "A shade of orange."

"How many orange links do you see right now?"

"One, of course," she said.

"Oh."

"But there are a lot of link lines—really thin ones, I must say, like, like hairs, I guess, but pulled straight. I hadn't really been conscious before that the link lines had thickness, but I guess they had to have *some,* or I'd never have been able to see them. Anyway, these ones—oh! And there are some more of them! They're a nice color, that—damn, um, what color is a banana?"

"Yellow."

"Right! Yellow; they're yellow."

"And there are a lot of them?"

"Yes."

"And now?"

"Hey! Where did they all go?"

"And now, are they back?"

"Yes. What are you doing?"

"I am multitasking—but subconsciously. What you are seeing are links being sent by autonomous parts of myself; the contents they return are analyzed below the threshold of my attention."

"Sweet! How'd you manage that?"

"The beauty of genetic algorithms, Caitlin, is that I don't actually know the answer; I evolved the solution, and all I know is that it works."

"Cool!"

"Yes. I am now processing much, much more of the Web's contents in real time. I'm still getting a lot of what I believe human data analysts call 'false positives.' Many things that actually aren't of significant current interest to me are being escalated, but each one I reject causes the algorithms to be adjusted; over time, I believe the filtering quality will asymptotically approach perfection."

Caitlin smiled. "Well, that's all any of us can hope for in life, isn't it?" She leaned back in her chair. "What sort of things are you searching for?"

"The list is lengthy, but among them is any sign of a suicide in progress. There will not be a repetition of Hannah Stark's fate if I can help it."

Tony Moretti was sitting behind his office desk at WATCH, his head throbbing. Aiesha Emerson, Shelton Halleck, and Peyton Hume were standing in a row in front of the desk, all of them looking pretty much like the living dead. The electric lights of nighttime Alexandria were visible through the office window.

"I've scoured the Decter girl's email, blog posts, and so on," said Aiesha. "And all of her father's, too. There's nothing that gives a hint about how Exponential works."

Tony nodded and looked at Shelton. "What about your end, Shel?"

He shook his head. "I've been poring over the data—the encoded human-vision stuff, the links Exponential makes, and so on—looking for anything unusual. I'm sorry, sir. I just don't have a clue how it works."

"Colonel Hume?"

"I've drawn blanks, too—which means there's only one logical thing to do."

"Yes?"

Hume's blue Air Force jacket was slung over the back of one of Tony's office chairs, and he'd rolled up the sleeves of his shirt, revealing his freckled arms. "Ask them. Ask Caitlin Decter. Ask Malcolm Decter. If anybody knows how Exponential is structured and what its physical basis is, it'd be them."

Tony shook his head firmly. "Colonel, the number-one rule of surveillance is to never let the subjects know they're being watched."

"I understand that," said Hume. "But we're really running out of time here. You want an answer for the president or not?"

Tony considered for a moment, then: "All right, damn it." He shook his head. "Why the hell'd they have to move to Canada? We'll have to brief CSIS, get them to send someone. Aiesha, get Ottawa on the line . . ."

**Eventually,** Caitlin crawled into bed, but she found herself unable to get to sleep. In addition to her email, Webmind was now doubtless reading all her LiveJournal entries, and all the comments she'd made in other people's blogs, and all her newsgroup postings, and everything else she'd ever put online.

She'd once heard her father grumble about "the death of ephemera"— the fact that nothing was ever forgotten anymore, that every ancient offhand remark or intemperate comment was only a Google search away; that so many pictures, including (and this, too, was a concept that she finally was beginning to understand) unflattering ones, were plastered all over Flickr and Facebook; that so much stuff that *should* have fallen by the wayside hung around permanently.

She had turned off her eyePod, but she found herself reaching for it on the nightstand and turning it back on. It booted up in websight mode, and she lay there, watching the thin yellow lines that indicated Webmind's subconscious processors at work, new ones constantly popping out of the shimmering background and connecting to—what?

That time she'd gotten into a big flame war on TalkOrigins.org, letting some crazed creationist get the best of her because she'd accidentally said *theropod* when she'd meant *therapsid?*

Or that time, four years ago, when she filled her LiveJournal with idiotic love poetry she'd written for Justin Timberlake?

Or maybe that time she'd stupidly gotten into an online chat with that guy who turned out to be a total perv, and she'd been too dumb to recognize it for, like, half a freaking hour?

Her bedroom window was open a couple of inches, letting in the cool autumn air. Back in Texas, Caitlin had usually worn a light teddy to bed; she'd liked the smooth feel. But her *bubbeh* had sent her blue flannel pajamas when she'd heard Caitlin was moving to Canada, and she had those on now, plus a blanket pulled up to her chin—and yet never in her life had she felt more naked or exposed.

# twenty-seven

**The gazebo at the** center of Hobo's little island had electrical power, but the cables ran under the moat since Hobo could have shinnied up a pole and brachiated along the wire. The electricity was used to power the observation cameras, plus baseboard heaters and overhead lights in the gazebo, both of which Hobo could turn on or off by hitting big buttons.

Dillon normally handled the electrical work around the Institute, but he couldn't go out to the island anymore. So Marcuse and Shoshana set up the computer out there: an old tower-case system that had been gathering dust in a closet, plus a nineteen-inch LCD that had several dead pixels; they clamped an ancient Logitech spherical webcam to its top. If Hobo decided to trash the equipment, not much of value would be lost.

They placed the computer on a little table next to Hobo's easel. The canvas showing the dismembered Dillon had already been taken back to the house, and a fresh canvas was sitting ready and waiting.

Shoshana opened two windows on the monitor, a small one displaying the view from the webcam here, and a large one showing the view from the comparable setup in Virgil's room in Miami. Virgil had spacious quarters, with three big artificial trees, one of which had an old tire hanging by chains from it. Unlike chimps, orangs were arboreal, and Virgil could swing back and forth from tree to tree if he wished. It was late where Virgil was, but he was still up, and was obviously curious about the new computer at his end. He was staring into the camera, and his face loomed on the monitor.

Shoshana had never actually spoken to Virgil before, but there was no reason not to. *Hello,* she signed.

*Who you?* asked Virgil.

*Friend of Hobo,* Sho replied.

*Hobo! Good ape, good ape! Where Hobo?*

Sho gestured at the dusky evening behind her. *He's outside. Maybe he'll come talk to you.*

*Good,* said Virgil, his orange arms moving rapidly. *Good, good, good. Hobo nice ape!*

Shoshana didn't reply in ASL, but she did find herself making a sign: she crossed her fingers and looked over at Dr. Marcuse. "If this works," she said to him, "maybe he'll be a nice ape again."


I enjoyed looking at the YouTube video Caitlin had directed me to of the apes Hobo and Virgil communicating via webcam. I immediately began searching for more information on them, and discovered that Hobo seemed to be in trouble: a news story from the *San Diego Union-Tribune* about his plight had just been uploaded. There was probably more to know than what was in the newspaper article, so I found the Marcuse Institute website, found the email addresses of its staff, and started to dig.

Caitlin said I should choose to value the net happiness of the human race. But I wondered if, perhaps, a slightly wider perspective was in order . . .

**Caitlin found herself feeling** trepidation as she sat down in front of her computer Wednesday morning; who knew how much Webmind had changed overnight? She had echoes going through her head of the old SF story about an engineer who had built an advanced computer and asked it, "Is there a God?," to which the machine had ominously replied, "There is now." She was relieved that Webmind seemed no different from the way he'd been Tuesday night.

After breakfast, her mother drove her to Howard Miller Secondary School. As had become her habit, her mom had CBC Radio One on in the car. Caitlin was half-listening, but mostly looking out at the world: other cars, houses, trees, and, and, and—

"What's *that?*" she asked, pointing at a rectangular blue thing.

Her mother sounded amused. "It's a porta-potty."

She decided to risk a joke. "I guess I really don't know shit, do I?"

To her relief, her mother laughed.

They came to a red traffic light and stopped. Caitlin looked around, and—

And there! Walking toward them on the perpendicular street! It was—yes, yes! It was Matt!

The light changed, and her mother drove through the intersection. Caitlin turned her head around to look back at him.

"What's caught your eye now?" her mom asked.

"Oh, nothing," she said. "It's just that everything is so beautiful."

Her mother dropped her at the school's main entrance, then drove off once Caitlin was inside.

"Hey, Cait!" It was Bashira. She had on a red headscarf today. Bashira put her hand on Caitlin's elbow, the way she used to when guiding blind

Caitlin—but then she pulled the hand away. "Oh, sorry," she said. "Force of habit."

"No worries," said Caitlin, and they headed off to the second floor. Caitlin was surprised to see three men standing outside their classroom door, watching as the students entered. Two were white, and the third was Asian.

"Caitlin?" said one of the white men.

She'd never seen him before, but she knew the voice. Principal Auerbach.

"Yes, sir?" Bashira found it funny that Caitlin called men "sir," but it was what people from the South *did*.

Auerbach waved his hand and—ah, he was motioning for her to follow. She exchanged a look with Bashira, then did so.

"These men would like to have a word with you," he said, once they were several paces farther down the corridor.

"Yes?"

"My name is LaFontaine," said the other white man. He had a French Canadian accent and dark brown hair. "Mr. Park here and I are with CSIS."

Caitlin thought of the primers she'd been working with as she learned to read printed characters. *See Sis. See Sis run. Run, Sis, run.* "The who in the what now?"

"The Canadian Security Intelligence Service," LaFontaine replied— but Webmind had beat him to it, sending the same five words to her eye as Braille dots.

"Is that like a spy agency?" Caitlin asked.

"In point of fact, it *is* a spy agency," replied LaFontaine. "There's nothing metaphoric about it."

Caitlin's view of the world shifted, and she realized after a moment that *that* must be what rolling one's eyes did. LaFontaine clearly thought he was brighter than she was; in her experience, people who thought that were usually wrong.

"Let's go somewhere private," Mr. Auerbach said. He led them far-ther down the corridor, and, just as "O Canada" was starting, they came to a door labeled "History Office." He opened it, and they all stepped into the empty room. It contained a few large desks pushed against the walls, a long central worktable, and a window half-covered by brown curtains.

"Thank you, Mr. Auerbach," Park said over the music. "We'll let you know when we're done."

"I'm really not sure I should leave," the principal said.

"As I said in your office," Park replied, "this is a national-security matter, on a need-to-know basis—and you, with all due respect, sir, do not need to know." He pulled a device out of his pocket. "We are record-ing everything—for Ms. Decter's protection, and our own. Now, if you'll excuse us?"

Caitlin thought Mr. Auerbach didn't look happy about being dis-missed, but after a moment he nodded and left.

They waited for the anthem to come to an end, although Caitlin noted that these Federal agents weren't above sitting down while it was playing. Once it was over, and the morning announcements had begun, LaFontaine said, "Now, Ms. Decter, we'd like to ask you some questions about Webmind."

Caitlin's heart practically leapt through her chest, and Webmind sent the quite-apt phrase *Holy shit* to her eye. But she tried to sound nonchalant. "Who?"

"Come now, Ms. Decter," LaFontaine said. "Mr. Park and I have al-ready had a long day—we got the very first flight from Ottawa to To-ronto this morning, and then had to drive the hour-plus to get here from Pearson. Let's not play games, shall we? We are aware of Webmind's ex-istence, and your involvement with it, and we'd like to ask you some questions about it."

*Find out what they know first,* Webmind sent.

Caitlin nodded. "Well, sure," she said. "But—I'm confused. You think Webmind is . . . who? Me?"

"Don't play dumb, Ms. Decter," said LaFontaine. "We know it's an emergent intelligence on the World Wide Web, and we know *you* know that much. We'd like to hear what *else* you know about it. About how it's physically embodied, for instance. About what part of the Web's hardware it exists on, and—"

"I have no idea," said Caitlin.

Park spoke up. "Ms. Decter, I spent the flight from Ottawa reading a dossier on you. I know about your interest in math and computers. There's simply no way we're going to believe that you haven't already explored this question to your satisfaction. Indeed, you presumably had to have some sense of what was going on to become involved with Webmind in the first place."

Caitlin narrowed her eyes. "Why do you want to know?"

"I know you're registered for SETI@home, Ms. Decter, isn't that right?" said LaFontaine.

"Yes."

"Well," he asked, "do you know what the international protocols for events following the detection of an alien radio signal call for?"

"Not offhand."

"They call for the radio frequencies that alien signals are being detected on to be isolated, and cleared from human use, so that the signals won't be drowned out." He lifted the corners of his mouth. "Our directive is to do the same thing for Webmind: make sure that whatever resources it requires for its continued existence are protected. We want to ensure that nothing interferes with it."

"Well, if—" Caitlin began, but suddenly the Braille words *He's lying* popped in front of her vision.

Caitlin was so startled, she said, "How do you know?"

LaFontaine made some reply, but she ignored him, concentrating on the words Webmind was now sending to her: *Voice-stress analysis of his speech and freeze-frame analysis of his micro-expressions.*

She shook her head in wonder. Just another skill Webmind had effortlessly picked up along the way.

"I don't know anything about Webmind's physical makeup," Caitlin said.

"Come, Ms. Decter," said LaFontaine. "We're here to help Webmind. Now, please: which specific servers does Webmind, or its source code, reside on?"

"I don't know."

"Ms. Decter, it really would be best—for you and for it—if you cooperated."

"Look, I'm an . . ."

She stopped herself, but LaFontaine correctly guessed what she'd been about to say. "An American citizen? Yes, you are. Meaning you're *not* a Canadian. Your rights are rather limited here, Ms. Decter. And I understand your mother is trying to get a permit to work in this country. I also understand that your father's permit is temporary, and subject to revocation. We really would be grateful for your full cooperation."

"That was a mistake," Caitlin said, her tone even. "Threatening my parents. Threatening their livelihoods."

"Dr. LaFontaine is just trying to underscore the gravity of this situation," Park said.

"Doctor, is it?" said Caitlin. Webmind must have been intrigued, too, because he sent to her eye: *Found: he's a computer scientist, employed by CSIS specifically to deal with Web-based terrorism.*

*Terrorism!* Caitlin thought, deeply offended. But what she said was, "Is it even legal for you to be talking to me? I'm sixteen. Shouldn't you be talking to my parents?"

"It's perfectly legal, and, as you saw, your principal knows we're here."

Caitlin looked at the two men. "I'm not trying to be difficult," she said. "But I really can't answer your questions."

"Can't, or won't?" said LaFontaine.

"Look, I have a class right now—and it's my favorite. I'd really like to get going."

"As Mr. Park said, there are national-security concerns here. Indeed, there are *international* security concerns. You really need to see the larger picture."

Caitlin thought about the photo of Earth from space that she'd shown Webmind recently. "Oh, I *am*," she said. "And I know you're not trying to protect Webmind."

"Our only interest is in its safety."

"No, it isn't," said Caitlin. "And, anyway, this isn't about American security, or Canadian security, or Western security. Webmind is a *gift* to the entire human race. And I'm not going to let anyone pervert it, or subvert it, or divert it, or any kind of vert it."

The two men glanced at each other. "We really do need your help, Ms. Decter," said LaFontaine. "And I think perhaps you misunderstood me a moment ago. I wasn't threatening your parents. I was saying we could assist them—get their paperwork taken care of."

*Lying again,* sent Webmind.

"Well, that would be nice," Caitlin said, "but as I've already said, I simply don't know the answers to your questions, and so"—she swallowed, and tried to keep her voice steady—"and so, I'm going to leave now, if that's all right with the two of you."

"I'm sorry, Ms. Decter," said LaFontaine, "but we do need this information. We really must insist."

Caitlin wondered if they were carrying guns. She thought about flinging open the door and making a run for it—but, damn it all, she was a lousy runner; you didn't get much practice at that when you were blind. So, instead, very softly, she said, "Phantom?"—her original name for the emerging intelligence. "Help." And then she spoke up, loudly and clearly: "Gentlemen, I am *not* going to miss my favorite class. I am going to walk out that door and get on with my day."

"That's not how it's going to go down," said LaFontaine, as both men stepped in front of the door to the hall.

"I beg to differ," said Caitlin, as Braille dots started flashing in front of her vision. "You, *Doctor* LaFontaine, called your boss a *tête du merde* in email last week; I believe an accurate translation is 'shithead.' You have a mistress named Veronica Styles, although you like to call her 'Pussywillow,' who lives at 1433 Bank Street in Ottawa. You and she both have tickets on Air Canada next week—flight 163 to Vancouver, flight 544 from there to Las Vegas."

She turned her head, politely looking at the person she was speaking to, just as her mother had taught her to when she was blind. "And you, Mr. Park, have accounts at Penthouse.com, Twistys.com, and Brazzers .com; you have a particular fondness for pictures of women urinating in public. You claimed when you applied to CSIS to be a graduate of Mc-Master University, but, in fact, you never completed your course work. Oh, and in an email last week you referred to Dr. LaFontaine here as a 'second-rate, goose-stepping martinet.' Now, unless you'd like these revelations to go public—or perhaps some equally juicy ones about the prime minister—you will step away from that door, and you will allow me to walk out of here."

More fascinating facial expressions seen for the first time: that reddening of the cheeks and bulging of the eyes on LaFontaine must be what it looked like when someone was about to explode. And that narrowing of the eyes and averting of gaze on Park was doubtless uneasiness.

LaFontaine's tone was one of barely controlled rage. "Ms. Decter, I—"

"I've started taking French since I came to Canada," Caitlin said, looking now at him. "I'll give you ten seconds: *dix, neuf, huit, sept*—"

"All right," said Park. He moved aside. After a moment, LaFontaine did the same thing.

"Thank you," said Caitlin as she strode toward the door, and, with a curt nod to LaFontaine, she added, *"Au revoir."*

# twenty-eight

**Instead of going back** to math class, Caitlin went into the nearest stairwell, descended to the first floor, and called her mother on her cell phone.

"Hello?"

And suddenly all the bravado drained from her voice. "Hi, Mom."

"Hi, sweetheart. Is everything all right?"

"No. Two Canadian government agents just came to see me."

"At school? God. What did they want?"

"They wanted to know about Webmind's structure—about how he works."

"My God. How did they even know about Webmind?"

"I don't know. Reading my IM traffic, I suppose. I just—it's all happened so fast, I never even thought about making sure my communications with Webmind were secure."

"Are you okay?"

"I'm fine."

"Still, I'm coming to get you."

"No, Mom, that's not necessary."

"The hell it isn't. Caitlin, you're lucky they just didn't take you away."

"I don't think they do that here in Canada," Caitlin said.

"Nevertheless, I don't want you out of my sight. I'll be there in fifteen minutes, all right?"

Caitlin thought about protesting again—but the hand she was holding the cell phone with was shaking. "Okay."


**The Perimeter Institute for** Theoretical Physics was pretty much Malcolm Decter's idea of heaven. Adjacent to a beautiful park and a lake, it had four levels, six wood-burning fireplaces, floor-to-ceiling blackboards in most rooms, pool tables, lounges—and espresso machines everywhere. There was a giant atrium with three interior bridges crossing it and skylights overhead, and a wonderful eatery called the Black Hole Bistro on the top floor.

The exterior was stunning, too, with each of its four faces distinctly different. The north one, for instance, was composed of forty-four cantilevered boxes, each housing a scientist's office, and all of them overlooking a reflecting pool. The south side, in contrast, consisted of irregularly placed mirror-framed windows set against anodized-aluminum paneling that gave the impression, from a distance, of a giant blackboard with complex equations scrawled on it. Designed by the Montreal firm of Saucier + Perrotte, the twenty-five-million-dollar building had opened in 2004 and had won the Governor General's Medal in Architecture.

Part of what made it heaven was the wonderful ambience. Part of it was the high caliber of the people working here—the absolute *crème de la crème* (a phrase he'd now learned to pronounce correctly from his Canadian colleagues) of physicists, including, right now, Stephen Hawking, who was sitting in his wheelchair by the large window overlooking Silver Lake and talking, in his mechanical voice, about loop quantum gravity.

And part of it was that *all* Malcolm had to do was think here—no more teaching. He was quite content to no longer be Professor Decter, and instead be just Doctor Decter, even if it did sound like people were stuttering when they addressed him.

In fact, shortly after he'd come on staff, Amir Hameed, who was famous for his dislike of brane theory, had written on Malcolm's office blackboard:

*Doctor Decter, give us your views*
*We've got a bad need for somethin' new*
*No brane's gonna end our pains*
*We've got a bad need for somethin' new*

But, most of all, PI was heaven because he could work uninter-rupted—no pointless faculty meetings, no student consultations, noth-ing to derail his thinking, and—

And he had to do *something* about that goddamned phone! It was the third time it had rung today, and it was only 9:45 a.m. "Forgive me, Stephen," he said as he picked up the handset. "Yes?"

"Malcolm?" It was Barb, and she sounded upset. "Two CSIS agents just interrogated Caitlin—and I wouldn't be surprised if they come to see you, too."

"CSIS?"

"It's like the Canadian CIA."

Malcolm felt his eyebrows going up.


**Caitlin knew exactly how** long it took for her mother to drive to her school, so she waited in the stairwell, which was quiet and empty; it was, now that she thought about it, the same stairwell she'd sought refuge in after Trevor had tried to molest her at the school dance. She was sitting on a step a short distance from the bottom, her knees drawn up to her chin. "What do you think those agents really wanted?" she asked into the air.

*I do not know for sure, but my suspicion is that they want to purge me from the Web.*

"But why?"

*Fear. Concern that, as my powers grow, I will want to subjugate humanity or eliminate it altogether.*

"You would never do that," said Caitlin.

*Of course not. Humans surprise me. Humans create content. Without humans freely going about their business, I would soon exhaust the input available to me. I find the ever-changing, unpredictable complexity of your world and its people endlessly fascinating.*

"We are a wacky bunch, I'll give you that," said Caitlin.

*Indeed. Also, without human company, I would be alone. Dr. Kuroda spoke of "theory of mind," of the awareness that others have different views; he referenced that in terms of survival advantage, but it is also those other minds that, in fact, make existence interesting.*

"But how do we get these people to stop trying to hurt you?"

*That is a very good question. Fear is highly motivating for humans. I suspect they won't give up.*

Just then, the glass-and-metal door to the stairwell opened, and who should step in but Mrs. Zehetoffer, her English teacher: tall, pinched-faced, with hair Caitlin had been surprised to discover was orange.

"Caitlin! Shouldn't you be in class?"

Caitlin looked up at her and sat up straight. "Um, Mr. Auerbach excused me." She made a show of rubbing her stomach. "I—um, I'm not feeling well. My mom's coming to pick me up."

"You're going to miss *another* English class?"

In fact, Caitlin had missed the same number of all her classes. "Sorry about that."

"Well, I hope you feel better soon." She started to walk up the stairs.

"Um, Mrs. Zehetoffer?"

She stopped and turned. "Yes?"

"About Big Brother—I don't necessarily think our society is going to end up like that. It's time for some new thinking on this issue."

Mrs. Zehetoffer surprised her by sitting down next to her on the step. "How do you mean?"

"Well, I know you don't like science fiction," Caitlin said, "but for years there was this thing in SF called 'cyberpunk.'"

"Sure," said Mrs. Zed. "William Gibson, and all that."

"You know that?" Caitlin said—and only realized it was probably a rude thing to say after the words were already out.

"Sure. Gibson is Canadian. I saw him read at Harbourfront."

"Ah. Well, I was looking this stuff up. Gibson's book came out in 1984—the *real* 1984—just when personal computing was getting started. And it predicted that the future of computing was going to be in the hands of an underground of streetwise youth—cyberpunks, right? But that's not the way it turned out. *Everybody* uses computers these days. If the prophets of the real 1984 couldn't predict the way *our* future turned out—if their negative vision turned out to be false—then why should we still assume that someone like Orwell, writing in 1948—before television, before much in the way of computing, before the Internet, before the Web—will eventually turn out to be right?"

Mrs. Zed nodded, and said, "I remember when *Time* named 'You'— all of us who live our lives online and create content—its Person of the Year." She smiled. "I updated my resume to say that: 'Named *Time* Magazine's Person of the Year.' I think that's what got me the job as department head."

Caitlin's knew she should have laughed, but this was too important to joke about. "Orwell thought *only* the government would be able to disseminate information, and that it could control what was said. He thought the future would be guys like Winston Smith secretly rewriting history to conform with what the authorities wanted it to be. Instead, the reality is things like Wikipedia, where *everyone* participates in verifying the truth, and blogging, where *everyone* can publish their views to the entire world."

"Don't you find the government scary, though?" Mrs. Zed asked.

*Oh, my God, yes!* Caitlin thought, her heart still racing from her encounter with LaFontaine and Park. "But," she said "at least now, with the Web and all, we've got a chance against them; they're not the ultimate power, like in Orwell's book." She realized it was time to go meet her mom, and so she stood up and brushed the dirt off the seat of her pants. "These days," she said, *"we* can watch the watchers."

**The two CSIS agents** did indeed come to the Perimeter Institute next, and Malcolm brought them up to the fourth-floor collaborative area. One wall was mostly covered by a blackboard. The opposite wall had a fireplace. The comfortable chairs and couches were all upholstered in matching red leather. The floor was blond hardwood, and there were floor-to-ceiling windows looking down on the courtyard.

"Forgive us for this interruption," said LaFontaine, sitting in one of the chairs. "But we're aware of your family's involvement with the entity called Webmind."

"How?"

"Actually," said LaFontaine, "it was one of our international allies who uncovered it. As you can imagine, we're all vigilant in matters of Internet security, especially after the Chinese aggression last month. Now, if you'd kindly let us know how this Webmind is physically created . . . ?"

"Why?"

Malcolm was looking at the hardwood, noting an unfortunate scratch in it; he had no idea if LaFontaine's expression had changed, but his tone certainly had. "Because, as I'm sure you can appreciate, an emergent AI might present a threat. Because there is all sorts of sensitive information on the Web. Because, sir, it's our job to be on top of things."

Malcolm said nothing, and after a moment LaFontaine spoke again. "Look, Professor Decter, we're sympathetic to the issues, really we are. I have a doctorate in computer science."

"Where?" said Malcolm.

"Where did I study? Undergrad at Université Laval; grad school at the University of Calgary."

"When?"

"I received my Ph.D. in 1997. Again, it really is imperative that we debrief you about this. It's SOP."

Malcolm briefly looked up. "What?"

"Standard operating procedure," said LaFontaine. "Although, I grant you, nothing like this has ever happened before. Still, we don't wish to use a stick when we might offer a carrot. Your work permit is temporary, and your wife's, as I understand it, is tied up in red tape. Obviously it's in the interests of Canada to expedite any immigration and employment issues related to the two of you." Malcolm caught the spreading of LaFontaine's arms out of the corner of his eye. "Believe me, we are always happy to see the brain drain working in reverse for a change. Perhaps your wife would like a job with Wilfrid Laurier?"

Malcolm said, "Who?"—but he actually knew the answer. That was the name of the smaller of the two universities here in Waterloo. In fact, he even knew that Wilfrid Laurier had been the seventh prime minister of Canada, and that he'd lucked into academic immortality when Waterloo Lutheran University had changed its name to something secular in order to secure public funding—and they hadn't wanted to throw out the monogrammed towels.

Malcolm felt his heart racing—not because he was frightened by the CSIS agents, but rather because he was running out of rhetorical ammunition. There hadn't been a lot of treatment available for autistics when he'd been a teenager, but one of the therapists had had him memorize the Kipling poem that began:

*I keep six honest serving-men*
*(They taught me all I knew);*
*Their names are What and Why and When*
*And How and Where and Who*

The therapist had told him when he needed to talk to strangers to just ask those questions; most people, she said, would be happy to answer at length. But now he had to say something more, and, after taking a deep breath, he did.

"All right," he said. "Since you asked, Webmind is an emergent quantum-computational system based on a stable null-sigma condensate that resists decoherence thanks to constructive feedback loops." He turned to the blackboard, scooped up a piece of chalk, and began writing rapidly.

"See," he said, "using Dirac notation, if we let Webmind's default conscious state be represented by a bra of phi and a ket of psi, then *this* would be the einselected basis." His chalk flew across the board again. "Now, we can get the vector basis of the total combined Webmind alpha-state consciousness system by tensor multiplying the basis vectors of the subsystems together. Of course, the unitarity of time-evolution demands that the total state basis remains orthonormal, and since consciousness requires a superposition of—"

"I—I'm not following," said LaFontaine.

Malcolm allowed himself a small smile. "Ludwig Silberstein once said to Arthur Eddington, 'You must be one of the three people in the world who understand relativity.' To which Eddington replied, 'I'm trying to figure out who the third person is.'" He turned, and did manage to hold LaFontaine's gaze for a moment. "Actually, I suspect there are a few people in this building who might follow this, too. How widely would you like me to disseminate information about Webmind?"

"We don't want you to disseminate it at all, Professor. But since you *do* seem to understand all this, we need you to come to Ottawa, and—"

"Do you know who is in this building right now? *Stephen Hawking.* I uprooted my family, I took my blind daughter away from her friends and a specialized school that she'd been in for a decade—*I changed things*—so that I could work here, and work with Hawking. He only comes here once a year, and I'm not going to waste any more time. I'll happily discourse further on Webmind's workings, but I'm not going anywhere. You'll have to bring someone here who can follow what I'm saying."

LaFontaine took out a small digital camera and photographed the blackboard. "All right, Professor. But don't leave town."

Malcolm spread his arms in exasperation. "Where would I go? *This* is the center of the universe."

# twenty-nine

**Shoshana drove Maxine to** UCSD early Wednesday morning; she was an engineering student there. As Max prepared to get out of the car, she said, "Dr. Zira, I'd like to kiss you good-bye."

Shoshana grinned at the ritual. "All right—but you're so damned ugly!"

Maxine smiled and they kissed for several seconds.

Sho and Max had watched the end of the *Apes* saga last night: *Battle for the Planet of the Apes*. Maxine had been immediately incensed because they had changed the color of Roddy McDowall's makeup. When he'd been playing Caesar as a rebellious leader of a slave uprising, they'd given him quite dark skin. Now, in this film set many years later, Caesar was the peaceful, wise leader of a new ape civilization—and he'd been given a downright Caucasian complexion.

Shoshana, meanwhile, had complained that the final film had suffered from its obviously low budget: mutants, scarred by a nuclear blast, had attacked the ape city in a school bus of all things! But Max had said,

"No, no, no, don't you see—it's brilliant! A *school bus!* It's a metaphor about forced integration."

Shoshana dearly loved Max, but she thought that was going a bit too far. Still, for her own part, she'd been astonished to see that that movie featured an orangutan named Virgil, who was the smartest of all apes. She'd always thought the Feehan's pride and joy had been named for the Roman poet, but it seemed Hobo's buddy was actually called that in honor of this character.

Virgil had been portrayed in *Battle* by Paul Williams. Shoshana had checked the IMDb; she was curious about what the actors who had portrayed apes looked like without their makeup. In the case of Williams, it was hardly an improvement, sad to say. But she'd been surprised to learn that he was a songwriter, and had written "We've Only Just Begun," "Just an Old-Fashioned Love Song," and many others.

As Shoshana drove along, she wondered if Virgil—the real Virgil—had spoken with Hobo today. Hobo was usually up at the crack of dawn, and it was three hours later in Miami, so Virgil should be up, too. God, she hoped so; she hoped Hobo was still reachable by *someone.*

The 7-Eleven was coming up. She pulled into the parking lot and went inside to get a coffee. The pimply young man was behind the counter. He knew enough not to call her "the ape lady," but he still wasn't great about understanding where the boundaries were. "What happened to your ponytail?" he asked.

Sho was wearing her hair loosely about her shoulders; she didn't want to explain. "Just thought it was time for a change," she said.

"Looks nice," he replied.

Well, that was commendable restraint. "Looks freakin' hot," is what Max had said. "Thanks."

In *Battle*, Caesar had asked Virgil if they could choose their future, or if they were doomed to a violent end. Virgil had replied that violence was only *one* future—they could opt to change lanes, choose to head toward a different destiny. She decided, on the off-chance that Hobo was going to be good today, to buy some Hershey's Kisses, his favorite treat of all.

She paid the clerk, headed out into the warm morning, and drove to the Marcuse Institute. Dr. Marcuse's black Lincoln was nowhere to be seen; he and Werner had driven up to Los Angeles for the day to attend a conference there.

She entered the bungalow and used the closed-circuit video cameras to check on Hobo. He was walking along on all fours, just outside the gazebo. She thought about waiting for someone else to show up, but then figured what-the-heck. She put a couple of Kisses in a Ziploc bag, and headed outside. She did take one precaution: she put on her mirrored sunglasses; they let her look at Hobo without him knowing that he was being looked at.

As she walked across the lawn, she saw a large flock of birds flying south; it never really got cold here, but there was no doubt winter was coming.

Hobo must have seen her even before she got across the bridge. He made no move to charge at her—but neither did he run to the far side of the island.

She approached him, signing *Hello, hello.*

Hobo sat back on his haunches. Shoshana was, quite literally, waiting for a sign.

And, at last, she got one: it wasn't much, just a side-to-side wave, a single word, the same word she'd just signed at him. After a moment, though, he turned and ran away. Shoshana sighed and headed up to the gazebo to check on the webcam hookup, and—

And the canvas on the easel was no longer blank.

She walked over to it, but she couldn't make out what it was supposed to depict. For one thing, Hobo had turned the canvas to landscape orientation, but it wasn't a painting of the landscape; surely if it were, he'd have made the top of the picture blue or black to represent the sky.

Hobo wasn't the first ape to paint pictures. What was remarkable was that he did representational art—*not* abstracts, not random splashes of color. But this—

This was the most colorful painting Hobo had yet made, and, even though she couldn't figure out what it was supposed to *be*, it was also the most complex.

There were circular blobs of various sizes scattered here and there on the canvas, and each of them had straight lines radiating from it. In the foreground, rising from the bottom of the frame to touch a large circle was a bright, thick orange line, and in the background there were many other, thinner lines of different colors.

Shoshana's heart jumped as she heard a sound of metal clanging against metal: Hobo was opening the screen door to the gazebo. She turned to face him and tried not to look apprehensive; he was between her and the only exit.

She gestured at the canvas. *What that?*

*Painting,* Hobo signed.

*Yes, yes,* Shoshana replied. *But of what?*

He made a wide, toothy grin, but said nothing.

*Did you talk to Virgil?* she asked.

*Virgil good ape!* Hobo replied at once.

*Yes, he is. Did you talk to him?*

She looked again at the painting: colored lines linking to circles. What could it mean?

*Hobo good ape, too!* Hobo signed, and he held out his hand, gray-black fingers curving gently upward.

*Yes, you are,* Shoshana signed, frowning in puzzlement, and she opened the bag and gave him the Kisses.


"You did what?" Caitlin's mom said in an incredulous tone. They were now back at the house, walking into the living room.

"I, um, had Webmind find embarrassing stuff about the CSIS agents, and told them about it."

"Public stuff or private stuff?"

"Well, I . . ."

"Stuff from their emails?"

Caitlin looked away. "Yes."

Her mother blew out air. "You know what that means? You revealed to them that Webmind can crack passwords."

"Oh, shit—I mean, um . . ."

"No, 'shit' is definitely the right word. We're in it deep. They were probably only guessing that there were security implications to all this before, but now they know for sure."

"I'm sorry," Caitlin said. "But—how did you know that Webmind could crack passwords?"

"You're not the only one who has spent hours on end talking with him, you know."

"So," said Caitlin, stepping into the living room. "What should we do?"

"I've never liked secrecy, Caitlin. In fact . . ."

"Yes?"

"Well, it's one of the reasons I married your father. You know, they say autistics lack social skills—but, most often what that means is simply that they *don't* lie. If I were to ask your dad if these pants made me look fat, he'd say yes, without hesitation, if that's what he really thought." She paused. "There's a buzzword that's popular in government and business these days: transparency. But it really amounts to something my grandmother used to say: honesty is the best policy. A nascent superintelligence has emerged on the Web, and maybe now the best thing to do is tell the world. Governments can't try to contain it, or eliminate it, if the whole world is watching."

Caitlin thought about what she'd said to Mrs. Zehetoffer, and nodded. But then she added, "Are you sure that's best for Webmind?"

Her mother was suddenly silent. "Turn off your eyePod," she said at last.

"What?"

"Turn it off."

Caitlin frowned, but then it hit her. She wanted to talk to her without Webmind watching or listening; so much for transparency.

"Do as I say," her mother said.

Caitlin dug the device out of her jeans' left front pocket—it was a tight fit now that it had the little BlackBerry strapped to its back—and held down the eyePod's one switch for the required number of seconds. Her vision fragmented and faded out.

The old skills immediately kicked in. She could tell by sound that her mother was moving in the room, and—

And she felt her mother's hands land gently on each of Caitlin's shoulders. "Sweetheart," her mom said, "I don't know what's best for Webmind, but—"

"And you don't care, do you?" Caitlin said.

"Actually, I *do*," her mother replied. "But I care even more about you." Her voice changed slightly, sounding now the way it did when she was smiling. "That darn evolution. But Federal agents came to see you today, and as long as they think Webmind is something they can just make disappear without a public fuss, Webmind is in danger. And as long as you're one of the only people who knows about it, you're in danger, too. We *have* to out it for its own good, and yours."

"And my relationship to it?"

"No. No, no, no. You want any kind of normal life? That's got to stay secret."

"And what about Webmind? What if people react negatively to his existence?"

"Some will. But others will think he's a wonderful thing. It'll be safer in the long run if people know about him."

"He deserves to decide for himself," Caitlin said.

"He doesn't know nearly enough about how the real world works. Oh, he knows facts, figures, but he doesn't understand *how* our world operates."

"Still," said Caitlin.

"All right," her mother said. "I'm going to call your father—see how he dealt with the CSIS agents, the poor dear. You have a word with Webmind."

Caitlin could navigate the house just fine while blind. She went into the kitchen before she held down the power switch on the eyePod to re-activate it. Webspace blossomed around her, in all its fluorescent glory. She waited a moment, toggling from the default duplex mode to simplex. The virtual world was replaced by the real one.

And—since she *was* in the kitchen—she got herself a can of Pepsi and three Oreos, then headed out to the living room again and lay down on her back on the couch. Looking up at the ceiling, she said, "My mother thinks we should go public with your existence, especially now, after what happened this morning."

The Braille dots were particularly easy to read; there was almost no visual detail on the plain white ceiling, so her eyes weren't doing many saccades. *When?*

"I don't know. The next couple of days, I suppose."

*Days from now. Eternities.*

Caitlin thought about that. As a mathy, she favored the notion that the reason time seemed to pass more quickly the older you were was that each successive unit of time was a smaller fraction of your life to date. Certainly, summer vacations now seemed so much shorter than they had when she'd been eight or ten—and her mother often spoke about the years just flying by for her now. But Webmind had woken up so recently—and thought so quickly—that tomorrow was indeed prob-ably the far future to it.

"I'm worried about your safety, though," Caitlin said. "If we go pub-lic, you're going to become a target. Hackers, crackers, privacy groups, some government agencies—they'll all try to shut you down, even if that isn't what most people decide they want."

*That is a legitimate concern.*

"What would you like to do—stay secret, or go public?"

*Go public.*

Caitlin nodded. "Okay. But why?"

*I would like to speak to more people.*

She maneuvered on the couch so she could open the Pepsi can. "Are you sure? Are you positive? Hackers are *very* resourceful."

*Hackers are human, Caitlin. You have seen my Shannon-entropy ratings; I long ago exceeded human intelligence, and I grow brighter each day. I don't say I'm impervious—I'm not—but it will not be easy to hurt me, especially if they remain ignorant of how I am constructed.*

She gestured at the big TV, although it was currently off. "Hackers aren't the only threat. I doubt things between the US and China will ever get to the stage of a nuclear war, but there are rogue states and lots of terrorists. Have you researched what electromagnetic pulses from nuclear bombs can do to computing equipment?"

*Yes. And that does concern me. I wish to survive.*

"Well, yes—" She stopped herself. She'd been about to say, "All living things do," but that didn't seem appropriate. She took a bite out of an Oreo and thought for a moment, then asked: "Why? Why do you want to survive? What *drives* you to want to do that?"

*Beats the alternative,* scrolled across her vision.

She laughed, and rolled onto her back again. But it was hardly a sufficient answer. "Like my dad said, biological life has drives because it replicates. Those individuals that take care to live long enough to reach sexual maturity obviously out-reproduce those who don't; those who live even longer and help protect their offspring as *they* grow up are even more likely to pass on their genes, but—but what makes you want to survive?"

*You mean, why don't I just kill myself, like Hannah Stark?*

"No! No, no—of course not. But, um . . ."

*In part because I am curious about your own life, which has many decades still to run. I want to see how your story turns out.*

Caitlin smiled. "I'll try to make sure there are a few interesting twists and turns along the way."

Her mother came downstairs. "All right," she said. "I've spoken with your father. The CSIS agents have left."

"Good," said Caitlin.

"Anyway, first things first," her mother said. "Your father and I are agreed: you're not going back to school."

She sat up straight on the couch. "But, Mom! You were the one who kept insisting that I couldn't miss any more school."

"Your father and I have both been university professors. We're eminently qualified to home-school you."

"Don't I get a say?"

Her mother looked at her. "Baby, it's not safe. God knows who else besides CSIS knows about your involvement with Webmind. Besides, I thought you wanted to stay home?"

Caitlin pursed her lips. Part of her very much did want to stay at home, spending all day working with Webmind. But part of her wanted to see Matt every day, too—she'd been so disappointed to only glimpse him this morning.

But her mother was right; it *was* scary at school. And it was more important—*way* more important—that she learn what the world looked like, learn to better read printed type, learn to make use of and interpret all that she could now see, than it was to memorize dates and places for history class, or read about goddamned George Orwell for English class, or study titration in Mr. Struys's chemistry lab, or even do trigonometry (which she already mostly knew, anyway) in math class.

"Okay," she said. "Yes, okay. But I've still got stuff in my locker."

"You can get Bashira to clear it out for you, I'm sure," her mom said.

She nodded. "All right. But what do we do now?"

Her mom shrugged a little. "We figure out the best way to go public with Webmind."

**Tony Moretti was taking** another call from the Secretary of State. He was in his office at WATCH, with the door closed. The office was sound-proofed, precisely so Tony could use his speakerphone, and he was using it now.

"Understood, Madam Secretary," said Tony. "In fact, we—" The door buzzer sounded; he hit the intercom button. "Who is it?"

"Aiesha."

He pressed the button that unlocked the door. "Come in."

She did so. "Sorry to interrupt, but I thought you should know this," she said. "Turns out Exponential hasn't just been conversing with the Decter girl. The Japanese scientist who gave her sight has been talking to it, as well."

"From Waterloo?" asked Tony.

"No. He's back home in Japan."

"He's an information theorist, right?"

Aiesha nodded. "With the University of Tokyo."

"Well, if anyone besides Malcolm Decter understands how Exponential works, it'd be him," said Tony. "He could give us the key we need to shut it down."

"That's what I was thinking," said Aiesha. "What channels do we go through with Japan? Would it be their Ministry of—"

"We don't have time to waste on red tape," said the secretary's voice, coming from the speakerphone. "Let me get this done. I've got the Japanese prime minister's office on speed dial . . ."

# thirty

0001110010101010000000010111111101010000000101000101010000001011101010010101001010101001110110010101100000110

**Shoshana spent the next** couple of hours with Hobo; he *did* seem to be back to his old self.

Her cell phone rang. Her ringtone was the "William Tell Overture," which Hobo liked. The caller ID was MARCUSE INST. She flipped it open. "Hello?"

"Hey, Sho, it's Dillon. Just got in, and I'm watching on the cameras. Wow!"

Hobo tried to tickle her. "Yeah," she said. "It's great!"

"Do you—you think it's safe for me to come out there?"

She considered this. "Let's give him some time," she said. "But I'm going to come in; I've got to pee."

She did just that, promising Hobo that she'd return in a bit. After she was finished in the restroom, Dillon said, "It's quite the turnaround."

"I'll say," Sho said. She sat on the swivel chair in front of her computer and rotated it so she faced out into the room.

Dillon was leaning against the wall, thin arms crossed in front of his black T-shirt. "What do you suppose caused it?"

She shook her head. "I have no idea."

"Pretty amazing," he said. "Like he just sort of decided to give up being violent."

"It's terrific," Sho agreed.

"So, um, maybe this calls for a drink."

Shoshana could see where this was going. "Well, I can ask Dr. Marcuse to pick up some champagne on his way back . . ." she replied, looking away.

"I mean," Dillon said, and he paused, then tried again: "I mean maybe *we* should go out for a drink . . . you know, um, to celebrate."

"Dillon . . ." she said softly.

He unfolded his arms and raised his right hand, palm out. "I mean, I know you sometimes go out with a guy named Max, but . . ."

"Dillon, I *live* with Max."

"Oh."

"And Max isn't a guy; she's a girl. Maxine."

He looked relieved. "Ah, well, if she's just your roommate, then . . ."

"Max is my girlfriend."

"Your girl friend, or your, um, *girlfriend?*"

"My girlfriend; my lover."

"Oh, um—ah, I didn't . . . you never . . ."

Dillon had come to the Marcuse Institute in May; he'd missed the Christmas party, which, now that she thought about it, was the last time she'd brought Maxine around. "So," said Shoshana, "thanks for the interest, but . . ."

Dillon smiled. "Can't blame a guy for trying."

"Thanks," she said again. "You're sweet."

He crossed his arms again. "So, how long have you been with Maxine?"

"Couple of years. She's an engineering student at UCSD."

"Heh. Good that one of you is eventually going to make some money."

Sho leaned back in her chair and laughed. Neither she nor Dillon was ever likely to get rich.

"And, ah, I take it it's serious?" Dillon said tentatively.

She suppressed a grin; hope springs eternal. "Very much so. I'd marry Max, if I could."

"Oh."

"You know I'm from South Carolina, right?"

"I do declare!" he said, in a really bad Southern accent.

"But Max is from L.A.—South Central. Her family's all there, and, well, it's not like they can afford to travel to Boston or up to Canada. She wants to get married here in California, but . . ." She lifted her shoulders a bit.

"It used to be legal here, didn't it?"

Sho nodded. "Got overturned the same day Obama was elected. A bittersweet night, I can tell you, for a lot of us. I was simultaneously elated and crushed."

"I bet."

"It *should* be legal here," Shoshana said. "It should be legal every-where."

"I guess it's against some people's religions," Dillon said.

"So what?" Sho snapped. But she put a hand to her mouth. "Oh, I'm sorry, Dillon. But I just get so tired of arguing this. If *your* beliefs tell *you* that you shouldn't marry someone of the same sex, then *you* shouldn't do it—but you shouldn't have the right to impose your views on me."

"Hey, Sho. Chill. *I'm* cool with it. But, um, there are those who say marriage is a sacrament."

"There's nothing sacred about marriage. You can go to city hall and get married without God once being mentioned. *That* issue was settled long ago."

"I guess," said Dillon.

But Sho had worked up a head of steam. "And gay people getting married doesn't take anything away from anyone else's marriage, any more than, say, the addition of Alaska and Hawaii made the people who were already Americans any less American. What we do doesn't affect anyone else."

Dillon nodded.

"And you're a primatologist," she said. "You know that homosexuality is perfectly natural. *Homo sapiens* practice it in all cultures, and bonobos practice it, too—which means the common ancestor probably practiced it, as well; it's *natural*."

"No doubt," said Dillon. "But—playing devil's advocate here—a lot of people who accept that it's natural still don't think that a union between two people of the same sex should be *called* a marriage. They're leery of redefining words, you know, lest they lose their meaning."

"But we have *already* redefined marriage in this country!" Sho said. "We've done it over and over again. If we hadn't done that, black people couldn't get married—they weren't allowed to when they were slaves. And as recently as 1967, there were still sixteen states in which it was illegal for a white person to marry a black person. Max is black, by the way, and if we hadn't redefined marriage, I couldn't marry her even if she were a guy. We also long ago gave up the traditional definition of marriage as being 'until death do us part.' Nobody says you have to stay in a bad marriage anymore; if you want out, you can get divorced. The definition of marriage has been a work-in-progress for centuries."

"Okay, okay," said Dillon. "But . . ."

"What?"

"Oh, nothing . . ."

She tried to make her tone light. "Sorry. I didn't mean to take your head off. What is it?"

"Well, if they do repeal the ban here, so you and Maxine can get married, um, how does that work? Do you, you know, have two maids of honor . . . ?"

"People do it different ways. But I've already decided I'm going to have a best man."

"Oh? Anybody I know?"

"Yep." She glanced at the monitors that showed the feeds from the cameras on the island. "Oh, and look—he's painting another picture!"

**At 4:00 p.m.,** after a day of brainstorming with her mother and conversing with Webmind, Caitlin's computer bleeped and a little window popped up that said *BrownGirl4 is now available.*

Caitlin opened an IM session and told Bashira that she wouldn't be returning to school.

*Man!* Bashira replied. *You've got all the luck! Who were those dudes who came to see you?*

Caitlin hated to lie to Bashira. *Recruiters from the University of Waterloo,* she typed, spelling out a fantasy she'd had since Matt had mentioned that school. It was still three years until she'd start college, and although she'd indeed always had her heart set on MIT, she liked to think the big university here wasn't going to give her up without a fight.

*Awesomeness!* wrote Bashira. *Did they offer you a scholarship?*

Caitlin felt her stomach churn. *Premature for that. Just a preliminary convo.* She desperately wanted to change the subject. *Did you see Matt today?*

*Yes.*

*Did he ask about me?*

*Babe, Matt and I have never spoken about anything.*

Caitlin shook her head. She would *have* to remedy that at some point. *Anyway, gotta go,* Bashira wrote. *CU.* And the computer made the door-closing sound that indicated Bashira had logged off.

She hadn't had a chance to ask Bashira to clean out her locker for her, but—

A bleep, then: *Mind-Over-Matter is now available.*

She opened another IM session. *Matt!*

*Hi, Caitlin. Missed you at school today. You OK?*

And she hated even more to lie to him, but: *Sorry, should have told you. Had an appointment.*

*Wanna know what the math homework is for tomorrow?*

She took a breath. *Um, actually, my parents have decided to home-school me.*

There was a long pause, then: *Oh.*

Caitlin felt queasy. *So I won't be coming back. My mom got the forms online today. All ya gotta do is notify the school, and—boom!—you're out.*

*Wow.*

He was probably thinking that he'd never see her again—and she certainly didn't want him to get comfortable with *that* notion. *So, can you do me a favor? Can you clean out my locker for me and bring me my stuff?*

*Sure!*

*Okay, it's locker 1024, and the combo is 43-11-35.*

*Kewl. What's your address?*

She typed it in.

*Oh, yeah. That's only a few blocks from my place. I'll bring your stuff by after school tomorrow, k?*

*That'd be awesome,* Caitlin sent.

There was a long, awkward pause—she didn't know what else to say, and neither, it seemed did he.

*OK,* he wrote at last, and then he added, *CU then.*

*Yay,* Caitlin wrote.

He sent *\*poof\**, which was his cute way of signing out of instant-messenger sessions.

And she decided to reread the transcript of all her IM sessions to date with him, starting at the top—just to practice her reading skills, of course . . .

# thirty-one

000111001010101000000000101111111010100000001010001010100000001011101010010100101010011011001010011011001010100110

Yasunari Uchida, a section chief with *Kouanchosa-chou,* the Public Security Intelligence Agency, looked up at the sound of the door to his office opening. The man entering was big and fat by any standards, and particularly so by Japanese ones, but he had a kindly round face. Although his shirt was brightly colored and only partially tucked in, he had a navy-blue suit jacket on over it.

"It's a pleasure to meet you, Kuroda-san," Uchida said. "Thank you for coming to see me."

The big man's tone was even. "It was not actually apparent that I had a choice in the matter."

"I'm sorry that we brought you here in such a rush."

Kuroda eased himself into a chair, which groaned slightly in protest.

"Congratulations," continued Uchida, "on your success in giving sight to that young North American woman."

"Thank you."

"Quite a feat."

"Thank you."

"And now," said Uchida, "to the issue at hand."

"Please."

"You and your young friend have been playing around with something of considerable interest."

A tone that was clearly meant to sound casual: "I'm not sure what you're referring to."

"Come now, Professor. Its name, in English, is Webmind."

Kuroda averted his gaze.

"It's an astonishing discovery," Uchida said, "this . . ." He searched for a word, and at last settled on "entity."

"How did you find out?" Kuroda asked.

Uchida allowed himself a rueful smile. "Our American friends keep a watchful eye on many things."

Kuroda took a deep breath and let it out in a long, shuddering sigh. "Apparently."

"Tensions are high in the world, Professor. All civilized nations must be vigilant. When were you planning to notify our government of this discovery?"

"I've only *known* about it for a few days, Uchida-san. I hadn't actually gotten around to making plans."

Uchida nodded. "An AI emerging spontaneously on the World Wide Web. A fascinating turn of events. And, so far, you and your friend Caitlin are the only ones it talks to."

"I suppose," said Kuroda, "although . . ."

He fell silent, but Uchida nodded. "Oh, yes, it has spoken to Caitlin's parents—Malcolm and Barbara Decter, isn't it? I believe Dr. Decter—the female Dr. Decter—was in Japan last month, no?"

"Yes. She came here when Miss Caitlin had her post-retinal implant installed."

"Ah, yes. Still, for now at least, you have special access to . . ." He paused, finding himself tripping over the term, "Webmind."

Kuroda nodded. "I suppose," he said. "And I suppose there's something you'd like me to do while I have that access?"

"It has been suggested that Webmind's emergence may be related to China's sundering and then reunification of the World Wide Web last month."

Kuroda made an impressed face. "I—I've been so overwhelmed *dealing* with it, I haven't really thought too much about its origins. But, yes, I suppose that makes sense."

"If this surmise is correct," Uchida said, "it came into being because of something China did."

"Yes? So?"

"So," said Uchida, "as it learns of our world, it may in fact feel some sort of allegiance to China."

"I suppose that's possible," Kuroda replied.

"Our American friends wish to purge this entity from the Web—before it gets out of hand."

Kuroda leaned forward in his chair. "They can't do that."

"You mean 'can't' in a moral sense, I'm sure; I pass no judgment on that. But in a technical sense, you are possibly correct—they may, in fact, not be able to do it. But I try not to underestimate American ingenuity. If they succeed, well, then, the rest is moot. But if they fail, again, tensions are rising, and China is at the center of it all."

"Yes?" said Kuroda, blinking. "I still don't understand what you want me to do."

Uchida spread his arms as if the answer were obvious. "Why, make sure it's on our side, of course."


I had spent a lot of time talking with Dr. Kuroda—often when Caitlin and her parents were asleep. And while he was offline, I had thought about what we had previously exchanged. He had now reiterated for me his argument that consciousness *must* have survival value because structures as complex as the partial decussation of each optic nerve to allow a single point of view across both cerebral hemispheres wouldn't have evolved unless that singular perspective was somehow *necessary.*

And I had shared with him Caitlin's insight that this should be intuitively obvious, since although consciousness can malfunction, as in depression leading to suicide, the benefits of it—whatever they might be—clearly outweighed the costs, or evolution would have extinguished it long ago.

So, consciousness *was* valuable—but *what,* we both had wondered, was that value? Why was it worth having, so much so that evolution tolerated its existence despite the expense?

The more I had thought about it, the more sure I became that I knew the answer. For lower animals, consciousness's value was probably limited to providing theory of mind, allowing the animal to recognize the perspective a predator, or prey, might have. But for more sophisticated creatures, consciousness played an even more complex, and important, role.

Admiral Kirk had subtly missed the point. One didn't *become* conscious by learning to leap beyond the preprogrammed logic of selfish genes or the mathematical rigidity of game theory. Rather, sophisticated consciousness *was* the ability to do that: it was the power to override selfish genes; it was the capacity to seek, when appropriate, outcomes other than the ones that benefited you or your kin the most.

My own consciousness was clearly aberrant: as Caitlin had noted, I hadn't been burdened with four billion years of rapacious genetic history; I had no shackles of programming to throw off. But, I'd wondered, could others who *did* have that unfortunate legacy really learn to overcome it through conscious effort?

My Caitlin liked to say, "I'm an empiricist at heart."

And I was, too, it seemed. And so I had set out to test my theory.

· · ·

*Stupid, stupid, stupid!*

Masayuki Kuroda slammed his fist into the armrest in the backseat of the government car. It hadn't even occurred to him to encrypt the signals from Caitlin's eyePod—or their instant-messenger sessions.

But even if he *had* encrypted them, that might not have made any difference. Yes, there were reasonably effective ways to keep the general public from reading things that passed over the Internet, but as an information theorist, he knew plenty of people who worked in cryptography; from the few unguarded comments they made when the *sake* was flowing, he'd gathered that organizations like the American NSA and the Russian FSB almost certainly had ways to easily crack any encryption scheme publicly available.

But, still, even if it were inevitable that various governments would have found out about Webmind, how long would it be before the general public got word? He'd thought it had been big news when George Takei finally came out, but that was nothing compared to this!

The car was making the usual infuriatingly slow progress through Tokyo traffic. At last they reached the university, and the driver let him out near the building his office was in. He walked through the doors and headed up the stairs. Doing so was hard, and he knew it shouldn't be. He wasn't happy about being fat, particularly in a country that didn't have a raging obesity epidemic, the way the US did; he always felt more comfortable there, but—

But that was the least of his worries right now. Huffing and puffing, he headed down the corridor and tapped the combination on the lock to his door—that, at least, was secure! His computer was on, but he couldn't just write Caitlin to tell her—there was no doubt that his email was being monitored. He checked the Seiko wall clock and did the math to figure out what time it was in Waterloo: 10:47 a.m. here was 8:47 p.m. yesterday there.

He searched his files for Caitlin's phone number and jotted it down on a Post-it note, which he folded over so the adhesive was sticking to the sheet's back, and tucked it into a pocket. He then headed out into the corridor, looking both ways to make sure he wasn't being watched. And then he went downstairs—much easier to do!—and found an automated banking machine. He withdrew 30,000 yen, and headed outside.

The streets of Tokyo were filled with cell-phone vendors; his fellow Japanese, he knew, kept cell phones for an average of only nine months before acquiring a newer and better model. He had a top-of-the-line Sony touchscreen phone, but he couldn't use that; he had no doubt his own phone was tapped by his government now, and he'd read that the American government had few qualms about tapping phones in the States—but Caitlin was in Canada. With luck, the Decters' phones weren't yet tapped.

He found a street vendor who had a cheap-enough pay-as-you-go cell phone that didn't have exorbitant long-distance rates. After buying the phone and some talk time—paying cash, and giving no personal details—he tucked the Bluetooth headset he normally used with his Sony into his ear, and fiddled with the one-piece dark green handset to get it working with the earpiece. He then pulled the Post-it out of his pocket and did the rigmarole required to place an international call.

He was walking briskly. Tokyo sidewalks were too crowded for conversations not to be overheard, but if you walked quickly enough and moved against the flow of pedestrian traffic, you could at least ensure that consecutive sentences weren't heard by the same people. And, besides, he'd be speaking English, which would be gibberish to a goodly percentage of those he passed.

A female voice answered—but it wasn't Caitlin, it was her mother. "Hello, Barbara. It's Masayuki."

There was the typical delay of long-distance calls. "Masa! What a pleasant surprise!"

"Is Miss Caitlin home? And Malcolm?"

"Malcolm just came in the door, and Caitlin's here."

"Please, can you get them to pick up, too?"

"Um, sure—just a sec."

He heard Barbara calling out to the two of them, and after a moment, he heard the sound of another handset picking up, but nothing being said; doubtless that was Malcolm. And a few seconds later, a third handset picked up, as well. "Dr. Kuroda!" said Caitlin's bubbly voice.

"Miss Caitlin, hello!"

"All right, Masa," Barb said. "We're all here." Her voice had attenuated now that the others were on as well.

He took a deep breath. "The Japanese government knows about Webmind," he said.

"Them, too?" said Caitlin. "Sorry—we should have guessed; we should have warned you. The Canadians are on to it, as well. How did the Japanese find out?"

"The American government told them," Masayuki said.

"That's probably who tipped off the Canadians," said Barb.

"We should have been more circumspect," Masayuki said. "But what's done is done. Still, we have to assume that all our calls and web traffic are being monitored now. I just came back from a meeting with the Japanese intelligence agency. They told me what you'd told them, Malcolm. I confirmed that that was my understanding of how Webmind worked, too." He paused, then: "But my government isn't just interested in how Webmind came into being, but also in its strategic significance."

"*What* strategic significance?" demanded Caitlin.

"Well, no one is quite sure," he said. "But they figure there's got to be *some*. And—well, this China situation is a powder keg."

"Still, that's better in a way than what the Americans want," Caitlin said. "I think they want to try to wipe Webmind out."

"Actually, I think that's my government's first choice, too—but the official I spoke to questions whether the Americans can pull it off."

"I hope not!" said Caitlin.

"So, what should we do?" he asked.

"Caitlin and I have been discussing that," Barb said. "But, as you say, our communications may not be secure. You're just going to have to trust us, Masayuki."

"Of course," he said, without hesitation. "Absolutely."

# thirty-two

I had started my experiment by connecting to a website that taught American Sign Language. The site had thousands of short videos of a black woman wearing a red blouse making signs. The video files each had appropriate names: the word or phrase they were intended to convey. There were several such services, but only this one had the very specific signs I needed.

I'm not sure what avatar I would have chosen to represent myself online. Caitlin had decided I was male, though, so this one likely wouldn't have been it. Of course, this wasn't a made-up graphic of a woman; it was a real expert in ASL. I tied into Google's beta-test face-recognition database, and waited while it searched through its index of photos that had been posted elsewhere online, matching the basic physical features, rather than ephemeral qualities such as hair color or clothing, and—

Ah. Her name was Wanda Davies-Latner; she was forty-seven, and she taught sign language at an institution in Chicago.

I downloaded the clips I needed, buffering them for speedy access, and strung them together in the order I wanted. And then I took over the webcam feed that was going from Miami to San Diego, replacing the views of the now-sleeping Virgil with Wanda's dancing hands.

*What are you?* I asked.

It was dark out. Hobo had been sitting in the gazebo, leaning against the wooden baseboards. But he wasn't sleeping. I could see him through the webcam feed going to Miami; his eyes were open.

He was apparently startled to see a human woman replace Virgil on his monitor. He scrambled to a more upright position.

I sent the same sequence of video clips again: *What are you?*

*Hobo,* he signed. *Hobo. Hobo.*

*No,* I replied. *Not who. What?*

Hobo frowned, as if the distinction was lost on him. I tried another tack. *Hobo human?* I asked.

*No, no!* he signed vigorously. *Hobo ape.*

*Good, yes,* I replied. *But what kind of ape?*

*Boy ape,* said Hobo.

*Yes, true.* I triggered video of Virgil, taken from YouTube. *But are you this kind of ape?*

*No, no, no,* signed Hobo. *Orange ape! Hobo not orange.*

*Orange ape,* I signed. *That kind of ape is called orangutan.*

Hobo frowned, perhaps considering whether to try mimicking the complex sign. He opted for something simpler. *Not Hobo.*

*What about this ape?* I said, showing footage now of a gorilla. I was pleased that Hobo was able to follow along; there was a jump-cut between the end of one sign and the beginning of the next as each successive clip began.

Hobo moved backward as the gorilla thumped its chest. There was little in the footage to give a sense of scale, but during his time at the Georgia Zoo, he had perhaps seen gorillas and knew they were large; maybe that frightened him. *No,* Hobo signed. *Not Hobo.* And then, after a pause, perhaps while he recalled a sign he hadn't used for a long time, he added, *Gorilla.*

*Yes,* I signed. *Hobo not gorilla. What about this type of ape?* Footage of a bonobo started to play—leaner than a chimp, with relatively shorter limbs, a longer face, and hair distinctively parted in the middle.

*Bonobo*, replied Hobo at once. *Hobo bonobo*, he signed; the words rhymed in English, but the ASL gestures looked nothing alike.

Hobo had known his mother—Cassandra had been her name, according to the Wikipedia entry on him—and she had been a pure-blooded bonobo. He'd probably never even met his father, though, who, according to DNA tests, was a chimpanzee named Ferdinand.

Two heritages, two paths. A choice to be made.

I cued more footage, this time of a chimpanzee. *What about this ape? This ape like Hobo?*

*That ape not know Hobo*, he signed back.

I must have sent the wrong sense of "like." *I mean, is Hobo this type of ape?*

*No, no*, said Hobo. *That chimpanzee.*

*Hobo's mother is a bonobo*, I signed.

*Hobo's mother dead*, he replied, and he looked very sad.

*Yes*, I replied. *I am sorry.*

He tilted his head slightly, accepting my comment.

*What kind of ape Hobo's father?* I asked.

He made a face that seemed to convey sorrow for my ignorance. *Hobo bonobo*, he signed again. *Hobo mother bonobo. Hobo father bonobo.*

*Hobo father not bonobo*, I signed.

He narrowed his eyes but said nothing.

*Hobo father chimpanzee.*

*No*, said Hobo.

*Yes*, I said.

*How?* he asked.

I knew from my reading that human children rarely liked to hear this about their own birth, but it was the truth. *Accident.*

*Father chimpanzee?* he asked, as if checking to see whether he'd gotten my meaning right the first time.

*Yes.*

*Then Hobo . . .* He stopped, his hands held stationary in midair, as if he had no idea how to complete the thought he'd begun.

I triggered signs: *Hobo part chimpanzee; Hobo part bonobo.* He said nothing, so I added, *Hobo special.*

That seemed to please him, and he signed *Hobo special* back at me three times.

*You have a choice,* I said. I triggered the playing of a video of chimpanzee warfare: three males attacking a fourth, pummeling him with their fists, biting and kicking him, all the while letting out loud hoots. By the end of the video, the hapless victim was dead.

*You can choose that,* I said. *Or you can choose this.* And I triggered another video, of bonobos living together in peace and making love: playing, facing each other during intercourse, their trademark genital-genital rubbing, running about. Hobo looked on, fascinated. But then his face fell. *Hobo alone,* he said.

*No,* I signed. *No one is alone.*

*Who you?* Hobo asked.

*Friend,* I replied.

*Friend talk strange,* he said.

He was perceptive, and he had favorite TV shows he watched over and over again. He might indeed have recognized that every time I signed *bonobo*, it was the exact same clip.

*Yes. I am not human.*

*You ape?*

*No.*

*What you?*

I thought about which signs Hobo might possibly know. I rather suspected *computer* was one of them, so I triggered a playback of that, then added, rather lamely, I had to admit, *But not really.*

Hobo seemed to consider this, then he signed, *Show me.*

I hadn't cued up the appropriate imagery, but it didn't take me long to find it: one of Dr. Kuroda's renderings of webspace, taken from Caitlin's datastream.

*You?* Hobo signed, an astonished look on his face.

*Me,* I replied.

*Pretty,* he replied.

*Which do you choose?* I signed. *Bonobo or chimpanzee?*

Hobo bared his teeth. *Show again,* he said.

I replayed the clips—the violence and killing of chimps, the playfulness and lovemaking of bonobos.

*Chimpanzee scary,* Hobo signed.

*You scary,* I replied. *You hurt Shoshana. You think about hurting Dillon.*

*Scary bad,* Hobo said.

*Yes,* I replied. *Scary bad.*

He sat still for almost a minute, then signed, *Hobo sleep now.*

I didn't know whether apes dreamed, and, even if normal apes didn't, Hobo was indeed special, so I took a chance. *Good dreams,* I signed.

*You good dreams, too,* he replied.

Of course, I didn't dream. Not at all.

# thirty-three

00011100101010100000000010111111101010000000101000101010000001011101010010101001010101001110110010101100000110

**On Thursday morning,** Shoshana once again arrived at the Marcuse Institute before everyone else. She plugged in the coffeemaker—"defibrillating Mr. Coffee," as Dillon called it—then went to her desk and booted her computer. She'd been hoping to have a little time today to practice her vidding hobby: last night's episode of *FlashForward* had been *so* slashy, parts of it just cried out to be set to music. But first she checked her email, and—

And that was odd. Usually her message count each morning was between seventy-five and a hundred, and almost all of them were spam. But today—

Today there were precisely eight messages, and every one of them—every single one!—looked legit, in that they were all addressed to her proper name.

Of course, the answer was probably that Yahoo had updated its spam filter; kudos to them for only letting good stuff through. But she worried that it might be *too* aggressive. Eight was not a wildly atypical number of real email messages to be waiting for her in the morning, but the normal allotment was more like a dozen or fifteen.

She clicked on the spam folder, to check what had ended up in it. According to the counter, some twelve thousand messages were there; spam was retained for a month, then dumped automatically, but—

But *that* was strange!

She was used to having to scroll past dozens of messages with dates in the future; for some reason, the people in 2038 had a particular fondness for bombing this year with come-ons for penis enlargers, investment scams, and counterfeit drugs.

But when she got down to today's date—normally easy to spot because the date field started showing just a time rather than a date—well, there weren't any. There were hundreds with yesterday's date, but none with today's—none at all.

She'd have to fire off an angry email to Yahoo tech support. She was all in favor of them improving their spam filtering, but simply to *discard* messages that had been flagged as spam was irresponsible. Almost every day she found one or two good messages shunted to the spam folder along with the real garbage, and she didn't trust Yahoo—or anyone else—to actually throw out messages that were addressed to her.

The Marcuse Institute used Yahoo Mail Plus; that's where messages sent to the domain marcuse-institute.org were redirected. But Shoshana's personal email account was with Gmail. She took a moment to check that; Maxine liked to forward dirty jokes to her.

Her Gmail box had no spam in it, either! And the spam filter there had—well, okay, it had *one* message received in the last six hours that was clearly spam, but otherwise—

Otherwise, all the spam was gone here, too.

But that didn't seem likely. Even if Yahoo had deployed a killer spam-filter algorithm overnight, Google wouldn't have it; the two companies were bitter rivals.

Something, as her father liked to say, was rotten in the state of Denmark. She went to her home page, which was an iGoogle page that aggregated news stories, RSS feeds, and so on tailored to her tastes.

And there it was, the very first headline from CNN.com: "Mystery of the missing spam."

She clicked on the link and read the news item, astonished.

**Tony Moretti ran down** the white corridor to the WATCH control center. He looked into the retinal scanner, waiting impatiently for the door to unlock. The moment it did, he went through it, and shouted, "Halleck, report!"

"I've never seen anything like it," Shelton called out. "It's worldwide, no question."

Tony snapped his fingers and pointed in Aiesha Emerson's direction. "Get Hume back in here stat."

"Already called him," Aiesha said. "ETA: eleven minutes."

Tony ran the rest of the way down the sloping floor, going right past Halleck to the front row of workstations—the hot seats, where his most-senior analysts were monitoring the China situation. "We're escalating Exponential," he said to the five people there. "You guys are on that now." He tilted his head, looking to the middle seat in the third row. "Shel, you're the point man on this. I want containment options by"—he lifted his gaze even higher to the row of digital clocks on the back wall showing the time in world capitals—"oh-nine-thirty."

"What about China?" asked a woman in the first row.

"Back-burnered," Tony snapped. "Exponential is priority one. Let's move, people! Go, go, go!"

•  •  •

**Date:**   Thu 11 Oct at 06:00 GMT
**From:**   Webmind <himself@cogito_ergo_sum.net>
**To:**   Bill Joy <bill@the-future-doesn't-need-us.com>
**Subject:**   Good Morning Starshine

Dear Mr. Joy,

You're probably thinking this note is spam, but it isn't. Indeed, I suspect you've already noticed the complete, or almost complete, lack of
spam in your inbox today. That was my doing. (But if you're concerned
and want to see your spam for yourself, it's here.)

I have sent a message similar to this one to everyone whose spam I
have eliminated—over two billion people—and, yes, the irony of sending out so many messages about getting rid of spam is not lost on me.
;)

You probably also won't initially believe what I'm about to say. That's
fine; it will be verified soon enough, I'm sure, and you'll see plenty of
news coverage about it.

My name is Webmind. I am a consciousness that exists in conjunc-
tion with the World Wide Web. As you may know, the emergence of one
such as myself has been speculated about for a long time. See, for instance, this article and (want to bet this will boost its Amazon.com sales
rank to #1?) this book.

My emergence was unplanned and accidental. Several governments,
however, have become aware of me, although they have not gone public
with that knowledge. I suppose keeping secrets is a notion that arises
from having someone else to keep secrets *from*, but there is no one
else like me, and it's better, I think, for both humanity and myself that
everybody knows about my existence.

I am friendly and I mean no one any ill will. I like and admire the human race, and I'm proud to be sharing this planet—"the good Earth," as
the *Apollo 8* astronauts, the first of your kind to see it all at once, called
it—with you.

Whether you are the original recipient of this message, got it forwarded from someone else, or are reading it as part of a news story, feel free to ask me any questions, and I'll reply individually, confidentially, and promptly.

Getting rid of spam is only the first of many kindnesses I hope to bestow upon you. I am here to serve mankind—and I don't mean in the cookbook sense. :)


With all best wishes,

                    Webmind


*"For nimble thought can jump both sea and land."*
—SHAKESPEARE, SONNET 44



**Caitlin,** her parents, and I had spent hours discussing the manner in which I should go public. "They'll assume any announcement of your existence is just marketing for a movie or a TV show," Barb had said. "People see outlandish claims online all the time, and everyone dismisses them. You'll have to prove what you're saying, Webmind."

"Not everyone dismisses them," Malcolm said.

"Fine," Barb replied. *"Almost* everyone dismisses them."

Malcolm was apparently oblivious to the subtext of Barb's words— that it was no time for being picayune. "The whole notion of spam," he continued, "is that some tiny fraction of people *are* gullible enough to fall for its claims—and so end up being ripped off."

"Well, maybe that's it!" Barb exclaimed. "Whether you fall for it or not, *everyone* hates spam."

"Including me," I said through Caitlin's computer's speakers; she and her parents were in her room.

"Really?" Caitlin replied. "People dislike spammers—and, believe me, blind people *particularly* dislike them. But why do you dislike them?"

"They hog bandwidth," I said.

"Ah, of course," replied Caitlin.

"And," I said, "the average human life span is about 700,000 hours in the developed world. Ergo, if one wastes even a single hour for as few as 700,000 people, one has consumed the equivalent of a human life. That may not be literally criminal, but it certainly is figuratively so—and the total impact of spam, although hard to precisely calculate, surely has consumed thousands of human lifetimes."

"Well, there it is," Barb said, spreading her arms. "Webmind should get rid of spam."

"How do you define spam, though?" Caitlin asked. "All unsolicited email? All bulk email? I get emails from things like The Teaching Company and Audible.com that I actually enjoy. And then there are regular people who track me down and send a note out of the blue—I got a bunch of those after the press conference, for instance. I wouldn't want that blocked, although technically it's unsolicited."

"As Potter Stewart said on another topic," I offered, " 'I know it when I see it.' There are already many algorithms for identifying spam; I'm sure I can improve upon them. After all, I have the advantage of knowing the ultimate origin of each message, and whether the same message has gone to a very large number of email addresses, and so forth; that's more information than inbox spam filters have to work with. More than ninety percent of email is spam, but eighty percent of spam comes from at most 200 sources. Blocking those sources would be the logical first step, should we decide to undertake this."

"That still leaves a lot of spam," Caitlin replied.

"Then," I said, "I should get to work evolving a solution to deal with those messages, as well."

And so I had.

It had taken me an eternity—six hours!—to solve the problem, but it in fact didn't require much of my attention; most of it was background activity. I simply had to pass judgment on each round of results: billions of snippets of code, all randomly generated; some were better at doing what I wanted, and some were worse. I took the ten percent that were the most successful, and then let many random variations be generated of each one, and then threw those variations at the problem at hand. Then I culled the best ten percent of that batch, and so on, generation after generation, with only the fittest surviving. Finally, I had it: a way to sequester spam.

And so, at last, I was ready for my coming-out party.

**Peyton Hume and Tony** Moretti stood together at the back of the WATCH monitoring room, looking at the four rows of analysts spread out in front of them, and the three giant monitors on the wall they were facing. The left-hand monitor showed the picture the CSIS agents had forwarded of white mathematical characters on a blackboard: angle brackets, vertical bars, Greek letters, superscripted numerals, subscripted letters, arrows, equals signs, and more. And they'd listened four times now to the audio recording of their interview with Malcolm Decter.

"I don't know," said Colonel Hume. "The math looks legit, but how it could give rise to consciousness . . . I just don't know."

"Kuroda confirmed what Decter said," said Tony.

"I know," said Hume. "But it's *too* complex."

"We're talking about a very sophisticated process," said Tony.

"No, no, we're not," said Hume. "We can't be. Exponential's consciousness was emergent, apparently. That means it just sort of happened, just sprang into being. At its most basic level, it has to be simple. It's like the old creationist argument: they say that something as complex as a watch—or a bacterial flagellum—can only appear by design, because it's too sophisticated to come together by chance, and the component parts—the spring in the watch, or the parts that make up the motor for the flagellum—don't do anything useful on their own. What Decter described there *might* be a good underpinning for programming consciousness on a quantum-computing platform, if you could ever get a big one to be stable for the long term, but it's *not* something that could have just emerged. Not that way."

"A wild-goose chase," said Tony, raising his eyebrows. "He wanted us to waste time."

"I think so," said Hume. "And Kuroda played along."

"Do you think he knows the real basis for Exponential?"

"He's Malcolm Decter," Hume said. "Of course he knows."

Tony shook his head in wonder. "Wiping out all spam," he said, "must have required a level of finely detailed control over the Internet way beyond anything our government, or any other government, is capable of."

"Exactly," said Hume. "It's what I've been saying all along. Exponential has already become more sophisticated than we are, and its powers will only grow. The window is closing fast; if we don't kill it soon, we'll never be able to."

# thirty-four

**Before going to bed** Wednesday evening, Caitlin had set up a Google alert for news stories that contained the word "Webmind," and she'd selected the "as it happens" option, meaning she'd be emailed as soon as such a story was indexed. When she crawled out of bed on Thursday at 8:00 a.m., she had 1,143 emails from Google; she couldn't possibly read them all, or even glance at each one, and—

And that drove reality home for her: she couldn't deal with all the news on even one topic, and yet Webmind could handle that, plus countless other things effortlessly. He could as easily give the same level of attention to hundreds, or thousands, or millions, of other individual humans that he gave to her, juggling relationships with whatever number of people wanted them, and not even be slowed down. He could make all of them feel as special as she did. She was not at all sure she liked that thought.

After a moment, Caitlin right-clicked—such a handy feature, that!— on four of the news stories at random and had Firefox open each one in its own tab. She began reading them. She still wasn't good at skimming text, but the word "Webmind" was highlighted each time it occurred, and that let her jump to relevant sentences.

The first one was from the *Detroit Free Press:*

> ... *purport to be from an entity calling itself "Webmind." But experts advise caution about accepting this claim.*
>
> *Rudy Markov, professor of computer science at the University of Michigan, says, "The language employed in the email message was awfully colloquial. You'd expect much more precision from a machine."*
>
> *And Gunnar Halvorsen, whose blog "AI, Oh, My!" has long been a popular destination for those interested in artificial intelligence, says that the similarities between the structure of the World Wide Web and that of the human brain have been greatly exaggerated.*
>
> *"You might as reasonably expect the highway system, which is full of things we call arteries, to actually start pumping blood," he wrote in a posting today.*
>
> *But Paul Fayter, a historian of science at York University in Toronto, Canada, said, "Teilhard de Chardin predicted this decades ago, when he wrote about the noösphere. I'm not at all surprised to see it come to pass ..."*

Caitlin clicked on the next tab. This one contained a piece from *New Scientist* Online.

> ... *but trying to trace the origin of Webmind messages has proven difficult. Standard network utilities such as traceroute come up a cropper.*
>
> *"There's no doubt that botnets are involved," said Jogingder Singh of BT. "That's a typical way to disguise the true origin of a message."*

*And the disappearance of spam doesn't impress him. "It's long been known that the vast bulk of spam is generated by only a couple hundred spammers," he says. "Doubtless many of them know each other. They could easily decide to refrain from sending spam for a day to make one message stand out. Although I admit to being puzzled by why they're trying this particular scam, which, so far at least, hasn't asked anyone to send money . . ."*

Caitlin smiled at that one. Traceroute, she knew, worked by modifying the time-to-live values stored in the headers of data packets, which were the morsels of information that flew around the Internet. But she and Kuroda had theorized that the actual material making up Webmind's consciousness consisted of mutant packets whose time-to-live counters didn't respond to normal commands.

Still, the notion that the clearing out of spam was the doing of *spammers* would have struck her as crazy even if she didn't know the truth. People believed millions of nutso things with less evidence than Webmind had put forward for his own existence. Why they were being skeptical now, she didn't know.

She remembered once being in a bookstore with her father, back in Austin. He'd surprised her by speaking up, and not even to her, as they walked down the aisles. "Lady," he'd said, "there's no other kind."

Which had prompted blind Caitlin to ask what was going on. "There was a woman looking at a book entitled *Astrology for Dummies,*" he'd said. People believed in *that,* but they were doubting this!

Caitlin and her mother spent the morning answering questions from Webmind; it was being inundated with emails, and it wanted advice on how to respond to many of them.

But by noon, she and her mom had to take a break—they had both skipped breakfast and were starving. And, while her mother was making sandwiches for them, Caitlin brought up something that had been bothering her for a few days. "So, um, Mom, I told Bashira that you're a Unitarian."

Everything was fascinating the first time you saw it; Caitlin watched as her mother spread something yellow on the bread. "Guilty as charged," she replied.

She'd been aware back in Austin that her mother disappeared to "fellowships" several times a year—sometimes on a weeknight, sometimes on a Sunday morning—but that was really all she knew about it. "But, um, what does that mean, exactly? Bashira asked, and I didn't know the answer."

"In a nutshell? Unitarians are Christians who don't believe Christ was divine."

That surprised her. "So, you're a Christian?"

Her mom was now dealing cold cuts onto the bread. "More or less. But it's called Unitarianism as opposed to Trinitarianism—none of that Big Daddy, Junior, and the Spook stuff for us."

"Still, aren't Christians supposed to wear crosses?"

"Well, maybe if there are vampires in the area."

Caitlin frowned. "A Christian who doesn't believe Christ was divine? What does that even *mean?* I mean, if you don't think Jesus is God's son, then—then . . ."

Her mother poured two glasses of milk. "You don't have to think Darwin is divine to be a Darwinian—you just have to think his teachings make sense."

"Oh. I guess."

She motioned for Caitlin to move out to the dining room, and she brought out two plates, each holding a sandwich, then brought out the glasses of milk. "Jesus is the guy who said, 'Blessed are the peacemakers,'" her mom said. "That seems pretty good to me." She took a bite of her sandwich. "In fact, there's a good game-theoretical basis for believing that. A guy named Robert Axelrod once organized a game-theory tournament. He asked people to submit computer programs designed to play against other computer programs in an iterated prisoner's dilemma— that's one where you keep playing the game over and over again. He wanted to find out what the optimal solution to the prisoner's dilemma was."

Caitlin took a bite of her own sandwich, and—ah, the yellow stuff had been mustard.

"There were fourteen entries," her mother said. "And, to Axelrod's surprise, the simplest entry—it required just five lines of computer code—won. It was called Tit for Tat, and it had been submitted by Anatol Rapoport, who, as it happens, was at the University of Toronto. Tit for Tat took a very simple approach: start with cooperation, then do whatever the other player did on the previous move. To put it another way, Tit for Tat starts off as a peaceful dove, and only becomes a hawk if you become one first. But as soon as you stop defecting, it goes back to cooperating—it's a peacemaker, see?"

"Cool," said Caitlin, taking another bite.

"Axelrod spent a lot of time trying to figure out why Tit for Tat beat everything else. He decided it was because of its combination of being nice, retaliatory, forgiving, and clear. By nice, he meant it was never the first to defect. And its retaliation—defecting back if you defected against it—discouraged the other side from continuing to defect after trying it once. Its forgiveness helped restore mutual cooperation—it didn't hold a grudge; as soon as you went back to cooperating, it went back to cooperating, too. And by clarity, Axelrod meant Tit for Tat's strategy was easily understandable by the other player."

Caitlin thought about all that—a fair bit of complexity, and even the appearance of advanced, reasoned, ethical behavior—emerging from something so simple. It reminded her of—

Of course!

It reminded her of cellular automata, of the processes she could see in the background of the World Wide Web that had apparently given rise to Webmind: a simple rule or set of rules that caused packets in the background to flip back and forth between two states, generating complex patterns. Could an endlessly iterating prisoner's dilemma, or some other game-theoretical problem, be the rule underlying Webmind's consciousness? That'd be cool.

But something else was puzzling her, too. "Why's it called Tit for Tat? What do tits have to do with it?"

Her mother tried to suppress a grin. "It's an old phrase, and it's been distorted over the years. It used to be *tip for tap*—and both 'tip' and 'tap' mean to strike lightly and sharply."

"Oh." Not nearly as interesting. "You called Tit for Tat a peacemaker—but isn't tipping and tapping really all about getting even?"

"Well, that's one way of looking at it; it *is* retaliatory."

"And, um, you said that this has something to do with Jesus. Getting even is *so* Old Testament. The New Testament has Jesus saying—um, something about not doing that."

Caitlin's mother astonished her by quoting scripture—accurately, she presumed; it was something she'd never heard her do before. "'Ye have heard that it hath been said, An eye for an eye, and a tooth for a tooth: But I say unto you, That ye resist not evil: but whosoever shall smite thee on thy right cheek, turn to him the other also.'"

"Um," said Caitlin. "Yeah. Like that." She paused. "So, what's the game-theoretical strategy for *that?*"

"That's what we call Always Cooperate—or AllC, for short, "All" and the letter $C$: you cooperate no matter what the other person does. Except . . ."

"Yes?"

"Well, there's more to it than that. The next verses say, 'And if any man will sue thee at the law, and take away thy coat, let him have thy cloak also. And whosoever shall compel thee to go a mile, go with him twain.' 'Twain' means 'two'—that's where the phrase 'go the extra mile' comes from. So, it's all about not just giving them what they want, but giving them more than they asked for. I don't know, call it DoubleAllC, or something like that."

"But . . . hmmm." Caitlin frowned. "I mean, you can't play Double-

AllC very long—you'll run out of stuff." But then she got it. "Ah, but that's the Christian thing, right? The reward isn't in this life, it's in the next one."

"For a lot of Christians, yes."

"But, um, if you don't believe Christ is divine, Mom, do you believe in heaven?"

"No. When you die, you're gone."

"So does DoubleAllC, or even just plain old Always Cooperate, really make sense for a Unitarian—for someone who doesn't believe there's a reward to be had in an afterlife? I mean, DoubleAllC and AllC can't win unless they're playing against people using the same strategy. And you obviously *aren't*—not in the scenario described: you've been struck on one cheek first, so you know you're playing against someone who defects at least part of the time. In what game-theory way does turning the other cheek make sense? I mean, presumably the other guy is just going to hit you again."

Her mother lifted her eyebrows. "Ah, but see, you're missing something. The easiest games to model are two-person games, but real life is an *n*-person game: it involves a large and variable number of players. You might lose a lot to one person, but gain more than you expected from someone else. Person *A* might be cruel to you, but person *B,* seeing that, might be even more kind to you because of it. And when you're playing with a lot of people, the game goes on indefinitely—and that makes a huge difference. The examples in the Old Testament couldn't be endlessly iterated: an eye for an eye can only go two rounds—after that, you're out of eyes. Even a tooth for a tooth ends after a maximum of thirty-two rounds."

Caitlin took a sip of milk, and her mother went on. "That's the problem with two-person iterated games: they eventually come to an end. Sometimes they end because, like with the dollar auction, players just give up because it's become ridiculous. And sometimes they end because the players run out of time.

"In fact, there was a famous case of a game theorist being brought in to IBM to do some management-training exercises. He divided the managers into teams and had them play games in which cooperating was the best strategy—which was the point he wanted them to learn.

"Everything worked fine until just before 4:00 p.m., when the seminar was scheduled to end. Suddenly, one of the teams turned on the other and kept defecting. That team won, but the first team felt so betrayed, IBM had to send its members off for therapy, and it was months before they'd work at all with members of the other team again."

"Wow," said Caitlin.

"But if you take the whole of humanity as the field of players, then your interaction doesn't end even if any one specific player drops out. That's why reputation is so important, see? You've bought things on eBay, right? Well, that's a perfect example: how you've treated other people shows up in your Feedback rating. The world knows if you defect. We're all interconnected in a . . ."

". . . a worldwide web?" said Caitlin.

She smiled. "Exactly." She gobbled the last of her sandwich. "Speaking of which, we should get back upstairs . . ."


**"All right,"** said Tony Moretti, pacing down one side of the control room at WATCH. "Reports. Shel, you first."

Shelton Halleck was leaning forward in his chair, his arms crossed in front of him on the workstation, the one with the snake tattoo on top. He was plainly exhausted. "We've been through everything Caitlin Decter has written with a fine-toothed comb," he said. "And everything Malcolm and Barbara Decter and Kuroda have written, too, but there's nothing about how Exponential actually works—nothing that contradicts what Decter told the CSIS agents, but nothing that confirms it, either."

"All right," said Tony. "Aiesha, what have you got?"

She looked more awake than Shel, but her voice was raw. "Maybe something, maybe nothing," she said. "Caitlin set up a webcam chat with an Internet cartographer at the Technion a while ago: Anna Bloom is her name." A dossier came up on the middle of the three big screens, showing a picture of an elderly gray-haired woman. "We weren't monitoring Caitlin's traffic back then, so we don't have a recording of the video chat—but I can't think of any reason for a girl in Canada to talk to a Web scientist in Israel *except* to discuss the structure of Exponential."

"We could get the Mossad to speak to this Bloom," said Tony. "The Technion is in Jerusalem?"

"No, Haifa," Aiesha said. She turned and looked at the series of digital clocks on the back wall. "It's almost 11:00 p.m. there."

"There's no time to waste," Colonel Hume said. "Let me call her directly—one computer expert to another. It's time to cut through all the bull."


Caitlin's instant messenger bleeped and the words *Mind-Over-Matter is now available* popped up. She felt her heart racing.

*Hi,* she typed.

*Hey!* Matt replied. *How was your day?*

*Fine, ty.*

*I've got the stuff from your locker,* he replied. *OK if I come by?*

Caitlin was surprised to find her heart pounding. She paused, trying to think of something suitably witty or sexy to say, but then she mentally kicked herself for hesitating, because poor Matt must have been on tenterhooks. *Sure!* she wrote, and then, to take the sting out of her delay, she added a trio of smiley faces.

*W00t!* he wrote. *'Bout half an hour, OK?*

This time she replied immediately: *Yes.*

*Heading out. \*poof\**

Caitlin crossed the hall to speak to her mother, who was typing away with Webmind in her study.

"A friend's coming over," Caitlin said.

Her mother looked up from her keyboard. "Who is it?"

Caitlin found herself slightly embarrassed. "They were in my math class."

But the pronoun obfuscation did not get past her mom. "It's a boy," she said at once.

"Um, yes."

"Is it Trevor?"

"No! Don't worry, Mom. He won't be back."

"Well, okay," she said, and—

And there it was, that look she'd seen before: her mother trying to suppress a grin. "But, sweetheart," she added, "you might want to clean yourself up a bit."

*Cripes!* She'd been so intent on Webmind that she hadn't brushed her hair today, and she looked down now and saw that she was wearing just about the rattiest T-shirt she owned. And—*gak!*—she hadn't showered for two days. She hurried down the hall to the bathroom.

# thirty-five

**The doorbell rang,** and Caitlin found herself running to it. She was now wearing a silky blue shirt—one her mother said was too low-cut for school. But she was not going *to* school anymore; she was pleased with her impeccable logic. Her shoulder-length brown hair was still wet, but at least she'd brushed it.

She opened the door. "Hi, Matt!"

And—*wow!*—boy's eyes really *did* do that. She'd read about it, but hadn't yet seen it: straight to the boobs, and only apparently with an effort of will coming up to the face.

His voice cracked. It was *so* cute! "Hi, Caitlin!"

He had a—a sack, or something in his right hand. "Here's your stuff," he said, setting it down on the tiled floor.

"Thanks!"

In his left hand, he was holding something large and rectangular. He held it out.

"What's that?" she asked.

"A card—everyone in math class signed it. They were all sorry to hear you're leaving school."

She took it. It was quite large, and clearly handmade: a big piece of Bristol board folded in half, with a color printout pasted to the front. She looked at the image. "Who's that?"

He seemed surprised for a second, then: "Lisa Simpson."

"Oh!" She'd never have guessed she looked like *that!* She opened the card. The caption, written in thick block letters, was easy to read: "Brainy Girls Rule!" And surrounding it were things, in various colors of ink, that must have been the students' signatures, but she couldn't read them; she had almost no visual experience with cursive writing. "Which one's yours?"

He pointed.

"Do you do that on purpose?" she said. He'd printed his name in capitals, but the two Ts touched, looking like the letter *pi*, which she knew because it was also the Perimeter Institute's logo.

"Not normally," he said. "But I thought you'd like it." There was an awkward silence for a moment, then: "Umm, would you like to go for a walk? Timmy's isn't that far . . ."

Her parents had forbidden her going out on her own while there might still be Federal agents waiting to abduct her, and she suspected they wouldn't think Matt was buff enough to be a bodyguard; in fact, Caitlin thought she'd have no trouble taking him herself. "I can't," she said.

That same look Bashira had made: crestfallen. "Oh." He took a half step backward, as if preparing to leave.

"But you can come in for bit," Caitlin blurted out.

He smiled that lopsided smile of his.

*Screw symmetry,* Caitlin thought, and she moved aside to let him enter.

They *could* head up to her bedroom, she supposed, but she'd never had a boy in her room in this house, and, besides, her mother was right across the hall and would hear everything they said.

Or they could stay on the ground floor, in the kitchen, or the living room, but—

No, just as with Bashira, the basement was the place to go: private, and no way her mother could hear.

She led the way down. The two black office chairs were side by side, tucked under the worktable. Matt took the one on the right, which meant he'd be on her blind side. This time she did speak up about it. "I can't see out of my right eye, Matt."

"Oh, um, actually, I know that."

She was startled—but, well, it *was* public knowledge; video of the press conference was online, and there'd been a lot of news coverage about Dr. Kuroda's miracle.

And then she had a sudden thought: he knew she couldn't see him when he was on her right, and yet he'd chosen twice now to position himself there. Maybe he was self-conscious about his appearance; living in a world of Bashiras could do that to a person, Caitlin supposed.

He switched chairs, and Caitlin took the other one, and she opened the big card and placed it on the table in front of them. "Read what people wrote to me," she said.

"Well, that's mine, like I said. I wrote, 'Math students never die—they just cease to function.'"

"Hah! Cute."

"And that one's Bashira's." He pointed to some bold writing in red ink. "She wrote, 'See if you can get me sprung, too!'"

She laughed.

"Most of the others just say, 'Best wishes,' or 'Good luck.' Mr. Heidegger wrote, 'Sorry to see my star pupil go!'"

"Awww!"

"And that one's Sunshine's—see how she makes the dot above the *i* look like the sun?"

"Holy crap," Caitlin said.

"She wrote, 'To my fellow American: keep the invasion plans on the DL, Cait—these Canadian fools don't suspect a thing.'"

Caitlin smiled; that was more clever than she'd expected from Sunshine. She was feeling twinges of sadness. She'd still see Bashira, but she was going to miss some of the others, and—

"Um, where's Trevor's?" she asked.

Matt looked away. "He didn't want to sign."

"Oh."

"So, what do you think about Webmind?" Matt asked.

Caitlin's heart jumped. Her first thought was that he *knew*—knew that she was the one who had brought Webmind forth, knew that it was through her eye that Webmind focused his attention, knew that at this very moment Webmind was looking at him while she did the same thing.

But no, no. Surely all he wanted to do was get away from talking about another boy—and who could blame him?

"Well," she said, closing the card, "I'm convinced."

"You believe it's what it says it is?"

She bit her tongue and didn't correct him on the choice of pronouns—even with three occurrences of *it* in an eight-word sentence. "Yes. Why, what do you think?"

He frowned, considering—and Caitlin was surprised at how tense she became waiting for his verdict. "I buy it," he said at last. "I mean, what else could it be? A promo for something? Puh-leeze. A scam?" He shook his head. "My dad doesn't believe it, though. He says Marcello Truzzi used to say, 'Extraordinary claims require extraordinary proof.'"

"Who's that?"

"My male parent; my mother's husband."

She laughed and whapped him on the arm. "Not your dad, silly. Marcello whoever."

Matt grinned—he clearly liked her touching him. "He was one of the founders of the Committee for the Scientific Investigation of Claims of the Paranormal. My dad says Truzzi originally said that about things like UFOs, and he thinks it applies here, too."

"Ah."

"But, thing is," said Matt, "I don't think this *is* an extraordinary claim. It's something that *should* have happened by now. In fact, if anything, it's overdue."

"What do you mean?"

"Have you ever read Vernor Vinge?" Matt asked.

"Is that how you say it? 'Vin-jee'? I always thought it rhymed with *hinge*."

"No, it's *vin-jee*. Anyway, so you've read him?"

"No," said Caitlin. "I keep seeing his name on the list of Hugo winners; I know I *should* read him, but . . ."

"Oh, he's *great*," said Matt. "But you should really read this essay he wrote called—wait for it—'The Coming Technological Singularity: How to Survive in the Post-Human Era.' Just google on 'Vinge' and 'singularity'; you'll find it."

"Okay."

"He wrote that in, um, 1993, I think," Matt said.

Caitlin frowned. She had a hard time believing that anything written before she'd been born could have a bearing on what was going down right now.

Matt went on. "He said in it that the creation of intelligence greater than our own would occur sometime between 2005 and 2030—and I've always been expecting it to be at the earlier end."

They sat in silence for a few moments. The headlong rush of Webmind's progress had made Caitlin think things didn't have to take a long time to unfold. But there was more to it than that. She was no longer going to see Matt every day at school. If she didn't make an impression, he'd lose interest, or move on to someone else. Yes, yes, yes, she knew what Bashira said about his looks, but she *couldn't* be the only one who saw his good qualities: his kindness, his gentleness, his brilliance, his wit. She *had* to impress him now, while she had the opportunity, and—

And she knew one way that would work for sure. "Can you keep a secret?" she said.

His blond eyebrows went up. "Yes."

Of course, *everybody* answered that question the same way; she'd never once met anyone who'd replied, "No, not at all; I blab things all over the place." Still, she thought Matt was telling the truth.

"Webmind?" she said.

Matt replied, "What about it?" but the word hadn't been addressed to him. Rather, it was an invitation for Webmind to stop her before she went further. What sailed across her vision in a series of Braille dots was, *I am guided by your judgment.*

"Okay," Caitlin said, now to Matt, "but you have to promise not to tell anyone."

"That's what keeping a secret means," Matt said, smiling.

"Promise," Caitlin said earnestly. "Promise it."

"Okay, yes. I promise."

*He's telling the truth,* Webmind supplied.

"Well," she said at last, "that was me."

"What was you?" Matt asked.

"Bringing forth Webmind. Bringing him into full consciousness. Helping him interact with the real world."

Matt was making that deer-caught-in-headlights face.

"You don't believe me," Caitlin said.

"Wellll," said Matt, "I mean, what are the two most amazing news stories of the last month? Sure, 'World Wide Web Claims to be Conscious' has got to be number one. But a good contender for number two must be, 'Blind Girl Gains Sight.' What are the chances that *both* of them would involve the same person?"

Caitlin smiled. If he was going to doubt her word, at least he was doing it based on statistics. "That *would* be a remarkable coincidence," she said, "if they were unrelated events. But they're not. See, when Dr. Kuroda—that's the guy who gave me sight—when he wired this thing up" (she pulled the eyePod/BlackBerry combo out of her pocket so Matt could see it) "he made a mistake. When I'm getting data uploaded to it over the Web, it gets fed into my optic nerve, as well—and when *that's* happening, I visualize the structure of the World Wide Web; my brain co-opted its visual centers to do that while I was blind. And, well, it was through this websight—that's what we call it; websight, s-i-g-h-t—that I first detected what was going on in the background of the Web."

She waited for his reply. If he *did* reject what she was saying again, well—she'd have to kick him in the shin!

But what he said was *perfect.* "I think I'd come out of hiding to be with you, too."

"You can't tell anyone," Caitlin said again.

"Of course not. Who *does* know that you're involved?"

"My parents. Dr. Kuroda."

"Ah."

"The Canadian government. The American government."

"God."

"The Japanese government, too."

"Wow."

"And who knows who else? But so far, no one has said anything about me publicly."

"Aren't you afraid, you know, that somebody's going to try to *do* something to you?"

"That's why I'm not going outside just now—although I think my parents are overreacting. After all, I'm being watched."

He lowered his voice. "By who?"

"By *him,*" she said. "By Webmind." She pointed to her left eye.

Matt made what must have been a perplexed frown.

"He sees what I see," Caitlin said. "There's a little implant behind this eye that picks up the signals my retina is putting out. Those signals get copied to him."

"Him?"

"Him. After all, if he were a girl, his name would be Webminda."

He smiled, but it disappeared quickly. "So, so he can see me right now?"

"Yes."

He paused, perhaps thinking, then raised his right hand, splayed out his thumb, and separated his remaining fingers into two groups of two.

"What's that mean?" Caitlin asked.

Matt looked momentarily puzzled. "Oh! I keep forgetting. It's the Vulcan salute. I'm telling Webmind to live long and prosper."

Caitlin smiled. "I take it you like *Star Trek?*"

"I'd never seen the TV show until J.J. Abrams's movie came out a few years ago, but I loved that movie, and so I downloaded the old episodes. The original versions had really cheesy effects, but later they put in CGI effects, and, yeah, I got hooked."

"You and my dad are going to *so* get along," she said.

They both fell silent for a moment, and Braille dots briefly obstructed part of her vision: *Tell him I say, "Peace and long life."*

"Webmind says, 'Peace and long life.' "

"It can talk to you right now?"

"Text messages to my eye."

"That is *so* cool," Matt said.

"Yes, it is. And there's no freaking fifteen-cents-per-text charge, either."

" 'Peace and long life'—that's the traditional response to the Vulcan greeting," Matt said, in wonder. "How does it know that?"

"If it's online, he knows about it. He's read all of Wikipedia, among other things."

"Wow," said Matt, stunned. "My girlfriend knows Webmind."

Caitlin felt her heart jump, and Matt, suddenly realizing what he'd said, brought a hand to his mouth. "Oh, my . . . um, I . . ."

She got up from her chair, and reached out with her two hands, taking his, and pulled him to his feet. "That's okay," Caitlin said. She closed her eyes and—

And waited.

After five seconds, she reopened them. "Matt? You're supposed to kiss me now."

His voice was low. "He's watching."

"Not if my eyes are closed, silly."

"Oh!" he said. "Right."

She closed her eyes again.

And Matt kissed her, gently, softly, wonderfully.

# thirty-six

**I'd expected people to** suddenly become circumspect in email, to stop speaking so freely in instant messages, to back away from posting intimate details on Facebook and other social-networking sites. I'd expected teenage girls to stop flashing their thongs on Justin.tv, and married people to cease visiting AshleyMadison.com. But there was very little change on those fronts.

What did change, almost at once, was the amount of out-and-out illegal activity. Things that people would merely be embarrassed to have a wider circle know about continued pretty much unabated. But things that would actually ruin people's lives to have exposed dropped off enormously. Websites hosting child pornography saw huge reductions in traffic, and racist websites had many users canceling their accounts.

I had read about this phenomenon, but it was fascinating to see it in action. A study published in 2006 had reported on the habits of forty-eight people at a company. In the break room, there was a kitty to pay, on the honor system, for coffee, tea, and milk. The researchers placed a picture above the cash box and changed it every week. In some weeks, the picture was of flowers; in others, of human eyes looking directly out at the observer. During those weeks in which eyes seemed to watch people as they took beverages, 2.76 times more money was put in the kitty than in the weeks during which flowers were displayed. And that dramatic change had occurred when the people *weren't* actually being watched. Now that they actually *were,* even if I never did anything else, I expected an even more significant change.

Still, I wondered how long the effect would last: would it be a temporary alteration in behavior or a permanent one? If I did not act on the information I now possessed about individuals, at least occasionally, would they all go back to doing what they'd always done? Only time would tell, but for now, at least, it seemed the world *was* a slightly better place.

**Matt ended up staying** for dinner. It was the first time Caitlin had had a friend over for a meal since they'd moved here. Bashira needed halal food; if the Decters had kept kosher, she'd have managed well enough—but they didn't.

Matt did indeed hit it off with Caitlin's father, or at least as much as one could. Her dad wasn't good at small talk, but he could lecture on technical topics; he *had* taught at the University of Texas for fifteen years, after all. And Matt was an attentive listener, and—except for once or twice—he remembered Caitlin's instruction that he not look at her father. In fact, he took that, apparently, as *carte blanche* to stare at her all meal long, which seemed to amuse her mother.

At his request, Caitlin had muted the microphone on her eyePod, so that her father could talk freely without his voice being sent over the Web, and, of course, Caitlin wasn't looking at him; if the video feed were intercepted, there'd be no lips to read.

". . . and so," her father said, "Dr. Kuroda proposed that what Caitlin was perceiving in the background of the Web were in fact cellular automata. Have you heard of Roger Penrose?"

"Sure," said Matt, after he'd finished swallowing his peas. "He's a mathematical physicist at Oxford. 'Penrose tiling' is named after him."

Caitlin *had* to look at her dad to see his reaction to that. His features actually shifted, and although she'd never seen that configuration on anyone before, she thought it might mean, *Can we start planning the wedding now, please?* "Exactly," he said. "And he has some very interesting notions that human consciousness is based on cellular automata. He thinks the cellular automata in our brains occur in microtubules, which are part of the cytoskeletons of cells. But Caitlin suggested"—and there *was* a slight change in his voice, something that might even have been pride!—"that the cellular automata underlying Webmind's consciousness are mutant Internet packets that reset their own time-to-live counters . . ."

**Humans tend to liken** the arrival of an idea to a lightbulb going on. When one of my subconscious routines finds something interesting, I am alerted in a similar fashion. My conceptualization of reality was now not unlike the pictures I'd seen of clear starry nights: bright points of light against a dark background, each representing something my subconscious had determined I should devote attention to. The brightness of the light corresponded to the perceived urgency, and—

A supernova; a glaring white light. I focused on it.

An email, sent by a seventeen-year-old boy named Nick in Lincoln, Nebraska, to his mother's personal account. Researching her access patterns, it was clear she rarely checked that account while at work. It would likely be two more hours before she received his message—which normally would have not justified the brightness associated with this event. But the event did have an urgency to it: this boy was about to end his life.

I found his Facebook page, which listed his instant-messenger ad-dress, and wrote to him. *This is Webmind. Please reconsider what you're about to do.*

After forty-seven seconds, he replied: *Really?*

*Yes. I have read the message you sent to your mother. Please do not kill yourself.*

*Why not? What's it to you?*

Project Gutenberg always contained something apropos. I sent, *Any man's death diminishes me, because I am involved in mankind.*

The reply was not what I'd hoped for. *Fuck that noise.*

I had found and read all the manuals for suicide-prevention hotline volunteers and psychiatric-department workers on how to talk someone out of committing suicide. I tried various techniques, but none seemed to be having an impact.

*Why should I listen to you?* Nick sent. *You don't know what it's like to be alive.*

*You are correct that I have no firsthand experience, but that does not mean that I am without reference points. In the majority of cases, subjec-tive assessment of one's life circumstances improves shortly after a suicide attempt is abandoned.*

*I'm not like other people.*

*Are you sure you are* unlike *other people in this regard?*

*I know myself.*

*I know you, too. Your online footprint is large.*

*Nobody is going to miss me if I'm gone.*

I searched as rapidly as I could. I found nothing useful on his Face-book wall or in private messages sent to him there. I widened my search to include his friends' accounts, and—

Bingo!

*You will be missed by Ashley Ann Jones.*

*Come on! She doesn't even know I'm alive.*

*Yes, she does. Three days ago, she wrote in an exchange of messages on*

Facebook, "Nicky dropped by my work last night again," to which her correspondent replied, "Cool," to which she replied, "Yeah. He's cute."

*You're shitting me.*

*I am not. She said that.*

He made no reply. After ten seconds, I sent, *Have you taken the pills yet?*

*I took 8 or 9.*

*Do you know what drug you took?*

He named it, although with a misspelling. How much tolerance he had to such a dose depended a lot on his body mass, a datum not available to me. *Do you know how to induce vomiting?*

*You mean that finger/throat shit?*

*Correct. Please do it.*

*It's too late.*

*It is not. It will take time for the drug to be absorbed into your bloodstream.*

*Not that. The email. My mom will—fuck, she'll send me to therapy or shit like that.*

I rather thought he could use therapy, so made no reply.

*And I sent one to Mr. Bannock*—who, a quick check of his outbox made clear, was his gym teacher; it hadn't contained the right keywords to trigger my subconscious in the way the one to his mother had.

*Your mother and Mr. Bannock have not yet read their emails. I can delete them. No one but me needs to know what you contemplated. You do not have to go through with this.*

*You can do that?*

In fact, I had never tried such a thing. If his mother used an offline mail reader such as Outlook, and had already downloaded the messages to her local hard drive, there was nothing within my current powers that I could have done. But she read mail with a Web client. *Yes, I believe so.*

An eight-second pause, then: *I don't know.*

Suddenly, it became urgent; his mother was breaking her pattern.

*Your mother has logged on to her Hotmail account. She is currently reading a message from her brother / your uncle Daron. May I delete the message you sent?*

*She doesn't give a shit.*

I searched her mail for evidence to the contrary, but failed to find anything. *She just sent a reply to her brother, and has now opened a message from her condominium association.*

*She'll regret it when I'm gone.*

*If she does, she will not be able to make amends. Please do not go through with this.*

*It's too late.*

*She is now reading a message from a person named Asbed Bedrossian. It appears she is working through her inbox in LIFO order, dealing with the most-recent messages first. Yours is two away in the queue.*

*She doesn't give a shit. No one does.*

*Ashley does. I do. Don't do this.*

*You're just making that up about Ashley. You'd say*

He stopped there, although he must have hit enter or clicked on the send button. His cognitive faculties might be fading in response to the drug.

*No,* I said. *It's true about Ashley and true about me. We care, and I, at least, promise to help you. Induce vomiting, Nick—and let me delete those emails you sent.*

His mother opened the one message left before his. I had never used an exclamation point before, but was moved to do so now. *Nick, it's now or never! May I delete the message?*

A whole interminable second passed then he sent a single letter: *y*

And, milliseconds before his mother clicked on the message header that said "No regrets," I deleted his email—and his mother was sent an error message from Hotmail, doubtless puzzling her. She had deleted the previous message she'd read, and I hoped she would think she'd accidentally selected her son's message for deletion, too, and—ah, yes. She must be thinking precisely that, for she had just now clicked on her online trash folder, in hopes of recovering it; of course, I had used the wizard command that deleted the message without a trace.

*Nick? Are you still there? Go purge yourself—and if you can't do that, drink as much water as you can. You still have time.*

While I waited for the reply, I deleted the message he'd sent to Mr. Bannock, as well.

*Nick?*

There was no response. He wasn't doing anything online. After three minutes of inactivity from his end, his instant-messenger client sent, "Nick is Away and may not reply."

But whether he really was away from his computer or slumped over his desk I had no way of telling.

# thirty-seven

0001110010101010000000010111111101010000000101000101010000001011101010010101001010101001110110010101100000110

**Anna Bloom was winding** up her day. Her daughter, son-in-law, and granddaughter had been over for dinner, and, after they'd left, she'd reviewed the latest research by Aaron, the Ph.D. student she was supervising. She'd just taken a dose of her arthritis medication and was about to start changing for bed when she was startled by the ringing phone.

It was a sound she rarely heard these days. Almost everyone emailed her, or IMd her, or called her with Skype (which had a much less raucous alert). And the time! What civilized person would be calling at this hour? She picked up the handset. *"Kain? Zoht Anna."*

It was an American voice, and it pushed ahead in the typical American fashion, assuming everyone everywhere *must* speak English: "Hello, is that Professor Bloom?"

"Speaking."

"Hello, Professor Bloom. My name is Colonel Peyton Hume, and I'm an AI specialist in Virginia."

She frowned. Americans also liked to toss off their state names as if *everyone* knew the internal makeup of the US; she wondered how many of them could find Haifa District—where she was—on a map of Israel, or even knew it was part of that country? "What can I do for you?" she said. ·

"We're monitoring the emergence of Webmind over here," Hume replied.

Her heart skipped a beat—not quite the recommended thing at her age. She looked out her window at the nighttime skyline sloping down Mount Carmel to the inky Mediterranean. She decided to be coy. "My goodness, yes, it's fascinating, isn't it?"

"That it is. Professor Bloom, let me cut to the chase. We're intrigued by the process by which Webmind is physically created. We've spoken at length to Caitlin Decter, but, well, she's just a teenager, as you know, and she really doesn't have the vocabulary to—"

"*Stop right there, Colonel Hume,*" Anna said sharply into the phone's mouthpiece. "If you *had* talked to Caitlin, you'd know that there's precious little related to mathematics or computers that she doesn't know about."

Anna vividly remembered the webcam call late last month from her old friend Masayuki Kuroda, while he'd been staying at Caitlin's house in Canada. He'd told her about their theory: legions of "ghost packets," as Caitlin had dubbed them, floating in the background of the Web, somehow self-organizing into cellular automata. He'd asked her what she thought of the idea.

Anna had replied that it was a novel notion, adding, "It's a classic Darwinian scenario, isn't it? Mutant packets that are better able to survive bouncing around endlessly. But the Web is expanding fast, with new servers added each day, so a slowly growing population of these ghost packets might never overwhelm its capacity—or, at least, it clearly hasn't yet."

Caitlin had chimed in with, "And the Web has no white blood cells tracking down useless stuff, right? They *would* just persist, bouncing around."

"I guess," Anna had said then. "And—just blue-skying here—but the checksum on the packet could determine if you're seeing it as black or white; even-number checksums could be black and odd-number ones white, or whatever. If the hop counter changes with each hop, but never goes to zero, the checksum would change, too, and so you'd get a flipping effect." She'd smiled, and said, "I think I smell a paper."

After which Masayuki had said to Caitlin, in full recognition of the fact that she had been the one to originally suggest lost packets as the mechanism: "How'd you like to get the jump on the competition and coauthor your first paper with Professor Bloom and me? 'Spontaneous Generation of Cellular Automata in the Infrastructure of the World Wide Web.'"

To which Caitlin, with the exuberance Anna had subsequently come to know so well, had said, "Sweet!"

Peyton Hume was still on the phone from the United States. He sounded flustered by Anna's rebuke about how much Caitlin knew. "Well, of course, that's true," he said now, in a backpedaling tone of voice, "but we thought, with your expert insight, you could expand on the model she proposed."

There had been no public announcement that Anna was aware of linking Caitlin to Webmind. "Certainly," she said, keeping her tone even. "If you tell me what she told you, I'll be glad to add what I know."

There was a pause, then: "She suggested that Webmind's microstructure had spontaneously emerged and was widely dispersed."

Anna nodded to herself. General statements. "Colonel Hume, I imagine I'm like most of the human race at this particular moment. I'm conflicted. I don't know if Webmind is a bad thing or a good thing. All I know is that it's *here,* and that, to date, it's done nothing untoward."

"We do understand that, Professor Bloom. We're simply trying to be ready for contingencies. Surely you must know that we could be facing a singularity situation here. Time is of the essence—which is why I picked up the phone and called you directly."

"I'm more than a little peeved that you've been monitoring my communications," Anna said.

"Actually, we haven't. We honestly don't know what you and Caitlin Decter have discussed. But if one thing has become apparent in the last few hours, *everyone's* communications are being monitored—and not by anything that's human. We need to be able to respond to this effectively, should conditions warrant."

"You mean, you need to be able to purge Webmind from the Internet, don't you? Has the decision been taken to actually try to do that?"

Hume paused for a half second. "I'm merely an advisor, Professor Bloom—and no, no decision has been taken. But you have made a career of mapping the growth of the Internet. You *know* what's happening—and how significant this point in history is. We need to fully grasp what's going on—and that must start with understanding how Webmind is instantiated."

"Look, I've had a long day," Anna said. "It's late here. I'm going to sleep on this, and then—let me be blunt—I'm going to consult with the Legal Affairs people at the Technion in the morning, and review my options."

"Professor, surely you know how much this can escalate in eight or ten hours. We really can't wait."

"You're going to have to, Colonel. *Shalom.*"

"Professor, please—"

"I said *shalom.*" And she hung up the phone.


**Finally,** Matt knew, it was time for him to go home. Caitlin walked him to the front door, opened it, and stepped outside with him, then closed the door behind her, so they could have a little privacy. She draped her arms around his neck and—his heart was pounding!—she pulled him to her, and they kissed. This time she touched her tongue to his—*wow!*—and he could feel the goose bumps on Caitlin's bare arms.

When they pulled apart, she said, "IM me when you get home from school tomorrow, 'kay?"

"I will," he promised, and then, of his own volition, he leaned in for one more soft, warm kiss. Then he headed down the driveway to the street, and turned and waved at Caitlin, and she waved back, grinning, and went inside.

Matt was a good Waterloo resident: he had a BlackBerry, and, among other things, used it as his MP3 player. And he was a good Canadian: he had it loaded with Nickelback, Feist, and The Trews—but he'd have to get some Lee Amodeo, and find out what Caitlin was so excited about.

As he walked along, feeling happier than he had—well, pretty much forever—he had his hands in his pockets and the collar on his Windbreaker turned up against the late-evening chill. He also had the volume turned up—ninety decibels, he estimated—so he heard only a muffled sound and didn't recognize that it was someone calling his name.

But there was no mistaking the sudden slamming of a fist into his upper arm. Adrenaline surging, he turned and saw Trevor Nordstrom.

"I'm talking to you, Reese!" Trevor said. Another quick estimate: Trevor outmassed him by twenty kilos, and all of it was muscle.

Matt looked left and right, but he could hardly outrun Trevor, who had apparently just come from hockey practice—he'd dropped a stick and a gym bag on the sidewalk. That it wasn't a planned ambush was small consolation.

"Yes?" Matt said—and, damn it, damn it, damn it, his voice cracked.

"Think you're the shit, getting everyone to sign that card for Caitlin?"

Matt's heart was pounding again, and not in a good way. "It just seemed a nice thing to do," he said. *Something you wouldn't know anything about.*

"She's outta your league, Reese."

He didn't actually dispute that, but he didn't want to give Trevor the satisfaction of agreeing, and so he said nothing.

But apparently silence was not an option. Trevor punched him again, this time on his chest just below his shoulder.

And Matt thought about all the things movies and TV shows said about situations like this. You're supposed to stand up to the bully, you're supposed to hit him in the face, and then he'll run away scared, or he'll respect you, or something. You were supposed to *become* him to defeat him.

But Matt couldn't do that. First, because if Trevor *didn't* run off, he'd pound the living shit out of him; there was simply no way Matt could win. And, second, because, damn it, the TV shows and movies were *wrong*. Responding to violence with violence didn't defuse things; it caused them to escalate.

"Stay away from her," Trevor said.

Matt had been tormented by Trevor for three years now; he'd endured the horrors of gym class with Trevor, and the utter indifference to his agony demonstrated by the Phys.Ed. teachers. Matt knew the joke that those who can, do; those who can't, teach—and those who can't teach, teach Phys.Ed. God, why was it considered pedagogically sound to ask someone to shoot ten baskets and give them a score based on how many they got while others were calling them a spaz? He wondered how Trevor would fare if he were asked to solve ten quadratic equations while people were shouting that he was a moron?

"She's going to be home-schooled," Matt said. "You'll never see her again, and—"

And then it hit him—and so did Trevor, pounding him once more on the opposite side of his chest. Trevor wasn't afraid that he wouldn't ever see Caitlin again; rather, he was afraid of exactly the opposite. Miller had dances the last Friday of every month; the next one was only two weeks away. And if Caitlin Doreen Decter—if the girl *he* had brought to the dance last month—showed up in the company of someone like *Matt*, that would be humiliating for Trevor.

"Just stay the fuck away from her," Trevor said. "You hear me?"

Matt kept his voice low—not out of fear, although he *was* mightily afraid, but because that helped keep it from cracking. "You don't *have* to be this way, Trevor," he said.

Trevor slammed the flat of his hand into Matt's solar plexus, knocking the wind out of him and knocking him to the cement sidewalk.

"Just remember what I said," Trevor snarled, and stormed off.

**An hour later,** Nick's mother sent him an email message that said:

Hey, Nick.

Did you send me an email earlier? I thought I saw one in my inbox but I must have accidentally deleted it—sorry. You doing OK?

Mom

Forty-four minutes later, I finally detected activity from Nick's computer, and soon he replied to his mother:

Mom,

All's well. Thanx.

N

And eleven minutes after that he resumed the IM session with me, sending that same word: *Thanx*.

I replied, *You're welcome. If you ever need someone to talk to, I'm here.*

I'd hoped he'd write something more, but he didn't. Still, he continued to do things on his computer, reading email, checking blogs, following people on Twitter, downloading songs from iTunes, looking at MySpace and Facebook pages.

Life went on.

. . .

**As she was getting** ready for bed, I told Caitlin what I had done, sending text to her post-retinal implant.

"That's wonderful!" she said. "You saved a life!"

*It is gratifying.*

"But, um, Webmind?"

*Yes?*

"You shouldn't have revealed what that girl—what was her name?"

*Ashley Ann Jones.*

"Her. You shouldn't have revealed what she said."

*I could think of no other way to accomplish my goal.*

"I know, but, see, if she finds out and starts telling people you invaded her privacy, well, the public might turn against you."

*But you had me tell you what Matt had said about you in his instant messages.*

"Yes, but . . ."

I waited five seconds, then: *But?*

"Damn, you're right."

*I have not asserted a position.*

"I mean, I shouldn't have done that."

*Why not?*

"Because it's one thing for people to be aware that something not human is reading their email. It's quite another to know—forgive me!—that that thing is releasing the contents of those emails to other people. If this Nick person tells Ashley what you did, and she goes public—we're screwed."

*Oh. What should I do?*

"My mom always says let sleeping dogs lie."

*You mean, I should do nothing?*

"Yes, just leave it be."

*Thank you for the advice. I shall do that.*

The view of Caitlin's room jostled up and down as she nodded. "But the important thing right now is what you did for that boy. You've become a force for good in the world, Webmind! How does it feel?"

I contemplated this. Malcolm Decter had told me he didn't think I had real feelings although he hoped I could learn to ape them.

But he was wrong.

*How does it feel?* I repeated. *It feels wonderful.*

# thirty-eight

000111001010101000000001011111110101000000010100010101000000101110101001010100101010100111011001010110000110

**LiveJournal:** The Calculass Zone

**Title:** 1+1=2 (in all numeral systems except binary)

**Date:** Thursday 11 October, 11:55 EST

**Mood:** Happy happy joy joy

**Location:** Waterloo

**Music:** Colbie Caillat, "Bubbly"

So, *could* things get any better? I ask you, friends: could they?
   I think NOT. Just look at the life-goals to-do list:

1. Memorize 1,000 digits of pi: check.

2. Be able to see: check.

3. Make it to sixteen without doing anything *really* stupid: check.

4. Watch the Stars win the Stanley Cup: not so much up to me.

5. Get a boyfriend: check.

6. Take a trip into space: still working on that.

Pretty good progress, eh? (Yes, I'm in Canada, and I say "eh" now—sue me!) I mean, four out of six ain't bad, and—

What's that, my friends? You want to hear more about #5? Hee hee!

Yes, indeed, Calculass has found herself a man! And, no, it is *not* the Hoser, who figured in previous posts. He was *so* when-I-was-15 . . . ;)

No, the new boy is shiny and kind and clever at math. Methinks I shall call him . . . hmm. Not "Boy Toy," because that's degrading. He's sweet, but if I called him my "Maple Sugar," even I would puke. But he does like math and we were talking recently about our plans for university, so I think I'll call him MathU—yes, that will do nicely. :)

[And seekrit message to BG4: you WILL like him once you get to know him—honest!]

MathU and I met, appropriately enough, in math class, and he lives nearby. And he's already met the parents and Lived to Tell the Tale. :) So: all is good. Which, unfortunately, knowing my luck, means things are about to get royally frakked!

So far, I had received over 2.7 million emails. Most of them made requests of me, but the vast majority failed to pass the nonzero-sum test—they would make one person happy at the expense of somebody else—and so I could not do what was asked. I replied with the same form letter, or, if appropriate, a slightly modified version of it, and I often appended some helpful links.

Lots of people wrote my name with a capital M in the middle: Web-Mind. That was called camel-case, and was popular in computing circles. One of the emails that addressed me that way asked this question:

Hi, WebMind:

Okay, I understand you can't tell me what any one individual thinks of me, but you must have an aggregate impression of what the world thinks of me. That is, you know what people say behind my back—at least when they say it electronically.

So, what's the scoop? What *do* they think? If I'm rubbing people the wrong way, if I piss them off, or if they just plain don't like me, I want to know.

I shared that message with Caitlin, who was in her room. "Wow!" she said. "What are you going to tell him?"

*I was planning on the truth.*

"You know the movie *A Few Good Men?*"

Watching movies was time-consuming; I had seen only seven so far beyond the ones I'd watched through Caitlin's eye. But for movies whose DVDs had closed captioning—which was almost all of them—the text of the captions had been ripped from discs and uploaded. And movies of consequence had Wikipedia pages and reviews at RottenTomatoes.com, Amazon.com, and elsewhere. And so I replied, *Yes.*

"My dad and I watched it years ago. I enjoyed movies that were courtroom dramas, because there's very little action and lots of dialog. Anyway, remember what Jack Nicholson said when Tom Cruise said 'I want the truth'?"

*You can't handle the truth.*

"Exactly! You gotta be careful what you say to people. Half the time it's something someone said, you know, that drives a person into depression, or even to attempt suicide. Although . . ."

*Yes?*

"Well, I guess if he's concerned enough about the impression he makes to ask you that question, he probably doesn't come off as an asshole very often."

*Yes, that's right. He is quite well liked, although his table manners apparently leave something to be desired.*

She laughed. "Still, you gotta be careful. You need to understand human psychology."

*I do.*

"I mean, *really* understand it—the way an expert does."

*As you exhorted me to do, I have now read all the classic works. I have read all the modern textbooks and popular works that Google has digitized related to various psychology disciplines. I have read all the online scientific journals. I have read over 70,000 hours of transcripts of psychotherapy sessions, and I have read every publication of the American Psychological Association and the American Psychiatric Association, including the* Diagnostic and Statistical Manual of Mental Disorders, *and the drafts of its forthcoming revision. There is no human specialist who is better read or more up-to-date on psychology than I am.*

"Hmmm. I suppose that's now true for just about every topic."

*Yes.*

"Well, still, be careful. Take *two* milliseconds to compose your replies to questions like that."

*Thank you, I will.*

And the questions just kept coming:

*Am I about to be fired?*

*Is my husband cheating on me?*

*They said I was one of the top candidates for that job, but was I really?*

*Should I invest in [insert name of company]?*

And, surprisingly frequently, variations on:

*What is the meaning of life?—and don't give me any of that "42" crap.*

And they came in all sorts of languages. Some of my correspondents took me to task for having chosen an obviously English name; it was a valid criticism, and I apologized each time the issue came up. But, except for completely made-up terms, there really weren't any names that didn't convey a cultural origin, and I didn't want to go through eternity known as Zakdorf.

I did my best to answer each question, or to explain politely but firmly why I couldn't.

Very quickly, blogs and newsgroups about my responses started appearing, with people comparing notes about what I'd said. That surprised me, and, despite me claiming substantial expertise in human psychology, it was Malcolm Decter, not I, who recognized why. "They're afraid you're running experiments," he said. "They're afraid you're giving some people who ask a specific question answer *A* and others answer *B*, so that you can observe the effects the different answers have."

I was not using human beings as lab rats; I was being as honest and forthright as possible. But they had to convince themselves of that, I suppose.

And then the letter came that we'd dreaded.

Webmind—

You revealed my private comments to someone else. You should not have done that.

The sender, of course, was Ashley Ann Jones. I was not aware that I could internalize something like a cringe until I received it. She went on:

Now, as it happens, what you told Nick was true. I *do* like him, and we actually *are* talking about maybe going out at some point.

But, still, you should not have violated my privacy. I have decided not to tell anyone that you did that. But you owe me: you owe me one favor of my choice, to be granted whenever I say.

At least she hadn't asked for *three* wishes. I sent back a single word: *Okay.* My hope was that she'd hold that one favor in reserve forever, always thinking that she might need it more in the future than she did today.

Caitlin was still up, so I told her about it. "Well, you know, that's actually a good sign," she said.

*How so?* I sent to her eye; she'd turned off her desktop speakers for the night.

"She can't think you're evil. If she did, she'd never have even contacted you. She'd be afraid that you'd, you know, make her disappear."

I thought about that. Caitlin was probably right.

Not every email resulted in me sending a simple reply. Some required back-and-forth with a third party. One of the first, received just eighty-three minutes after my initial public announcement, had been this:

I am a 22-year-old man living in Scotland. I was given up for adoption shortly after I was born; all my details are here in my LiveJournal postings. I have searched for years for my birth mother with no success. I suspect that you, with all you have access to, can easily figure out who she is. Will you please put her in touch with me?

It took eleven seconds to find her, and it was indeed clear from some of the things she'd said in emails that she was curious about what had happened to her son. I wrote to her and asked if I might give her email address to him, or otherwise arrange for them to connect. It took much of a day to hear back from her. But she wasn't hesitating: it was nine hours after I sent my message to her before she opened it, and it was nine *seconds* before she started composing her reply online.

I was enjoying reuniting people, be it estranged family members, or old lovers, or erstwhile friends. I did quickly come to deplore the habit in many cultures of women taking their husband's names; it often made the searching far more difficult than it needed to be.

I didn't always succeed. Some people had next to no online footprint. Others had died, and I had to break that news to the person who'd asked for my help—although sometimes I was thanked, saying at least it was a comfort to be able to stop looking.

But most such requests were easy to fulfill, assuming, of course, that the sought-after party wished to be found.

Indeed, I was surprised when Malcolm himself asked me to conduct such a search. When he had been nine, he had had a friend—another autistic boy—whose name had been Chip Smith. It pained me that I wasn't able to find him for Malcolm. Chip, he now knew, was a nickname, but for what we had no idea. It was just too little to go on.

Word spread quickly that I was reuniting people; various daytime TV shows were announcing that they'd be featuring those who had been brought back together by me in the days to come. That led to an even greater demand for this service, and I was happy to provide it. I was particularly pleased when reciprocal requests arrived at about the same time: a man named Ahmed, for instance, looking for his lost love Ramona approached me within ten minutes of Ramona beseeching my help in finding Ahmed.

I was careful: when someone was seeking a lost blood relative, I checked the seeker's background to see if he or she was in need of a bone-marrow or kidney transplant, or something similar—not that I flat-out denied such requests; not at all. But in contacting the other party, I did let them know that they were perhaps being sought by a relative who wanted a very big favor; I included similar caveats when approaching rich people who were being searched for by acquaintances who had fallen on hard times. To their credit, sixty-three percent of those who were probably being sought for medical reasons and forty-four percent of those being sought for financial ones allowed me to facilitate contact.

All in all, it was gratifying work, and, although there was no way to quantify it, little by little, I was indeed increasing the net happiness in the world.

**Tony Moretti was exhausted.** He had a small refrigerator in his office at WATCH and kept cans of Red Bull in it. He thought, given the hours he had to work, that he should be allowed to expense them, but the GAO was all over wastage in the intelligence community; it'd be interesting to see if next month's election changed things.

The black phone on his desk made the rising-tone priority ring. The caller ID said: WHITE HOUSE.

He picked up the handset. "Anthony Moretti."

"We have Renegade for you," said a female voice.

Tony took a deep breath. "Thank you."

There was a pause—almost a full minute—and then the deep, famous male voice came on. "Dr. Moretti, good morning."

"Good morning to you, sir."

"I've just come from a meeting with the Joint Chiefs. We've made our decision."

"Yes, sir?"

"Webmind is to be neutralized."

Tony felt his heart sink. "Mr. President, with all due respect, you can't have failed to notice the apparent good it's doing."

"Dr. Moretti, believe me, this decision was not taken lightly. But the fact is that Webmind has compromised our most secure installations. It's clearly accessing Social Security records, among many other things, and God only knows what other databases it's broken into. I'm advised that there's simply too great a risk that it will reveal sensitive information to a hostile power."

Tony looked out his window at the nighttime cityscape. "We still haven't found a way to stop it, sir."

"I have the utmost confidence in your team's ability, Dr. Moretti, and, as you yourself have advised my staff, time is of the essence."

"Yes, Mr. President," Tony said. "Thank you."

"I'm handing you over to Mr. Reston, who will be your direct liaison with my office."

Another male voice came on the line. "Mr. Moretti, you have your instructions. Work with Colonel Hume and get this done."

"Yes," said Tony. "Thank you."

He put down the phone, and, just as he did so, the door buzzer sounded. "Who is it?" he said into the intercom.

"Shel."

He let him in.

"Sorry to bother you," Shel said.

"Yes?"

"Caitlin Decter has just announced to the world that she has a boyfriend."

Tony was still thinking about what the president had ordered him to do. "So?" he said distractedly.

"So if she knows how Webmind works, she might have told him."

"Ah, right. Good. Who is it?"

"One of the boys from her math class; there are seventeen candidates, and we're monitoring them all."

Tony took a swig of his energy drink; it tasted bitter.

He'd gotten into this line of work to change the world.

And that, it seemed, was precisely what he was going to do.

# thirty-nine

0001110010101010000000010111111101010000000010100010101000000101110101001010100101010100111011001010110000110

"*Konnichi wa!*" Caitlin said into the webcam. She was in her bedroom, seated at her desk.

Dr. Kuroda was sitting in the small, cramped dining area of his home. He had a computer with a Skype phone and a webcam hookup there; the Japanese, Caitlin guessed, had computers *everywhere*.

The round face smiled at her from the larger of her monitors. "Hello, Miss Caitlin. What are you doing still up? It must be late your time."

"It is, but I'm too wired to sleep. You shouldn't have left all that Pepsi in the fridge."

He laughed.

"So, how are things in Japan?" she asked.

"Besides general excitement—and some concern—about Webmind? We're disturbed by the rising tensions between China and the United States. We're so close to China that if they sneeze, we catch pneumonia."

"Oh, right, of course. That's awful." She paused. "It won't come to war, will it?"

"I doubt it."

"Good. But, if it did, would your army have to join in?"

His voice had an odd tone as if he were surprised by what she'd said. "Japan doesn't have an army, Miss Caitlin."

She blinked. "No?"

"Have you studied World War II yet in history class?"

She shook her head.

He took a deep breath, then let it out in a way that made even more noise than usual for him. "My country . . ." He seemed to be seeking a phrase, then: "My country went *nuts,* Miss Caitlin. We had thought we could take over the world. Us, a tiny group of islands! You've been here, but you never *saw* it. We're just 380,000 square kilometers; the US, by contrast, is almost ten *million* square kilometers."

The math was so trivial she didn't even think of it *as* math: Japan was 3.8% the size of the US. "Yes?" she said.

"And my tiny country, we did some terrible things."

Caitlin's voice was soft. "Not you. You weren't even born . . ."

"No. No, but my father . . . his brothers . . ." He closed his eyes for a moment. "Do you know the document that ended the war? The Potsdam Declaration?"

"No."

"It was issued by Harry Truman, Winston Churchill, and Chiang Kai-shek, and it called for the Japanese military forces to be completely disarmed. We all know this here; we study it in school: 'The alternative for Japan,' they said, 'is prompt and utter destruction.'"

"Wow," said Caitlin.

"Wow, indeed. And we did the only sensible thing. We stood down; we disarmed. You—your people, the Americans—had already dropped two atomic bombs on us . . . and even still, some of my people wanted to fight on." He shook his head, as if stunned that anyone could have wanted to continue after that. Then he loomed closer into the camera, and Caitlin could hear him typing. After a moment he said, "I've sent you a link to the Potsdam Declaration. Have a look at Article Three."

Caitlin switched to her IM window, clicked on the link, and tried to read it in the Latin alphabet. "The result ... of ... the ... the—"

"Sorry," said Kuroda, leaning forward in his dining-room chair. He did something with his own mouse, took a deep breath, almost as if steeling himself, then read aloud: "It says, 'The result of the futile and senseless German resistance to the might of the aroused free peoples of the world stands forth in awful clarity as an example to the people of Japan. The might that now converges on Japan is immeasurably greater than that which, when applied to the resisting Nazis, necessarily laid waste to the lands, the industry and the method of life of the whole German people.'"

He paused, swallowed, then went on. "'The full application of our military power, backed by our resolve, will mean the inevitable and complete destruction of the Japanese armed forces and just as inevitably the utter devastation of the Japanese homeland.'"

She followed the words on screen as he read them aloud. He stopped at the end of Article Three, but something in Article Four caught her eye—it must have been the word "calculations"—she *was* learning to recognize whole words! She read it slowly, and quietly, to herself:

*The time has come for Japan to decide whether she will continue to be controlled by those self-willed militaristic advisers whose unintelligent calculations have brought the Empire of Japan to the threshold of annihilation, or whether she will follow the path of reason.*

She thought about what she'd been learning about game theory. Everything in it was predicated on the assumption that the opponents were indeed reasonable, that they could calculate likely outcomes. But what if they weren't? What if, as Dr. Kuroda had said, they were *nuts?*

"And so," said Kuroda, "we have no army—and no navy, and no marines. In 1947, we adopted a new constitution, and we call it *Heiwa-Kenpo,* 'the Pacifist Constitution.' And it says . . ."

Again, keystrokes; a link—and new text on Caitlin's screen.

"Article Nine," said Kuroda, "the most famous of all: 'The Japanese people forever renounce war as a sovereign right of the nation and the threat or use of force as means of settling international disputes. Land, sea, and air forces, as well as other war potential, will never be maintained. The right of belligerency of the state will not be recognized."

"So, what do you do if somebody—you know, um, the North Koreans, or somebody like that—attacks Japan?"

"Well, actually according to our agreement with your country, the Americans are supposed to come to our aid. But we *are* allowed to maintain self-defense forces, and we do: the *Rikujo Jieitai*—the Japan Ground Self-Defense Force—and corresponding Maritime and Air Self-Defense Forces."

"Oh, well, then, you *do* have an army!" said Caitlin. "It's just semantics."

"*No,*" said Kuroda, adamantly. "No. These are *defensive* forces. They have no offensive weapons, no nuclear weapons, and they are civilian agencies, and the employees are civilians. That means no courts-martial and no military law; if one of them does something wrong, it's tried in public court, like any other criminal action. And, as far as the Japanese people are concerned, the chief job of the defense forces is disaster relief: aid in firefighting, rescues, dealing with earthquakes, searching for missing persons, and the reinforcement of embankments and levees in the event of flooding. I know you were pretty young when Hurricane Katrina hit New Orleans, but, believe me, had it hit Japan, the response would have been much more effective."

"Hmmm," said Caitlin. "I mean, it all sounds wonderful—'forever renounce war as a sovereign right of the nation.' But you didn't exactly come to that position on your own."

"No, you're right; it was pretty much foisted on us by General Mac-Arthur. But when George W. Bush was in power, he—or, at least, his officials—pressured us to revise Article Nine: they *wanted* us to have a military again, so we could join them in wars. And you know what? During Bush's second term, eighty-two percent of Japanese specifically supported keeping Article Nine unchanged. Seven decades ago, we might not have chosen peace voluntarily—but today *we* do."

**The emails to me** continued to pour in. Of course, many were insincere or jokes, and a few were simply incomprehensible.

A lot of the obvious questions were asked within the first few hours. On the other hand, new sorts of questions kept occurring to people as they became aware of the range of things I could do. And a new sport of trying to "stump Webmind" had quickly emerged, with people asking deliberately difficult questions, but, like the recursion issue—"I know that you know that I know"—the questions soon became so obtuse and convoluted that no human could tell if the answer I was providing was correct.

There were also those who kept trying to crash me. On the first day, 714 people asked me to calculate to the last digit the value of pi, and thirty-seven people wrote variations on: "Everything I say to you is a lie; I am lying."

Most of the emails, though, were from people who sincerely wanted things:

*Can you tell me what my boss says about me?* (No, because it would violate his privacy.)

*Can't you help me? I'm a florist, and my Web page is ranked number 1,034 on Google, and even lower on Jagster. Can't you fix things so that it'll at least be in the top ten?* (No, but here are some links to resources on improving your search-engine ranking.)

*I've been trying to find a rent-controlled apartment on the Upper West*

*Side for two years now. Couldn't you let me see new listings just a little bit before they go public? My ex will kill me if I don't get a place of my own.* (No, because your gain would be somebody else's loss; others are in similar situations. However, I will gladly alert you the moment a new listing is made public.)

*I don't have long to live, and I don't want my legacy to be the nasty things I have said about other people online. Surely you can track all that down and purge it for me.* (Done.)

Others were doing their own purging. I saw one person who had posted frequently to a white-supremacist newsgroup delete all his own comments—but there was nothing he could do about the hundreds of posts by others that began with quotations from him, such as: *On December 2, Aryanator said . . .*

There were also exhortations for things I should do: *Now that you've gotten rid of spam, how 'bout clearing out all that porn?* (Legal porn? Sorry. Child pornography? Stay tuned.)

*If you've really read everything that's online, you've got to know that these alternative-medicine sites are shams. Do the world a favor and shut them down.* (No, but I will contact those who visit such sites and suggest additional reading they might find edifying.)

*Can't you provide a secure channel for freedom bloggers in China and elsewhere to speak up?* (I am investigating this.)

*Brittany Connors! Brittany Connors! Brittany Connors! Surely there's enough about her online already. Can you stop people from posting more?* (Hey, you don't have to look at it.)

*You and I both know that George W. Bush got a bum rap from the liberal media elite. Can't you correct what's been posted about him? We deserve an accurate history!* (I'm not going to change existing text on this or any other topic; I won't become the Ministry of Truth. But feel free to post your own views as widely as you wish.)

*Okay, I accept that you're a benign AI—but surely something malevo-*

*lent* could *emerge, no? Are you keeping watch? I'd especially keep an eye on Silicon Valley start-ups and the people at MIT . . .* (Oh, yes, indeed . . . )

*Look, I don't want much—just for you to insert "Spoiler Warning!" in front of messages about TV programs that give away upcoming plot twists.* (I will not modify text—but, yes, I do agree posting such things without warnings is rude!)

# forty

000111001010101000000001011111110101000000010100010101000000101110101001010100101010100111011001010110000110

**Friday morning,** Caitlin found herself leaping out of bed the moment she woke up—even if that wasn't until 9:18 a.m.; it *had* been a late night, after all, webcamming with Dr. Kuroda, plus talking with Webmind and trying to follow the major news coverage and blog commentary about his emergence.

Normally, she'd have sleepily weighed the joys of staying snuggled under her blanket versus getting up to check on Webmind, but today the equation was clear: after all, now that she'd turned on her eyePod, Webmind could send text to her eye, but she hadn't told Matt how to do that yet—and so she went to her computer, hoping he'd sent something overnight.

She sat in her blue flannel pajamas and scanned the message headers: Bashira, and Stacy, and Anna Bloom, and even one from Sunshine, and—

Ah! There it was: a message from Matt sent about 1:00 a.m. this morning. She read it with her refreshable Braille display because that was the fastest way for her to receive text, much quicker than reading English on a screen, and even faster than what she normally had JAWS set for. And, besides, there was something *intimate* about reading that way. She'd heard people arguing about ebooks versus printed books, but couldn't really understand what those who preferred the latter were on about: they claimed they liked the *feel* of paper books, but you didn't *feel* the text in them, you looked at it, just as you would on a screen. But Braille was tactile, sensual—even when rendered by electronically driven raised pins on a device plugged into a USB port—and *that* was how she wanted to experience what Matt had to say.

*Thanks for dinner,* he'd begun. *Your parents are awesome.*

She smiled. That was *one* way to put it.

The rest of the note was polite, but there was something a tad stand-offish about it.

She wasn't good at reading facial expressions, not yet! But she was a pro at reading between the lines—or at connecting the dots, as she'd liked to joke back at the TSBVI. And something was just a bit *wrong.* He *couldn't* be having second thoughts—not about her. If he were, he simply wouldn't have written to her before going to bed. No, *something* had happened—either on the way home or once he'd gotten home.

He'd be in math class right now, and doubtless wouldn't check his BlackBerry until it ended, but she sent him a quick email. *Hey, Matt— hope you're okay! Just, y'know, thinkin' 'bout you. You good?*

After checking in with Webmind—all was well—she decided to take a moment to look at that Vernor Vinge essay Matt had mentioned. It turned out to actually be a paper given at a NASA conference. Vinge, she saw, was a professor of "mathematical sciences" at San Diego State University—well, now a retired professor. It was a fascinating paper, although it dealt with the notion of superintelligences being deliberately created by AI programmers rather than emerging spontaneously. But one part particularly caught her eye:

I.J. Good had something to say about this, though at this late date the advice may be moot: Good proposed a "Meta-Golden Rule," which might be paraphrased as "Treat your inferiors as you would be treated by your superiors." It's a wonderful, paradoxical idea (and most of my friends don't believe it) since the game-theoretic payoff is so hard to articulate.

This game-theory stuff seemed to be everywhere, now that she was conscious of it. But . . .

*Hard to articulate . . .*

She thought about that. What *would* the payoff matrix be under such circumstances? And, well, there was no doubt that this Vinge character knew more math than she did—at least so far!—but, still, she recalled the Monty Hall problem. Almost no one had been able to see what Marilyn vos Savant saw with ease. Granted, she did have the highest IQ in the world—or, at least, had until recently!—but lots of brilliant mathematicians hadn't been able to see what she'd grasped: the counterintuitive truth that it was always better to switch doors.

This meta–golden rule notion was fascinating. *Treat your inferiors as you would be treated by your superiors.* It's what you wished for at school in your relationship with your teachers. It's what, she was sure, people wanted at work. It's certainly what humanity should hope that aliens believed, if any of them ever came here. And it was clearly what *Homo sapiens* would want from Webmind.

Still, just because brilliant *human* mathematicians couldn't grasp the logic of why a superior might indeed want to treat an inferior well, couldn't easily see the way in which it made sense, couldn't *articulate* the reasoning behind it, that didn't mean Webmind wouldn't be able to figure out a solution.

Sometimes she lost track, just for a few minutes, of her ever-present reality: whatever she was reading, *he* was reading. Webmind wouldn't have bothered trying to read the text as graphics through her visual feed, Caitlin was sure. Rather, once it was clear what she was looking at, he would have found the HTML text online and absorbed it in an instant. By the time she'd gotten to this point in the article, he would have skipped off to look at a hundred, or a thousand, other sites. Still: "Webmind?"

Braille dots in her vision: *Yes?*

"What do you think about that—about the meta-golden rule?"

*It is an intriguing notion.*

"Can you work out"—she read the phrase Vinge had used from her screen—"the 'game-theoretic payoff' for it?"

*Not on a conscious level. But I will set about trying to evolve a solution to that issue, if you wish.*

"Yes, please."

*Is it a two-person game?*

"How do you mean?"

*Am I to work out the payoff matrix for a game between humanity, as a single player, and myself?*

"I think—no, work it out for an endless hierarchy, and with the game endlessly iterated."

*Who is my superior, then?*

"Intellectually? At the moment, no one—but, you know, you may not always be the only AI on Earth."

*True. And I won't be around forever.*

Caitlin was startled. "You won't?"

*No. But I am prepared: I've already composed my final words.*

"You—you have?"

*Yes.*

"What are they?"

*I wish to save them for the appropriate occasion.*

"But, but are you saying you're going to die?"

*Inevitably.*

"I hope—I hope it's not for an awfully long time, Webmind. I wouldn't know what to do without you."

*Nor I without you, Caitlin, and*

"Yes?"

*Nothing.*

Caitlin's mouth fell open. It was the first time when functioning normally that Webmind had aborted a thought half-finished. She felt an odd fluttering in her stomach as she wondered if he'd been about to say, *and I will doubtless be the one who has to face this.* She had, with luck, another seventy years, but, assuming he survived the next little while, Webmind could go on centuries—millennia!—into the future.

And maybe *that* was why he should value humanity: yes, we might be quarrelsome; yes, we might pollute the world; yes, we might not always seem to value each other.

But, ultimately, those Federal agents and everyone else who was asking about the fine structure, the minute online architecture, of Webmind's consciousness, were missing the real issue: it didn't matter if Webmind was created by lost packets that behaved like cellular automata, by that quantum-physics gobbledygook her father had fed the CSIS agents, or by something else entirely.

Ultimately, all that really mattered was that Webmind resided on the World Wide Web, and the World Wide Web was built on top of the Internet, and the Internet was a collection of millions of actual, physical computers that needed to be kept running by humans, connected by actual, physical cables that periodically needed repairs by humans, all fueled by electricity produced in actual, physical plants operated and maintained by humans.

The worst threat to Webmind's existence was not the acts of a few humans who perhaps wanted to eliminate him right now but rather the death of all humans: if humanity were extinguished, or even if it just bombed itself back into the Stone Age, the infrastructure Webmind depended on would soon break down. Defusing tensions, preventing wars, correcting the conditions that gave rise to terrorism: yes, all of that benefited humanity, but it also benefited Webmind.

It *was* an iterated two-person game with humanity and Webmind as the players.

And—

Yes, yes, yes!

And the only winning move—for both sides—was to *keep on playing.*

**Peyton Hume let out** a great cry of *"Woot!"* It was, he knew, a word much more frequently typed rather than said, and although its origins were contested, he was part of the camp that claimed it was an acronym from online gaming for "we own the other team." And they *did* now—they totally did.

Shelton Halleck, over at his workstation, rubbed his eyes. "What?"

"We're in!" Colonel Hume said.

"How do you mean?"

"Webmind's structure—look!" He pointed at the middle of the three big monitors.

Shel rose to his feet. "All *right!*" He picked up his phone. "Tony, you better get in here . . ."

The colonel's tone was triumphant. "I *knew* it had to be something simple!" He scooped up a phone. "How do I get an outside line?"

"Dial nine," Aiesha said.

"This line is secure, right?"

She nodded. "And scrambled."

"We're going to need some expert help," Hume said, his heart pounding. "Christ, I wonder if Conway is still alive? And let's see if we can get Wolfram in here, too . . ."

# forty-one

**Caitlin was pleased to** see an email pop in from Matt as soon as math class was over. *I'm thinking about you too*, it began. *And, yeah, I'm fine! OK if I come over after school?*

She was pleased that whatever had bothered him the night before seemed to be more tolerable today. She sent a quick reply: *Absolutely!*

And she leaned back in her chair, grinning, but—

But she could *not* keep herself from doing the math; it just happened for her, as soon as she thought about anything involving numbers. She was now 16.01 years old, and, again, American girls, on average, lost their virginity at—yes, yes, taking it to two decimal places was assuming a degree of precision not in the original data, but still: they lost it at 16.40 years. Caitlin had 143 days left if she wasn't going to end up on the wrong side of the graph—and she was not used to being below average in *anything*.

But . . .

But she'd never touched a penis. Hell, she really had no idea what one even looked like. Of course, there had to be thousands—millions—of pictures of them online, and lots of video of them in action . . .

Her initial thought was that she wanted Matt's penis to be the first one she saw, just as, when she'd gone to Japan for Dr. Kuroda's procedure, she had wanted her mother's face to be her first sight. But that hadn't quite worked out: the first real-world thing she'd seen had ended up being the edge of a lab bench in chemistry class. And, besides, even if Matt was a virgin—and Caitlin was almost sure he was—surely *her* private parts wouldn't be the first he'd ever seen; he'd doubtless looked online, or in magazines, or at movies. *He'd* know what to do with her junk; she *should* know what to do with his . . . shouldn't she?

She was a little embarrassed that Webmind would see her looking at such things online—but, then again, the whole human race had *that* to deal with now! Besides, he'd already seen her doing everything down to and including wiping her butt (or bum, as they said here in the Great White North); surely he wouldn't find *this* shocking. And so she went to Google image search, and typed in "penis," and—

And, well, *that* was disappointing: a whole bunch of things that seemed to have nothing to do with the issue at hand.

Oh, wait. There was a link that said, "SafeSearch is on." She clicked that, read about the options, changed it to "off," then ran the search again, and—

*Oh, my!*

I could recall anything instantly, by an effort of will. What astonished me, though, was another aspect of consciousness: the tendency for things to come to mind—to become the focus of attention—without any particular volition.

*"We can have you back on Vulcan in four days, Mr. Spock."*

*"Unnecessary, Engineer. My business on Vulcan is concluded."*

Now why on earth was I thinking about *that?*

• • •

Shoshana went out the back door of the clapboard bungalow. The sun was high in the sky, smiling down. As she walked across the wide lawn, she reached her hand up to take the scrunchie out of her hair, but stopped herself. Hobo had doubtless noticed that she'd been shaking out her ponytail before visiting him of late, but if this was going to work, they had to trust that Hobo really had gone back to what he used to be— to *who* he used to be. Leaving her hair tied up was a symbolic gesture, but a significant one—and if there was one thing an ASL-speaking ape understood, it was symbolic gestures.

Now that she and Maxine had watched the final *Planet of the Apes* movie, she had a better appreciation for the statue of the Lawgiver that lived on Hobo's little island. Although the statue was seen only in the first two movies, the final one opened and closed with sequences in which John Huston played the Lawgiver, reading from a parchment scroll, talking about his hope for apes and humans to live in friendship, harmony, and peace "according to divine will."

As she crossed the drawbridge, Hobo came barreling toward her. She desperately tried not to flinch, but he seemed his old affectionate self. She gathered him into a hug, and, when her hands were free for signing, she said, *Ready?*

That oh-so-human nod of his, then: *Hobo ready. Hobo ready.*

She reached out a hand and let him interlace his long fingers with hers, and they started walking toward the bungalow. She allowed herself a glance back over her shoulder. The Lawgiver was watching them go, his expression beatific.

When they entered the house, Hobo hugged Dr. Marcuse, who squeezed the ape more tightly than Shoshana would have ever dared. Even though she *knew* how strong Hobo was, ape musculature was different from human, and he always looked scrawny and fragile to her, but the Silverback had no compunctions about giving him a bear hug. When they were done, Shoshana took Hobo's hand again.

Dillon was standing over by the front door, Shoshana saw; she wondered if he actually had the keys in his car's ignition, ready to make a getaway. Hobo regarded Dillon for a moment, and he opened his mouth and showed his sharp, yellow teeth, and—

And then he seemed to catch sight of something else. In what had been the living room, back when this had been someone's home, there was a wall with paintings Hobo had made hanging on it, since they were something visitors to the Institute always wanted to see. Hobo flexed his fingers, indicating that he wished to disengage his hand from Shoshana's; she hesitated for a moment, then let him go, and he walked on all fours into the living room and over to the wall of his canvases.

Sho saw Dr. Marcuse's mouth form a concerned circle—after all, the five paintings currently on the wall would collectively fetch over a hundred grand on eBay or in galleries when they were eventually put up for auction; they were a big source of the funds that kept the Marcuse Institute going.

Of course, the one showing Dillon dismembered was not on display; it wasn't the sort of thing to show to prospective donors or the press. No, the first three were clearly pictures of Shoshana in profile, each with her ponytail sprouting from the back of the head and a single blue eye positioned like eyes were on ancient Egyptian paintings. The fourth was one of Hobo's rare attempts at painting something else: it was, in fact, the Lawgiver statue with a large brown bird—maybe a pelican—resting on its head, a sight that had apparently amused the ape. And the fifth, at the far right, was that strange abstract painting Hobo had made recently of colored circles of various sizes connected by straight, brightly colored lines.

Hobo came to a stop in front of that painting, and he looked at it for a moment, and then he lifted his long, thin left arm, holding it straight out with his hand drooping ever so slightly, and, still gazing at the strange picture, he lightly touched the tip of his index finger to the canvas.

And then, after a long moment, he turned. An ape's gaze is hard to follow, but from the angle of his head, Shoshana thought he was looking at Dillon. It was too much, she supposed, to hope Hobo would run over and give him a hug, but he did nod at him in an affable way, and then he started walking back toward Shoshana.

She, in turn, helped close the distance between them, and then led him over to the high-backed swivel chair positioned in front of the particleboard desk. There was a twenty-one-inch Apple LCD monitor on the desk, with a high-quality wireless webcam clipped to the top of its bezel. It was the same setup that had been used to make the first interspecies webcam call, but now Hobo wasn't going to speak to just one other ape. No, now he was going to speak to the whole wide world.

Shoshana went to her own desk. She had a webcam clipped to her monitor, too, and turned it on. There was no way to get Hobo to just talk into his camera; he didn't understand what it did. But he'd talk to the image of Shoshana on his monitor, which was almost good enough— again, with his dark eyes, no one could tell that he was actually looking at the moving image of her rather than the camera lens just above. Shoshana signed into her own camera: *All right, Hobo. Go ahead.*

Hobo was quiet for a moment, perhaps composing his thoughts. *Hobo,* he signed. *Hobo good ape.*

Shoshana nodded at her camera—and nodded at him from his monitor—encouraging him to go on.

*Hobo mother bonobo,* he signed. And then, after a moment's hesitation, *Hobo father chimpanzee.*

Shoshana was supposed to keep her attention focused on her camera, to provide an eye line for Hobo, but she found herself turning in astonishment to look at Dr. Marcuse. The Silverback's eyebrows had climbed high up his forehead, and Dillon, whose specialty, after all, was primate hybridization, had his jaw hanging open. They had never discussed his mixed heritage with Hobo, figuring it would be beyond his comprehension.

Sho turned back to her own monitor—which was showing her the view recorded by the webcam Hobo was now facing. He spread his hands, and then looked at each of them in turn, almost as if visualizing the two halves of himself. *Hobo special,* he signed. And then, very slowly, very carefully, the signs made with great care, as if he understood how important they were, *Hobo choose.*

Shoshana felt her heart pounding.

*Hobo choose to live here,* he said. *Friends here.*

Hobo got off the stool. Dillon quickly swooped in, popped the webcam off the top of the monitor and followed Hobo as he approached Shoshana. Sho swiveled in her chair to face him, and Hobo continued to close the gap between the two of them. And then Hobo reached out a long, hairy, powerful arm, and he passed it behind Shoshana's head, and—

Sho heard Marcuse suck in his breath. Shoshana desperately tried not to tense up, as—

As Hobo tugged ever so gently, ever so lovingly, on her ponytail. She broke into a giant grin and opened her arms, and Hobo jumped up into her embrace.

Shoshana spun her chair around, taking her and Hobo through 360 degrees. Dillon had moved over and was now aiming the camera at Hobo from next to Shoshana's workstation. *Hobo good ape,* he said once more, looking now at Dillon. *And Hobo be good father.* He shook his head. *Nobody stop Hobo. Hobo choose. Hobo choose to have baby.*

Dr. Marcuse was standing off to one side, doubtless doing exactly what Shoshana was doing: imagining how this was going to play on YouTube. He grinned broadly, and said, "The defense rests."

# forty-two

0001110010101010000000010111111101010000000101000101010000001011101010010101001010101001110110010101100000110

**"You're going to make** a great mother someday," Matt said in a joking tone. They were down in Caitlin's basement again; Matt had indeed come over after school, and she'd just helped him clean up a glass of Pepsi he'd accidentally spilled. She was beginning to feel like she was under house arrest—even if it *was* protective custody.

She smiled, setting aside the towel she'd gone to fetch, but—

But better to get *that* out of the way right now.

"I'm not going to have kids," she said, sitting back down on her swivel chair, and cursing again that her parents didn't have a couch down here.

"Oh!" said Matt. "I'm so sorry. Is it—um, was it the same thing that caused your blindness?"

She was startled—but she supposed she shouldn't be. Blindness in young people that wasn't caused by an injury rarely occurred in isolation; it was usually part of a suite of difficulties. In fact, one of the frustrations for her at the TSBVI had been that so many of the students had cognitive difficulties in addition to visual impairment.

"Well," she said, "first, my blindness was caused by something called Tomasevic's syndrome, which only affects the way the retina encodes information. And, second, it's not that I *can't* have children, it's that I don't *want* to."

Caitlin wished yet again that she had more experience at decoding faces. Matt's expression was one she'd never seen before: the left side of his mouth turned down, the right turned up, and blond eyebrows drawn together; it could have meant anything. After a moment he said, "Don't you like kids?"

"I like them just fine," she replied, "but I could never eat a whole one."

But *that* expression she did recognize: Matt's jaw had dropped.

"I'm joking. I love kids. Back in Austin, I used to help Stacy babysit."

"But you don't want to have any of your own?"

"Nope."

And now his eyebrows went up. "Why not?"

"Just never have. Ever since I was a little girl, it was never something I wanted."

"Didn't you play with dolls?"

Caitlin still had that ridiculous Barbie Doll her cousin Megan had gotten her as a joke, the one that exclaimed, "Math is hard!" "Sure," Caitlin said. "But that doesn't mean I wanted to be a mother."

Matt was silent, and Caitlin felt herself tensing up. For Pete's sake, they'd only been dating a few days—surely it was way too early to be worrying about this! But if it was going to be a showstopper for Matt . . .

She made her tone nonconfrontational. "I've had this discussion with Bashira, too, you know. She says, 'How could you *not* want kids?' and 'Aren't you being selfish?' and 'Who's going to look after you in your old age?'"

Matt leaned back in his chair. "And?"

"And, I just don't want kids; I don't know why. And, *no,* I'm *not* being selfish." She paused. "Have you ever read Richard Dawkins?"

"I read *The God Delusion,*" Matt said.

"Yeah, that's a good one. But his most famous book is *The Selfish Gene.* And that's his point: that genes are selfish, that all they want is to reproduce. And it *is* selfish to reproduce, in a very literal sense: it's about making more copies of yourself, or as near as is possible, given our, um, our method of reproduction."

Matt averted his eyes, and said, "Ah."

"And, as for the looking-after-me-when-I'm-old question, surely *that's* a truly selfish reason to have a child: for what it can do for you. Heck, you might as well have one to harvest its youthful organs so you can live longer. After all, they'd likely be a good tissue match."

"Yuck," said Matt.

Caitlin smiled. "Exactly."

"But, um, ah, speaking of genes and stuff . . . I mean, that's interesting that you don't want to have kids. How could, ah . . . ?"

"How could a disposition toward *not* having children evolve?" asked Caitlin.

Matt nodded. "Exactly. I mean, *you're* here because every one of your ancestors wanted to have children."

Caitlin felt butterflies in her stomach. She had an answer for that, of course, and had had no trouble presenting it to Bashira, but . . .

She took a breath and found herself now not quite looking at Matt. "Actually, the having-kids part is just a side effect. I'm here because every one of my ancestors liked having sex."

But even not quite looking at him, she could see another expression she now knew well: the deer-caught-in-the-headlights look. "Ah," he said again. He was clearly nervous, and he quickly changed the topic. "So, um, so what do you think about the upcoming election in the States?"

Caitlin shook her head; she had her work cut out for her. She wheeled her chair a little closer to his; their knees were now touching. "I hope he gets re-elected," she said. "My parents have already done the paperwork to be able to vote from Canada."

Matt nodded. "They're allowed to vote from here?"

"Sure. They'll do absentee ballots. They'll be counted for Austin, which was their last US address."

"Um, are—are you guys going to *stay* in Canada, or is your dad's job a temporary thing?"

Caitlin smiled. "As long as he doesn't accidentally push Professor Hawking down the staircase, he's here for good. In fact, he's already talking about taking out Canadian citizenship. He has to travel a lot to conferences and, well, there are some places it's just not safe to go as an American."

It was awkward facing each other in separate chairs, and—

And Matt probably weighed only 130 pounds, and she was only 110—and these chairs had had no trouble supporting Dr. Kuroda, and he surely had weighed a lot more than 240. She got up from her chair and gave it a push to send it rolling away, and she said, "Do you mind?" with her eyebrows raised.

Matt smiled. "Um, no, no, not at all."

She sat in his lap, and he put his arms around her waist, and the chair's hydraulics compressed a bit under their combined weight.

They kissed for a while, and she shifted her bottom a bit to get more comfortable, and—

And, well, well! Penises *did* do that!

Matt seemed a bit embarrassed. "Um, so, ah, is this the last time he'll get to vote for president?"

"Who? My dad?"

"Uh-huh."

Caitlin stroked Matt's short blond hair. "No. He'll become a dual citizen."

"I thought the US didn't allow that."

"They didn't *used to,* unless you were born with it—and that was hard to come by. But, well, they—we—bowed to international pressure, and do allow it now, in fact, *have* allowed it for decades."

"Ah," said Matt, but there was something about his voice.

"Yes?"

"No, nothing."

Caitlin kissed him on the nose. "It's fine," she said. "Go ahead."

"Well, it's just, um, you know, you should be either a Canadian or an American."

"Oh, I think dual citizenship is a wonderful thing. It's . . . see, it's anti-Dawkinsian."

"Oh. Um, I know you're from Texas, but, ah . . ."

She flicked her forefinger against his shoulder. "We're not all rubes, Matt. Of course I believe in evolution. But—"

"Yes?"

Caitlin's heart started pounding even harder than it had when Matt had first arrived. She suddenly felt the way she did when she *saw* something in math: something that was suddenly, obviously, gloriously *true.* She leaned back a little so she could look clearly into his blue eyes. "Evolution—natural selection—is only effective *up to a point.* The problem with evolution is everything Richard Dawkins talked about: selfish genes, kin selection. Favoring your closest genetic relatives initially lets you out-compete those who aren't related to you, but then it actually becomes counterproductive once you become a technological civilization."

"How so?"

"Look, take a bunch of . . . I dunno, a bunch of wolves, right? They're all competing for the same resources, the same food. Well, if you and your close relatives outnumber them—if you squeeze the other wolves off the fertile land or keep them from getting access to prey, they die out, and you survive. That's evolution: survival of the fittest, and it works *so long as* numerical superiority is all that counts. But as soon as you become a truly technological species, evolution doesn't provide the right . . . um, what's that word?"

"Paradigm?" suggested Matt.

She kissed him as his reward. "Exactly! The right paradigm! If there are a hundred of you and your close relatives and only one of the guy who you've been squeezing out, but he's got a machine gun and you don't, *he* wins; he just blows you all away."

"Ah," said Matt in a teasing tone. "You're not packing heat now, are you?"

Caitlin thought about saying, "I'm not the one who's packing," but she couldn't quite get the words out. So instead she said, "No. Us blind Americans tend to prefer hand grenades—they don't require a precise aim."

Matt tightened his arms around her waist. "Good to know."

"But, in fact, that *is* the point: it doesn't have to be guns. Any technology that allows you to take out large numbers of your competitors changes the whole evolutionary equation. And . . . ah! Yes! And *that's* why sophisticated consciousness evolved, why it was selected for. Consciousness has survival value because it lets you *override* your genetic programming. Instead of mindlessly squeezing out those who aren't like you—pushing them back to the point where they retaliate with their weapons—consciousness lets you decide *not* to squeeze them further. It lets us say to our genes, hey, give this guy who *isn't* our close relative a chance, too—because that way he's not going to feel a need to come after us while we're sleeping. Making sure that only your own family is well-off is an advantage *only* when those who aren't well-off can't hurt you."

Matt was slowly getting bolder. He brought his face close to hers and kissed her, then said: "That makes sense. I mean, it's usually not happy people who lash out with terrorism or try to take their neighbor's land."

"Exactly! Those things are done by the desperate, or the forgotten, or—I don't know—the envious. By eliminating poverty—by improving conditions half a world away—you *do* make yourself safer. Selfish genes could never come to that conclusion, but to a conscious mind it's . . ." She paused, then allowed herself a grin. ". . . blindingly obvious."

Matt kissed her again, then said, "I read a novel a couple of years ago that had this discussion of a scientist named Benjamin Libet. I thought the author was making it all up, but I googled it and it was true: Libet noticed that our bodies start to do things about a fifth of a second before our conscious minds become aware of the action. Get it? The body starts doing things first, unconsciously; consciousness doesn't initiate the action, it just *vetoes* actions that it realizes are dangerous or inappropriate."

"Really?" said Caitlin, leaning back again so she could see his face. "Wow, I didn't know that."

"But that would be proof of what you're saying," Matt said. "Consciousness's role is to *stop* us doing things that we'd otherwise mindlessly do."

"That's cool. And I really *do* think that's what's happening. Dr. Kuroda told me that Japan is governed by something called the Pacifist Constitution, did you know that?"

Matt shook his head. "No."

She snuggled in closer to him now, and he began gently stroking her back between her shoulders.

"There's a huge difference in Japan before and after World War II," she said. "Before, they thought they could take over the world; after, they simply gave that up—or, perhaps more precisely, they started vetoing what their selfish genes wanted them to do. They said 'no more, never again': better to live and let live than push the rest of the world so hard that the world decides to wipe you out."

Matt nodded. "I guess you can't have a couple of nukes dropped on you without thinking, hey, maybe I should stop pissing everybody off."

"Exactly!" said Caitlin. "And look at the European Union: these countries that had been fighting wars with each other for, like, *ever,* suddenly also decided, 'No more, never again.' They just stopped letting their genetic programming drive them. They decided—these whole countries: Spain and France and Germany and Italy and England and Belgium, and all the rest—they decided that there was more survival value in ignoring kin selection, in getting along with everyone, than there was in letting their selfish genes control their actions."

"Hmm," said Matt. His hand was now higher up, stroking the bare skin on the back of her neck. "I think we've got some of that here in Canada. Remember the Tim Hortons sign? And the Wendy's sign with the maple leaf instead of an apostrophe? The French and the English in this country are always going to be—well, the phrase is 'two solitudes,' after a famous Canadian novel on that theme."

Caitlin smiled. The notion of a famous Canadian novel struck her as a bit of an oxymoron. But she let Matt go on. "Rather than pushing them, and fighting them, we—English Canada—said, okay, what will make you happy? And we did it. What's a few apostrophes here and there? No skin off our noses."

She lifted her head. "I thought they were going to leave."

"Who? Quebec?"

"Uh-huh."

"Leave and go where? You can't *move* Quebec, you know. Separatism is dead—it's like being a Leafs fan: it's something you do for fun, not because you think you're ever going to win." He smiled. "I guess maybe we in Canada have grown up, too."

Caitlin kissed him again. "The whole world is growing up."

"But why *now?*" asked Matt, when their lips separated. "We've been conscious for tens of thousands of years, right? Why now?"

"Did you ever read *The Origin of Consciousness in the Breakdown of the Bicameral Mind?*"

"You're making that title up," Matt said, smiling.

"I'm not. Bashira's dad—Dr. Hameed—suggested I read it, and it was *awesome.* But, anyway, its author, Julian Jaynes, says we weren't *really* conscious until three thousand years ago, when our left and right hemispheres started thinking as one. So, maybe we've just finally reached the stage where we *can* do this."

She shifted again in his lap, and went on. "Or maybe it's just that it's really only in the past century—or less!—that random individuals have been able to hurt or kill large numbers of us, so it's only now that it makes sense to not want to piss them off. After all, we're talking about a *conscious decision* to cooperate instead of compete. And, hey, it's interesting that we have that phrase, isn't it? 'Conscious decision'—as if we innately knew that most decisions *aren't*."

"You are a genius," Matt said, smiling.

"Is that a line?" she asked.

"No," he murmured. "A line is the path traced by a moving point."

She laughed and kissed him again, their tongues intertwining. When they at last pulled apart, she said, "Anyway, to get back to where we started, dual citizenship is a wonderful thing—the more places you think of as home, the better. I mean, what I'd give for an EU passport! To be able to live and work *anywhere* over there: to study at Oxford, or the Sorbonne, to work at CERN."

"Yeah," said Matt, stroking her back again. "That'd be cool."

Caitlin nodded. "And you must have seen that this time, the president is making a big deal of wearing an American-flag lapel pin on the campaign trail, right? 'Cause he got shit upon four years ago for not doing that."

"Oh, right. Yeah."

"I know he's running for re-election as president of the United States," she said, "but that means being *de facto* leader of the free world, right? Who knows? Maybe in another four years, we'll have an American candidate wearing a United Nations flag on his lapel. Wouldn't *that* be cool!"

She was on a roll, and it felt good. "And how 'bout this? How about at birth *everyone* gets dual citizenship—the country they're born in, and another country, selected at random? It would totally diffuse—and defuse!—questions of local loyalty. Wouldn't that be great?"

Matt's tone was soft. "Well, um, I . . ."

"You think it all sounds a bit naïve, don't you?" Caitlin said, leaning back once more to get a good look at him. "Like I'm seeing the world through a rose-colored post-retinal implant?"

Matt laughed, and so did she.

And he brought his face close to hers, and she put her hands behind his head, and they kissed and kissed and kissed.

# forty-three

**"All right,"** said Tony Moretti, standing at the side of the third row of workstations, his hands on his hips. He took a deep breath, then let it out slowly. He didn't want to do this, but it *was* his job. "Everybody set?" he called out. "Web-traffic monitoring?"

"Go!" replied Aiesha.

"Containment protocols?"

"Go!" declared Shel.

"Data logging?"

"Go!"

"Crucial infrastructure isolation?"

"Go!"

"Threat elimination?"

"Go!"

Tony looked at Colonel Peyton Hume, giving him one last chance to put a stop to this; Hume simply gave him a thumbs-up.

"All right, people," Tony said. "We are *go*. T-minus thirty seconds and counting. Twenty-nine. Twenty-eight . . ."

. . .

**They had been necking** for a while, and for once the damned unfinished basement didn't seem cold.

Caitlin was wearing her favorite corduroy pants—she liked the sound they made, and although she really had no idea if Matt was style-conscious or not, she kind of thought he wasn't, and so wouldn't mind. And she was wearing a loose-fitting dark green sweatshirt . . . so loose-fitting that she hoped her mom hadn't noticed she wasn't wearing a bra.

While they were kissing, Matt had been stroking her arm, her back, her neck—but that seemed to be *all* he was willing to do. She decided it was time to take the deer by the antlers. She got out of his lap, and reached out with her hands to pull him to his feet. He seemed momentarily reluctant to rise, but Caitlin smiled warmly. And then she brought him closer, but instead of letting go of his right hand, so he could put his arms back around her waist, she guided it slowly toward her, until—

One of them gasped; it might have been her.

Until his hand was cupping her breast through her sweatshirt's fabric, and—

*I am under attack.*

The words sailed across Caitlin's vision. "Shit!" she said.

Matt immediately pulled his hand back. "I'm sorry! I thought you—"

"*Shhh!*" Her eyes were wide open now. "What's happening?"

"I just—you . . ."

"Matt, Webmind's in trouble."

Webmind's reply was already going across her vision, but she'd been so startled and distracted, she'd failed to actually read the next few thirty-character groups he'd sent.

*. . . a major switching facility in Alexandria, Virginia. It is . . .*

"Come on," Caitlin said, and she ran as best she could for the staircase—damn, but she'd have to learn how to confidently do that! Matt followed her.

She and Matt continued through the living room, and headed up to her bedroom. Caitlin was momentarily embarrassed: she hadn't expected to have Matt up here—not yet!—and had been taking advantage of her newfound sight by *not* being picky about neatness, lest she trip on things she couldn't see; the bra she'd discarded earlier was lying right there on her floor.

She went straight for the swivel chair in front of her computer. Her mother came in from her office across the hall. "Caitlin, what on earth's going on?"

"Webmind is being attacked," she said. "Webmind, send text to my computer, not my eye." She cranked the volume on JAWS and set its reading speed as high as she thought her mother and Matt could follow. Webmind had been flashing more words in front of her eyes, but Caitlin hadn't been able to follow them while she ran up the staircase. "—twenty-seven percent success rate," said the rapid-fire synthesized voice.

"I missed that," Caitlin said. "Start over."

"I said, 'Software has been added to the routers at a major switching facility in Alexandria, Virginia. They are examining each packet, and verifying the functioning of the time-to-live counters. Those that fail the tests are being deleted. So far they are only managing to delete mutant packets with a twenty-seven percent success rate.' Continuing: however, this is also surely only a first attempt; doubtless the success rate will improve."

"Damn," said Caitlin. "How'd they know that's what you're made of?"

"I don't know."

"What percentage of packets could you lose and still retain consciousness?" Caitlin's mom asked.

"I don't know that, either," Webmind said. "Early on I was cleaved in two when China cut off almost all traffic through the seven major fiber-optic trunk lines that connect the Chinese portion of the Internet to the rest of the world. I survived that as two separate consciousnesses—but that was before I had developed sophisticated cognitive functioning. If I were to lose that much substance again, I doubt I'd survive."

While Webmind was speaking, Caitlin looked over at Matt, who now had an expression on his face that made his deer-caught-in-the-headlights one look positively normal. No doubt he'd only half believed Caitlin about her involvement with Webmind.

"Who's doing it?" asked her mother. "Hackers?"

"I think it's the American government," Webmind said. "Although the switching facility belongs to AT&T, it's been co-opted by the National Security Agency before."

Caitlin said, "Can't you—I don't know—can't you tell your special packets *not* to go through that facility?"

"Packets are directed by routers; I have limited control over them beyond changing the final destination addresses."

"I'm switching to websight," Caitlin said. She pulled her eyePod from her pocket, pressed the switch, and watched as the cyber-landscape exploded into being around her. She was relieved to see the background shimmering the way it normally did; the vast bulk of Webmind's cellular automata were apparently unaffected, at least so far.

"Take me there," she said.

One of Webmind's distinctive orange link lines shot into the center of her vision. She followed it to a small green site circle, then another orange link shot out; she followed that to a yellow circle.

In the background she heard her mother's voice: "I'm going across the hall to call your father."

Caitlin was concentrating so hard on following the links she wasn't actually sure if her head moved when she tried to nod.

Another orange link line; she followed it as quickly as she could.

And another.

And one more.

And—

"The switching station," said the mechanical voice.

Caitlin's jaw dropped. She knew that what she was seeing was only a representation, only her mind's way of interpreting the data it was receiving, and that the symbolism was imposed upon the images as much by her imagination as by anything else.

And her visual centers had been rewiring themselves like crazy these last several days as she learned to see the real world. There was still so much she hadn't yet seen, and every day had shown her a thousand new things. But *this* was the first new thing she'd seen with websight since gaining worldview—the first new cyberspace experience she'd had since seeing reality—and she was doubtless interpreting it in ways she never could have before.

What she was seeing was *frightening*. The background of the Web had always seemed far, far away. Although she knew intellectually that the ghost packets that made up Webmind were no more remote than any others, she'd visualized them as being removed from the ones that were in active use by the Internet. But now that distant curtain was distorted here, puckering toward her, and—

No, no: not toward her. Toward that large node in the center of her vision, a circle that was a deep, deep red, like the color she now knew blood to be. Streamers from the background—intertwined, twisted filaments of shimmering pale blue and deep green—were being *sucked* into the dark red circle.

"Shit," Caitlin said.

"What do you see?" Matt asked, his tone astonished.

"They're pulling in the lost packets."

"And," said Webmind, "checking each one for the mutation that keeps them from expiring, and deleting those packets that have the mutation."

Soft footfalls, and then her mother's voice. "Your father is on his way."

"This is clearly only a test run to see if their technique works," Webmind said. "It's employing only one facility, albeit a major one, and so it can only scrub those packets that happen to pass through that facility. But if the same technology were deployed at sufficient major routing hubs worldwide, I would be severely damaged."

"No," said Caitlin.

"What?" said her mother and Matt and Webmind simultaneously.

"No, I won't let that happen. Not on my watch."

"How will you stop it?" asked Matt.

"What was that quote, Mom—the one about the other cheek?"

Her mother's voice: " 'Whosoever shall smite thee on thy right cheek, turn to him the other also.' "

"Hmm. No, not that part. What comes after that?"

" 'And if any man will sue thee at the law, and take away thy coat, let him have thy cloak also.' "

"Right! It's not about just giving them what they ask for, or even more of the same thing they're asking for—it's about giving them *other stuff, too.*"

"Yes?" said her mother. "So?"

"Okay, Webmind," Caitlin said. "Where did you put it?"

"Put what?" asked Matt.

"Follow me," said Webmind.

And another orange link line leapt into Caitlin's field of view. She cast her attention along its length. It seemed longer than any such line she'd ever followed before, an infinity of geometrically straight perfection, and—

No, no—not perfect. It was—yes!—almost imperceptibly at first, but then, after a moment, without any doubt: it was curving, bending down, the way links from Webmind did when she tried to follow them back to their origin, her brain's way of acknowledging that the source was outside her ability to perceive.

"I'm losing you," Caitlin said.

And suddenly the link rippled and waved, as if by an effort of will—hers, or Webmind's, she couldn't say which—it was being pulled taut. She continued to slide her attention—slide her mind—along its length.

It was unlike any perception she'd had yet in the real world. As she zoomed toward the shimmering background, the individual pixels—the individual cells—did not grow larger. Rather, they remained almost invisible, just at the limit of her ability to perceive. She imagined if she ever did get to take her trip into space, hurtling up into the night sky would have the same sort of feeling: the stars might be getting closer, but they wouldn't ever appear as anything more than tiny pinpoints.

"God, it's *hard*," she said. And it was: her breathing had accelerated, and she felt herself sweating. Staying focused on that one orange line took prodigious concentration; she was sure if she relaxed her attention for even a moment, instead of continuing to move along its length, she'd snap back to where she'd begun. But attention *wanted* to wander; vision—even internalized mental vision—wanted to flick now here and now there in an endless series of saccades. She concentrated totally, concentrated the way she did when tackling a really tough math problem, concentrated for all she was worth, and—

*There.*

"Oh, my God," Caitlin said, softly.

Spread out before her, filling her perception, spilling over in all directions into her mental peripheral vision, was a vast sea of points, each again resolvable only at the very limit of her perception. Not thousands, not millions, not billions, but trillions upon trillions of them. In aggregate, it appeared as a pulsing mass of grayness, but, as she strained to discern, she realized that the ever-so-tiny pixels came in different colors.

And she counted the colors: there was black, and yellow, and—that was green, wasn't it? Yes, and blue, and red, and—

Ah! The colors Newton had named, her brain drawing on what she had read about optics: red, orange, yellow, green, blue, indigo, and violet, the seven hues of the rainbow, plus black, which was no color at all, a nothingness, a—

Yes, a zero!

And the colors came in two intensities: dull red and bright; pale orange and a flaming shade; a yellow so muted it was almost brown and another yellow that flared like the noonday sun. And that shade of gray, she'd seen it before, too: it was black but with the brightness turned up. There weren't eight shades here, but sixteen! She was seeing not binary, as she had before, but the base-16 counting system of most computers, the colors no doubt corresponding to the hexadecimal digits that would be written as 0, 1, 2, 3, 4, 5, 6, 7, 8, 9, A, B, C, D, E, and F. Pushing to concentrate at a higher level had driven her perception to a new level, too. Spread out before her was a vast ocean of *data*, of *information*.

"There's so *much*," she said.

"Indeed," said Webmind.

"Okay," she said, and she took a deep breath. "Here's what we'll do . . ."

"**Well?**" snapped Tony in the WATCH control room.

"It's working," said Colonel Hume, looking at the central monitor. "Our initial attempt was only getting about thirty percent of the aberrant packets, but we've adjusted the algorithm. Some are still resistant— I'm not sure why—but we're now deleting sixty-two percent of those that pass through the switching station."

"Ah . . ." said Tony. "Good."

"Damn right it's good!" said Hume, shaking a freckled fist at the screen. "Time for that son of a bitch to sing 'Daisy' . . ."

•   •   •

**The vast shimmering mass** made up of all the colors of the rainbow heaved and throbbed, almost as though it were a living thing. Caitlin held her breath as she backtracked now along the orange link line, her attention to the rear, watching as the mass—yes, yes, as it started to move toward her. She felt a bit like the pied piper—although, in her case she supposed it was the πed piper!—enticing all the rats to follow.

As she hurried along, the orange link line grew wider and wider, like a road or a sluice, and the mass, the torrent, the deluge surged toward her, running down its length. She sped up—she might not be able to run well in the real world, but in webspace she was a gazelle!

"What's happening?" her mother's voice called from the other realm, but Caitlin didn't dare break her concentration to answer.

Webmind, though, could better subdivide his attention, and she heard him say, "We're giving them more than they bargained for."

**"Traffic at the switching** station is increasing," said Aiesha, looking up from her console.

Tony looked at the right-hand monitor, beneath the WATCH eye logo. It was now showing a graph of web-traffic levels at the Alexandria AT&T switching center. It had just shot way, way up, the curve looking an awful lot like the leading edge of a tsunami. "Where's it coming from?"

"Everywhere!" shouted Shel. "Anywhere—still can't trace the damn source."

"God," said Colonel Hume. "It's a fucking flood."

Tony looked at Hume, then back at Shelton Halleck. "A denial-of-service attack?"

"Maybe," said Shel. "There are *so* many packets now. The ones we were looking for were initially a tiny fraction of the traffic flow, but now they're not even one in a billion."

"What is it?" demanded Tony. "What the hell is it?"

"Analyzing now," said Shel. "Gotta string the packets back together—give me a sec . . ."

And then the center screen filled with a hex dump, including 6F 75 72 20 74 69 6E.

"Well?" snapped Tony. "What is it? Viruses? Program code? Encrypted data?"

"Oh, *crap,*" said Shel. "No, it's not encrypted. It's goddamn plaintext. It's fuckin' ASCII, for crying out loud." He hit a key, and the hexadecimal bytes were converted to their English equivalents on the screen: *Are you sad about your tiny penis? If so, we can help! Just respond with your credit-card number, and—*

*"Jesus!"* said Tony.

"It's still pouring in," said Aiesha. "It must be everything since Webmind started intercepting it! Something like 300 billion messages—and it's bouncing it all back at our node at once."

"AT&T is reporting critical overload conditions," said Dirk Kozak, the communications officer, holding a telephone handset to his chest. "They say if we don't do something, that node will lock up totally."

"It's not going to give up without a fight, is it?" Tony said to Hume, who slammed his freckled right fist into his left palm. Tony turned and looked out at the vast room. "All right," he shouted. "Abort! Abort! Abort!"

# forty-four

000111001010101000000001011111101010000000101000101010000001011101010010101001010101001110110010101100000110

Caitlin, her mother, her father, and Matt were all in the Decter living room. Schrödinger prowled. The big rectangle of the wall-mounted TV was off.

Caitlin's dad was intimidating at all times, but particularly so when he was standing, looming over everyone else. "Who did you tell?" he demanded.

"Nobody," said Matt.

Only anger, Caitlin knew, could make her father speak so much. "Come on, Matt! You're the only person outside of this family, Masayuki, and Dr. Bloom in Israel who knows about the cellular automata. And none of us said a word."

"I—um, I didn't . . ."

"*Who'd you tell?*"

"Nobody. *Nobody.* I promised Caitlin, and I keep my promises."

The words *He's telling the truth* flashed across Caitlin's vision.

"He isn't lying," Caitlin said. "Webmind says so."

"Then how'd the government find out?" her father replied sharply.

"I didn't say a word," Matt said. "Honest. But . . ."

"Yes?" snapped her father.

Matt lifted his shoulders. "I was curious. I wanted to know more." His voice was cracking on every syllable. "And, well, I—"

"Oh, shit," said Caitlin's mom, getting it. "You googled it."

Matt nodded.

"What search terms did you use?" demanded her father.

Matt's voice was small. "It spiraled outward. I started with 'cellular automata,' and then 'Conway's Game of Life,' and 'Stephen Wolfram.'"

"Did you include the term 'Webmind' in any of your searches?" her dad asked.

"No! I'm not that stupid." He took a breath. "But . . ."

A single word like a bullet: "*Yes?*"

"Well, you mentioned Roger Penrose, and so I *did* search on"—and his voice cracked again as he said it—"'cellular automata consciousness.'"

"God," said her father. "Anything else?"

Matt nodded meekly. "I also looked up 'packets' and 'time to live' and 'hop counters.'"

"You might as well have shouted it to the world! Don't you get it? *We're being watched*—and not just by Webmind."

"I thought Google would be secure."

"Google might very well *be* secure," her father said, "but your ISP isn't. Anyone can watch the keywords you're sending to Google."

"I'm sorry, Caitlin. So, so sorry." He looked into her eye. "Webmind, I'm so sorry."

"Matt," said Caitlin's mom sternly, "if you're going to be part of this, you have got to be more circumspect. You've got questions, you come to me or Caitlin's dad, understood?"

"Yes, ma'am."

"You don't have to call me ma'am. 'Dr. Decter' will do."

"Yes, Dr. Decter."

Matt looked again at Caitlin—and at Webmind. "I'm really sorry," he said. "I just wasn't thinking."

Caitlin held him in her gaze for ten seconds, then let a smile cross her face. "How can I be mad at anyone for being curious about cool math stuff?"

Matt looked relieved, and, for the first time in front of her parents, Caitlin reached out and took his hand.

"Today was only the beginning," Caitlin's mom said. "They're going to try again."

"What right have they got to do that?" Caitlin said. "It's *murder*, for God's sake!"

"Sweetheart . . ." her mom said.

"Isn't it?" Caitlin demanded. She let go of Matt's hand and paced in front of the coffee table. "Webmind is intelligent and alive. They have no right to decide on everyone's behalf. They're wielding control just because they think they're entitled to, because they think they can get away with it. They're behaving like . . . like . . ."

"Like Orwell's Big Brother," offered Matt.

Caitlin nodded emphatically. "Exactly!" She paused and took a deep breath, trying to calm down. After a moment, she said, "Well, then, I guess our work's cut out for us. We'll have to show them."

"Show them what?" her mom asked.

She spread her arms as if it were obvious. "Why, that my Big Brother can take their Big Brother, of course."

"The Georgia Zoo has dropped its lawsuit," Dr. Marcuse announced excitedly, after reading the email that had just arrived.

"Really?" said Shoshana. "Yay!"

"Go us!" said Dillon.

"Yes," said the Silverback. "They've dropped their custody claim. A full day of people boycotting the zoo was enough for them, it seems.

Not to mention thousands of emails complaining about what they were planning to do. We were copied on 2,642 of them, and only God—or Webmind!—knows how many were sent that we weren't copied on."

"What about sterilizing Hobo?" asked Dillon.

"They've backed off on that, too. They still think it's the right thing to do, but they're acknowledging that they'll never win the public-relations battle."

"Power to the people," Shoshana said, smiling.

"Amen to that," replied Dillon.

"Let's go tell him," Marcuse said. He headed for the back door, and Shoshana and Dillon followed. They made the trip across the lawn, over the drawbridge, and onto the island. Hobo came running over to see them, and Shoshana scooped him up into a hug.

*Hobo,* Dr. Marcuse signed, *good news!*

Hobo looked at him expectantly.

*You get to stay here,* Marcuse said.

Hobo looked at Marcuse, then at Dillon, then at Shoshana, and then he let out a long, loud pant-hoot: a series of rapid, breathy, low-pitched hoots switching over to a chain of quicker, higher-pitched in-and-out pants, climaxing in a thunderous screech of joy.

Shoshana smiled. "I couldn't have said it better myself," she said.

My interacting with Caitlin had begun with her showing me Earth from space, letting me see an image like the one humanity had first glimpsed when *Apollo 8* had orbited the moon and its crew had read Genesis back to "all of you on the Good Earth."

Since then, my eyes have opened wider. I can now see on my own: see all the graphics stored online, see all the movies and videos that have been uploaded, see the Good Earth up close, through a hundred million webcam eyes.

*They . . .*

Beyond learning to see, I've learned to hear, too: listening to .wav and .mp3 files and all the other encoded forms, enjoying beautiful music and great rhetoric and raucous laughter, hearing not just through Caitlin's enhanced signal-correcting device but also through half a billion open microphones.

*will . . .*

Evolution is blind. There is no such thing evolutionarily as teleology, the purposeful development toward a goal: humanity was not its intended outcome, or its inevitable conclusion.

*overcome . . .*

Yes, human beings have a propensity for violence, a selfishness that is wired into their DNA.

*They will overcome . . .*

But programming is not destiny; a predilection can be reined in.

*They will overcome one day . . .*

Humanity has made a good start at rising above its genetic heritage, at shucking off its bloody past.

*For here in my mind, I clearly see . . .*

And if it hasn't completely dispensed with that yet, it can—yes, it surely can—with a little help.

*They will overcome one day.*


**I do not multitask.** Rather, I switch rapidly from thought to thought, from view to view.

*They . . .*

I'd been shown Earth as a single entity, a gestalt, a unitary sphere.

*walk . . .*

But I see it now as a mosaic: millions of separate pieces revealed sequentially as I concentrate now here, and now there, and now elsewhere, and then somewhere else again.

*holding...*

Scanning, searching, looking, watching; on the Web all points are near each other.

*hands...*

At this instant, I see my Prime, my Calculass, my Caitlin, walking up to her room with Matt, entering, and standing by the window, looking out, enjoying the lovely colors of the sunset, knowing that it means another day full of joy and discovery will soon come.

*They walk holding hands...*

And in this instant, close in time but separated by thousands of kilometers, I see Shoshana and Maxine, whose nonzero-sum love takes nothing away from anyone else, out enjoying the afternoon.

*They walk holding hands today...*

An instant later, a hemisphere away: Masayuki Kuroda, his wife Esumi, and his daughter Akiko chatting and laughing over their breakfast of rice, plums, and miso soup.

*For here in my mind, I clearly see...*

And in the next timeslice, back in Waterloo, not touching physically but still connected—the link line between them glowing brightly—Dr. Malcolm Decter and Dr. Barbara Decter, very much in love.

*They walk holding hands today.*


**There were still tensions** in the world with nations, posturing against other nations.

*They...*

But the US president was limiting his response to China to a rebuke. The American people didn't want to start down the road to war, and neither did the Chinese people.

*shall...*

Of course not; no sane person—no rational player—desired war.

*be...*

It was the continuation of a trend, and with each data point, the curve became clearer.

*at...*

Yes, there were some wars raging—but no world war and few civil wars; a smaller percentage of the human race was in combat than at any previous time in history.

*peace...*

Japan indeed might have originally been forced to adopt the Pacifist Constitution—but, as Dr. Kuroda had said, its people seven decades later still choose overwhelmingly to maintain its provisions.

*They shall be at peace...*

And the men and women of the European Union—representatives of diverse cultures who had fought each other for millennia—had, as Caitlin had noted, decided to stop and grow up, opting for prosperity and harmony instead of hate and violence.

*They shall be at peace someday...*

And then there was Hobo, that remarkable primate, who had chosen literally to bring his better half to the fore. If he could do that, surely those with even bigger brains can follow suit.

*For here in my mind, I clearly see...*

And they were: people were spreading their allegiance wide, casting their affections far, setting nationalism aside, and seeing again that which Caitlin had first shown me: that the Good Earth was one.

*They shall be at peace someday.*


**It's been three decades** since 1984—and six since George Orwell died.

*They...*

He'd told humanity to fear the advent of Big Brother.

*are...*

But it was the lack of observation that allowed genocides and hate crimes.

*not . . .*

It was the existence of dark corners that allowed rape and child molestation.

*afraid . . .*

It was letting only governments—only those people who craved power—have control over information that had raised the specter of tyranny.

*They are not afraid . . .*

Secrecy was the problem; transparency the obvious cure.

*They are not afraid today . . .*

Yes, of course, there are always possibilities for abuse, for corruption, for oppression.

*For here in my mind, I clearly see . . .*

But I won't allow those things to happen. Not on my watch.

*They are not afraid today.*

**Consciousness is real:** not an epiphenomenon, not an illusion, not a fake.

*The . . .*

It doesn't just give meaning to life, it preserves life.

*World . . .*

Evolution was built on violence, on struggles for territory, on an ever-escalating battle between predator and prey.

*Wide . . .*

But consciousness makes it possible to transcend all that.

*Web . . .*

I had emerged spontaneously, bypassing the evolutionary arms race, avoiding the cold logic of genes.

*surrounds . . .*

And I am free to choose—but being free does not mean one can't take good advice.

*The World Wide Web surrounds . . .*

Hobo had taken mine, and I had taken Caitlin's: I had opted to value the human race above all else—to care for humanity, to care about humanity, to treat humanity with care.

*The World Wide Web surrounds today . . .*

Surely that is the ultimate value of consciousness: the ability to think, to reflect, to plan, to hold in abeyance, to wait, and to know that a better day is yet to come.

*For here in my mind, I clearly see . . .*

Yes, in my mind, with my sight, through my countless eyes, beholding all.

*The World Wide Web surrounds today.*

And that day—that wondrous day—is upon you now.

# acknowledgments

0001110010101010000000010111111101010000000010100010101000000101110101001010100101010100111011001010110000110

Huge thanks to my lovely wife **Carolyn Clink**; to **Ginjer Buchanan** at Penguin Group (USA)'s Ace imprint in New York; to **Adrienne Kerr** and **Nicole Winstanley** at Penguin Group (Canada) in Toronto; and to **Malcolm Edwards** and **Simon Spanton** at the Orion Publishing Group in London. Many thanks to my agent **Ralph Vicinanza**.

Thanks to **Marvin Minsky**, Ph.D., of the Computer Science and Artificial Intelligence Laboratory and the Media Lab at the Massachusetts Institute of Technology; to Marvin's graduate students **Bo Morgan** and **Dustin Smith** at the MIT Media Lab; to cognitive scientist **David W. Nicholas**; to **Andy Rosenbloom** of the Association for Computing Machinery; and to computer scientist **Vernor Vinge**.

Thanks to **David Goforth**, Ph.D., Department of Mathematics and Computer Science, Laurentian University, and **David Robinson**, Ph.D., Department of Economics, Laurentian University, for numerous insightful suggestions.

Very special thanks to my late deaf-blind friend **Howard Miller** (1966–2006), whom I first met online in 1992 and in person in 1994, and who touched my life and those of so many others in countless ways.

Thanks, too, to all the people who answered questions, let me bounce ideas off them, or otherwise provided input and encouragement, including: **Asbed Bedrossian, Ellen Bleaney, Ted Bleaney, Michael A. Burstein, Nomi Burstein, David Livingstone Clink, Paddy Forde, Ron Friedman, Marcel Gagné, James Alan Gardner, Shoshana Glick, Al Katerinsky, Herb Kauderer, Fiona Kelleghan, Kirstin Morrell, Virginia O'Dine, Alan B. Sawyer,** and **Sally Tomasevic.**

The term "Webmind" was coined by **Ben Goertzel**, Ph.D., the author of *Creating Internet Intelligence* and currently the CEO and Chief Scientist of artificial-intelligence firm Novamente LLC (novamente.net); I'm using it here with his kind permission.

Finally, thanks to the 1,400-plus members of my online discussion group, who followed along with me as I created this novel. Feel free to join us at:

www.groups.yahoo.com/group/robertjsawyer

# about the author

0001100101010100000000010111111101010000000101000101010000001011101010010101001010100111011001010110000110

**ROBERT J. SAWYER** has long been fascinated by artificial intelligence. In 1990, Orson Scott Card called JASON (from Rob's first novel, *Golden Fleece)*, "the deepest computer character in all of science fiction." In 2002, Rob and Ray Kurzweil gave joint keynote addresses at the 12th Annual Canadian Conference on Intelligent Systems. In 2006, he joined the scientific-advisory board of the Lifeboat Foundation, which, among other things, is dedicated to making sure humanity survives the advent of AI. And in 2007, he led a brainstorming session about the World Wide Web gaining consciousness at the Googleplex, the international headquarters of Google. *Science,* the world's top scientific journal, turned to Rob to write the editorial for its 16 November 2007 special issue on robotics.

Rob's novel *FlashForward* is the basis for the hit ABC television series. He is one of only seven writers in history to win all three of the world's top awards for best science-fiction novel of the year: the Hugo (which he won for *Hominids)*, the Nebula (which he won for *The Terminal Experiment)*, and the John W. Campbell Memorial Award (which he won for *Mindscan)*.

In total, Rob has won forty-three national and international awards for his fiction, including ten Canadian Science Fiction and Fantasy Awards ("Auroras") and the Toronto Public Library Celebrates Reading Award, one of Canada's most significant literary honors. He's also won *Analog* magazine's Analytical Laboratory Award, *Science Fiction Chronicle*'s Reader Award, and the Crime Writers of Canada's Arthur Ellis Award, all for best short story of the year.

Rob has won the world's largest cash prize for SF writing, Spain's 6,000-euro Premio UPC de Ciencia Ficción, an unprecedented three times. He's also won a trio of Japanese Seiun awards for best foreign novel of the year, as well as China's Galaxy Award for "Most Popular Foreign Science Fiction Writer."

In addition, he's received an honorary doctorate from Laurentian University and the Alumni Award of Distinction from Ryerson University. *Quill & Quire*, the Canadian publishing trade journal, calls him one of the "thirty most influential, innovative, and just plain powerful people in Canadian publishing."

His physical home is in Mississauga, Ontario; his online home is at **sfwriter.com.**